SHADES
OF DEATH

THOMAS DUNNE BOOKS.
An imprint of St. Martin's Press.

SHADES OF DEATH. Copyright © 2001 by Aline Templeton.
All rights reserved. Printed in the United States of America.
No part of this book may be used or reproduced in any manner
whatsoever without written permission except in the case of
brief quotations embodied in critical articles or reviews. For
information, address St. Martin's Press, 175 Fifth Avenue,
New York, N.Y. 10010.

www.minotaurbooks.com

ISBN 0-312-29024-1

First published in Great Britain by Hodder & Stoughton
A division of Hodder Headline

First U.S. Edition: May 2002

10 9 8 7 6 5 4 3 2 1

SHADES
OF DEATH

Aline Templeton

THOMAS DUNNE BOOKS
St. Martin's Minotaur
New York

For LOISIE and RUTHIE
with love.

Prologue

The scary, awful screaming and howling seemed further away now, though it was hard to tell because of the echoes.

Snuffling and choking in terror, with her hand over her mouth to stifle the noise of her uncontrollable sobbing, she groped her way along in the impenetrable dark, still too frightened to use the small blue torch she had in the pocket of her thin summer dress. Her fat feet in their Start-rite sandals kept stumbling over rocks and into potholes she couldn't see; she couldn't remember how many times she had fallen, but her fleshy knees and her hands were sticky with blood.

She was lost now. She hadn't gone far – she couldn't have, moving so slowly – but she didn't know which way she was facing and in the caves there were these huge horrible holes you could just fall down and then they would never even find your dead body. She'd been well warned never to go in; she always just said, 'Oh, Mum, don't go on about it', but was she ever wishing now she'd done as she was told!

It was really creepy, walking in the dark like this, but it would have been worse to let them catch her. It was the darkness that had let her escape, just like she was invisible or something. She'd cowered down, watching the flares and the lights from their torches flickering, casting giant shapeless shadows on the walls of the passage beyond, heard them yelling like savages as they rushed past. Hunting her . . .

Yes, the noise was definitely further away now. She let out

a long, shuddering sigh and put up her hand to wipe her eyes. Her cheeks felt stiff where the salty tears had dried.

The silence seemed to be gathering itself together again as the animal sounds faded, until it was part of the thick, endless, terrible blackness. It was dead cold too. She pulled the blue cardie her mum had knitted tight over her dress, but it didn't help much.

She couldn't hear them at all now, but strangely that didn't make her feel any better. There was still a faint sort of whispery sound, sort of like, well, like a huge animal breathing . . . She was almost scared to take the little blue torch out of her pocket and switch it on, for fear of what she might see. But then, she was scared of the dark too.

With her groping, outstretched hands she could feel a wall in front and another beside her. She turned round, shrank further into the corner, huddling down, and took out the torch.

When, taking a deep breath, she switched it on, the feeble pencil beam didn't go very far. She shone it round about; she was in a little, shallow sort of cave, and all there was to be seen were rocks and stones and a puddle or two. Nothing awful, nothing like – oh well, *eyes* or anything.

She shuddered at the thought, then shone the torch down to look at her injuries. Both knees were badly bruised and gashed, and blood had trickled down her stocky legs on to the neat white socks which were filthy already with mud and dust. There was a huge triangular tear in her dress too. She didn't know when that had happened. Mum would kill her when she got home – she was dead fussy, was Mum.

If she got home. Just as the thought came to her, the torch flickered and she gasped in alarm. She switched it off and it was as if her eyes were shut; she blinked them once or twice, just to make sure they were actually open. She was really scared now, really really scared, even more scared than she had been when they were after her, but in a different way.

'Spying on our mysteries! Get the spy! Get her! Get her!' Someone had caught a glimpse of her and screamed, then they'd all started screaming like they'd gone crazy or something and she had run away in what had seemed like real terror. Then.

But in a sort of way she hadn't quite believed it was anything but a mean, horrible game. She was used to them slagging her off and calling her names. Like 'sneak' and 'snitch' when all she'd ever done was say what was true. And just suppose they'd caught her – they wouldn't have dared to hurt her, not really. Not once they'd cooled down.

So that panic wasn't like this. This was worse, much worse. This was a cold deadly chill that seemed to be seeping into her very bones with the icy damp.

Her teeth had started to chatter. She'd no idea where she was now. Even if her torch battery didn't run out, she could wander for ever if she took a wrong turning. She could starve to death, if she didn't pitch into one of those dreadful holes, screaming uselessly as she fell . . .

But that wouldn't happen. They'd have to come back, look for her, say sorry. Or tell someone where she was, if she wasn't back for dinner time.

Of course they'd have to. She had begun to cry again; she sniffed dolefully, and wiped her nose on the back of her hand. To cheer herself up, she thought of how she'd make them pay for frightening her like this. They'd be in trouble and no mistake, once she told her mum what they'd done to her.

But what if they didn't come back? What if they were scared she'd tell, what if they just went home and pretended they didn't know where she was? No one else even knew that the others came here.

She wasn't going to think about that, not yet, anyway. They'll come back to find me before I count to a thousand, she told herself, trying not to hear the sound of her racing heart.

She had reached six hundred and thirty-five when she saw it – the faint, bobbing beam of a big torch somewhere down the further passage. Only one beam, no voices. They must have separated to search for her, realised they'd have to say sorry and beg her not to tell . . .

The torchlight was nearer now, shining along the passage she had escaped into, towards the mouth of her little cave. She stepped forward. 'Who's that?' she called. 'I'm in here, and you'd better come and get me out or I'll tell what you all did—'

The beam of light swung sharply round, picking her out ruthlessly, shining directly into her face. She couldn't make out who was behind it; she put up her hand to shield her eyes.

'Who is it?' she demanded again, more shrilly this time. 'I can't see you – put the light down lower.'

But the beam didn't waver. As the person holding it advanced slowly, silently, menacingly, she took a step backwards and then another step.

'Stop it! Stop it! You're scaring me! *Who is it?*'

She turned away, trying even in that confined space to slip past, to vanish into the darkness as she had somehow managed to do before. But this time she was skewered by the dazzling light which drove her back, back into the corner she had come from.

Deathly fear clutched at her throat so that she could hardly breathe. 'No, no,' she whimpered, turning away, burying her face in her arms against the rock face. 'No, no!'

Something hard and heavy struck the back of her head. She knew a second of searing pain and she screamed. Then her legs buckled beneath her, the bright light faded and the darkness came surging in to swallow her up.

Chapter One

———————◦———————

Lindy could sense the cave all about her, almost like a malevolent presence, as behind the others she stumbled out into it from the cramped, tortuous passageway. She could hear its echoing vastness in the hollow sounds the men's boots made on the rocky floor. The powerful beams from the miners' lamps in the helmets they wore gave only glimpses of its immensity, and currents of air from other passages and shafts and crevices whispered across her face like some slow, menacing exhalation.

She straightened up painfully, easing her back and neck and rubbing the bruises on her plump arms and legs. Lindy wasn't built for wriggling through confined spaces, not like Doug and Ally, who were thin as whippets and lithe as eels. As was bloody Andrea, who was on her first ever caving outing too, but was loudly loving every minute of it.

Lindy wasn't. She hated the darkness and the clammy damp and the dank smell and the crushing feeling of having hundreds of tons of earth and rocks above her head. She was muddy and wet and cold and here in the main chamber it seemed colder than ever, a deathly ice-house chill that seemed to go right through to her bones.

From the dense shadows above, water dripped through a billion trillion pores in the limestone, a perpetual rain which had formed pale crystalline pillars or was dropping now with a sharp, delicate ringing sound into the clear stream coursing along the channel it had carved out for itself over millions and millions of years. Lindy couldn't get her mind round that sort of time.

Doug and Ally whooped as they reached it, prancing round boulders scattered on the floor like building bricks after a giant toddler's tantrum, their lamps throwing distorted silhouettes on to the craggy walls. Andrea jumped down neatly to join them, and their high excited voices awoke echoes long-dead and better, Lindy thought uneasily, left undisturbed.

She shuddered. Like a cathedral, Doug had told her lyrically when she'd met him at the End of Year Dinner, like some great beautiful temple of nature, where you could feel as if you just might be the first person in the world ever to step into this secret place. Awesome, he had told her as he chatted her into signing up for the University Caving Club the following year. Looking into his bright blue eyes, she had decided there and then that she would follow him, if not to the ends, then certainly to the bottom of the earth. Now she wished she'd gone down whenever term finished and was safely at home in Middlesex instead of in this dreadful place.

She couldn't complain that he'd hyped it. It reminded her more than anything of the description of Hell in *Paradise Lost*, which she'd done for A level. Something about rocks and caves and shades of death.

Still, here at least you could stand up and walk normally, which was more than you could do in the passage she had just struggled through, where the ground rose and the roof came down without warning and you had to crawl into terrifying narrow funnels through puddles and even little streams. Or else the walls came together so that you were squeezing painfully sideways between rocks greasy with the sweat of damp while cold drips from above landed suddenly on your face like the touch of a clammy finger on your skin, but you couldn't scream, because this was what Doug and Ally had casually described as an afternoon stroll, and bloody Andrea was greeting each new torment with fetching cries of delight.

So, gritting her teeth, she managed to say, 'Brilliant!' when Doug came back to ask her what she thought of it and help her across the stream where she was hesitantly looking for a way to cross. She joined in the laughter when Ally made a joke, but as the laughter reverberated away into the dim recesses it seemed to take on a mocking life of its own. Never, in all her eighteen years, had Lindy felt so coldly and unreasoningly afraid.

The others were moving to the far end of the cave and she hurried clumsily to join them, wincing as she caught her ankle on an unnoticed projection. With his torch, Doug was proprietorially highlighting the curious profiles to be picked out in the chemical streaks on the walls and the hollow straw stalactites hanging like icicles from the roof.

And there, right at the back of the cave was the Cataract. He had told them about it, a sort of petrified waterfall spilling from a hole near the roof, its sculpted folds like crumpled yellowing lace.

Yes, it was awesome, and beautiful too, Lindy acknowledged, in a bleak, inhuman, scary sort of way. She had to compress her lips to trap the wail, 'Can we go back now?' which was threatening to escape.

'God, this is just so, like – well, I don't know. Mind-blowing!' Andrea was squealing. 'It's sensational – how come you didn't tell me it would be like this?'

Lindy could see, even though his helmet shadowed his face, that Doug was beaming fatuously. Ally, showing off, had scaled a rough pile of rocks to shine his torch behind the Cataract. As it sprang into gleaming life, every flow-edge and ripple glistening, even Lindy gasped and Andrea shrieked. A thousand eldritch shrieks chimed a spectral chorus.

Ally had vanished behind the curtain of calcite. 'Hey Doug,' he called, his voice a little muffled, 'have you been up here? Did you know there's a passage behind?'

'Really?' Doug went up the rocks like a Barbary ape, and disappeared too.

'Gosh, isn't this thrilling?' Andrea gave a giggle of excitement, and Lindy repeated hollowly, 'Thrilling!' You didn't need to be reading psychology to work out what would happen next.

When they reappeared, Ally called down, 'We're just going to do a quick recce. There's quite a wide lead-off back here—'

'Of course, it may not go anywhere, or there may be a shaft, or water.' Doug's excitement was obvious. 'We just want to check it out for the Club next year, OK? We won't be long – you two just wait here—'

'Forget it!' Andrea was already nimbly scaling the steep blocks. 'Less of the girlie stuff. Lindy and I are right there with you, aren't we, Lindy?'

Doug, looking down at Lindy standing unhappily below, said doubtfully, 'Well, I don't know – it could get a bit iffy—'

Andrea followed his gaze, then said contemptuously, 'Oh, if Lindy doesn't fancy it she can just wait here, can't she?'

Wait alone here, in this sinister temple to who knew what dark deity, with the shadows encroaching on her as the light from the others' lamps disappeared behind the Cataract?

'No, no, I'm coming,' Lindy said hastily.

'Fine, why not?' Ally's tone was a little too hearty, but Doug came down to help her – well, haul her up as she scrabbled awkwardly for footholds.

Once she was up, in fact, it was straightforward enough and the passage which yawned darkly ahead was wider than the one they had come in by. At its mouth Doug paused.

'Now look, we haven't checked this out. Caving can be seriously unpredictable, so don't crowd us, right? And remember what I told you at the start – mind your head, don't get left behind, and don't under any circumstances wander off the main drag, even if you see the Taj Mahal in calcite ten yards down a side passage. OK?'

Lindy was all too ready to promise, and Andrea nodded solemnly. They set off in single file, Ally leading.

They had to splash along through a shallow stream, but otherwise the going was easy. Here and there another opening gave a glimpse of labyrinthine passages, created millennia before, when the rushing waters which had hollowed them out fell again in some later subterranean convulsion. Once Doug shone his torch into a crevice and a miniature cave sprang briefly to light, a tiny fairy cave with pink crystals forming a little forest of stumpy stalagmites. Lindy almost enjoyed that.

'Just think,' Andrea said, 'we could be the first people ever to see that. It's sort of weird, isn't it?'

'Maybe,' Doug said, 'but you can bet people will have gone behind the Cataract before. You more or less have to dive nowadays to find virgin territory.'

The tunnel was getting smaller now, both lower and narrower. Lindy swallowed hard, trying not to think of suffocation and entombment, but even so when Ally stopped suddenly her heart missed a beat.

Ahead, in the light of his miner's lamp, they could see that the floor, which had been sloping gently, started to shelve more steeply and the roof dipped dramatically down. The little rivulets at their feet were running faster now and a loose stone from above, disturbed by their passing, bounced down and clattered on Ally's helmet.

He lowered his voice. 'It looks as if it might be going into a shaft. Doug, you'd better take the girls back while I check to see if it might be worth a proper expedition with ropes. Don't go singing rugby songs at the top of your voice, will you – I don't fancy being under a roof-fall.'

With a wistful glance Doug turned back obediently, shepherding Andrea and Lindy in front of him. Lindy was thankful to turn back; she was shivering now, only partly with cold.

It was even colder when they stopped moving. Neither Lindy nor Andrea had the purpose-made protective clothing the men wore, and now Andrea, annoyed at being sent back, started shivering ostentatiously.

'It's too cold to stand still,' she complained. 'Can't we explore here, just a little bit, while we're waiting?'

'We-e-ell.' Doug hesitated, looking back down the tunnel to where he could still see the light from Ally's lamp receding. 'Oh, he'll be a minute or two yet. I saw a cross-passage just along here, and if we stay in sight of the main passage we won't miss him when he comes back. Lead on, Lindy – maybe we'll find the Taj Mahal after all.'

Stamping to try to bring some feeling back into her numb toes, Lindy walked back to where the passages met, not far from the fairy cave. The other rose sharply, at right angles to the one they were in, and she could see that only a little further on there was a fork.

'In here?'

'Yes, why not? It won't do any harm to sus out this one as well, if we're going to come along here another time.'

At least, at least, he wasn't suggesting they should follow it now, so once Ally rejoined them, surely they would head back. With her spirits lifting just a little, Lindy led the way, her head bent to let the light from her borrowed helmet illuminate the uneven footing. At the fork, she paused.

'Which way?'

Doug peered into both, then considered. 'I don't think the right-hand one goes anywhere, from the feel of the air. Stick your head in there, Lindy, and make sure, and I'll go on a little further down the other one.'

Andrea promptly attached herself to him, and Lindy un- willingly walked a little way into the right-hand opening. She couldn't say she was afraid when she didn't even know herself what she was afraid of.

This hardly seemed more than a deep crevice, with projec- tions and rock buttresses making it narrow, though it was high overhead when she looked up. As Doug had said, the air was very still and without the draughts it wasn't quite so cold. When she looked straight ahead the light from her lamp seemed to bounce off a solid wall of rock.

'I think it's a dead end,' she called, as much for the reassur- ance of hearing another voice reply as to share information.

'Fine. Come round here, then,' Doug called back. 'There's a nice calcite flow you might like to see.'

She turned. The beam from her head light swung in a low arc, picking up a glimpse of something white, down near the ground behind a projecting rock. Stalagmites, perhaps?

She swung back. No, not stalagmites. There seemed to be some rags in the corner there, and—

The terror she had been fighting engulfed her. Her screams,

in that confined place, produced echoes which crashed endlessly about her, terrifying her still more with their amplification. Her hands hiding her face in horror, she stumbled blindly out, blundering into Doug who grabbed at her.

'What's happened? What's the matter? Lindy, stop it! You're all right!'

He shook her, but somehow she couldn't make herself stop. Andrea, coming up behind and pale with alarm herself, took in the situation and slapped her face hard. The shock silenced her; Lindy stopped screaming and subsided into hysterical sobs.

Ally's voice came from the outer passage. 'What the hell's going on? Is it Lindy? She could have started a roof-fall, the silly cow.'

Doug had his arm round Lindy's heaving shoulders. 'Panic attack,' he said briefly. 'It's OK, Lindy – it affects some people that way. You should have told us you were feeling bad.'

Lindy shook her head vehemently. 'No, no!' she gasped between sobs. 'There, there!'

The beams from the powerful lamps converged as their heads turned to follow her pointing finger, giving a harsh theatricality to the scene.

Lying in the corner formed by the rough buttress, still clad in rags stiff with dirt, still with a pair of rotting sandals grotesquely clinging to its bony feet, its skull empty-eyed and grinning hideously, was a human skeleton.

They did not pause to take in details, did not even speak. With one accord, like the frightened children they so nearly were, they turned and fled.

On the day after Lindy's ordeal, Juliette Darke was lying on a rug in the orchard of her grandmother's house in Ambys, near Limoges, feeling the heat of the sun soak into her, gently loosening all the knots of tension. Already her olive skin – sallow under the cool northern skies – was turning gold.

Overhead, the dappled shade of the apple trees cast patterns of shadow on her half-closed eyelids, though in the still heaviness of the Sunday afternoon the leaves were barely moving and even the crickets' grating cry seemed muted.

In the dark interior of the shuttered house she could hear the sounds of Grandmère stamping about her kitchen, swearing at the cat and the stove, clattering pots and plates, as she assembled her speciality, *Civet de Lapin au thym*, for the family meal this evening. Everyone would be there, Elise Daubigny's wiry black hair was showing signs of grey and her small bony frame had started shrinking but her will was as strong as ever and not one of her large sons would have had the courage to defy a maternal edict. Altogether there would be twenty-three people of three generations gathered in Juliette's honour around the long table on the terrace, spread already with a starched tablecloth so white that looking at it in the strong sunlight was almost painful.

The dark little mews house in London which had insidiously become Juliette's prison seemed strangely insubstantial in her mind, like a nightmare from which she had drifted back into this comfortable, drowsy state.

I've left him for ever, she said to herself, shaping the words with her lips as if to reassure herself that this, at least, was no dream. It's all over. I've escaped.

She had planned it with infinite care, so that he could have no suspicion. She had packed an item at a time, always with an excuse ready to explain if need be why she should be going into the cupboard where the suitcases were kept.

Then, when he had gone to his weekly meeting at the headquarters of the computer company which employed him to work from home, she had broken a window, hoisted her luggage through it and fled. She had left no note; he would be able to see what she had done on the surveillance cameras when he came home. She had been icily calm until she reached the airport; then she had started shaking so much that she couldn't hold the medicinal glass of brandy she had prescribed for herself.

'*Tu ne lui as pas dit?*' Elise Daubigny had said, her thick black brows shooting up almost to her hairline, when her granddaughter explained briefly the reason for her sudden visit. 'You haven't told him?'

She was astonished, but so pleased that for once in her outspoken life she didn't say too much. She nursed a consuming hatred for the English who in the name of freedom had destroyed her native city of Limoges and killed her parents, and it pained her to think that Juliette, her favourite among the grandchildren (largely because she didn't see her often enough to notice the flaws she regularly pinpointed in the others) was making the same mistake as her mother in marrying one of the swine. And Juliette was very like her mother, with the same creamy olive skin, oval face and delicate features; if her eyes had been brown instead of dark blue, she would have been Marguérite all over again.

Elise's mouth still twisted with bitterness when she thought of Marguérite, the precious only daughter in a family of boys, who had defied her widowed mother by going to work in England, been fool enough to marry a perfidious Englishman with blue eyes like Juliette's, and had come home sick and heartbroken − as Elise had bluntly warned her that she would − only to die.

That was fifteen years ago, and Marguérite's memorials were a plaque in the family vault and this child who, apart from her eyes, had little that was English about her appearance. She was pretty like her mother, and foolish like her mother too, courting inevitable disaster with an English husband when there were honest Frenchmen like her third cousin Valéry − Elise liked to keep marriages within the extended family − who had only taken plump, stolid Anne-Marie when it was clear he couldn't have Juliette.

It was three years since she had last seen Juliette, and it was all too clear what that marriage had done to her. The sparkle had gone; she was nervous, too thin, and sorely in need of good food and good wine and the soothing village tranquillity in which Ambys had basked for the past six hundred years.

'If you had not left him, he would have killed you. They are all murderers, these English. Like your father,' she said mercilessly. 'Here in France you will recover.'

So Elise, who was up every morning by half-past six, and who disapproved of sunbathing, or indeed almost any form of leisure apart from sitting down outside the front door in the cool of the evening and commenting acidly on the antics of one's neighbours, had left *la petite* to sleep late this morning, and spread the rug under the tree herself so that Juliette could rest after a proper nourishing lunch of Elise's good soup, bread from M. Moreau's bakery and the cheese that Mme. Bouchet made herself with milk from her little herd of goats.

Banished from the kitchen, Juliette lay in the orchard with her eyes half-closed and thought about the past and the future.

Juliette had run away from Jay Darke once before. She had loved him as long as she could remember, but as student life drew to a close she found herself becoming more and more uneasy about his possessiveness.

She couldn't explain, even to her own satisfaction, why she shouldn't be happy enough to be possessed; there was certainly no one she had ever met who was as fascinating as Jay, no one else who had such crazy, off-beat, brilliant ideas. He was clever as well as having the sort of dark, dangerous, Heathcliff looks which meant that there were plenty of girls at university who would have been more than ready to take her place, if Jay had ever shown the slightest interest in anyone except Juliette.

He never had. He depended on her, confided in her; 'my other self', he called her, only half-mocking, and the phrase had started to haunt her. She felt stifled, sometimes, as if he was leaving no space for her own personality.

With his First in Artificial Intelligence, he had accepted a golden 'hello' from a computer firm in Sheffield. Juliette, with her sound degree in French and Italian, allowed him to believe that she was job-hunting in Derbyshire. She could never have told him about her misgivings; he had only to fix her with his compelling hazel eyes and she knew she would weakly capitulate.

Her father was more than happy to assist her in deception. Harry Cartwright was a tough-minded, hard-nosed self-made man who, if he didn't precisely worship his creator, was certainly pretty satisfied with what he'd made out of the raw material.

There was nothing wrong with the raw material, in fact; Harry had a good sharp mind and, if not exactly handsome, he was what they termed locally 'well set up' with a stocky build, fair hair, a pugnacious jawline and dark blue eyes which had misled more than one young woman into thinking him romantic.

A miner's son, Harry had grown up in a cottage with an outside privy in the Peak District village of Burlow; the house he had now was still in Burlow, but it had four bathrooms, three of them *en suite*. In his uncertain youth, he had modelled himself on the men he saw cutting the big deals, the men with the flashy cars and the big cigars, the hard men who knew how to handle themselves and ruthlessly carved him up the first couple of times he was brash enough to take them on. But Harry was a fast learner, quick to adopt the style as protective coloration for the business jungle, and now, in the way of these things, the clichés had become the man himself.

He saw nothing wrong with that, played up to the image, even. He'd always known what he wanted, and he'd got it, too. He'd made only one serious error – losing his head over a tasty little French *au pair* who might as well have come from another planet for all she understood about being the wife of an up-and-coming man in Derbyshire – but he'd put that right afterwards with Debbie. She knew how to enjoy herself, did Debbie. He liked that in a woman.

Being unreflective himself, he was wary of intellectuals and never quite knew what to make of Juliette, his clever only child. He loved her of course – and God help anyone who mucked Harry Cartwright's daughter about – but he understood her not at all. He certainly didn't understand her infatuation with Jay Darke, going as far back as their schooldays in Burlow.

Darke, where Harry was concerned, was a weirdo, too clever by half. He hadn't liked the Darke parents – the father a fly-by-night who had callously abandoned the family when the boy was eight, the mother a wispy woman who sighed a lot – and he disliked everything about Jay, from the length of his hair to the way he kept himself rigidly aloof from lesser mortals.

'Darke by name and dark by nature,' was another of Harry's pronouncements, but he had long ago given up hope that his daughter – flattered, like any woman, by unswerving devotion – would see sense. Hearing her say that she wanted to do a translator's course in London and that she didn't want Darke to know her whereabouts was the best news he'd had since Lomex dropped their opposition to his takeover bid.

Juliette was almost superstitiously careful about covering her tracks, and it took Jay three years to find her, working from home in a flat in Putney which she shared with three other girls. They were out all day; it was lonely work, translating trade publications into French, and by now the novelty of being independent and living in the capital had worn off.

There had been a number of men in her life, but somehow none of them managed to exorcise the ghost of her first love. They might be kinder, or more demonstrative, or less demanding, but the long association with Jay, rich with shared experience, made these new relationships seem shallow, superficial. As one after another they faltered, she found herself increasingly reluctant to begin again on the long, wearisome process of personal discovery – hip-hop or Hindemith or Haydn, pasta or potatoes, rages or sulks – when at heart she knew it was never going to come to anything anyway.

So when Juliette opened the door and saw Jay standing there, with his hair short now but so sweetly familiar in every other way, looking quizzical rather than angry – as he had every right to be – she had fallen into his arms with a sob of relief.

There was no need to ask about his tastes (Hindemith and pasta) or try to discover his true nature. Juliette knew it already, knew all about his perfectionism and his rages. She knew better than anyone how to handle them; after all, she had been talking him down since she was eleven years old. His possessiveness, which still troubled her, was a compliment, after all. They belonged together. She knew Jay as she knew herself.

Or so she had thought.

Harry accepted their engagement with resignation. Debbie, a buxom bottle-blonde with whom Juliette had nothing except Harry in common, threw herself into arranging a wedding suitable for Harry Cartwright's daughter.

Jay had been surprisingly accommodating. 'Don't worry,' he had said, when she apologised for the number of local councillors on the guest list. 'Why should I care about one day, when you're mine for the rest of our lives?' And Juliette, God help her, had thought that was romantic.

Mercifully, her French relations refused *en masse*; Juliette shuddered at the thought of Grandmère and Debbie in the same overswagged marquee. She submitted to all the horrors docilely enough. It was by way of being her parting gift to her father since she could see that in her married life with Jay he was unlikely to have much of a place.

What she hadn't quite realised was that neither would anyone else.

She had offered to come back to Sheffield, though not Burlow. Certainly not Burlow, with its small-town atmosphere. But Sheffield would be all right; her translating could be done anywhere, and with the gilt of London wearing thin, she was rather looking forward to picking up the threads of her earlier life, from university and even from school. There was Kate Cosgrove, for instance, one of her school friends; she was a solicitor in a top Sheffield practice now and running for parliament as a Liberal Democrat in the constituency round Burlow. And there was dear Abbie Bettison, her first-ever best friend, married to one of the local farmers. And Dave and Jan Brooks, good mates from university . . .

But Jay, without telling her, had fixed up a job with a multinational computer firm in London. Well, she was hardly in a position to complain about lack of consultation, and they were almost doubling his salary which was already twice what she earned herself. When he explained that he had fixed it so that he too could work from home, what could she say but 'Wonderful!' For a bride to display dismay at the amount of time she would be spending with her new husband was hardly tactful.

In any case, she told herself, if it got too much she could look for an office job.

Jay had found a tiny mews house for them in Westbourne Grove, with a garage that was just big enough to house Jay's little Golf gti. It had one bedroom upstairs, which Juliette used as a daytime study. Jay had his computer equipment downstairs, at the back of the main room which opened on to the mews, so it was unreasonable of her to mind that she could never decide to go out without telling him.

If she came down, to pop out for an errand, perhaps, he would say, 'Great! I'm just looking for an excuse for a break. Let's go and grab a coffee.' They shopped at the supermarket together, and he was even happy to browse around the dress shops, and pay the bills for her clothes. She'd had a credit card, in her maiden name: 'Why bother to renew it?' he had said. 'You don't earn enough, my love, for the sort of things I like to see you in,' and she'd agreed that she might as well cancel it. Fool that she was! They had a joint account too, only he so regularly paid for everything that she didn't even carry her cheque book.

When Juliette tried to explain to him that the girls' lunches she arranged with her former flatmates – the only friends she had in London – were just that, Jay laughed and accused her of sexism. 'I'd like to think Laura (or Carrie or Jess) was a friend of mine, too,' he would say, looking hurt, and after that she couldn't really stop him.

'I couldn't stand to see that much of *anyone*,' Carrie had said, laughing, at one of these lunches, while Jay was in the Gents. 'But it's sweet to see someone with such an adoring husband. I should be so lucky!'

Loyalty forbade the honest reply, but after that Juliette noticed that gradually the lunch invitations stopped.

After six months, she suggested she should look for an office job. Jay went dangerously quiet; reading familiar storm signs, she felt herself tensing up.

'Are you saying you don't love me any more?' he asked softly. 'Tired of me already?' He was staring at her, forcing her somehow to look into those mesmeric eyes.

'Oh Jay, of course not, don't be silly!' She tried to laugh it off, but she was aware of sounding nervous not amused. 'It's just that we do absolutely everything together, and—'

'And isn't that just how it should be?' he cut in before she could finish. 'Modern marriages come apart because other things and other people get in the way, and I'm not taking any risks with you, my life, my only love.'

She sensed mockery in what he said, but what answer could she make? 'Fine,' she said feebly. 'It was only an idea.'

And the thing was, he was still, as ever, the greatest fun to be with. Even as a child, she had been flattered to be his chosen friend. The summer of the Egyptian Game, everyone had wanted to be in his gang because his ideas – bad, dangerous, cruel ideas sometimes – were the sort that no one else would think of. His fantasies became a sort of secret life for them all, deliciously scary at the time, even if they regretted it later.

That was all behind them, of course, forgotten as far as possible, but he'd never lost his talent for originality, and now he had money as well. For the first Valentine's Day of their marriage he gave her a fur hat, then took her to Krakow where it was thirty below so she could wear it. They rode the rollercoasters at adventure parks and watched *avant-garde* plays where they formed a third of the audience. They went clubbing in Amsterdam. He got tickets for a Tom Jones concert and for Glyndebourne and for an amateur pantomime in a village one Christmas which was funnier than anything the West End could offer. He'd found out where there was badger-baiting in darkest Somerset, but Juliette, with horror, refused to see it as a joke.

They even went to Egypt to see the pyramids at the height of the Foreign Office warnings about tourist terrorism. Well, of course, since Burlow Primary Jay had always had a sort of obsession with Egypt. They all had, then, but after the horrible business with Bonnie Bryant she had been plagued with recurring nightmares about the animal-headed gods, and even now had problems with Jay's elegant collection of Egyptian antiquities. She was glad to get home after that trip, and only partly because of the danger of bombs.

They had been married for two years before she noticed uneasily that, somehow, they had no friends. Her flatmates had married or moved away. Her neighbours might nod, but she didn't know them. Her father took them out to dinner occasionally when he came down to London, but apart from business contacts they entertained together, there was no one else they socialised with. They only had each other.

She began to dread their evenings in, when over the coffee cups after supper he would demand, 'Amuse me!' And since it was he who usually came up with the fun ideas, it seemed only fair that she should try, though it made her feel like a caged canary, kept for its entertainment value and obliged to sing.

For what was there to talk about? She had to cudgel her brain to think of something fresh; what could she tell him about the events of her day that he didn't know already? What opinions did she ever hear, but his own?

It got harder and harder. At last the night came – would she ever forget it? – when she wasn't prepared to try any longer.

'Sorry, Jay, I'm all talked out,' she said lightly, getting up to clear the table.

'Oh, I'm sure you can do better than that,' he drawled. 'I like to hear you try.' He glanced up at her, and that was when she saw cold malice in his eyes, and felt as if it had turned her blood to ice.

Oh, he covered up at once. He veiled his gaze, and then he was smiling, saying, 'But never mind! It doesn't matter. I'll put on a CD, shall I, while we clear up?'

It was *The Magic Flute*, of course, as she had known it would be. But as Juliette went mechanically about the domestic tasks, she knew what she had seen, and with Mozart's sublime *Isis and Osiris* aria filling the room just a little too loudly, everything fell relentlessly, horribly into place. She had been feeling like a helpless bird in a cage, because that was exactly what she was. She was friendless, because he had made her so. And knowing him as she did, how could she have been stupid enough not to realise before?

She, privileged to be his other self, had rejected him. He

would, with some justice, have seen her defection as cruellest treachery, and he was making her pay. How could she have imagined he had forgiven her? How could she have forgotten that Jay Darke never let an injury go unpunished?

His possessiveness was prompted by revenge, not devotion. Their little house was a prison, not a love-nest. Their partnership wasn't a marriage, but a custodial sentence.

She was the victim in one of his games, one of his bizarre, cruel, endless games. And she didn't know what to do.

In her precious breathing space, when he went to the Friday morning meeting, she phoned Laura, married now with an infant, but still living in London. Perhaps if she went to see her next week she could resurrect the old friendship, talk about her problem, get some of Laura's down-to-earth advice which might give her a proper perspective on things.

Laura was delighted to hear from her; it was easily arranged. She said nothing about it to Jay, but the next week he didn't leave at his usual time.

'Aren't you going to the office today?' she asked, carefully casual.

'There's nothing much on at the moment,' he said without looking up from the sports page of the *Independent*. 'We decided I might as well stay here.'

Juliette had no choice but to confess.

'Oh, that's nice,' he said blandly. 'We haven't seen Laura for ages. How lucky that I can come too.'

She saw that he had known about it all along. With his skills, bugging the phone would be child's play.

She could bear the elaborate deception no longer. Gathering her courage she said as temperately as she could, 'You're spying on me, aren't you, Jay?'

His anger, like sudden lightning tearing the sky, tore their marriage apart. She cowered under the lash of his spite and contempt; he didn't strike her, though she felt she would almost have preferred honest physical violence. At least the injuries he inflicted would have been visible.

After the storm, the calm. He phoned Laura to cancel the

visit, citing a forgotten engagement and laughing about Juliette's forgetfulness, promising they would both come and see the baby some other time. Then chillingly, he went on as if nothing had happened.

In the weeks that followed, he took her out, talked to her, made jokes and made love, as if this had been a married tiff like any other. Yet he didn't trouble to veil the cruelty in his eyes any more. He was playing with her, like a cat with a defenceless mouse.

Then he had the security cameras installed, which covered upstairs and downstairs in the little house, so there was no privacy at all any more. Even when he was asleep he could be party to her sleeplessness, review her restless wandering about the house, savour her wretchedness as she sipped tea in the middle of the night. He took to security-locking the windows and front door and taking away the keys on the mornings when he went to the office.

Juliette's work was suffering. She could settle to nothing; like a hamster in a wheel, her mind scrabbled round and round the problem without finding any fresh answers, and she was terrified of what in his ingenuity he might do if she tried to leave him and failed.

She could phone the police, but they were notoriously reluctant to interfere in domestic matters, and how could she claim imprisonment when their neighbours would declare that she was out with her husband almost daily? She could phone her father – but Jay would know before ever he arrived, and she didn't trust Harry not to do something outrageous, something that would get him into trouble. Jay would love that.

If she broke out, ran away, she had no money. She had looked, during one of his absences, for her cheque book on their joint account, but he must have destroyed it. He had taken even the small change out of her purse now.

If the money order from one of the French companies she did translations for hadn't arrived during one of his Friday morning absences, she would be his prisoner, his plaything, still.

She had laid her plans meticulously, and, mercifully, it hadn't occurred to him to remove her passport.

When she arrived in Ambys, she had phoned her father, despite her grandmother's bristling disapproval, to tell him what had happened. He had exploded in protective rage, as she had known he would, but she made him promise to do nothing until he met her in London when she came home. With his support she felt she could confront Jay and finish the whole sad game.

'But don't go by yourself, Dad, he's dangerous,' she warned again. 'Clever.'

Harry Cartwright had snorted. 'He's a sick bastard,' he said. 'He may have brains, but I can tell you when it comes to dealing with unpleasant customers I wrote the text-book. No –' as she protested, 'don't worry. I use the sort of lawyers who have boys like him for breakfast. They'll have him tied in so many legal knots he'll fall flat on his face if he takes a step in your direction.'

She still feared Jay's vengeance, but Dad's confidence was comforting. After all, he hadn't got where he was without making enemies, and all the evidence suggested that he could handle it.

She'd stay for another couple of days, and then she'd go home to draw a double line under that strange part of her life, and start over again. Perhaps she might even think about working in France. Grandmère would love that.

To the monotonous lullaby of the crickets, Juliette fell asleep.

Chapter Two

It was raining. It had been raining like this for three days now, as if, like a child left to cry for too long, it didn't know how to stop.

Typical July weather. Typical Monday. Tom Ward was in a sour mood as he left his tiny cottage in the hills of the Peak District for the large market town of Flitchford where he was a sergeant in the CID.

The view which he relied on to elevate his spirits when the grubbiness of the job started getting to him was invisible today, with grey sheets of rain veiling everything except the greyer dry-stone wall across the road and the scrubby bushes in the field below. He gave it a jaundiced look before locking the front door behind him, noticing with irritation that it needed a fresh lick of paint.

He had planned to go out for a run this morning – there was a marathon in just over a month – but he had failed to overcome his lack of enthusiasm for soggy, slippery ground, mud splashes and general drenching misery. Sloth had triumphed, and knowing he would be feeling better now if he'd made himself do it did nothing to improve his temper.

He got into his middle-aged silver Ford Capri, started the engine and flicked on the wipers. One was worn down, leaving an annoying uncleared patch right in his line of sight. He'd have to buy a replacement set at Halford's, then waste precious time trying to work out how to fit the damn things. He was scowling as he drove away.

It was being sent to London on that course which had deepened his present discontent. Or rather, to be fair, it was unwisely allowing himself the pleasurable pain of spending the weekend after the course with Mike and Toinette. Every so often he was dumb enough to test whether by now the wound might have healed, knowing full well it hadn't.

He and Michael Moore had been best mates at university. They had studied French together when they weren't playing rugby together or competitively sinking pints. Together they had gone to the same French university for their language year, where they both fell violently in love with Toinette Varenne. Didn't everyone?

Toinette was slim and dark with a peach-bloom olive complexion and huge velvet-brown eyes. She was studying English which she spoke with an entrancing French accent and she had the most delicious gurgling giggle in the world. Mike and Tom managed to see off the rest of the competition, but then it came down to the two of them.

Mike was a big man, loose-limbed, cheerful and warm-hearted. Tom was altogether a more complex character; tall and thin-faced, with crisp brown curly hair and sharp brown eyes, he was inclined to be introspective, with a clever, unruly tongue and maverick tendencies. Love, for Tom, was an agony of alternating ecstasy and despair; for Mike, it was the most natural thing in the world.

Toinette made her choice, and it wasn't Tom. Somehow he had never thought it would be.

He'd accepted it stoically – he hadn't so many friends that he could afford to lose the best one he had – and then bled in private. He had been Mike's best man, and made a witty, self-deprecating 'resignation speech', as he had termed it, at the wedding. But since then, in the relatively long and unsatisfactory procession of women which had wound its way through his life, he had never found one for whom he could feel even anything recognisable as the same emotion.

She'd made the wise choice, though, hadn't she, he mused grimly now, not for the first time, as he jiggled the control of the temperamental heater in an effort to persuade it to demist the windscreen.

He himself was the son of an inner city schoolmaster, an unsung hero who when he retired after thirty-eight years' hard labour still believed in the fundamental goodness of child nature despite determined efforts by generations of schoolchildren to disabuse him. Lacking his father's benevolent illogicality, Tom had chosen policework, but with a similar light of idealism in his eyes and the naïve conviction that money wasn't important in his heart.

Mike was a decent guy with an active conscience about his privileged public school background and a genuine commitment to service. He had none the less followed his father into merchant banking, paying his dues to society by working hard for a couple of charitable trusts, ruthlessly extorting five-figure sums for them from the business community on a regular basis.

Why didn't I think of that? Tom asked himself sometimes when the hairshirt of policework was particularly chafing. Like now, after the weekend. He ought to hate Mike, but he couldn't. No one could.

Mike and Toinette lived in a charming maisonette in a square on the smart edge of Fulham where it blurs into Chelsea, with the two little boys who had their mother's eyes and their father's sunny smile.

Toinette had never lost her accent. 'Darling Tom, 'ow do we never see you nowadays?' she greeted him when he presented himself on Friday night after the last of the lectures. She threw her arms round his neck.

He kissed her. She still wore the same cool, flowery, perfume.

'Darling Toinette, because I adore you and if I saw you too often the intensity of my passion might overcome me and I would be forced to kidnap you and carry you off to wildest Derbyshire.'

He slipped into French, partly because it was a treat to exercise his perfect fluency, and partly because the language lent itself to extravagant compliments, providing excellent camouflage for simple truth.

Toinette had not lost her giggle either. '*Méchant!*' she reproached him, wrinkling her small straight nose. 'Mike is bathing our little terrors – come and say hello. Then once the baby-sitter comes we're going to take you out on the town.'

They saw a clever, amusing play at the National Theatre, then ate late at a smart Armenian restaurant before a taxi whisked them home. On Saturday Mike, who had an interest in modern art, wheeled Tom round galleries in St James's where they greeted Mike as a valued customer; they went to Hatchard's and to Fortnum's and to Quaglino's for lunch. London, Tom reflected as Mike hailed yet another taxi, was a very seductive place. If you had the money.

On Saturday night, Toinette cooked dinner: a *daube de boeuf Provençale*, an exotic cheeseboard (so that they could finish off the château-bottled claret), then a *tarte aux pommes* made to a family recipe, with a couple of glasses of a golden *Muscat de Beaumes de Venise* by way of pudding wine.

They spoke French, arguing and joking and laughing, as they had always done. They managed not to say, 'Just like old times,' but it was a running sub-title to the action.

At last, pleading exhaustion from having laughed so much, Toinette tactfully took herself off to bed leaving the men together in the airy sitting room with its polished floor, its pale sofas and rugs and Mike's striking art collection on the parchment walls.

'Why don't you apply to join the Met?' Mike suggested as he handed him a liqueur brandy in a balloon glass of Danish crystal, so fine that it looked like frozen air, which Tom felt might shatter under the pressure of his fingers. 'Toinette and I were saying we don't see nearly enough of you. If you were here in London we could do this sort of thing all the time.'

Tom rolled the brandy in his glass, warming it with his hand, and as he took a sip of liquid luxury glanced round at the expensive, understated elegance of the room in this pretty house in its pleasant square. On the salary of a sergeant in the Met he could probably run to a two-room flat in Ealing, with a daily commute to work in a filthy, jolting tube, jammed shoulder to thigh against the other victims. He could just imagine the Moores coming to visit and being frightfully upbeat and positive about it all.

No, there were two Londons, and the one he liked he couldn't afford. And he did have his pride.

'You cannot be serious!' he said lightly. 'Swap clean air and a good local and ordinary decent criminals for the sort of rubbish you have down here? And you only need pictures on your walls because you can't look out of the window at High Neb for free.'

Mike grimaced. 'Oh, I hate to admit it, but you're spot on. It's getting to be a nasty habit with you, you know. I worry about raising city kids who grow up thinking that grass is something you lay like a carpet only outside instead of inside.'

'I wouldn't lose sleep over it, if I were you.' Tom couldn't keep the asperity out of his voice. 'In a year or two when you need more space, leafy Bucks will beckon and you'll buy a nice house with a good prep school down the road. You can join the gin and Jaguar set and assuage the old social conscience by going on the PTA.'

Mike was, as always, unruffled by the gibe. 'You are a sod, aren't you,' he said amiably. 'Fortunately I don't fancy Jaguars and I prefer wine, but I must admit Toinette's getting stressed already about the pollution. No, you're probably much better off where you are.'

'Absolutely,' Tom said, hoping that the reply didn't sound as hollow as it felt.

On Sunday, after a very late breakfast of coffee and croissants from the French pâtisserie round the corner, Tom reluctantly left for home.

The train journey north was dreary and slow, with Sunday diversions in operation. He picked up his car at the station and drove bleakly back in the teeming rain.

The silent house, when he opened the front door, smelled of loneliness to him – musty and depressing. Even though it was technically summer he started the central heating and put on the lights in an effort to lift his spirits.

He made a mug of tea, grabbed a packet of chocolate diges-
tives from the tin and went through to the little sitting room. He
had been quite pleased with it before, with the old rough stone
fireplace and the ancient leather chairs and Turkey-red
Axminster carpet he had picked up in a local auction. Now it
looked sad and tatty.

It wasn't actually cold enough to justify lighting the fire. He
sat down by the dead grate, took a biscuit from the packet and
settled back with his tea. The biscuit was slightly soggy, and after
a weekend of drinking from Toinette's white porcelain cups the
mug seemed unpleasantly thick and rough. He hadn't bothered
with a plate, and now there were crumbs on the carpet that he'd
have to hoover up later.

It was oppressively quiet, apart from the monotonous sound
of rain beating on the windows. It was odd how quickly you
became used to the noise of children, the babbling as they played,
the squeals, even the occasional tempest of rage.

He was thirty-two years old, and this house was all he had to
call home. It wasn't a home, though, it was the place where he
slept when he wasn't working. He badly needed to get a life –
one that wasn't wholly defined by the police career which he'd
embarked on with such cock-eyed idealism and which now
seemed no more than a labour-intensive way of earning a not
very good living. Not only that, but he had begun to realise that
he was bored. Crime was in general a sadly predictable business,
and he could almost feel discouraged brain cells curling up and
dying from disuse.

Yes, he definitely needed to sort himself out. The trouble was
that, short of putting the clock back, he hadn't the first idea
where to start.

All in all, it was unsurprising that DS Tom Ward was in a sour
mood as he drove to Flitchford police station that Monday
morning.

Jay Darke woke on Monday morning with a raging hangover.
He was lying fully clad on top of his unmade bed amid the

wreckage of his bedroom, in the stinking clothes which he had been wearing for three days.

When he had arrived home on Friday at lunch time and seen the broken window to the left of the front door, Jay had not immediately assumed his wife had fled. That was, after all, no part of his plan for her.

He entered, calling her name. He closed the door, stood waiting for the sound, or even the tell-tale stir of air, which would confirm her presence, but all he could feel was the cold draught coming through the missing pane. A hammer lay on the window ledge.

The house was empty, dead, cold with a cold which seemed to chill his nerves. His dark, heavy brows came together. He had no need to go upstairs to check the bedroom. He knew Juliette wasn't there.

Moving like a sleepwalker, Jay went to the walk-in cupboard which housed the control panel and screens for the security cameras and rewound the downstairs tape. It felt like rolling back time.

The jerky, poor quality film flickered before his eyes like an old silent movie. He watched as Juliette, in the casual shirt and jeans she had been wearing when he left, appeared at the top of the stairs, a suitcase in one hand and her lap-top in the other. She came down composedly, then deposited her burdens beside the window next to the front door and vanished from sight.

A moment later she reappeared, the hammer in her hand. She glanced out of the locked window then, apparently satisfied that she was unobserved, raised the hammer and smashed it as calmly as if this were her normal method of leaving the house. She spent a moment knocking out the jagged shards, then lifted her baggage through. She stepped across the sill, ducked neatly under the crossbar and was gone.

Frantically he turned to the tape from the bedroom camera. There she was once more, coming in carrying a case which seemed to be packed already, though he had previously observed no sign of her doing it. She collected an envelope from her working desk in the corner of the room, stuffed it into her bag and picking up the case and her lap-top went to the door.

Jay ran the downstairs tape again, looking in vain for signs of stress or agitation, for some gesture towards the cameras which she knew to be her absent husband's eyes. One moment she was there, his most prized possession, poised and cool and lovely, and the next she had vanished from the screen and from his life.

He left the tape to run. It showed a room in which nothing was alive, nothing moved apart from the surrealistic ballet of the screen-savers on the computers in his work area. He speeded it up, letting the static image pass in a blur before his unseeing eyes as he struggled with incomprehension.

She should have been incapable of doing this. By his careful calculations, she was entirely dependent, unable to act except under his control. He had dedicated two years to bringing her to this point of abject subjugation.

It had been a long, slow, subtle process, but he was never impatient when he was working on a project he enjoyed and it had been worth it for the sensual thrill it gave him when at last she recognised both his proprietorial hatred and his power. He had judged her at that moment broken; surely he had sucked out the blood of her independence.

And yet, and yet, behind that pale submissive face and the huge haunted eyes which seemed to speak to him reassuringly of total helplessness, there had lurked where even his watchfulness could not monitor it the spirit of rebellion. He didn't understand.

The first time, Juliette had betrayed the stifling intimacy which was what he thought of as love; now she had evaded the strangling surveillance of his revenge. His control had proved illusory. She had humiliated him yet again.

Suddenly, a red tide of rage took him and he was blindingly, blazingly angry. He wanted her there, so that he could pound his fists into her delicate features, grab the slim rounded neck and squeeze, smash her brown curly head against the wall again and again, kill her, kill her, KILL HER!

At this moment he understood what it meant to be beside oneself: the black shadow of fury which clouded his mind seemed almost a separate entity. It demanded that he tear things, smash things – he took the steep narrow staircase to the upper floor three steps at a time. He stumbled twice, clumsily.

In the bedroom, the nightdress she had worn only last night lay where she had discarded it on the unmade bed, a slippery column of cream satin with a froth of lace. He remembered it against her smooth, pale olive skin, and picking it up put it to his face. It still held the scent of her body, and he tore it savagely with his teeth, spitting out the strips of fabric as if they had been flesh torn off her bones.

Then he flung open the doors of the wardrobe. He was familiar with its contents; he had excellent taste, and dressing a living doll had been one of his pleasures. There was little missing, just jeans, shirts and a few things like that, as well as a suit which her father – Harry-the-bastard, as Jay called him – had insisted on buying for Juliette, but which Jay had never allowed her to wear.

The orderly rows of clothes he had bought her, expensive fetters, hung there like the sloughed skin of a snake and he pulled them to the floor, stamping on them, ripping what he could with hands and teeth. The heavier fabrics resisted; he went downstairs to fetch the sharpest kitchen knife and brought it up to slash and stab and slice to ribbons the designer outfits which had expressed his image of his wife.

He swept her collection of Victorian silver and crystal dressing-table ornaments to the carpet and ground them under-foot. He flushed away a hundred pounds-worth of perfume in the bathroom, and with the knife he made savage scores in the delicate marquetry of a dainty Edwardian *bonheur du jour* he had given her as a wedding present. Then he went downstairs to fetch the hammer which had aided her escape, and used it to reduce the little desk to matchwood.

He had screamed and cried and yelled obscenities while he did it all, but now the adrenalin surge had ebbed and his throat was raw and painful. He found he was becoming the self-conscious observer of his own actions, and slowly the frenzy left him. He looked about him at the havoc he had wrought, with something like dismay. He hated disorder. He found even his habitual clumsiness deeply disturbing, because it was beyond his control; this was worse . . .

And the chilling, inexorable truth was that it hadn't made any difference. He was helpless to change the one important fact, that he had not been able to keep Juliette – the one person in the world he had believed he understood – either through love or hate.

He dropped on to the disordered bed and curled into a foetal ball, eyes tight shut. Bitterly he thought, *I should be used to it by now.*

'It's not that I don't love you, lad. Don't ever think it,' his father had said. 'I'm proud of you too. Smart as a whip, you are. Only – well, it's just your mum and me don't get on like we used to.

'Oh, you'll understand when you're grown. These things happen, son, these things happen. You don't get a second chance, you see, that's the thing. We all make mistakes, and life's too short to stick around the mistakes you've made.'

The eight-year-old Jay looked up at him with pebble-hard eyes. He was a mistake, was he – and was he really supposed to go along with this crap, when his mother had moaned on endlessly about the woman she called 'That Tramp'?

Not that he'd ever been soppy around his folks, like some kids were – he was different from other kids, always had been. He'd never seen the point of kicking a stupid football, either, which was all boys seemed to do with their dads, and as for his mum – well, he'd put a stop to her pawing at him as soon as he could say 'Geroff!' and shove her away.

But they were his parents, weren't they? They belonged to him, that was the point, and yet he couldn't stop his dad walking out and leaving him alone to cope with his mother who was always whining and no doubt would whine a lot more now. His eyes brimmed with tears of rage and frustration.

Misinterpreting them, his father said hastily, 'No, no, don't cry now. Big lads don't cry – you know that. Tell you what – you can have a present, a good present. Tell your dad what you'd like.'

He'd told him, without hesitation, and held him to it with ruthless emotional blackmail. His father couldn't really afford the top-of-the-range computer Jay had set his heart on, but he was almost afraid of the strange, self-contained child. He weakly agreed to credit terms which, Jay had learned with considerable glee, had brought out the shrill side of That Tramp's personality.

Jay had discovered computers when he was six – rudimentary things they were then, compared to their later sophistication, but even so he plunged into a relationship with them more satisfying than any he had known before. He understood computers. They weren't messy and sloppy and unpredictable like people. Computers were better than the friends he'd never really been good at making.

While other children played with the games, he played with the computer's mind, stretching his own in the process. He relished the cool logic, the fascinating complexity, the functions available at the tapping of a button. He loved, above all, its obedience to his control. It was a powerful servant, and he was master of its ever-expanding universe. By the time he was ten, Jay had substituted an intellectual for an emotional life.

But then there was Juliette, the little girl who had always been in his class, but who, for reasons he didn't understand, became essential to him suddenly that summer. The Egyptian summer.

As he thought back to it now, Jay's eyes opened. He yawned, stretched himself from his cramped position, shivering from tension. He needed a drink.

He went downstairs like an old man, holding on to the stair rail. The broken window gaped; there was some discarded plywood in the garage and he fetched a piece which would more or less block it, pushing it awkwardly into position with hands that were still trembling. When he poured himself a brandy the lip of the heavy crystal decanter chipped the Waterford tumbler, but unheeding he gulped from it, wincing as the drink burned his raw throat, then topped his glass up and went to sit down.

Along the wall opposite him were the glass shelves where he kept his Egyptian collection, the treasured pieces of jewellery, the scarabs and little canopic jars he had picked up over the years in all sorts of places, with in the centre the stark black basalt figure of Anubis, the jackal-headed God of the Dead.

What was it that had made Ancient Egypt a lifelong obsession? Not old Maxton, for sure, the prosy, pompous headmaster of Burlow Primary who had considered himself an expert but didn't know half of what the eleven-year-old Jay had researched in three weeks. He'd been fascinated despite, not because of, Maxton.

Perhaps it was the complexity of the mythology, the labyrinth of cross-allusions which was almost like the connections within his computer world: if you 'clicked' on Osiris, that led you to his wife Isis and his son Horus and his murderer Set who cut up his body which was pieced together by Isis while Horus defeated Set, and so on and on.

Perhaps it was the clinical savagery of the 'Neters', the gods whose animal heads proclaimed their nature, gods who were merciless in punishment and revenge. It all made more sense to him than the Christian virtues of love and kindness they bored on about in school assembly: he could never quite grasp the one and the other he despised.

Or perhaps it was because, at some level, he believed in their occult powers. Perhaps he still did.

Certainly, that summer at Burlow Primary, in exchange for worship and sacrifice Jay had been endowed with a power he had never known. Always a figure on the sidelines before, the secret Egyptian Game had made him the centre of everything. In the name of Osiris, he had selected some to be Neters and rejected others, just as Anubis weighed the heart of the dead spirits against a feather to decide whether they should enter bliss or die again in the maw of a crocodile. He had been drunk with the heady wine of omnipotence – until It happened.

He didn't want to think about that. It had ended his reign; he had kept his hold over his Isis-Juliette, but his other acolytes had basely deserted him. They wanted to put it all behind them and Osiris-Jay was shut out of their lives.

Or so they thought. His eyes went to the screens at the back of the room, with their shifting images, his obedient slaves held in suspended animation, until he should choose to bring them to life again with a touch.

These were his spies, his windows into the lives of the Neters, who were, however little they knew it, Neters still. His secret knowledge gave him power over them even now, though he had not used it yet. He'd always known that one day it would fit into the destined pattern of his life. Perhaps the gods would tell him now that the time had come.

Occasionally he was uneasy with this near-belief. He tended to rationalise it, for his own peace of mind, as symbolism and metaphor. He could rationalise now, when the metaphor for justified revenge would be the gods' righteous punishment of Isis, who had rebelled against their decree that she was bound to Osiris, to death and beyond. But it wasn't only that, inside his head.

He needed another drink. He wasn't thinking clearly anyway, so he might as well get drunk. Then tomorrow – that was in the lap of the gods, as they said.

'Whom the gods would destroy, they first make mad.' The other saying came unbidden into his head, but he thrust the thought savagely aside, poured more brandy into the chipped glass and dedicated himself to achieving oblivion.

That had been on Friday. He remembered little of the weekend. He spent the rest of Monday recovering slowly, dealing with the consequences of his fury, restoring precious order to his home and contemplating his vengeance. He would repay his wife for his own folly in allowing her to matter in his life.

'Ah, sergeant, deigned to honour us with your presence once more after your little holiday, have you?'

Detective Chief Inspector Brian Little's voice assailed Tom Ward like a truncheon across the base of the skull just as he crossed the threshold of the Flitchford police station. Turning to close the door behind him gave Ward the chance to bite his tongue and compose his features before responding.

DCI Little had the sort of face which looked as if it would be greatly improved by having a fist planted squarely in the middle of it. He was a balding, bull-necked man, smug, self-important and famously thick-skinned.

The only thing known to get under his hide was the 'fancy brigade', as he termed the graduate entry into the police force, so putting Ward in his department was akin to tying a red rag to a bull's horns so that it was permanently in its line of sight.

Ward elaborately finished closing the door. His face was suitably expressionless when he turned round.

'Incident room in five minutes,' Little stalked off without waiting for any reply.

'Sir,' Ward said woodenly to his retreating back.

'I never know how you manage to make that word sound exactly like "prat".'

Ward turned as Alex Denholm, fellow-sergeant and fellow-sufferer, spoke at his ear. He was in his early forties, grey-haired, stocky, and sardonic, with humour lines about his mouth, an unambitious man who could never take himself seriously enough to enter the promotion stakes. He was simultaneously fascinated and alarmed by Ward's subversive attitudes, and had become a good friend almost against his better judgement.

'Hours of practice. Don't you reckon that even if he was a Master of the Universe and I was a slug I would be entitled to find his manner offensive?'

'You always did have ideas above your station. Since when did a DS rate as high as a slug in Little's world view? Anyway, you have to make allowances for him being over-excited.'

Ward raised his eyebrows. 'Been asked to organise the stripper for the Chief Constable's Christmas tea, then, has he?'

Denholm stared at him. 'Don't tell me you haven't heard? Flitchford's fifteen minutes of fame, and you blink and miss it. Lying in a drunken stupor somewhere in London, were you?'

'If you mean I had better things to do than watch telly, you're right. Something's happened?'

In fact, now he looked about him it was clear this wasn't your standard Monday morning in Flitchford with a couple of drunks and someone lifted for GBH waiting in the cells to be taken to the custody court. There was a lot of movement through the hallway and the phone at the reception desk had rung ten times in as many minutes.

'Oh, nothing much, nothing much. We've only been dealing with the "skeleton in the cave" mystery, that's all.'

'What? You mean someone's found one?'

'It's probably just some poor benighted bastard who went exploring the caves up on Long Moor years ago and couldn't get out, but as you can imagine it made a bit of a stir. An interview with Little's been shown on the news three times in the last two days and his empty head's so swollen it's a miracle he doesn't float up to the ceiling. Press statements, TV cameras, and so many reporters hanging about you almost had to scrape them off the sole of your shoe before you got into your car.'

Ward frowned. 'Were they around this morning? I didn't see anyone—'

'Oh, that was yesterday. Apart from the sensation factor, someone who got themselves lost in a cave isn't really a story they can run with until we have some human interest to flesh out the bones, you should pardon the expression.'

'Look, you'd better fill me in on what I need to know.'

'Fine, but we'd best get ourselves up to the incident room while we talk. The knives are out for you – Little was fit to be tied about the Super sending you on that course. Fancied a city break himself, I shouldn't wonder. Anyway, you're going to have to keep your nose clean for the next ten years or so.'

They headed together for the incident room upstairs.

Flitchford, a large, pleasant market town which served a far-flung rural population, was right in the heart of the Peak District. Year on year, an increasing number of tourists with shoe-size IQs and a theme-park approach to hill-walking equipped themselves with trainers and fashion leisure jackets for the purpose and flooded into the area to suffer totally predictable unforeseen emergencies and to find themselves involved in entirely un-surprising freak accidents. As a result there was at Flitchford a well-equipped incident room, disproportionate to the size of the police station itself.

Denholm outlined the basic facts of discovery by the students and the difficulties of the site. 'The conditions are bloody awful for getting cameras and equipment down there, let alone a police surgeon. They got Dr Robson to start with, then discovered he wouldn't fit through one of the passages in the tunnel they had to get down to reach the main cave.

'And then the rest of us have been combing missing persons registers. It's a bastard – only the most recent stuff on disk and everything else stuck in files in the basement here. Or even in the police station where the disappearance was reported. And go back far enough, and some of these stations don't even exist any more. Then of course, maybe he – she – whoever – didn't actually go missing from this area. Needle in a haystack stuff.'

'Surely if it's a skeleton the most recent records wouldn't be relevant anyway?'

'Yeah, you'd think so. But apparently, a few months down there in the damp, laddie, and that finely toned musculature that you're so proud of would be down to bleached bones. Less, if there were rats—'

Ward, notoriously squeamish, blanched. His companion grinned in ghoulish satisfaction as they started up the last flight of stairs.

'Anyway, rumour has it that Little's summoning us to unveil the results of the PM. He can't stand the parade passing him by when he's just got used to the roar of the greasepaint and the smell of the crowd, so he's milking it for all it's worth – drum rolls, dimmed lighting, opening up the incident room and all. It would have been a lot more helpful to have had the info as it came in – if they've even narrowed it down to male or female, it would have cut down the chasing-up we've had to do just to discover that good old Uncle Jimmie only took a couple of weeks' well-earned break from Auntie Jean, but no one bothered to let us know he'd come back.'

Ward shook his head. 'I still feel a bit bemused by all this.'

'Jet-lagged by the journey up from London, probably,' Denholm said sarcastically as he opened the door into the room where a dozen or so police officers had gathered already.

Chapter Three

DCI Brian Little rocked importantly to and fro on his heels and scratched reflectively at one of the rolls of fat on his neck as he stood at the window of the incident room on the third floor,beside the table with two chairs set for himself and Superintendent Chris Broughton, paper and pens laid neatly at each place.

Relishing the atmosphere of anticipation, he scanned the room where officers were gathering, chattering animatedly. Gobsmacked, they would be when he filled them in on the latest developments.

He clutched the thick file of papers he was holding possessively closer to his chest. And that was exactly how he had played it – close to his chest, sternly instructing the kids who had made the gruesome discovery to keep their mouths shut, however much the Press sweet-talked them, until he gave them the nod. And he wasn't about to do that until after the press conference he had called for ten-thirty.

After his weekend experiences, Little was looking forward to that. He was looking forward to the respectful silence that would fall as he entered the room, and the collective gasp when they heard what he had to tell them, to seeing their pens scribble across notebooks while their eyes never left his face, to the lights of the TV cameras and the machine-gun rattle of flashlights. He had become addicted. He had put on his best suit.

Since Saturday night, details had been coming in piecemeal.

Drip-feeding wasn't drama, though, and reckoning that there would be little more mileage to be had from the story he had hoarded the reports for one good final press conference. It was only on Sunday afternoon, after the pathologist's report, that he realised this one would run and run.

He hadn't expected to have it so quickly. You could wait a week for a standard is-it-isn't-it report on the commonplace, like the suspicious smothering of an elderly relative, but then Dr Dunne was a quirky academic who had been intrigued by the challenge of something so off-beat.

Little decided not even to brief the officers working on the case. After all, you could never be sure that one of them wasn't moonlighting as a mole for a tabloid, and he wasn't dumb enough to risk having someone else steal his thunder. Telling them now would be a dry run for what he considered the Real Thing.

The Superintendent had arrived. Broughton was a big, burly man with an easy manner; he was chatting to two of the uniformed constables, so that they'd get above themselves, no doubt, and Little would have to make a point of slapping them down later. Not that they'd take liberties with Broughton himself, of course; behind his gold-rimmed spectacles were eyes that pierced like a gimlet and there wasn't a man in the Force who didn't treat him with wary respect. But it was the principle of the thing – if uniformed constables didn't know their place, discipline went to pigs and whistles.

Little had no time for Broughton. Every smart copper knew, of course, that you had to make the politically correct noises nowadays to have a cat in hell's chance of getting on with the job in the time-honoured fashion. The trouble with Broughton was that he had sold out to the enemy; he believed in the spirit, not just the letter, of modern policing. And the Chief Constable, who had taken over five years ago from good old 'Nelson' Masters with his famous blind eye, was only a little better.

Just as well Little had made rank before either of them was in post. He sure as hell wouldn't get any further now, and he had been grimly marking off the days till his pension.

What he most definitely hadn't expected was to find himself

the man with the hottest ticket in town, the man in charge of investigating a high-profile murder. Once the case was solved and he'd left the Force, he'd be able to sell his story of the successful investigation for the sort of sum that would get Janine off his back about the pension her sister Moira's bank-manager husband had retired on. But Moira's gas had certainly been on a peep when Janine phoned her last night.

Little smirked involuntarily at the thought, then straightened his face into appropriate solemnity as Broughton came up to join him at the table. Nodding a greeting, he took up a pen and rapped it sharply for attention. As an expectant silence fell, the door opened to admit sergeants Denholm and Ward.

They were the thorns in his flesh – Ward with his smart-ass degree, and Denholm who should be bright enough to know which side his bread was buttered on and act accordingly, but somehow wasn't. His lips tightened into a sneer.

'Ah, excellent! Our cosmopolitan sergeant has decided to favour us humble provincials with his company, I see. Let's all just wait while these gentlemen find themselves somewhere to sit. We don't mind waiting, do we?' he asked rhetorically of his unresponsive audience. 'We're just grateful to you for sparing us the time.'

Only one young constable tittered sycophantically as the two men perched side by side on a table at the back of the room, their faces studiously blank and their arms folded across their chests in an almost comically identical body-language statement.

Glancing irritably round the politely unsmiling faces of the other officers, Little began.

'You all know why you're here today, but I daresay some of you may have been wondering why you haven't been provided with details of this case as it has progressed.

'Well, let me put you in the picture. You know as well as I do that this one's off-beat. There's been a lot of sensationalist and, need I say, unwelcome Press coverage, and I've been keeping everything under wraps to protect ordinary members of the public from unnecessary anxiety.'

Without turning his head or moving his lips, Denholm

muttered to Ward, 'And if you believe that you'll believe anything.'

Little's head swivelled suspiciously, but he could not identify the vague sound he had heard and Ward and Denholm both had their gaze fixed on him in exemplary concentration.

'I am now, however, in possession of three highly significant facts.' Little's small, piggy eyes were glittering; he licked his rubbery lips as if savouring physically what he had to impart.

'One, the skeleton is that of a child, ten to twelve years old. Two, it is female. And three, she was murdered by a blow to the back of the head.'

Yes, he'd got it right. That was effective. It had completely silenced them. And then, without respect for the dramatic pause Little had so skilfully engineered, Ward spoke.

'Any indication how long ago, sir?'

At Little's side, Broughton seemed to be nodding approval of this sharp interjection.

'I was coming to that, Ward, if you would have the courtesy to wait,' Little snapped. 'If everyone starts asking individual questions, we'll be here all day.

'According to the pathologist, she's been there a good number of years – fifteen to twenty, probably.'

The briefing went on for twenty minutes. Her skull had been fractured, possibly by a blow from a stone – they would be looking for that. Since they could assume that the cave had not been visited in the intervening period, there might be informative traces left there and even in the network of caves round about. She had a chipped front tooth which might have happened as she fell, but there were no other signs of violence, and because of the lack of tissue it was impossible to say whether or not she had been sexually assaulted. She had broken her wrist at some time in the past. Measurements suggested that she was between four foot ten and five foot, and remnants of her hair found beside the skull – even Little faltered, and Ward swallowed hard – showed her to have had mousy brown, wavy hair. A dental chart was being prepared which would be circulated to dentists within a fifty-mile radius, and laboratory analysis was being done on the fragments of rotting fabric and the shoes.

It was around nine-thirty when the briefing and allocation of assignments finished. Oozing self-satisfaction, Little dismissed them and led the way as he and Superintendent Broughton left the room.

Still sitting on the table at the back of the room, Ward and Denholm waited as the others filed out.

'Well, that's another nice mess you've got me into,' Denholm said acidly. 'The others get the interesting stuff, like going down the cave and seeing what they're doing at the sharp end, or dossing about doing liaison with the labs. And what do we get, because, as he quips, you've got "book learning"? We both – not just you, you notice, but me as well, me what moves my lips over the long words – get put on to trying to track down all the files every local police station has lost in the last twenty years. And I get hayfever just thinking about all that dust. Cheers!'

Ward too had been annoyed to be sidelined away from the active part of the investigation to tackle this mountain of dull and routine stuff, and he had been putting his mind to figuring out some way round it. 'Tom,' he remembered his English mistress saying at school, 'like most boys you will do any amount of thinking to avoid work.' (Girls, she had been accustomed to add darkly, would do any amount of work to avoid thinking.)

He had, he reckoned now, thought to some purpose. He levered himself off the table. 'Fun though it would be to sit and listen to your sparkling conversation all morning, I feel I must tear myself away. We have this and that to do.'

'I can make a start by dumping all the stuff I wouldn't have needed to dig out yesterday afternoon if he could have been persuaded just to hint that we weren't looking for adults, instead of being hell-bent on hogging the limelight. Then I suppose we'd better go down to dig around in Records—'

'Far be it from me to stop you, if that's your idea of a good time. I don't fancy it, though. Let's get ahead of the pack, and test out Little's blood pressure.'

He winked at the other sergeant, and headed off downstairs. It was a terrible thing to admit, given the tragedy which undoubtedly lay behind that pathetic collection of bones, but suddenly Tom Ward was feeling better about life, though it was plain that, not for the first time in their four-year professional association, DS Alex Denholm was both intrigued and irritated by his younger colleague.

When they reached the deserted CID room, Ward sat down at his desk, leaned back in his chair, stretched out his long legs, crossed his ankles and said provocatively, 'What would it take to get you to make me a cup of coffee while I make a phonecall?'

'More than you can afford.' Denholm glared at him and pointedly went to sit down at the next-door desk. 'It's bad enough playing Watson when you take one of your Sherlock Holmes fits, but Mrs Hudson – forget it!'

Ward had fished out a diary from the inside pocket of his jacket and flashed him a cheeky grin. 'Trust me,' he suggested, 'and hold good thoughts. If this goes the way I want it to, it could save us hours getting filthy down in the basement among the files. And remember your hayfever.'

'Tell me about it! Half a box of tissues I needed for that lot yesterday, and now they'll all just have to be put back.' Denholm gloomily tapped a tottering pile of aged, dusty folders on his desk.

'Go on, get me a cup of coffee. I'm more persuasive when I'm high on caffeine.'

Denholm groaned but got up. The electric kettle, which stood on a surface in one corner of the room, was empty.

'It's empty,' he objected.

'It always is.'

With another groan Denholm unplugged it and carried it across to the door, where he paused.

'Who are you going to phone anyway?' he demanded suspiciously.

Ward only tapped the side of his nose and making an obscene gesture Denholm went out.

When the door shut, Ward picked up the phone and dialled the number he had looked up. As the voice said, 'Yes?' abruptly in his ear he abandoned his lounging position and sat forward at his desk.

'Kay? It's Tom Ward here.'

The woman at the other end sighed elaborately. 'What do you want now, Tommy? And before you ask me, work out what you're going to tell me is in it for me.'

Kay Grattan always sounded as if she gargled with gravel every morning. She was the only woman to call him Tommy since his mother died, and she was a middle-aged Press harridan in the classic mould, tough and abrasive as coconut matting, with a nose for a story that would make a bloodhound appear olfactorily challenged.

They had met some years before when an interview Ward had been sent on as a PR exercise started out formally over tea in a hotel, degenerated into swapping slanderous stories off the record, and only finished at three in the morning in her flat when there wasn't anything left in the bottle of Islay Mist. They had still been known to kill a bottle of a good Highland Malt between them occasionally, when time had mercifully obliterated their recollection of the hangover from the time before.

Kay was news editor on the formidable *Midland Star* and, despite offers of the sort they must have reckoned she couldn't refuse from half a dozen London-based papers, had never been tempted to desert her home patch. She and Ward had a solemn agreement to keep quiet about their friendship during which, without rancour, they had strung each other along as often as they did each other favours.

Ward liked her a lot. 'What would you do for the lowdown on the "skeleton in the cave" story?'

'Not a lot. There's a press conference this morning. Come on, Tommy, don't insult me. You can do better than that.' She was impatient.

'Hang on, hang on. We can do each other a bit of good on this one.'

'When you say "each other" does that include me?'

'Would I be naïve enough to imagine it could work any other way? Kay, I need your help.'

'Of course you bloody do. You didn't phone because you were pining to hear my dulcet tones, did you?'

'Are your records computerised?'

'Aren't everyone's?'

'Not if you're operating with tax-payers' money. What I mean is, do you have back numbers of the *Star* on disk, going back, say, twenty years?'

'Back over the last eighty, to the first ever issue of the paper, but who's counting?'

'Listen. How long would it take you to find me a girl – ten to twelve years old – who went missing between fifteen and twenty years ago from this area?'

'Make it worth my while. I'm not in the business of saving idle coppers legwork. You spend far too much time sitting on your backside as it is.'

'Let's not get personal. What you don't know is that she was murdered. That's what Little's going to say at the press conference.'

There was a fractional pause. 'Was she, indeed,' Kay said slowly, and he could almost hear her nostrils flare.

'It's a hot story. Track down anyone you can, give me the names and I'll check them out and let you have what I find out in time for tomorrow's edition.'

'Done,' she said. 'I'll get back to you as soon as I can.'

Ward could hear Denholm's footsteps in the corridor. 'You've got my mobile number, haven't you?' He rang off as Denholm opened the door, and leaned back in his chair again, satisfied.

Denholm eyed him curiously. 'Get what you wanted?' he said, as he went to plug in the kettle.

'So far, so good. I'm expecting a phone call later.' He got up. The scent of the chase had made him restless, disinclined to accept meekly Little's edict taking him out of play. Rebellious.

'Why don't we take a spin up to Long Moor meantime and have a look at what they're up to there? It would be interesting, don't you think?'

Denholm gaped at him. 'Interesting! Well, probably, but not

as interesting as what Little will say if he finds we aren't getting on with the searches.'

Ward shrugged. 'With any luck we won't have to do them at all. And Little isn't about to come hunting round for us in the basement – he'd get his best suit dirty and then what would he wear for his next star appearance?'

'But—' Denholm protested helplessly, then gave up. 'Anyway, what about the coffee?'

'Oh, I've gone off the idea. Too much caffeine isn't good for you.'

He was smiling as he went out, and Denholm, though nursing a sense of grievance and still protesting, followed him. Behind them, the abandoned kettle boiled, then switched itself off.

It was still raining doggedly when they arrived up on the Long Moor, which rose behind the straggling village of Burlow. Under grey skies the rolling expanse of low hills with rock outcrops – so picturesque on a sunny day – looked bleak and forbidding. A few dismal-looking sheep, huddled together in sodden misery, looked up as the car stopped, then dropped their heads sadly once more.

There was a rough walkers' path across the moor and they lurched up it in Ward's car, leaving it eventually beside police cars, a police Land Rover, the scene of crime van and a couple of ordinary saloons belonging to other members of the CID.

The vehicles of the sickos who got their kicks out of sight-seeing at murder sites were being denied access, but even so when the two policemen reached the entrance to the caves there was a small anoraked crowd on the other side of the fluttering white-tape barriers, staring in greedily, as if content to stand there getting wet as mindlessly as any sheep if there was a chance, however remote, of witnessing some fresh horror.

The constable on guard in his dripping black waterproof jacket didn't look a lot more pleased with life than the sheep did. He was a local lad, normally cheerful and voluble, whose face brightened at the prospect of diversion as he recognised Ward and Denholm. He came to meet them, turning his back on the gawpers and drawing them out of earshot.

'Give you the creeps, them lot would,' he said. 'Don't talk or that, do they, just stare. I were going to have a bit of a chat, maybe, but every time I take a look, they sort of shuffle off, then when I stop looking, there they are back again. Arrest them on sus, I would!'

The two detectives grinned, glancing over his shoulder at the phenomenon which was repeating itself as the watchers – adults and even, horribly, children – realised that they themselves were being watched.

'Embarrassed,' Ward suggested. 'And so well they might be. We'll just go in for a quick look, if that's OK, Jeff?'

'No problem, sarge.' The constable sounded forlorn and Denholm added kindly, 'Drawn the short straw, haven't you, lad? Sorry we can't give you a bit of company, but we're pushed for time. Don't want to be away from the station too long, do we?'

He raised his voice pointedly as he said this, but got no reaction from Ward.

'That's all right, sir.' The constable, resigned to his fate, waved them towards the gap in the rocky hillside, an opening which was perhaps four feet wide at the base, rising to a lop-sided truncated arch.

'You go on there through the first cave, see, then there's sort of a tunnel as goes off. It's locked, usually – had this grid across it ever since someone broke an ankle exploring and got ten thousand quid off the farmer down there.' He jerked his head towards a grey-stone farmhouse on the edge of the moor road below them.

Ward was interested. 'So you have to get a key from them for access? How long ago was that done?'

The constable considered. 'Six, seven years, maybe? Just as well, to my way of thinking. Folks make mess enough in the cave there, courting couples and all. Disgusting, I call it.

'Any road, they've the generator in now, and some lights

strung up along the tunnel. Torches don't help much, not in there.'

It was still dark enough, in all conscience. Even though the day outside was so murky, it was hard to make out where they were going for the first few paces over the uneven, rocky ground. As their eyes adjusted, they could see they were in a shallow chamber, at the back of which an iron gate stood propped open to give access to a narrow passageway, feebly illuminated by a string of widely spaced, low-wattage lamp bulbs. There was, as the constable had said, the sordid evidence of casual human occupation, and the smell of decaying food from discarded pizza boxes, crisp packets and polystyrene trays. Some showed signs of having been gnawed or nibbled, and thinking of what Denholm had said about rats, Ward shuddered.

In the middle of the cave, the unwieldy bulk of a large portable generator shook and hummed. There was no one else around.

Ward eyed the generator. 'You wouldn't want that to break down when you were at the other end, would you?' he said warily. He'd never been below ground before, and in yielding to his rebellious impulse hadn't paused to work out what it would actually be like, going down into the bowels of the earth. Now he had a nasty feeling he wasn't going to enjoy it.

'I've got a torch,' Denholm said smugly, producing one from the inside pocket of his light raincoat. 'What I don't have is my thermal long-johns, though.' He shivered. 'Bloody cold in here, isn't it?'

The walls, as they went cautiously along the passage, were running with damp, but Ward had started to find the whole thing oppressive even before everything began to close in. He wiped away the sweat which was beading his upper lip as Denholm called with offensive cheerfulness, 'This must be where Dr Robson got stuck. Lucky we're both in such good shape.'

He bent down and started to crawl. Steeling himself, Ward stooped and followed him towards an aperture which seemed almost impossibly narrow.

When at last they reached the other end he was almost as

thankful as Lindy had been to straighten up, escape from the claustrophobic atmosphere and step out into the huge, bare, vaulting space. They were simultaneously silenced by the awe which struck most people entering the Cathedral cavern for the first time.

How extraordinary that rainwater could have done all this, rainwater falling on soluble rock, relentlessly seeking out every crack and weakness, forming rivulets to widen the cracks, rivers to follow their path and floods at last to scoop out these astonishing spaces which remained when the water drained away again. All this, from just water, and time.

The process hadn't stopped. The strange, soft pattering of internal rain was all about them, depositing sediment on stone or falling into the unnaturally clear, unnaturally swift and silent stream in its smooth rock channel, being carried away down below to some secret aquifer.

They were seeing it now under unprecedented conditions, as half a dozen gas cylinder lamps hissed out the brightest illumination the cave had ever known. The streaked chemicals in its rugged walls glowed with deeper colour; the frothing exuberance of the huge calcite flow at the far end had never in all the millennia of its construction glittered with such creamy extravagance.

But light casts shadows, shadows now more intense than ever. There was yawning blackness behind the rocky projections and the crevices seemed only to have an endless nothing beyond them.

It made Ward uncomfortable. He stared about him uneasily, trying to shake the fanciful thought that there was something unnatural, something ugly, about this place. '*Je suis le ténébreux* . . .' The hairs on the back of his neck rose as Baudelaire's phrase came unbidden to mind. 'I am Darkness . . .'

'Strewth!' Denholm said, apparently also moved. 'Quite something, this place, isn't it?'

'I'm lost for words,' Ward said simply, and his companion snorted.

'There's a first time for everything, I suppose. Look, there are two of the SOCOs. Let's find out what's going on.'

The men wearing the disposable white boiler-suits used by scene of crime officers were standing beside the waterfall formation, at the foot of what looked like an irregular rock staircase designed with giants in mind. There were more lights at the top, and they could hear sounds of human activity.

'Is that where it's all happening?' Ward asked, pointing.

One of them nodded. 'There's a passage in the back there leading to the cave where they found her. We're on our break, in theory. Not much of a break when there's no food and no coffee and you've been told to lay off the fags for ecological reasons as well.'

'Are you part of the detail from Flitchford?' the second man asked.

'Not exactly,' Ward said, and Denholm added, 'Actually, we're supposed to be confined to barracks under a pile of paperwork but *he* didn't fancy it.'

The others laughed. 'You'd better watch it, then. Your Super's up there, checking out how it's going.'

Denholm blanched, and even Ward looked a little taken aback. But he said nonchalantly, 'Oh, Broughton's OK. He can't stand Little any more than the rest of us can, and anyway, I've got a story.'

He was feeling better in the less confined atmosphere of the cave. He started athletically up the climb, leaving Denholm – stouter and distinctly less fit – to scramble up behind him as best he could, muttering darkly, 'It had better be a good one,' as he scrabbled for a handhold on one of the more awkward stretches.

Once they got behind the formation it was, thought Ward, almost like some scene from a Bond movie. They had concentrated most of the wattage down this passage, and the contorted shapes of boulders and the colours of the rocky walls were starkly highlighted. The sound of voices was being shaped by the echoes into a meaningless blur of hollow sound.

As the two men followed along the passage, they passed a policewoman on her hands and knees, checking the rocky floor with its shallow streams. She was concentrating hard, not even raising her head as they passed; in an unlit side-passage they could see a powerful torch bobbing along in the darkness, evidence of another search down there.

The centre of operations was only a little further ahead. A photographer was leaning against the wall, wrestling with his camera and swearing about the damp playing havoc with its electrical contacts.

A harassed-looking detective whom they didn't recognise – presumably the inspector in charge of the SOCOs – was giving directions to part of the Flitchford contingent which, it seemed, had just arrived. He had been living in a logistical nightmare, and was now trying to organise a search, under financial as well as operational constraints, for evidence which might be twenty years old. If it existed at all.

Behind him, a tape barrier was stretched across, a little way down the narrowing passage beyond. 'Don't go past that,' he was cautioning them as Ward and Denholm reached the group. 'It slopes down suddenly into a shaft, and if you slide into that we don't have the resources to get you out for another twenty years. Not that you'd care anyway, once you'd hit the bottom.

'If you go down a side-passage, watch where you put your size tens. You just might be the first person there since the kid was killed, so if there's rock dust be on the look-out for foot-prints, or anything lying about. We probably can't expect anything from the main drag here – a fair number of people will have been along over the years. But because apparently most of the other passages are dead ends, according to the experts, it isn't on the cavers' tourist route. So you never know.

'Anyway, make it thorough. This is our only chance, because once we figure out how to get the equipment back up, no one's ever going to bring it down again. OK? And for any favour don't wander off and get yourselves lost. We don't have time to look for you.

'Any questions?'

No one spoke; his audience nodded, then moved on up the forked passage just as the tall figure of Superintendent Broughton came out from the most brightly illuminated area, the right-hand opening which was where there was the greatest concentration of men in white boiler-suits.

'They think they may have got the chip off her front tooth,' he said to the detective in charge, then noticed Ward and Denholm hovering. He frowned. 'What are you two doing here? I thought you were detailed to wade through the "Missing" files.'

Denholm winced, but Ward was ready to say smoothly, 'We've got that in hand, sir – narrowed down, I think, but we just wanted to check on the latest evidence in case there was something to help with elimination.'

Broughton gave him a hard stare, his spectacles glinting in the artificial light, then said, with the air of a man who has problems enough of his own without shouldering other people's, 'Fine. I don't think we have anything new to give you though, do we, Grant?'

The other detective grimaced. 'Not so's you'd notice, sir. A sackful of stones that forensic might tell us includes the murder weapon – or might not. A rusted torch with a few flakes of blue paint on it, which probably belonged to the child herself. And a chip of tooth, if that's right, which tells us she fell forward and hit her mouth on the way down. Well, you would, wouldn't you, if you were clobbered on the back of the head. That's all, lads. Big deal.'

He turned away and went gloomily back up into the cave where they were working, and Broughton, after pausing for a word with the photographer, followed him.

'God, you're a jammy beggar!' Denholm shook his head. 'Smelling of roses again. Can we go back now? I keep thinking any minute I'm going to hear Little booming, "Sergeant, what the hell do you think you're doing here?" '

Ward squinted at his watch. 'Nearly eleven o'clock. How time flies when you're enjoying yourself! Yes, we'd better head back.' He wasn't much looking forward to the return journey, but there wasn't any point in putting it off. His mobile was out of action until they got back above ground, and if Kay had seen fit to pull the stops out there could be a message with the answering service by now.

As they returned along the main passage, the policewoman who had been close-searching the floor was standing up, brushing dust off her uniform trousers, and Ward recognised Lynn Carson, a sturdy, sensible, bright-faced woman seconded from Traffic. Having been at the briefing she greeted him with some surprise.

'Tom! What are you doing here? Bunking off?'

'Something like that.'

'What's it worth not to grass to Little?'

'You can't fool me, Lynn – you'd do anything for a half of shandy and a packet of pork scratchings. And even if he does find out I should have enough to keep him off our backs. Probably.'

She looked at him sideways, then said, 'But isn't this the weirdest place you've ever seen? It's incredible – look at this!'

She was holding a torch which she swung up to a fissure in the rock wall, at around waist height, a crack not much more than a hand's breadth from side to side and about fifteen inches high. In the light, Lindy's 'fairy cave' sprang into view with its stalactites and stalagmites – some of which had met to form pillars – in shades ranging from deepest salmon-pink to rose-tinged ivory.

'Brilliant, isn't it?' she said. 'And maybe no one's ever even seen it before. Makes you think, that.'

Denholm took the torch and looked in, exclaiming, then Ward took his place, marvelling at the profligacy of nature in creating such beauty to blush unseen – though it was, of course, arrogant to consider creation's purpose as being human delight.

He took one lingering, final look – because nothing in God's earth was going to get him back down here – and was turning away when something towards the back of the cave off to one side caught his eye. He angled the torch beam to illuminate it, then bent closer, frowning.

'You weren't the first, Lynn. Look – what on earth is that?' He drew back to let the others see past his pointing finger.

Something had been placed in the middle of four of the pillar formations which almost made an enclosure for it. It wasn't obvious; it was a similar colour to the natural features of the cave – a rusty beige – but this was not a natural feature. It had been painted that colour; some of the paint was flaking away and under it was some grey substance – clay, perhaps?

It was a primitive artefact about five inches in height, a long narrow body with a head with ears and a sharp pointed nose, a head like a dog's or wolf's. On it had been outlined, in patchy, faded black, staring eyes and a row of savage, pointed teeth, and it was curiously and powerfully unpleasant.

'Could have been left by anyone, of course,' Broughton pointed out. 'It's on the main passage, after all.'

'It's the sort of thing a kid might have made, though, sir,' argued Grant, desperate to find something to show for his men's labours. 'Using that little cranny for some sort of game, maybe.'

It wasn't the sort of game you would like to think of children playing, though. Ward felt the unease he had experienced before, a longing for the freshness of the upper air instead of this stale, stagnant dampness. He shifted uncomfortably as the two senior officers bent down to the crevice for another look.

They hadn't moved it yet; they'd want photographs and tests and fingerprints, just in case there was something useful even after all these years.

'Anyway,' said Broughton, 'that was good observation, Tom. Well done. *However,*' he added drily, looking beadily from Ward to Denholm, 'I shall be looking forward to reading your report on identification later today. Looking forward to it *very much.*'

'Yes, sir,' Ward murmured submissively. There were beads of sweat on his upper lip again, but the pressure that had caused them wasn't now entirely atmospheric. If Kay didn't come up with the goods, he might as well start scanning the Jobs ads in the *Midland Star*. Broughton's tone had made it clear that success was the only possible excuse for insubordination.

They had just turned to leave when an echoing shout came behind them. 'Sir! Sir! Along here!'

Grant spun on his heel; the noise had come from the dark side-passage opposite the tiny cave they had been studying. He and Broughton, followed by the others at a respectful distance, went across to join the uniformed constable who had been searching it. He was directing a beam of light into another, wider crevice in the wall, again about waist height, about ten yards from the opening of the passage.

His voice was shaky. 'It's bones, sir,' he said. 'More bones.'

Chapter Four

'Well, what did you make of that?'

Ward and Denholm had said little as they made their way back out of the caves; as they walked down the hill, Ward spoke first.

Denholm was inclined to be indignant. 'From the way he spoke, I thought we had another murder on our hands.'

'Disappointed?' Denholm snorted, and Ward went on, 'Unpleasant enough, don't you think, the bones of small animals?'

'Mmm. Rabbits, do you reckon?'

'Well, I only caught a glimpse, but the skulls didn't all look the same size.'

'Laid in a sort of pile, weren't they? Deliberate, that looked.'

'They hardly all climbed in there to die neatly, did they?'

'How many did you reckon there were? A dozen?'

'Thereabouts.'

They fell silent again, tramping down towards the car. Suddenly, Ward remembered the message he was waiting for. The smooth, plummy voice of his mobile answering service said, 'You have one message. Message one:—' and Kay Grattan's less refined tones rasped, 'Tommy, where the hell are you? Call me.'

'Ah,' he said, switching it off and putting it back in his pocket as they reached the car.

Denholm eyed him with naked curiosity. 'Got something?'

'It's – possible.' Better than possible, surely; if Kay had phoned back as quickly as that, she must have turned up something. The temptation was to phone her back immediately, but it would be wiser to wait. Deirdre, the secretary who presided over the office fax machine, had embraced all too enthusiastically the principle that knowledge is power, so he'd better be in a position to snatch whatever Kay sent as soon as it came through.

'I'll find out once I get back,' he said provokingly, starting the engine.

'Oh, don't tell me what's going on, will you? Just because I have a wife and children who'll be out on the street if I haven't something to show Little, don't feel you have to put my mind at rest.'

Ward grinned, pulling in to one side of the track as the mobile canteen van came lurching uncertainly up, to allow it a better run at the slope. Denholm's wife was a bank manager, earning roughly twice what he did for working the sort of social hours a copper could only dream about.

'Trust me,' he said once more.

'No wonder you can't keep a woman. You probably say that to them all without realising everyone knows it means "I haven't the first idea what I'm doing but it'll be in my interests not yours."'

'Ouch!' Ward said placidly, then, 'Changing the subject away from my personal defects as a human being, what did you reckon to the clay figure, Alex?'

Diverted, Denholm considered the question. 'Hard to say. Kids' game, Grant said – but it wasn't Ring-a-Ring-a-Roses, was it? It – it sounds daft, maybe, but there was something about it I didn't like. That dog's face . . .'

'Yes,' Ward said slowly. 'It's annoying me – it reminded me of something I can't quite pin down. Nasty, certainly. But face it – kids do have some pretty nasty ideas nowadays.'

'But that wasn't nowadays, Tom,' Denholm pointed out. 'Not if it's got anything to do with this case. That was twenty years ago when ten year olds were into *Blue Peter* not *Trainspotting*.'

They had reached the bottom of the track, and with some

relief that nothing crucial seemed to have fallen off the car Ward accelerated away in the direction of Flitchford.

'That little cave,' he said thoughtfully, 'you know what it suggested to me? Some sort of temple. The group of pillars – it was almost as if the figure had been set there in a kind of shrine.'

'Creepy anyway.'

'And the dog's head – I wish I could nail that association.' Ward was brooding. 'There's nothing more irritating – it's like an itch you can't scratch.'

Unimpressed, Denholm said, 'Try thinking of something else, and it'll come back to you. You could try thinking what we're going to do next.'

Suddenly, Ward exclaimed, 'Anubis!'

'*Gesundheit!*' Denholm said drily. 'What's that supposed to mean?'

'Anubis, the jackal-headed god – that's what it reminded me of.'

'Oh, *Anubis*, of course. Well, slap my wrist for not thinking of it!'

'They went in for gods with animals' heads, the Egyptians, didn't they? I'd this book about them when I was a kid.'

'I read the *Beano*, me.'

Ignoring him, Ward continued. 'There were hawks and bulls and all sorts. But I think Anubis was the one with a man's body and a jackal's head.'

'Go on, surprise me. Why a jackal?'

Ward shrugged. 'I'd have to look it up.'

Denholm thought about what he had said. 'Could be linked with those animals, couldn't it? Sacrifice, or something.'

'That did occur to me. Still, as Broughton said, there's nothing definite to link it with the skeleton.'

'Money on it?' Denholm suggested hopefully. They were inclined to liven up their policework by the occasional flutter on the outcome of a case, and since Tom was ahead by all of £2.50, Alex was keen to get his word in first on what looked to him like a dead cert.

'Not a chance. Unless you're planning to bet against a connection?'

'Not exactly. Can they get prints off something that could be that old?'

'No particular reason why not, is there?'

'Depends on the surface, probably.'

'And the atmosphere, maybe.'

As they were equally uninformed, there wasn't a lot more to say about it and they fell to talking about Alex's sixteen-year-old daughter who had now added a pierced eyebrow to the pink streaks in her hair that had so exercised her mother the week before.

'Maybe you could say something to her, Tom,' her father suggested not very hopefully. 'Say it makes her look weird or something. She thinks, for some unfathomable reason, that you're a cool dude.'

Tom grinned. 'Oh, no you don't. You do your own dirty work. The only reason your Tammy thinks I'm a cool dude is because I don't say things like that. I'll need all the street-cred I've got for when she's a ravishing twenty-one and I'm on the slopey side of thirty-five.'

'She won't be ravishing if she's got as many holes as a colander. And anyway, the thought of a dirty old man like you'll be then dating my daughter isn't a consoling one.'

Swapping amiable insults they drove back to Flitchford. When they arrived at the police station they saw that the Press was back in force, a damp, dispirited group around the entrance. As Ward slowed to turn into the car park they came suddenly to life, shouting questions as the car swept unresponsively past. A couple of cameras flashed.

'We'll have some fast talking to do if they publish those and Little sees them,' Denholm said wryly.

Ward laughed. 'A blurred shot of a couple of unidentified guys in an unmarked car? They'll be far too busy trying to decide which of Little's poses to select – left profile, right profile, full face, three-quarters on . . .'

Back in the CID room all was quiet, with no urgent messages from anyone.

'Looks as if we got away with it,' Denholm said with relief. 'As long as we really can come up with something to show Broughton. Come on, Tom, put me out of my misery – what's all the mystery about?'

Ward hardly heard him. He was almost afraid of making the phonecall now. Perhaps, after all, Kay had called to say she couldn't help him, couldn't find anything . . . He picked up the receiver and got out his notebook to check the number.

Denholm parked himself defiantly. 'You needn't think you can get rid of me this time,' he said, preparing without shame to eavesdrop.

But Ward's end of the brief conversation wasn't revealing, confined as it was to monosyllables. Still, it was plain what he was hearing wasn't bad news.

'Right, you'll fax me then,' he concluded, giving the number. 'Give me a couple of minutes to get there ready to grab it.'

Denholm looked at him hopefully as he rang off. 'Well?'

'Promising,' was all Ward would say, but he couldn't altogether conceal his optimism. 'I'm just going to collect that fax.'

'I'll come.' Denholm got to his feet.

'We can't both go cluttering up the dreaded Deirdre's office. It's not big enough,' Ward pointed out with sweet reason. 'And you know how she is about people who have the nerve to inter-cept their faxes before she's read them.'

'Look, why don't you take those files back down to Records and I'll find you there? I'll be wanting to pick up some stuff anyway.'

'Got names to follow up, then, have you?'

'Might have, might have.'

He went out and Denholm, sighing heavily, collected the unwieldy pile of files from the desk, sneezed violently twice, and headed for the door.

Spewing out of the fax machine into Tom Ward's waiting hands, Kay Grattan's fax was ten pages long.

'Goodness,' said Deirdre from her desk with a sugary vivacity which emphasised rather than concealed her resentment at this impugning of her discretion. 'Writing a book at our expense, are they?'

Ward collected the sheets together and extricated himself as quickly as he could.

Walking back, he riffled through the dark, grainy, and in places barely legible sheets. Kay had turned up three girls for him, the youngest ten, the oldest thirteen, all reported missing locally during the relevant five years. He was determined, though, not to court disappointment by raising his hopes too high. Alive or dead, any or all of them could have been accounted for later, and he had limited the area for the sake of speed and simplicity, without evidence to pin it down so precisely.

Still, this was somewhere to start. At worst, it was something to produce for Broughton when he checked what they had to show for their morning's search. Reaching his desk again, Ward sat down and spread the pages out before him.

Looking at the pictures which accompanied the headlines, fuzzy and amateurish as such things inevitably were, he winced. Missing Persons' photographs always got to him.

Removed from a frame or prized out of the family album, they had a raw directness which not even the most skilful professional photographer could hope to reproduce. They drew you unwillingly into the intimacy of some ordinary family celebration, of Christmas or a play or a picnic, where someone had posed cheerfully and casually in harrowing ignorance of the terrible future use of this innocent record.

You knew what they didn't know, and the knowledge chilled your soul because you and your family had, like them, posed a hundred times for photographs just like these. Like them, you had smiled or pouted for the camera, like them never considering that in this fleeting image you might some day be grimly immortalised.

It was even worse, of course, with pictures of children. From the blurred pages on his desk, the three childish faces looked out at him with almost unbearable poignancy. Had any of them been spared to develop the adult face hinted at by those rounded, half-formed features?

He shuffled them into a rough order of probability. If any of them had survived, he would put his money on Trudi Walker. The photograph of Trudi showed her wearing a strappy party dress and long earrings, and even in this indistinct snapshot you could see that there was elaborate make-up on the pert little face. Thirteen going on thirty, he guessed. It seemed that her mother's live-in lover had banned her from going to a disco; Trudi had packed her bags and left in the middle of the night, clearing out his wallet and her mother's purse. She'd probably headed for London or Manchester and lived rough. And if she'd been lucky, if she wasn't dead of drugs or AIDS, she could be a mother herself by now, learning the hard way about problems with kids.

It would need following up, of course, but Trudi looked to him like a survivor. It would be good to think so, anyway.

The other two, Bonnie Bryant and Angie Morrison, were younger. Ward looked at their photographs and sighed. He wouldn't like to bet on the chances for either of them.

Angie was ten, a pretty, fair-haired child. Hers was a sadly familiar story: sent out just before dusk on an autumn evening to a corner store five minutes from her home on the outskirts of Matlock, she had never returned. 'Angie, our very own little angel, gone,' her distraught father had said with the triteness which is so often the hallmark of genuine grief.

Perhaps a check would reveal a happy ending, but Ward had been in the police force too long to cherish any illusion that this was a likely outcome. On the other hand, would Angie's abductor have been likely to drive her all the way to the Long Moor and drag her in darkness through difficult underground passages and caves, either before or after he had indulged whatever perversion had prompted taking her? And besides, as far as Ward could tell from the snapshot, her hair was blonde and straight.

He had kept the reports on Bonnie Bryant's disappearance until last. It had been an unfortunate choice of name; the fat plain child in the photograph glowering out from under a paper hat with a Christmas tree apparently growing out of it, was not in the least bonny. She was eleven; she had disappeared on a summer day when she had been given permission to go out and play on her bicycle, under strict instructions not to be late for lunch.

But what had caught Ward's eye, what had made him almost superstitiously read the other cases first as if to conceal his interest from some God of Investigations who might be jealous of mortal success, was the name of the village to which she had never returned.

Burlow. Burlow, the village he had driven through that morning, which straggled across the flank of the Long Moor, one of the villages peculiar to Derbyshire where the one-time miners' houses indicated an industrial past in curious contrast to their rural setting.

Not only that, but it looked, as far as he could see under the silly hat, as if her hair was brown and wavy.

Ward glanced at his watch. Twelve-thirty; any minute now other detectives would be returning. He picked up a notepad and scribbled down names and dates, then opened a drawer in his desk and swept the tell-tale copies of newsprint into it.

It wouldn't be long before other journalists, too, thought of running through the back numbers of their papers and homed in, as he had done, on Bonnie Bryant. For that matter, once the news was out that this was a child's skeleton, it wouldn't be long before people in Burlow with long memories started putting two and two together as well. He was owing Kay Grattan now, and in order to deliver he would have to move fast enough to keep ahead of the pack.

Denholm would be waiting impatiently in Records, too. He was a good man, was Alex, and he'd tried his patience far enough today already; he grabbed the notebook and hurried downstairs.

When Ward came in, Denholm was discussing football with Dan Collins, a stubbornly unimaginative sergeant with only a year to go before being put out to grass. He had been parked in the basement by Superintendent Broughton who, as he tried to get the Flitchford force up to speed with modern policing, reckoned Collins could probably do less harm here than anywhere else.

The present fortunes of Derby County were not an exhilarating topic and Denholm greeted Ward eagerly as he came in. His expression suggested someone who has paid good money for a magic show and, though sceptical, is prepared to suspend disbelief in the hope that it hasn't been entirely wasted.

Playing to the gallery was reprehensible but hard to resist. Ward closed his eyes, and pinched his brows in a pantomime of psychic concentration.

'It's coming to me now. Yes, I have it. Three files, Dan, if you'd be so good. Angie Morrison, Trudi Walker and Bonnie Bryant; 3 October 1983, 28 May 1978 and 12 July 1980 respectively. There, I've written it down for you.'

Unmoved, Collins nodded, took the sheet of paper Ward had torn from the notebook and plodded off into the catacombs behind him, the resting place for so many cases which would never again see the light of day.

'I suppose I'm expected to be grateful you've pulled the rabbit out of the hat yet again and my children can eat tomorrow,' Denholm said.

'We're not there yet. These may all come to nothing.'

'But you don't think so, do you?'

Ward hesitated, as if that same God of Investigations might be listening, alert to punish presumption in mere human practitioners of his art.

'No, I don't,' he risked saying.

Collins had never been a fast mover. It was nearly quarter of an hour before he succeeded in tracking down the three files requested, and he slapped them down on the counter with the air of one who has hacked his way through a tropical rainforest and made it to the other side.

'Not easy to put my hand on, those weren't,' he said. 'You have to know the system, see? I've told them I should've had someone long ago to train up. It's too late now. They'd need a couple of years' experience with me to show them the ropes properly – it'll be mayhem, bloody mayhem when I go. And if it's going to be like it's been the last couple of days, I should by rights have an assistant down here anyway. I've told them, but of course they just don't want to know.'

The other men made non-committal noises. It was an open secret that Broughton's technological revolution was being post-poned until Collins rode off into the sunset. They left him to make an afternoon's work out of replacing the files Denholm had returned.

Back in the CID room, Ward made no pretence of inde-cision. He laid down the other two thick files and picked up the one marked 'BONNIE ELIZABETH BRYANT dob 3.10.68' with hands which only just didn't shake with eagerness.

Denholm watched him sourly. 'Do I take it I'd be wasting my time if I went checking through the other two elements of the three card trick?'

Ward showed no sign of having heard him. 'It's her height I need to know. Height, height, we must have it here somewhere.' He flicked impatiently through the pages.

Denholm picked up the Angie Morrison file. The photo-graph taped to the cover was the original of the one Ward had seen in the paper, but much clearer. 'This one's blonde,' he said. 'Look! And Little said the hair was brown, didn't he?'

Again, Ward ignored him. 'Here we are,' he exclaimed. 'Height four foot eleven. That's within the parameters the pathologist set. And mousy-brown, wavy hair, and she lived in Burlow.'

'Burlow! But that's the village right below the moor—'

'You've noticed too. Right. So we need to talk to someone who can tell us whether she once broke her arm, and then we can get on to DNA testing.'

'Dental records first,' Denholm suggested. 'Quicker.'

'You're right. I knew there had to be a reason for hanging out with you. Let's go and see if we can time it so that Little's out of his office and we can go direct to the Super.'

'What are you going to say if he asks where you got the information?'

'"Just a wild guess, sir," I should think. Only he isn't dumb enough to ask a question like that when he knows he won't get an answer.'

'Not like me, you mean?'

Fortunately, the door opened before Ward was obliged to reply, and the two officers assigned to liaison with the labs came in, grinning when they saw the other two men.

'Had a good morning?' Crozier said.

'Not looking as dusty as I expected,' Barclay chimed in. 'How far have you got, lads? Past the letter A yet?'

Ward and Denholm watched them laugh, then Denholm said, 'We've not had a bad day, in fact. Just on the way up to the Super with a hot lead.'

They looked gratifyingly astonished. 'That was lucky!' Crozier exclaimed.

'Not luck,' Denholm indulged himself by saying smugly. 'Skill.' He avoided meeting Ward's eye.

'How's it going at the lab?' Ward asked. 'Are they doing a dental chart?'

'Working on it, along with all sorts of other things,' Crozier said. 'It's quite interesting down there. A bit gruesome, but interesting. They send the parts off to different departments, you see—'

'Dental chart?' Ward prompted, anxious to cut short the ghoulish recital Crozier seemed to be embarking on with considerable relish.

'Someone's got the jaw and is examining it, then they'll chart – oh, fillings and that sort of thing. Then they'll circulate dentists and hope one of them can match it up—'

'We'll probably be able to save them a bit of time. We could have the name of the child's dentist in the next day or so.'

'What've you got, then?' Barclay was openly curious.

Denholm gathered up the files possessively. 'That,' he said with dignity, 'is for us to know and you to guess.'

His grand exit was spoiled by Ward suddenly recollecting his chief concern. 'Oh, by the way, you don't know where Little is, do you?'

'Passed him on the way down to the canteen,' Barclay replied. 'You'll catch him there, I should think.'

'That wasn't – er – what we had in mind,' Ward said, and they were laughing as he closed the door.

Broughton looked up as Ward and Denholm entered the Superintendent's office.

'Ah, that's handy,' he greeted them with dangerous sweetness. 'I was going to send down for a report on how you were getting on.'

'I'm afraid I haven't had time yet to write any sort of report, sir,' Ward said circumspectly, 'but we've come up with three files. We haven't checked them out yet, but there's one that looks so promising I thought we should let you see it as soon as possible.'

He took Bonnie Bryant's file from Denholm and put it down on the desk in front of the Superintendent. Broughton said nothing, merely pulling it over to him and opening it.

He had been looking distinctly sceptical, but as his eye fell on the address, he exclaimed, 'Burlow!' His bushy grey eyebrows shot up as he took the photograph attached to the report and studied it with sudden interest.

'The hair's right, as far as you can tell,' he said. 'And she looks around the right age too.'

'She is, sir, and the date she disappeared fits. And the height matches.'

Broughton was sifting through the reports in the file. 'I must say, it looks very promising. Very promising indeed. Amazing that you've managed to put your finger on it so quickly.'

He looked searchingly over his glasses at Ward.

'Thank you, sir,' Ward said stolidly.

Broughton held his gaze for a moment, then said, mildly enough, 'What about the others?'

Denholm, shifting uncomfortably, had looked down at the files he was holding to avoid the Superintendent's eye and was leafing through Trudi Walker's, which was uppermost.

'This inquiry's actually been closed, sir,' he said. 'There's a record here of a phonecall from her received a year later when she was in Birmingham. And she'd have been fourteen by then.'

'Right. And the other one?' Broughton held out his hand.

'That's Angie Morrison,' Ward said. 'I've got a nasty feeling she's probably in a shallow grave somewhere.'

As Broughton looked at the file, Ward outlined his earlier conclusions about her case. 'After checking out the caves this morning, sir, it struck me that it would be extraordinarily difficult to get someone who was either resistant or inert through some of the trickier parts of that passageway, wouldn't you say?'

Broughton nodded, and Ward became aware that Denholm was looking at him strangely; of course he knew Ward hadn't so much as glanced at the Morrison file, and he was no fool. It wouldn't take him long to work out where such detailed information was to be found. Well, he'd felt a bit of a rat keeping Alex in the dark anyway.

'Right,' Broughton said. 'It looks as if we should follow up on the Bryant child, doesn't it? They found her bike, apparently, but not a body.'

Ward spoke eagerly. 'Perhaps we might go up to Burlow this afternoon, see what we could turn up?'

Broughton put his fingers together, considering. 'Yes, why not? But I don't think it needs two sergeants. We have a manpower problem here, with so many people tied up in the cave search. And with such a promising lead, there's no point in doing any more searches in the records until this is sorted out one way or the other, is there? So one of you can go down to Belper this afternoon – there's been some vandalism in one of the smarter streets down there, and the residents are making waves. Don't think we're taking it seriously enough, apparently.'

There was an awkward pause before Denholm, doing the decent thing, immolated himself. 'I'll go down to Belper then, sir,' he said, and Ward, as he relaxed, realised that his nails had been digging into the palms of his hands. If it had been left to Broughton, Ward wouldn't have put it past him to take subtle revenge by sending Denholm to Burlow, knowing that Ward was likely to have instigated the flouting of orders.

'Do you think you need a constable, Tom?' Broughton asked. 'Because—'

'No, no,' Ward said hastily. It would suit him very well to be a free agent. 'I won't be taking statements or anything, just getting background to see if we can get further confirmation. There might still be someone around who would remember if she ever broke her arm, for instance.'

'Twenty years is nothing in these villages,' Broughton said. 'You shouldn't find it too difficult. Good luck!'

'Thank you, sir.' Ward picked up the Bryant file. 'Should I wait to tell DCI Little what's happened? We did look for him before we came here, of course, but he wasn't in his office.'

Did Broughton's mouth twitch? It was hard to tell, but anyway he said, 'No, just get on with it, Tom. I'll put him in the picture.'

As they shut the door, Ward said to Denholm, 'Thanks, Alex. I owe you one.'

'Yes you bloody do. More than one. Several, in fact, the very next time we're in the pub. An afternoon massaging the ego of articulate middle-class trouble-makers – thank you very much.'

'Just tell them broken windows are part of a New Labour initiative for job creation. An informal kind of on-the-spot taxation to help in the redistribution of wealth.'

Alex scowled at him. 'Always such a help. Just don't let Little find out that you've got a Press source, that's all. No one's allowed to have contacts with the media apart from him.'

'Actually, I do feel bad about giving you the runaround over all that,' Tom said with a genuine pang of conscience. 'It's just that my contact and I are sworn to secrecy—'

Denholm groaned. 'Don't tell me, it's a woman, isn't it?' Glamorous, sexy—'

'Not exactly. She's a great lady, but – mature, shall we say.'

'God, I don't know about you. Sixteen year olds one minute, grandmothers the next. Is there a woman in the entire country who's safe?'

Chapter Five

———————⋙●⋘———————

Burlow was an odd little town – or was it a large village? Tom Ward had never been clear in his own mind about the distinction between the two. He parked his car at one end of the main street and set off on foot.

Despite its idyllic rural setting, this was a creature of the Industrial Age just as much as Birmingham, say, or Manchester. From those prettified cottages running along the hillside there, much prized for their view of patchwork fields outlined by neat, ruler-straight gritstone walls, miners had gone out to toil underground and spinners and weavers had walked to their work in the mill, a humid hell of noise and dirt.

Its belching chimney had been levelled long ago, its only legacy the grimy streaks that marked the stonework of the older buildings. The mine was now an attraction in the burgeoning business of industrial tourism, but apart from that Burlow was undistinguished – an ordinary high street, an ordinary church, ordinary houses, with few pretensions to the picturesque.

Even so, it had a chintzy tearoom and a couple of shops that reeked of potpourri and aromatic candles and sold 'gifts' – that curious category of artefacts whose common feature is to be without purpose, whether practical or aesthetic. There was a smart delicatessen catering to the Sheffield commuters who had colonised an 'executive development' on the outskirts.

On the rainswept pavements, two or three disconsolate groups of tourists in light waterproofs that offered them little protection from the spiteful gusts of wind, peered dispiritedly in at shop windows. A smart woman in jeans and a Barbour jacket came out of the deli, hurried across the road and jumped into an Isuzu Trooper parked on the other side.

There didn't seem to be any customers in the shops Ward passed. In one of the gift shops, with a window display consisting mainly of pastel-coloured dragons and freshly caught fairy folk in jars, a plump, middle-aged blonde woman wearing a cream trouser-suit and a lot of gold jewellery was standing with her arms folded, staring out gloomily at the rain. Catching Ward's eye she smiled, but not hopefully.

Mixed in with the tourist traps was a handful of shops serving the daily needs of the local community: alongside the contrived, cutesy charm of their neighbours, they looked almost defiantly grim. Most of them still had their seventies frontage, heavy on the plate glass with aluminium trim.

The newsagent's had a fly-blown layout of faded plastic toys and paperback books with curling covers. The dress shop next door but one was this month featuring crimplene suits in variegated shades of mud and slime in one window, and baby clothes that would need ironing in the other. The Spar mini-mart, with its windows almost completely obscured by lottery posters, looked so unwelcoming that Ward felt it would be awkward to go in without a letter of introduction.

Most telling of all, there was a charity shop with rails of felted woollens and drooping jackets from men's outworn suits. What people felt able to discard said a lot about prosperity: there clearly weren't too many people with money to throw around here, despite the deli and the gift shops.

When he thought about it, there seemed to be a marked divide. The shabby high street shops gave an air of depression to the place that must make it harder for shopkeepers trying to make their living from tourism. Indeed, their shabbiness almost looked like an act of sabotage.

It was surprising, really, that Burlow still supported the sort of shops which had altogether vanished from most places of this size. But then, of course, the nearest supermarket was at

Flitchford, twenty-five minutes away with a clear run, and considerably more than that when the roads were clogged by visitors with nothing better to do than drive from one set of gift shops to another.

It was getting on for two o'clock now, and it seemed a very long time since breakfast. Surely he'd noticed a pub when they drove through on the way to the caves this morning? Oh yes, there it was.

The Cavendish Arms, with its smart cream paint and the beer-garden at the side, clearly saw itself as catering to the upper end of the tourist market. The menu outside in its wrought-iron frame offered the delights of scampi, lasagne and chicken tandoori rather than pie, beans and chips.

But today the wooden bench tables were sodden and the pink and purple petunias in the window-boxes were bruised and bedraggled from the rain. When Ward glanced in one of the windows, only two of the beaten copper tables were occupied and the fruit machine in the corner was winking and flashing to itself.

Not really the sort of place where he was likely to be able to find Burlow natives, was it? Unmoved even by the promise of breaded garlic mushrooms with a sour cream dip, Ward walked on. There must be, surely, another watering-hole catering to the other side of the Great Burlow Divide?

There was, indeed, another pub further along on the opposite side of the street. It was an old building in Derbyshire limestone, with small windows obscured to half-way up by opaque glass. *The Three Tuns* was written on a badly weathered sign over the door and the paintwork had been perpetrated in tobacco-brown wood-grained varnish.

On the frosted panel of the door was etched an advertisement for a long-forgotten stout and a peeling sticker claimed 'Good Food Here'. Ward, eyeing it with the cynicism born of painful experience, pushed down the old brass thumb-plate and opened the door. It certainly looked the sort of place where Burlow society could feel itself safe from tourist invasion.

It was dark inside and the mock-Tudor wall lamps with deep

red shades did little to lighten the gloom. The smell, familiar from a hundred other similar pubs, was a mixture of stale beer, cigarette smoke, and the underlying hint of indeterminate vegetables being relentlessly overcooked.

There was no one sitting at the tables with their chipped black varnish. A middle-aged woman wearing a soiled pink overall was wiping them with a cloth that didn't look as if it had been clean even before she started.

Nothing cooked, then, Ward decided as he walked across to the bar. A cheese and pickle sandwich, perhaps – that shouldn't be too much of a health hazard.

Behind the bar, a man with thin, receding dark hair and a hangdog expression was morosely drying glasses. The only customer was an elderly man sitting in one corner at the counter with a half-pint mug in front of him, half full. Somehow it had the air of a drink which has been nursed for an inordinate length of time.

The woman glanced up indifferently, then went back to her work. She was emptying ashtrays into a plastic bag now, then wiping them round with the same cloth.

The barman set down his dish-towel and came forward, unsmiling.

'Sir?'

'A pint of bitter please. Am I too late for a sandwich?'

'We stop serving come two o'clock,' he said, glancing up hopefully at the yellowing plastic of the 'Guinness is Good for You' clock above the bar. The toucan, which formed one of the hands, indicated that it was no more than five to, and he sighed heavily.

'I'll see what I can do. Annie!'

He raised his voice and the woman turned round. She had shoulder-length, stringy grey hair and the sallow complexion of the heavy smoker.

'Gentleman wants a sandwich. Can you do him one?'

'Right,' she said listlessly, picking up the bag and the cloth. Ward saw her wipe her hand down the side of her overall and suppressed a shudder.

'Cheese or ham?' the barman was asking, but Ward said hastily, 'Actually, I've changed my mind. Don't bother. I'll just have a couple of bags of crisps instead. Cheese and onion if you've got them.'

'Suit yourself.' The man shrugged his shoulders and jerked his head at the woman who plodded back again to her task. He picked up a glass and began to pull a pint.

Feeling uncomfortably as if he had invaded someone's private sitting room only to insult them with impertinent demands, Ward perched on one of the bar stools. For all he was likely to get out of mine host or Mrs Glum there, he might as well have succumbed to the breaded mushrooms.

The old boy in the corner was his best bet. He was wearing a sort of blazer, but it looked as if his gents' outfitter was the charity shop across the road. The stringy, red-spotted cravat round his jowly neck was tied with a certain panache, though, and the rheumy blue eyes were sharp and curious.

'Can I get you another of those?' Ward offered, gesturing towards the glass which now had little more than half an inch in the bottom.

His companion brightened. 'Don't mind if I do. Make it a pint this time, Jim,' he said, downing the remainder and pushing the empty glass across the bar. Ignoring another heavy sigh, he turned to his benefactor.

'Thank you, sir, that's uncommonly civil of you. Stranger here, aren't you?'

Ward took his pint and the crisps from the tight-lipped Jim and as he took out his wallet to pay offered, 'And one for yourself?'

'No thanks.' Jim pulled the second pint, then dumped it down in front of him with a bad grace so that it slopped on the beer-mat, and went back to his glass-drying.

Ward slid it along the bar. 'Cheers. Yes, I just came up from Flitchford. Tom Ward.'

'Your very good health, Tom. A liberal man, clearly. Percy Willis is the name, Perce to my friends, and any man who buys Perce Willis a pint buys entry to that select company.'

Ward grinned and raised his glass. 'Thank you, Perce. Honoured, I'm sure.'

A snort came from Jim's direction.

'Now what, I was asking myself,' his new friend went on after a long and satisfying pull at his pint, 'is a likely lad like you doing in this sad place where the landlord has never been known to crack his face and there isn't so much as a pretty barmaid to gladden your eyes?'

Nettled, Jim swung round. 'You're welcome to take your custom – for want of a better word – elsewhere, Perce Willis, if there's anywhere else you can find. Wouldn't have you at the Cavendish, I can tell you that for free. Lowering the tone.'

'My mission in life,' Perce said solemnly. 'Lowering the tone.'

'Funny you should say that,' Ward interjected. 'I'm a policeman.'

He was used by now to the drop in temperature, the withdrawal whether open or covert when he declared himself; here, Jim's reaction – if you could call it that – was complete lack of interest, while Perce noticeably perked up.

'Police – ooh, it's that skeleton in the cave, isn't it?'

'Could be. Tell me, Perce, how long have you lived in Burlow?'

'How long? Seventy-eight years, that's how long. Burlow born and bred, with a few years serving king and country with courage and distinction in North Africa—'

'And a few more serving at Her Majesty's pleasure a bit nearer home.' Jim couldn't resist the acid comment.

Perce looked at him reproachfully. 'And what, may I ask, was there for a man of my tastes and talents to do around here, if not to try to improve the lot of my fellows? Was it my fault that the bank so churlishly reneged on our arrangements?'

'Not what the judge said, were it? The judge—'

'Does either of you,' Ward cut across their squabble with the authority of office, 'remember the disappearance of a child named Bonnie Bryant?'

The crash that came from behind him startled them all equally. When Ward spun round, Annie was standing staring at him, with her mouth gaping open and at her feet the shattered remains of a large china ashtray.

'Bonnie?' she said, her lips trembling. '*Bonnie?*'

'*Now* look what you've done!' Lifting the counter flap Jim came out from behind the bar and bent to pick up the shards, leaving Ward at least in some doubt as to which of them had been addressed. It was he who reached the woman first, urging her gently into the nearest chair.

'You knew her,' Ward said carefully. If by some evil trick of fate this was the child's mother he could be in some very insalubrious surroundings with a paddle missing.

'Niece,' she replied, her mouth quivering. 'She were my niece. But she were in the lake, weren't she? All them years, every year – flowers and everything – we took them to the lake. Nobody ever said about caves. Her bike, see—'

She began to cry, rocking to and fro, and her sobs took on a keening pitch. As if the sounds she was making encouraged her, her distress reached hysterical pitch.

United in helplessness, the three men looked at each other in dismay.

'I'd best get Doreen,' Jim said at last and disappeared through a door behind the bar, coming back a couple of minutes later escorting a large woman with high colour wearing a hand-knitted maroon sweater that strained across her substantial bosom. She withered Ward and Willis with a glance, then went over to put her arm round Annie's heaving shoulders in a grasp which looked more controlling than comforting.

'Now, Annie, you're upsetting yourself. We can't have that.'

At her steely tone, Annie's sobs noticeably subsided.

'That's better. Now, you come through with me and I'll make you a nice cup of tea and it'll be all right.'

Annie got to her feet submissively. As Doreen prepared to sweep her past them, Ward said desperately, 'I'm sorry, could I just ask, if it wouldn't be too much, did Bonnie ever break her arm?'

Annie, wiping her face frantically with her hands, hardly seemed to hear him, but Doreen paused.

'Well, of course she did.' Her tone was scathing. 'Broke it the autumn before, day after she got that flashy new silver bike for her birthday – though why they needed new I could never see, a second-hand one were good enough for our Shane – and then what did Bonnie do but fall off and break her arm. And after that – well, it just shows you.'

Without explaining precisely what it just showed, she pushed Annie ahead of her through the doorway off the bar and they could hear her voice saying, 'Now, Annie, that's quite enough, do you hear?'

It was getting on for six o'clock when Tom Ward arrived back home. The weather had relented at last; it was dry now and the evening sun was warm. He fetched a folding chair and set it up in the garden on the west side of the house where he could look at the view, then got himself a beer and the cordless telephone. Sitting down with a sigh of pleasure he took a swig from the can, then dialled Kay Grattan's number.

'Nice one, Tommy,' she said when she had listened to his story without interruption.

'Paid in full?'

'Paid in full. I've got the "Is this little Bonnie?" story ready to run, just waiting to check that you weren't going to shoot it down in flames, and I'll just have to give it a tweak or two based on what you've told me.'

'I can't guarantee an exclusive,' he warned. 'I've done my best for you, but in fairness I have to say there was an old chancer in the bar who might well think of trying his luck with the tabloids.'

Kay groaned. 'There's always one. Can't be helped. But just remember your friends, Tommy, if you turn up anything special.'

'In your own words, Kay, what's in it for us?'

He grinned as she swore at him amiably, then switched off the phone. He would never be fool enough to double-cross Kay, but he'd been careful not to give her any information that hadn't been publicly discussed, and if Perce Willis were indeed inspired to look to the gutter press for beer money, he wouldn't break his heart. He'd left DCI Little gloating over the dainty dish he had to set before tomorrow's press conference, and he'd be ready to wring necks when he saw the spoiler in the *Midland Star*. Ward would be right up there at the top of the list of suspects, and it would be good to be able to suggest with perfect truth that some other little bird must have begun to sing.

He was certainly solidly in good with the Super, who'd been both pleased and impressed with his informal report, not least because with such strong suggestive evidence on identity and no immediate urgency about the investigation, they could scale down the operation almost at once. They had completed the search of the caves and the equipment was being brought up; two or three officers would be detailed to take formal statements in Burlow tomorrow, and once they had firm ID – provided they kept quiet about the off-beat stuff like animal bones and figurines – the Press would lose interest in a murder that was twenty years old. Yes, Broughton had been very pleased.

Tom sat back in his chair and crossed his legs, half-shutting his eyes in the welcome warmth. It had been a good day's work.

He had found himself, once Annie had been removed from the scene and a visibly shaken Jim Archer had locked the pub door and poured himself a drink, in the ideal position to get the kind of information that isn't included in police files, the sort of information, he suspected, that the natives of Burlow were not in the habit of sharing with outsiders. And he had, of course, another bombshell to drop into the conversation. He just had to choose his moment.

Archer, sitting down at one of the tables, sighed yet again, even more gustily than he had before. 'Doreen won't be best pleased if that's Annie off with another of her turns,' he said gloomily. 'Hard enough to get someone to work here, with them lot over the road paying their fancy prices for summer season.'

'Always were like that, the Martin girls,' Perce pointed out. 'Set each other off with their carrying-on, if you ask me. That's what went wrong with Bella, after it happened.'

Archer grunted, staring sadly into space.

Perce had wanted to ask questions, but with practised skill Ward had diverted him into talking about the Bryants instead. Bonnie had been a twin, apparently; her brother Barry had done well for himself, gone off 'somewhere in the south', got himself qualified as a teacher and now was back in Burlow as headmaster of the primary school he had attended himself.

'Now Barry, you see, took after his father,' Perce explained. 'Don Bryant started out as an electrician, but he was a smart fellow. You'd never have taken Barry and Bonnie for twins.'

'Do her parents still live locally?' Ward asked.

There was a pause, then Archer shot a warning glance at the older man. 'No need to go talking about them things. Nobody's business but hers.'

Ward was wise enough to say nothing. Perce, looking uncomfortable, said at last, 'They'll find out soon enough, won't they? She's – delicate, Bella.'

'Delicate?'

'Well,' he shifted uneasily, with a glance at Archer, who scowled back. 'She's not right. Never the same after Bonnie went, being her favourite, you see. And Don – well, she'd always given him a hard time and that finished it. Got a manager's job in Birmingham or somewhere. Headed for the bright lights, anyway.'

'America,' Archer interjected. 'Went to America, is what Annie said.'

'You couldn't blame him, could you? Chance to see the world, get out of this place—' Perce's contemptuous gesture goaded Archer into response.

'All very well for him, taking off that way. It all came on Annie, didn't it, and Doreen's had to listen to it for years. And Doreen's not an easy woman when things is difficult. It's been a bit better since they got Bella into that Norwood House, but now this—'

He took another sip of his drink, then addressing Ward directly for the first time, said roughly, 'This – skeleton, then, it's Bonnie, isn't it? Not very nice to think of her, dying there, not able to get out . . .'

Not yet, Ward thought, not yet. 'We'd need to do tests and so on to be sure. It seems likely. But what was that about her bike?'

'Abandoned, they found it, up by the lake,' Perce said, then corrected himself, 'well, not a lake exactly, is it? It's the old quarry — steep sides, you see, and the edges all loose stones. Natural enough she should fall in, if she went playing round there.'

'Dragged it for days after that,' Archer added with a certain gloomy relish. 'Divers and all sorts. Didn't find her of course, but with all them ledges and crannies, seemed natural enough. Annie used to take Bella up every year to throw in flowers.'

'Not that Bella accepted it, mind you. She would have it Bonnie wouldn't have gone up there herself because she'd been told not to. But then, the young 'uns were all well warned never to go near the caves either, so all her talk about foul play—'

'No need to go on about that rubbish,' Archer said sharply, and Perce, to Ward's regret, subsided. He made a mental note to ask Perce later, but this seemed a good time to play the murder card.

'Funny you should say that,' he said for the second time.

He was glad, afterwards, that he hadn't mentioned it before. Usually, shock loosened people's tongues; in this case, it had the opposite effect. After their initial expressions of horror and amazement, both men clammed up. Even the voluble Perce, in a telling display of body-language, shifted on his bar stool so that he wasn't facing Ward directly any more. They wouldn't be drawn on Bella's speculations — just ramblings, Archer said firmly. They didn't remember anything about events before Bonnie's disappearance. They hadn't really known her, except as a kiddie running about the place. They didn't know who her friends were. They hadn't any idea about her habits. Or if they did, they certainly weren't telling a policeman who had blown in and made everyone in Burlow a suspect for murder and possibly sexual assault as well.

'Her brother,' Ward said, making the best of a bad job. 'Is he around?'

Perce was prepared to tell him that he lived just along the road in a cottage with a blue door, and Archer added, 'He's not there, any road. Taken a party of kids off to York to see the museums. Be back Wednesday.'

Ward managed to extract the addresses of a couple of parents who would know where they were staying, then got up.

'Thank you very much,' he said. 'You've been very helpful. Just one more thing. I do need to get information about Bonnie at the time of her disappearance. Is there anyone who lives round about here who would have known her well – a teacher, perhaps?'

They hesitated, and he could almost read their minds: *He'll find out anyway.*

'Try Arthur Maxton,' Perce said. 'He's retired over in Statley on the other side of the Moor, but he was headmaster here when it happened. He's a bachelor, in his seventies now, a bit of an old woman – he'll rabbit on, given half a chance—'

Archer cut in. 'Drink up, Perce, I'm wanting to close up now.' He didn't speak to Ward but the look he gave him was unfriendly.

Writing down Maxton's address, Ward said, 'I won't take up more of your time. If you think of anything helpful, officers will probably be here tomorrow taking statements.'

Don't hold your breath, Archer's rigid posture proclaimed, but Perce looked thoughtful. 'And the newspapers too, I shouldn't wonder,' he said, and Ward, as he took his leave, had thought there was a speculative gleam in his eye.

It had proved easy enough to get the address of the guest house in York where Bryant and his pupils were staying, but he was less lucky with Maxton. Statley was only two or three miles away as the crow flies, but twenty miles by road round the edge of the Long Moor. It was a slow journey, and when he arrived at the neat terraced house where Maxton lived there was no one in, either there or in the houses on either side. There had been nothing to do except return to Flitchford to report.

Still, Tom reflected now as he watched the sun start to outline the hills with a dusky golden haze, it had been a pretty satisfying day.

The police in York would be contacting Bryant tonight, and the matron at Norwood House, where Bella was living out her twilight existence, had been warned to expect a police-woman tomorrow to break the news, always supposing Bella could understand.

Broughton had given his blessing to setting up an interview with Maxton; so as long as the man wasn't on holiday or some-thing, that should turn up a few more lines of enquiry to pursue tomorrow.

And then, of course, they could start to consider the big questions: who had smashed in little Bonnie Bryant's skull, and why? And what had Bonnie been doing in the caves, anyway?

That unpleasant figure came into his mind again. Anubis, and those little fragile animal skeletons— He had no proof that it had anything at all to do with the case, yet somehow . . .

Suddenly, Tom shivered. The sun had dipped right down below the horizon, and without its direct rays the air was cold. He finished his can of beer and stood up, realising that not only was he cold, he was hungry as well. He'd grabbed a sandwich at a petrol station shop on the way over to Statley, but that and a couple of packets of crisps since breakfast was barely enough to keep body and soul together.

Starting to cook something substantial would take time, and the Bell, after all, was only a ten-minute walk away. Tom locked up and set off, whistling. The only problem exercising his mind was whether to have a mixed grill or one of Stan's justly famed steak and kidney puddings.

It did occur to him that there were at least some advantages in having no one to consider but himself.

Barry Bryant came back into the lounge in the York guest house looking weary. He had been with the police for nearly an hour before phoning Norwood House, where his mother lived, and it was after eleven o'clock. His naturally fair skin looked waxy and almost transparent, with the marks of strain showing round his eyes.

Gina Lambert and Maggie Black – one short, dark and plump, the other tall, fair and plump – greeted him with identical expressions of maternal concern. Their children's young headmaster ('Well, doesn't really seem like a headmaster, does he?') was very popular, particularly since instead of staying in the south where he'd done his studying and been doing ever so well in schools, he'd chosen to come back home to be near his mum. There weren't a lot of men would do that, particularly seeing she wasn't herself any more, but Barry was like that – nice, he was, to the kids as well, though he wasn't a pushover either. It was just awful seeing him so upset.

The two women had come on the school trip to York as pupils' mums just to help out, but when the shocking news came they took over Barry's responsibilities without hesitation. They had despatched the children to bed using blatant emotional blackmail – 'Poor Mr Bryant's had bad news and is very sad, so be specially good for him' – backed up by straightforward threats – 'or else no one will be going to the Yorvik Centre tomorrow.'

'You look shattered, Barry,' Gina said. 'What you need is a nice cuppa – there's still one in the pot.'

She gestured to the tray on the coffee table in front of her and taking no answer for consent poured out a cup for him.

Maggie patted the beige flock-velvet settee beside her invitingly. 'Come and have a sit-down. The children's all settled. I've been up to the boys too and they're being ever so good, so you needn't go up.'

He sat down obediently, running his hands tiredly through his curly hair.

'Thanks. It's very good of you. I'm – I'm sorry about all this.' He said the words as if someone had told him what to say, but they were without meaning for him.

'Hardly your fault, is it?' Gina said robustly.

'No. No, I suppose not. It just feels . . .' His voice trailed off.

The two women exchanged glances, then Maggie said gently, 'Your mum – how's she taking it?'

'They haven't told her yet. I offered, of course, but the matron said they're sending someone out tomorrow. No point, she said – she doesn't think she'll take it in anyway.' That obviously distressed him too.

'Oh dear,' Maggie said helplessly, but Gina urged, 'You just go if you want, Barry. Everyone'll understand. The kids may be disappointed, but then that's life. Got to learn, don't they?'

Barry grimaced. 'And spoil their trip, when they've saved up and looked forward to it? If there isn't any point?'

He lapsed into silence again, and after a moment Maggie said sympathetically, 'You'd best talk about it, you know. Don't bottle it up – cry if you want to, we don't mind, do we, Gina?'

'We're here for you, Barry,' the other woman assured him.

'It's – it's kind of you, but it's not like that, really.' He tried to smile, failed, then said suddenly, as if he couldn't contain himself, 'I ought to cry, shouldn't I, be grief-stricken, or something. But quite honestly, I can barely remember her. Isn't that awful? I ought to have memories of how it felt at the time, of horrors that would come flooding back, but I don't. I was the same age as some of these kids at the time, and all that I really remember is how distraught everyone was – and then my mother, afterwards—'

He stopped, then bent forward over his tightly clasped hands. 'I'm sorry, I've probably shocked you.'

Maggie reached across to pat his hands and Gina cried, 'Course you haven't, Barry! That's just kids, the way they are. Dave's mum died last year, and we'd have said as our Lee were close to her gran but she just said could she wear her platform trainers to the funeral. Quite upset, Dave were, and that's what I said to him, "It's just kids, isn't it? Lee were fond of her gran, you know that."'

Barry sighed. 'Well, perhaps I was fond of Bonnie too. All I seem able to remember is that we quarrelled all the time.'

'That's just brothers and sisters,' Gina said firmly. 'My two fight the whole time – drive you mad, they would – and me and my brother come to that. It were only after we both grew up we started getting on.'

It was intended as consolation. To her dismay, he was visibly upset.

'Yes,' he said with difficulty. 'Only we didn't have the chance to grow out of it, did we? When I think about my dead twin sister, all I can come up with is that we didn't get on. Surely I owe her more than that.' He got up. 'Sorry – I didn't mean to embarrass you. I'm going to go to bed, if you don't mind – I'll check the children on the way up.'

He went out, leaving his untouched cup of tea cooling on the table.

'Oh dear,' Maggie said again, inadequately. 'Poor Barry. Ever so hard, isn't it?'

'And not going to get any easier either,' Gina pointed out. She sighed, then said, 'Oh well. Could you fancy another chocolate cream?'

Chapter Six

On Tuesday morning Kate Cosgrove was wakened by the sun streaming through the layers of cream muslin that curtained the east-facing windows of her bedroom. Hers was a modern loft flat, one of half a dozen created from an old warehouse in the centre of Sheffield.

She was pleased with it. She liked its open living-space and its honey-coloured wooden floors and its white walls. She liked its stark, uncompromising lines and angles. Such furniture as she had was modern, expensive and carefully chosen, but she liked it uncluttered. Just the way she liked her life.

On her white Egyptian cotton sheets, Kate turned over and stretched luxuriously. There weren't too many mornings in this dismal summer when the sun had wakened her, but she was habitually an early riser and once awake she was eager to get on with the day.

Tuesday. Usually she spent Saturday and Sunday at the cottage in Burlow, which it had suited her political ambitions to keep on after her parents died, but this weekend she'd been away in Amsterdam seeing a client. It had been late last night before she got back, so there would be a backlog to shift today.

She took a lazy moment to review the day ahead before she got out of bed: a consultation with a barrister for one of her big corporate clients at ten o'clock, a couple of appointments, a partners' lunch, paperwork, paperwork, paperwork. Then at six o'clock she was to meet her political agent, for a drink.

Afterwards, it was on to deliver a meticulously prepared after-dinner speech to an association of small businessmen, who would on past experience turn out to be conspicuously large business-men, probably as a result of too many dinners like this evening's.

Her smile was contemptuous as she swung her own well-disciplined body in its black silk jacquard pyjamas out of bed, pushing her expensively tailored mane of wavy dark blonde hair back from her face. She squinted at the clock – quarter-past six. Good! She could be in the office with all the newspapers read well before eight o'clock.

She spent quarter of an hour running hard on the treadmill in the corner of her bedroom, then went through to the gleam-ing, icy-white bathroom and turned on her power-shower. While it was reaching its pre-set temperature she went over to the wardrobe which ran the full length of one wall in her bed-room to lay out clothes for her working day. She selected a black linen shift dress and jacket, found a black and white scarf of twilled silk to go with it. She could fasten it at the neck with the heavy silver Victorian brooch that had been a lover's gift one Valentine's Day, just when she had made up her mind to give him the push. She liked the brooch, though; it had bought him a fortnight's grace.

Kate invariably dressed for breakfast. Her mother had always slobbed around the house in an old dressing-gown, none too clean, until she had seen her off to school, and Kate, fastidious even at that age, had made a childhood vow never to leave her bedroom until she was ready for the day.

She had also vowed never to have children, which had so far proved a smart decision. She had nightmares about children sometimes – noisy, damp, clinging creatures who wouldn't let her escape. In one dream, vividly recollected, she had drowned a crying baby: it had seemed at the time the logical solution to an unpleasant problem.

Yes, she was perfectly satisfied with her life, in so far as an attitude of perpetual striving could be described as satisfaction. Through self-discipline, ruthlessness and sheer hard graft she was, at the age of thirty-one, a junior partner in the top firm of corporate lawyers in Sheffield, she had been selected by the Liberal Democrats for a seat that was winnable – just – and she had two years in which to cut her political teeth before the next general election.

Between them, she and her agent were nursing the constituency around Burlow to some effect, and with her looks, professional status and local background she was attracting an extremely good press. The sitting tenant was a Tory with a wafer-thin majority which private soundings indicated was crumbling fast, so unless something went wrong – badly wrong – she should be home and dry.

It was five past seven when Kate emerged from her bedroom into the huge airy space that was sitting room, dining room, office and kitchen. There were a couple of paintings, enigmatic abstracts, on the white walls, and on a low rosewood chest stood a powerful Victorian bronze sculpture of a lioness, hunched over the limp body of its prey, the magnificent, savage head half-lifted, snarling. As she always did, she caressed it as she passed.

The newspapers should have arrived by now. Kate frowned; she had a generous financial arrangement with the paperboy to make sure they did. She was just calculating how much to dock him when they began spewing through the extra-wide letterbox in a torrent of newsprint.

Kate took half a dozen daily newspapers and gutted them systematically for anything that might affect the interests of the constituency. On a good day, she read the law reports as well.

She picked them up as they landed, piling them neatly without looking at them. She had a set pattern for dealing with them that never varied; laying them down on the limed oak refectory table and picking up *The Times* to glance at the main headlines, she ground the coffee beans, boiled the kettle, toasted a slice of organic wholewheat bread and squeezed a couple of oranges on the Philippe Starck squeezer which had been a present to herself after a successful case.

There was a political row brewing between the left and right wings of the Labour Party; she read the report with interest and sardonic amusement.

When she sat down with her breakfast, she sorted through the pile to find the *Midland Star*, her invariable starting point. Whatever the political squabbles or world disasters, what the *Star* chose to say to her future constituents was what counted as important to Kate Cosgrove. Just how important it could be had not occurred to her until she picked up that morning's edition.

Kay Grattan had not stinted. There was a blown-up photograph and a full banner headline across all six columns. 'Is this little Bonnie?' it screamed, then in quieter type below, 'Skeleton in Cave could be Murdered Child.'

Kate set down her white porcelain cup in its saucer with a crash. The world seemed to tip crazily about her.

There was only one thing in cold, calculating Kate Cosgrove's well-planned life which could tarnish her image seriously enough to blight a glittering political career. And there, before her horrified gaze, was a headline she had never expected to see. Instinctively, she raised her eyes to the powerful sculpture of the lioness opposite her across the room, and shuddered.

Then she jumped up. She must get to her office; there was something hidden deep in her computer system, something protected by a secret password, something which she had known she was a fool to keep and which she must even now destroy. She should have done it long ago.

Abbie Bettison didn't reach the papers until rather later in the day. She too had been up at six; on these summer mornings Sam had to take advantage of the light, and today in particular when it looked as if the sun was at last planning to shine he was keen to get out into the fields as soon as possible.

She often worried about how hard Sam had to work. He was farming the land his father and his grandfather had farmed before him, but the previous Sam Bettisons hadn't had to cope with the quotas and the directives and the VAT. Sometimes Sam's cheerful, weather-beaten face was seamed with lines of worry and tension quite at odds with his cheerful nature.

Abbie liked to be up to give him tea and toast and a kiss to set him on his way before she got on with her own morning chores – letting the dogs out, feeding the hens, stoking the old-fashioned Aga – so that she had them done before Sammie woke up. Once he was trotting round under her feet everything took twice as long.

Then there was breakfast to cook for Sam and his two farm workers when they came in at half-past eight, a proper solid breakfast with porridge and bacon and eggs and toast and tea. They needed it with all the hard physical work they had to do.

Abbie didn't need it, but somehow the delectable fragrance of cooking bacon sapped her resolve. The half-stone she'd put on when Sammie was born had settled, with another few pounds to keep it company. There just wasn't much incentive to deprive herself when all Sam said when she bewailed her lack of willpower was, 'You look pretty good to me, love.'

Well, someone else might not consider that a particularly romantic statement, but it satisfied her. She loved him very much, and she loved her little son, and she loved her busy life as a farmer's wife, ruled by the age-old rhythm of the seasons, of spring lambs and summer harvests and the harrowing of brown bare winter fields. She was as contented as the insecurities of farming would let her be, and at least Sam was level-headed enough not to get into trouble with borrowing, and smart enough to understand the latest idiotic ruling made by someone in Brussels who'd never got mud on his boots. Once Sammie – and Sammie's little brothers or sisters, hopefully – went off to school, she'd start doing farmhouse holidays. She liked cooking and baking and looking after people, so she would enjoy doing it, and it would take some of the burden off Sam.

Today she got them all out to work again after breakfast, then washed the dishes and whisked round upstairs. By the time she'd done that, it was almost ten o'clock.

'Sammie!' she called. She could hear him in the playroom off the big farmhouse kitchen, making 'vroom-vroom' noises and chatting to Floss, the elderly sheepdog who was no doubt lying in a patch of sunlight savouring the joys of retirement.

Samuel Bettison, the fourth of that name, appeared in the

doorway clutching a large yellow tractor, a miniature version of his father in dungarees and a T-shirt.

'Teletubbies!' he crowed.

His mother laughed. 'That's right. Now here's your biscuit, and I'll bring your milk.'

He took the oatmeal cookie she held out to him and stomped back into the playroom to sit on a red beanbag in front of the television. Floss, sniffing hopefully, raised her head and Sammie frowned.

'No, Floss! Sammie's biscuit,' he said firmly.

Abbie set down the mug on the floor at his feet, turned on the set and as the familiar music started retreated thankfully into the kitchen. This was her time, the one blessed spell of peace in her hard-working day. The kettle on the back of the Aga was singing quietly; she lifted the lid off one of the rings and pulled it on to boil.

One of the yard cats had sneaked in through the back door and established itself on the cushion of the sagging armchair beside the stove. They were usually too timid to come inside, but this one was bold, a handsome beast with a sleek black coat and a head like a miniature panther.

'Scat, cat!' Abbie didn't like cats, hadn't since she was a child, not after – But she tried not to think about that. She just didn't like cats, that was all.

The cat glared at her haughtily without moving. When she pushed it, it bared needle-sharp teeth with a tiny hiss, but jumped down and stalked resentfully out through the open back door, its tail held straight and stiff.

Abbie took her mug of tea, picked up the newspaper that always came with the mail, and sank back into the seductive embrace of the old chair, sighing with satisfaction.

She liked the *Midland Star*. They got it mainly for the local news and the animal stock prices towards the back of the paper; the stories that hit the main headlines Abbie would glance at, shaking her head over the follies and miseries of the world out there in much the same spirit as she deplored similar events in *Emmerdale Farm*, her favourite soap.

So it was with a sense of shock which drained the blood from her round rosy cheeks that Abbie saw, in headline type unusually large for a quality provincial paper, the horrifying question, 'Is this little Bonnie?'

The skeleton in the Burlow caves had, of course, been in the news over the weekend. Abbie had discussed it with Sam and with her parents who still farmed on the outskirts of the town where she had grown up and gone to school. A nasty business, they had all agreed, some poor soul gone in and got lost, and there was a lot of talk about it locally, but it had never crossed her mind until this moment that it could have anything to do with Bonnie Bryant. That shameful memory, she thought, had been drowned long since beneath the waters of Quarry Lake.

Abbie's nature was gentle, sunny and uncomplicated. In her thirty-one years there was little she had done that she was truly ashamed of, which she would have wanted to hide from Sam, who loved her.

With one exception. There was one sin that lay on her soul, a sin so black that she had never told anyone about it. The other seven knew, of course, indeed had shared in the Egyptian Game, but after what happened they never mentioned it again.

It was, she had told herself a thousand times, when the memory that haunted her resurrected itself in uncharacteristically troubled sleep, not a bit like her to have done it. She was kind, soft-hearted even . . .

Sometimes she found herself blaming Jay; sometimes, shabbily, Juliette, since there was no way Abbie would have been considered as a member of the Neters if Juliette hadn't been her best friend.

But of course, when it came right down to it, she had been part of the madness. She had even gone along with the hunt right up to the moment when they had lost Bonnie, when they stopped uncertainly, when the torches, made with rags soaked in paraffin stolen from Ed's father's garage pump, began to die and the frenzy which had fuelled the chase began to die too. She didn't know what they might have done if they had caught

Bonnie, but she didn't think, whatever it was, that she would have held out against it.

Even now she was tormented by the fear that somewhere deep inside, where she didn't want to look, the cruel wicked being who had taken possession of her in those crazy weeks of the Egyptian Game was lurking still, could at some stage reappear. The loving devotion to family, the warm concern for friends and neighbours, the charity work – these might be no more than a thin piece of plywood laid across a cesspit and liable to break under pressure.

And then how could Sam, who had decency stamped right through him like a stick of Brighton rock, who teased her so fondly about being a soft touch, go on loving her?

Abbie looked at the photographs on the newspaper's front page through a mist of tears. There was a big one of fat, smirking Bonnie, pathetic now and dreadfully, horribly young. There was a picture of the entrance to the caves, and one of Bonnie with her mother and Barry.

Barry – oh, poor Barry. It must be so much worse for him. She bit her lip.

She just didn't understand how Bonnie could have been in the caves. There was no doubt that she'd left home on her bike in the morning, and finding it abandoned up at the lake was what had alerted everyone to Bonnie's fate.

Abbie had seen it all so clearly in her mind's eye: the panic-stricken Bonnie stumbling out of the caves, pedalling off on her bike as fast as her fat legs would go in case they came pouring out after her like the hounds of hell, pedalling all the way up to the lake to put distance between them. And then . . .

Perhaps she had just gone walking round it, and slipped. That was what Abbie hoped. She had always feared that the victimised Bonnie had thrown herself in.

When the news about Bonnie spread through the town, Jay had summoned the Neters to a last secret meeting, had made them swear by Anubis never to tell what had happened in the caves, on pain of the dread vengeance of the God of the Dead.

Despite Jay's protests, they had refused to meet again after that, or even talk about it, and as far as she knew they had all kept their pact. To this day, in some primitive part of her mind, Abbie still half believed in the threat.

But if they had told at the time, as Abbie had known she should, there might have been search parties checking the caves just in case, and Bonnie wouldn't have been left in awful darkness to starve or freeze to death.

The tears that had blurred her sight spilled over, and she got out a hankie to wipe them away, blowing her nose fiercely. She had to read this properly, find out what had actually happened, find out, oh dear God, what could be laid to her charge. What would they do to you if, as a child of eleven you had by your silence caused the death of another child?

A sob escaped her, and she wiped her eyes again. It was only then that she focused on the sub-heading, 'Skeleton in Cave could be Murdered Child.'

Murder! She began to shake so that she had to steady the paper on the arm of the chair, but shock dried her tears so that she could see to read.

Limited as the information was, they seemed to be saying that Bonnie had not died as a result of being lost in the caves. Abbie frowned, unable at first to make sense of what she was reading. Were they really saying that this child had been *murdered*, deliberately killed by a blow to the head? Yes, they were quite definite about that, at least.

Abbie's first reaction was one of overwhelming relief; she put her head in her hands and thought a prayer of thankfulness. She hadn't caused Bonnie's death, or even, as she had always feared, been part of the reason Bonnie would have taken her own life. She was guilty of cruelty, yes, but then children were cruel. Bonnie herself had revelled in threats and blackmail.

The difference was that Abbie had been given the chance to grow out of that childish vice. Bonnie hadn't. Someone, apparently, had found her hiding-place and killed her. Had it been someone who had been part of the hunt, someone who had known where she was and sought her out later once it was over and they had scattered – one of the Neters?

It was Jay who had christened them, Jay who as Osiris had been their overlord and directed their ceremonies and their horrid sacrifices, Jay who had somehow taken possession of their thoughts and controlled their actions. It was Jay who had made the image of Anubis, the jackal-headed God of the Dead, and installed him in the cave shrine where they all had to take the blood-oath that bound them to the Neters till death and beyond. Abbie had been uneasily flattered to be allowed to join them under the name of Bastet, the cat-goddess; she could still remember, despite the horror and the nightmares, the heady, unhealthy excitement of it all. Ever since, she had hated cats.

None of us was more than eleven, for heaven's sake, she thought. Just kids at primary school. How could a child do that? Yet there were child killers as brutal as adults, of course there were. And her stomach knotted when she thought of some of the things the Neters had done.

Perhaps Bonnie had been followed to the caves by someone else. Abbie snatched at the saving thought. Bonnie had tracked them down; perhaps someone else had stalked her.

But why would anyone else want to kill Bonnie? It was the Neters who knew Bonnie would go home and tell, the Neters who knew they had gone too far, who knew that punishment would be severe.

She remembered going home herself that day, feeling cold and sick at the thought of what her parents would say – and do. She remembered, too, God forgive her, being relieved that now Bonnie was dead they would never find out. Who might have been so afraid that they killed Bonnie to silence her?

Abbie needed to talk to someone. She couldn't tell Sam about that strange, sick period in her childhood, not yet, not unless she must.

Perhaps she could phone Juliette. She had her number some-where, though she hadn't seen her since she married Jay, or even been in contact except through Christmas cards. It would be good to talk to Juliette, who had always known what to do. Abbie had missed her friendship.

She didn't want to talk to Jay, though. He had been a cold, unnatural child, and on the few occasions when she'd talked to him in adult life, she had always felt he was mocking her unpleasantly, but it was more than that. Something in her shrank from him, almost as if she believed he could take control of her again, call back the cat-goddess Bastet, her hidden demon . . . Oh, please let it be Juliette who answered the phone!

Happy Teletubby noises were still coming from the playroom. She went to the dresser, rummaged around for her address book and dialled the number.

Jay's voice, silky and rather high-pitched, answered. She had forgotten his voice; with unthinking revulsion she hung up – a gut reaction, foolish in these days of number recall. She stepped back, eyeing the phone as if it were a ticking bomb, and jumped when inevitably, a minute later, it rang.

Her cheeks burning, she picked it up, controlled her voice. 'Hello?'

'Who am I speaking to?' Jay's hateful drawl.

'Oh Jay! It's Abbie – Abbie Bettison. I – I was trying to phone you—'

'Good gracious, dear little Abbie Bettison! Well, fancy that! And what did I say to make you panic?'

Annoyance steadied her. 'Don't be silly, Jay. I had just dialled the number when one of the pans on the Aga boiled over. I didn't realise you had answered the phone.' She was deplorably proud of the way the lie tripped off her tongue.

'I see. Well, if your Aga crisis is under control and you can tear yourself away from your pans, how may I be of service?'

'Actually, I just wanted a chat with Juliette.'

Did he know? Had he seen the papers? If not, she certainly wasn't going to tell him.

'Juliette? Oh, you mean Juliette, my wife? That Juliette?'

He was clearly bitter, angry about something. Abbie hesitated, and he went on, 'When you find her to have a chat with, perhaps you would let me know where she is this time?'

Abbie stammered stupidly. 'She's – she's not there?'

'Marriage and the bucolic life in Derbyshire must suit you,

my dear. I'm sure you never used to be quite so quick off the mark.'

Paradoxically, the cheap sneer was helpful. She wasn't still little Abbie Fenner and he wasn't Osiris, God of the Underworld, and she didn't have to take that sort of rudeness from anyone. She was Abbie Bettison, Sam's wife and Sammie's mother, and Jay Darke was no part of her life any more.

She said bluntly, 'If by that you mean that Juliette's left you, Jay, I can only say I don't blame her in the very slightest. It's not before time, and I'm delighted. I can't think why she ever put up with you.'

She banged down the receiver without waiting for his reply. As she turned away the Teletubby music signalled the end of the programme, and Sammie came trotting through.

'Floss got Sammie's milk,' he announced with satisfaction. 'On floor.'

'Oh, Sammie, for goodness' sake!' Abbie groaned routinely, but it was a relief to have a problem of the normal, trivial, domestic sort to deal with.

At the sound of the phone being slammed down at the other end, Jay Darke gave a short, mirthless laugh and replaced his own receiver.

He had disliked Abbie, right from primary school days. She would never have been one of the Neters, if Juliette hadn't insisted. Abbie was a reluctant neophyte, and it had taken the full majesty of his Osiris persona to establish a proper hold over her, prevent her from infecting Juliette with her own mawkish doubts.

With her insipid, feather-brained niceness she totally lacked the fascination which all of the others – even Juliette – showed for the unholier delights of power. She had somehow eluded him, and he had been offended, too, by her open distaste on the few occasions when they had met as adults. Apart from Brian who had emigrated and Dick who was dead, she was the only one of the Neters on whom he had no useful files – largely because her life was the most boring of open books, most likely.

But why had she phoned today? Not a word from her for years, and now she rings for no apparent reason just when Juliette has walked out. Coincidence, or what?

He didn't believe in coincidence. There had to be a reason.

Brooding, he went to make himself a cup of coffee. Could Juliette have been trying to make contact with her friend, left a message on the answer-machine, perhaps, without mentioning where she was? Did that mean she'd gone to Derbyshire?

Jay had thought that was what she would do, run back to Daddy. He'd even thought of pursuing her there, just because she was his, and he wanted her, wanted to make her pay for what she had done to him. But beating on the door and demanding her return wasn't likely to be effective, and he was afraid of what Harry-the-Bastard might be capable of in his own little fiefdom where he kept the police force in his back pocket. It wouldn't do to underestimate Harry-the-Bastard – he should take pre-cautions, perhaps, so if he were threatened he could warn him off. Yes, he'd better see to that.

He took down the coffee jar and discovered that it was almost empty. He looked in the cupboard for a fresh packet; there was none, and his eye fell on the Memo board where the reminder 'Coffee' was written in Juliette's lacy script. Of course, in that other life which had ended at Friday lunch time, they would have taken the car and gone to Sainsbury's for the usual weekly shop.

Without warning he was hit by such a pang of desolation that it made him gasp. He didn't know what love meant – never had – but he recognised loss, and he could hardly bear it. Whatever she had done, she was still his other half, and without her he was maimed.

The anger which had seized him on Friday surged through him again and he hurled the green jar with its mocking gold legend 'Coffee' to the tiled floor where it exploded into shards which scattered to every corner of the room.

This time the spasm was short-lived. It made him feel worse, not better, and now he had this mess to clear up as well. Destruction didn't solve anything. Jay vowed grimly, as he wielded dustpan and brush, to take control of the black monster of temper that seemed to be lurking permanently at his shoulder.

He hadn't been out for three days, so perhaps he was going stir-crazy. He could pop round the corner to the '8 till Late'; he needed a few other things besides the coffee anyway.

Jay opened the front door warily but the mews, as usual at this time of the working day, was deserted. He was glad not to have to field 'neighbourly' interrogation about the window that he'd only got fixed yesterday.

He had picked up the groceries he needed and was waiting in the small queue to pay when it caught his eye – the familiar 'Missing' snapshot, hugely enlarged, of Bonnie Bryant. His stomach lurched; he did not need the tabloid headlines to tell him that her body – or 'pitiful remains', as the rag put it – must have been found.

He stood very, very still, his eyes dilated with shock, and the woman at the checkout had to speak to him twice to get his attention.

'I'll take this as well.' Jay added the newspaper to his purchases, then carried them home.

He sat down on the sofa in the sitting room, his desire for coffee forgotten, and spread the newspaper out on the low table in front of him.

There was a photo of old Perce Willis too – trust him to get in on the act, and fleece them for whatever rubbish he told them too, no doubt. There hadn't been official identification yet, or a proper police statement, but Perce had said that when the police found her body in a little cave she'd been hit on the head with a stone, perhaps even assaulted as well.

He sat back, eyes narrowed in thought. So that was why Abbie Bettison had been phoning. Things were stirring in Burlow, dark forgotten things creeping out from under the stones where they had been hidden. This could give shape to his plans, which were at the moment formless.

He looked up at the black gleaming figure of Anubis on its shelf, with its enigmatic expression and blank eyes. He had been waiting for a sign from the gods, hadn't he, and what sign could be plainer than this? A chill – part exhilaration, part fear perhaps – passed down his spine and he shuddered.

He rose like a sleepwalker and went over to his work area, to the machines that never betrayed him, never defied his will. He woke one, his hands caressing the keyboard as tenderly as a lover.

Jay worked feverishly until hunger made him look at his watch, then pushed back his chair, stretching. It was all very satisfactory, and he had made a good beginning to the elaborate design that would punish all those who had made their vows and then deserted him, and above all punish his errant Isis. If she had truly determined to take herself wilfully out of his life, then this would punish her in a way she would never be able to expunge from her mind.

But if it was all so satisfactory, why did he feel as he sat in the silent house like the last person on a dying planet watching the sun grow cold?

Chapter Seven

DCI Little came out of the press conference and bellowed his fury and frustration like a bull maddened by the darts planted by picadors and denied the satisfaction of charging his aggressors.

'Where the hell is Ward? I want an explanation!'

WPC Matthews, who was assigned to Public Relations – not normally at the cutting edge of policework in Flitchford – timidly suggested the CID room. She had been sitting helplessly at Little's side while the ladies and gentlemen of the Press tore chunks out of his self-esteem to indicate their displeasure at being scooped by two of their number.

Little snorted. 'Wasn't there earlier, was he? Keeping his head below the parapet, most likely, as well he might.'

However, he headed off in that direction with the police-woman trotting meekly behind. When he flung open the door, Ward, Denholm and Crozier were working at their desks with the ostentatious concentration of schoolboys who have heard the master's footsteps approaching the classroom.

Copies of the two newspapers which had between them ruined the Chief Inspector's day were spread out on one of the unoccupied desks. Little strode over, jabbed the tabloid with a quivering finger and said awfully, 'How do you explain this, Ward – this breach of security? How can they have got hold of this story when I gave strict instructions it was to be kept under wraps until this morning?'

Judging by the inset photograph of Perce Willis on the front page and the extensively quoted interview with him, it wasn't hard to guess. It also seemed likely that he would be in beer money for some time to come.

Ward, like the others, had got to his feet. 'I'm afraid I can't help you there, sir.'

'This – this Willis man. Where did he get his information?'

Thinking he might well stand Perce a grateful pint or two himself, Ward could say, with perfect truth, 'Well, sir, it's obviously not possible to question members of the public without giving away the sort of information that will have the Press putting two and two together, if someone chooses to contact them.'

'But didn't you explain, didn't you instruct them to keep their mouths shut—'

At this PR heresy, WPC Matthews drew in her breath sharply and Ward allowed his eyebrows to rise just ever so slightly. 'I didn't think it would do us any good to have the police accused of trying to gag people, sir. And anyway, with money probably changing hands, I couldn't hope to make it stick.'

Little glared at him. 'It's all very fine for you sergeant. But I have just been subjected to a most unpleasant half-hour, most unpleasant, as a result of your lack of grip.'

Ward achieved an expression of suitable concern. 'Perhaps we should consider releasing items of information as they come to hand, sir, instead of saving them up for a press conference.'

'I did suggest that, sir, if you remember,' WPC Matthews joined in with suicidal eagerness. 'I know the Press would welcome extra time for questions instead of a long statement—'

'Oh, for God's sake, woman,' Little snarled, 'I daresay you were born hen-witted, but you could at least try not to be any more brainless than you have to be.' He stormed out.

The girl's face was pink. 'Oh dear,' she said inadequately. 'I'd better—' She hurried out after him without finishing her sentence.

With the door safely shut the three men, again like naughty children, exchanged grins.

'Mauled, was he, do you reckon?' Crozier asked.

'Couldn't you see the clawmarks? Serves the bastard right. Though you do sometimes wonder where the papers get their information,' Denholm said, looking pointedly at Ward, who ignored the implied question.

'He won't be so keen to take press conferences after this. Just watch him throw poor little Jenny Matthews to the lions instead.'

'I'm getting out of here.' Crozier was collecting up papers from his desk. 'I'm checking out a country house hotel which conveniently burned down just after the fire department ordered major safety improvements. Are you two still on the caves job?'

The others nodded. 'I'm taking a couple of constables up to Burlow this morning to take some statements. Trying to find out the girl's dentist is top priority, to see if we can get formal ID. But our boy wonder here,' Denholm jerked his head towards Ward, 'gets to go off and do his own thing, reporting direct to Broughton – no wonder Little's baying for blood. And smirking isn't pretty, Tom.'

Provocatively, Ward hummed a couple of bars of *Jealousy* as Denholm followed Crozier out. He was in upbeat mood, relieved to have avoided awkward questions over the *Midland Star* and basking in the Super's approval. Once he got this report finished he could head off to Statley for the ten-thirty appointment he'd arranged with Arthur Maxton.

Maxton had a dry, precise voice, and had asked rather too many questions before assuring Ward that he would be more than delighted to do anything which lay within his power to assist the police to some sort of successful conclusion to their distressing enquiries. Which sounded as if the interview, while possibly informative, was unlikely to be a laugh a minute.

Ward had an idle habit of construing a person's appearance from their voice on the telephone, and he arrived in Statley with a clear picture in his mind of a tall, thin, shabby pedagogue. It was something of a shock to find himself greeted on the doorstep by a short man, in his early seventies perhaps, sporting a yellow spotted bow tie. He was portly and dapper with a pink complexion, a neat pink mouth and a bald head so shiny it looked as if he must set about it with Pledge and a duster every morning.

A vain little man, Ward judged, as Maxton swayed on the balls of his feet. In that incongruous, dusty voice he was saying he had always flattered himself that he had a natural gift for knowing his pupils.

'And remarkable recall, people have been kind enough to say, *remarkable*,' he added, preparing to make good this threat as Ward took out a notebook and settled gloomily back in his chair. They were sitting in a sun lounge at the back of the house looking out on a small garden with weedless flowerbeds containing plastic-looking lobelias, french marigolds and geraniums, and a lawn which might as well have been astroturf.

'You must first of all understand Burlow,' Maxton began magisterially, and Ward resigned himself to a recital of the three hundred years of history leading up to the summer of 1980.

It wasn't quite as bad as that, and Maxton's sketch of Burlow's social climate was useful. As Ward had sensed himself from a cursory look at the main street, there was a lot of unemployment in Burlow and such jobs as there were tended historically to be low-paid, in savage contrast to the prosperous commuters and beneficiaries of the growing tourist trade.

'The haves and the have-nots – it's the story of most rural communities,' Maxton pontificated. 'What one family can afford, another can't—'

Hoping to bring the meeting to order, as it were, Ward interjected, 'And what about Bonnie's family?' but the other man brushed aside his attempt with the practised ease of one who has spent a professional lifetime ignoring dangled red herrings.

'However, that aside, within the school we were a happy community. Left to themselves, children tend to get along very naturally.'

'OK,' Ward agreed cautiously. 'But—?'

Maxton sighed. 'Ah, yes indeed, sergeant, there you have it. *But*. I have to tell you, that summer was the most unpleasant of my whole teaching career. I was thankful when the term was over. And then of course, just afterwards, that tragic business—'

Intrigued now, Ward said, 'What was so bad about that summer?'

'There were two major problems: the eleven-plus, and Jay Darke. It was always a stressful time, of course, a very busy term with a great deal to cram into it. Sports, you know, and—'

'Hang on, you've lost me. The eleven-plus?'

Maxton looked at him as if he had muffed a simple question in a mental arithmetic test. 'The eleven-plus – the sheep and goats exam, I always called it, where the blessed were permitted to enter the spangled heaven of Grammar School and the accursed were relegated to the infernal regions of the Secondary Modern with a merit in woodwork as the height of their aspiration—'

It wasn't the first time he had trotted that out, obviously, and Ward's interruption was a little testy. 'Yes, yes, of course I remember the eleven-plus. But why was it significant?'

'Ah.' Maxton hesitated, almost as if he regretted having mentioned it. 1980, it seemed, had been something of a golden year academically for Burlow Primary. Normally, three grammar school places out of a class of twenty-odd would have been good; this year there were seven out of twenty-two, all of them in Jay's gang.

Ward was impressed. 'A clever lot, then.'

Maxton picked it up eagerly. 'That's right, they were. Oh, I'm not denying there were a couple of surprises, but there were some very bright children. Jay, of course, and Juliette Cartwright and Kate Cosgrove – well, Kate wasn't as naturally talented but when she made up her mind to do something she'd do it. Oh, they were clever, no doubt about it. No doubt at all.'

The words 'whatever anyone said' were almost audible. Curious. Maxton still hadn't really explained why this academic success should have been anything other than a feather in his cap. Ward asked the next question before making a note.

'And – Jay Darke? Was that the name you mentioned?' He probably imagined that he had felt a pricking of his thumbs as he said the name. Maxton hesitated.

'Jay Darke,' he said at last, 'was without doubt the cleverest child I have ever taught. But strange, very strange. Held himself aloof, you know – no good at sport, total lack of co-ordination. Never seemed to make friends until that summer. And then—'

He paused again, and this time Ward made no attempt to prompt him. The silence lengthened, then Maxton said heavily, with unexpected humility, 'I hope I misjudge him. I hope that perhaps I am being uncharitable because I resented his attitude to authority. But after that summer, I think I would say he is the only coldly evil child I have ever encountered.'

It was an astonishing statement, delivered in that flat, emotionless voice. Ward said simply, 'Why?'

Maxton put his hands together, made a neat steeple of his fingers, then studied them. 'He gathered together a gang. I don't know how he did it, or why, but it became all the rage – what they call now "cool", I believe.' He allowed himself a small smile at his own mastery of contemporary slang.

'But Jay made it – well, not so much just "cool" to be in as social death to be out. He had a wicked tongue and he managed to make every child in that class feel a total failure if they didn't belong.

'It affected morale. It sparked off feuds, jealousies, persecutions. There was vandalism, stealing; I had more complaints of bullying in that term than I had in the whole of the rest of my career put together, but nothing I said or did made any difference. I knew it was Jay who was behind it, but there was never anything you could pin on him, and if you were one of his gang – well, you were impervious. He was running the place like a medieval court.'

'So who was in and who was out? You don't keep school photos, by any chance?'

He did, and was piqued not to have thought of that himself. He led Ward through to a room at the front of the house which seemed to serve as sitting room and study, motioning him to a chair while he went over to a pair of filing cabinets in one corner.

As he idly took stock of his new surroundings, a flash of colour caught Ward's eye. On top of one of the bookcases which ran on either side of the fireplace, striking in blue and gold, was a small reproduction of the famous mask of Tutankhamen.

Further along, there was an elegant black figurine, a vaguely Egyptian-looking cat with earrings which Ward was sure was a copy of a famous museum piece. Under the lamp which stood on a table beside him was a shiny, highly polished scarab which could have been genuine, and in the neatly ordered bookcases he could pick out a shelf of books with an Egyptian theme. Well, well, well.

Meanwhile, with a cry of satisfaction, Maxton was holding up a group photograph mounted on yellowing card.

'I do pride myself on my filing system,' he said smugly, bringing it over. 'School leavers, 1980. I have a complete record, you know, of every year when I was headmaster.'

Ward took it. There were two rows of children, the girls sitting in front on either side of a younger, though still bald, Arthur Maxton, the boys standing behind. The youthful faces looked back at him, cheerful or surly, dark or fair. He recognised Bonnie, stolid and lumpish, with her heavy face set in lines of discontent despite the artificial smile. Why was it that black-and-white photography as a medium seemed so much more revealing than colour?

'Which is Jay Darke?' he asked, though he reckoned he knew already.

There was a boy right in the middle of the back row, tall but slightly built, with a thatch of dark hair and a sharp intelligent face. He was unsmiling, his dark eyes meeting the camera with a stare which was – what, challenging? Contemptuous?

Maxton, leaning over Ward's shoulder, confirmed it with a double tap of his finger. 'And that's Ed Jennings beside him. He's running his father's garage in Burlow now – a thoroughly bad lot, I may say, *not* one of Burlow Primary's successes. And there's Barry, Bonnie's twin.'

Barry Bryant, on Jay's other side, was a smallish, pleasant-looking lad with fair curly hair who looked younger than his years and bore no resemblance to his sister.

'He wasn't one of the academic stars, but he's got there through sheer hard work. I did what I could for him when he applied for my old job, and he's been excellent. But he and Ed

– that summer they acted as Jay's henchmen, his slaves, really. Not healthy, I thought, not healthy at all, but there was nothing I could do about it.'

'What about the others in the gang? Any girls?'

'Now let me see.' He had fetched half-moon glasses, which he perched on the end of his nose. He pointed. 'Well, that's Kate Cosgrove there – she belonged, though goodness knows why.' His voice softened as he talked about an obvious favourite. 'She has a cottage in Burlow still, comes back at weekends. She's our parliamentary candidate, you know – prime minister one day, I shouldn't wonder. Still has time to chat about old times, though, if I'm chairing one of her meetings.'

The girl he indicated was striking rather than pretty, with strong features and a composed, enigmatic smile. Ward found himself wondering cynically how much time she would spare her old headmaster if he wasn't a political asset. But perhaps that was unfair.

Maxton was going on, 'Oh, there's Dick Stevens – dear me, I'd forgotten about him, poor fellow. Nice lad, son of a bank manager – killed himself on a motor-bike at seventeen. And Abigail Fenner – sweet girl, Abbie, a farmer's daughter and married to another local farmer now. Not as bright as the others – the only one of Jay's little coterie who failed the eleven-plus – went to that convent school in Flitchford instead. It was surprising, really, that he chose her, but of course she was very friendly with Juliette Cartwright, and Jay was – perhaps obsessed with her isn't putting it too strongly. He married her in the end – they live in London now.'

'Which is she?' Ward ran his eye along the unidentified girls' faces. None of them really looked like a *femme fatale*.

Maxton checked. 'Oh, she's not there. Must have been off ill that day, or something – I don't recall. She was a very interesting girl, with something about her. Very appealing, very charming – French mother, of course – not that *that* lasted.'

'So that was the lot – seven of them?'

'Yes – no, wait a minute. Brian Thorburn – I'd forgotten

about him. There he is, see? The family emigrated to Canada not long after that.'

'But Bonnie, I take it, wasn't in with the in-crowd.'

The other man laughed, a dry titter. 'Bonnie? Hardly. *Au contraire*, you might say.'

'So who were her friends, then?'

Maxton looked uncomfortable, pursing up his neat pink mouth. 'It hardly seems right to gossip,' he said stiffly. '*De mortuis*, you know—'

And *noblesse oblige* and *nil desperandum* to you too. Ward retained his patience with some difficulty. 'I'm afraid in a murder inquiry social niceties like not speaking ill of the dead have to go by the board.'

It was rather as if Maxton had been reassured that he wouldn't think the worse of him in the morning. He licked his pink lips and began with relish. Bonnie, it seemed, was the school sneak. Bonnie had no friends. The friends she wanted wouldn't have her, and she made it all too plain that she despised the others.

'She was spoiled by Bella Bryant, of course.' Maxton was enjoying himself now. 'Bonnie was her mother over again – a most unpleasant, mischief-making woman, Bella, though she's a poor sad creature now. Barry took after Don, and his mother held that against him – Don was a nice chap, but – well, easily led, as you might say. But that was hardly Barry's fault, and I used to feel quite sorry for him, poor lad. It wasn't easy, and he's been a good son to her, even now.'

'And Bonnie resented Barry being in Jay's gang?'

'Jealous as a cat. Kept telling tales and getting her mother to come and complain that they wouldn't play with her, which of course made everything worse.'

'Well, it would, wouldn't it?' Ward glanced at his watch. 'Right – you've been immensely helpful, and I've taken up far too much of your time. But I'd be grateful if you'd indulge me with just a couple more questions.'

Fishing in his pocket, he took out a transparent evidence bag.

He set it on the low table beside him, and smoothed it out so that Maxton could see the clay figurine inside.

'I'm sorry I can't take it out, but the forensic people may want to check it again. Does this mean anything to you?'

Maxton stared at it. 'Good gracious,' he said blankly. 'Is it – is it meant to be Anubis?'

'That was my guess too. Would there be any reason for linking it to Bonnie or her classmates?'

'Well—' For the first time he seemed at a loss for words. 'Anubis. Of course, as you can see I have a particular fascination with Ancient Egypt myself. The Tutankhamen exhibition – that was seventy two. It made a deep impression. It became a sort of hobby, and of course, it was an ideal theme for study. Under it you could subsume history, geography, art, mythology – even maths through a little bit of elementary trigonometry if they were bright enough. So I always did it with Primary Seven.'

'I don't suppose you would remember whether they showed any special interest that year?'

The schoolmaster bridled at this implied slight to his memory. 'Well, of course I do. As you would expect from such an intelli-gent group, they took it up with great enthusiasm. I flatter myself that I really caught their imagination. Some of the work was outstanding, quite outstanding – Jay, for example, became completely absorbed, compiled a particularly impressive folder on it, with a lot of external research.'

'Any connection between that and the caves?'

'The caves?' Maxton looked surprised. 'No, not that I know of. I certainly never heard anything—'

'Fine. It was just a thought.' Ward put the plastic bag back in his pocket and stood up. 'Thank you. You've been very helpful.'

Maxton, looking regretful at this sign that the curtain was about to come down on his performance, stood up as well. 'And the second question?' he prompted. 'You said there were two.'

'Ah yes. That's a little more delicate. Do you, by any chance, remember whether there was any adult who appeared to be taking a particular interest in Bonnie?'

Maxton's face stiffened. 'Was she – was she *assaulted*?'

'We have no reason at all to think so, but it is obviously a line of enquiry we can't ignore.'

His brow cleared. 'Oh, you've been talking to Bella Bryant! You really have to remember, sergeant, that in the first place she was quite unhinged by Bonnie's death, and in the second place she was always a peculiarly malevolent and unreliable gossip.'

'I – see.' Ward decided not to admit to ignorance; Alex Denholm was scheduled to go along with a policewoman to talk to Mrs Bryant in the afternoon, and it sounded as if she wouldn't hesitate to name names. 'But there was nothing that gave you concern at the time?'

'Good gracious no. And I would caution you to be on your guard. The most dangerous people, the people who mislead one most, are those who are themselves convinced, however mistakenly, that what they are saying is the truth.'

'That's a profound remark,' Ward said, heading for the door. 'I'll keep it in mind. Thank you for your time.'

It took him another ten minutes to extricate himself, but he felt it had been time well spent.

Determined not to miss his lunch this time, Ward made a detour to a pub where he sometimes ate when he was out hill-walking, then fortified by an excellent Lancashire hotpot drove back by way of Burlow.

He had time, he reckoned, to do one interview before he went back to Flitchford. Arthur Maxton had been able to give him addresses for Abbie Fenner, now Bettison, for Kate Cosgrove's weekend cottage and for Ed Jennings' garage; since Ms Cosgrove would presumably be in Sheffield and the Bettison farm was out of Burlow to the north, Jennings' garage was the obvious choice.

The garage was on the main street, near the centre. It had a petrol forecourt with a few second-hand cars lined up at one side, a workshop at the back where three mechanics were working on a couple of cars, and a run-down-looking office.

As Ward came in, the girl operating the till looked up without much interest from the magazine she was reading, indicating a door on the farther side when he asked for Mr Jennings. He knocked and went in.

The man who got up from behind a desk where papers were untidily piled around a computer monitor was wearing a short-sleeved navy shirt which exposed a dragon tattoo on his left forearm. He was powerfully built and swarthy, with a five o'clock shadow already showing. When he saw Ward, his dark eyes narrowed.

'Yeah?' His pose was defensive.

Ward introduced himself, flipping out his warrant card.

'That's what I thought. What's your problem now? But just let me tell you before you tell me, whatever it were, I didn't do it. Right?'

'No one is—' Ward began, but he was cut short.

'You lot never give up, do you? Just because I've a bit of previous you say to each other, "Oh yeah, let's go round and lean on Jennings," every time you come up with a cut-and-shut. It's harassment, that's what it is—'

'Mr Jennings,' Ward raised his voice, 'may I explain? It's nothing to do with the garage. I was wanting your help over another matter entirely – may I?'

He indicated the chair in front of the desk, and Jennings shrugged. 'Can't stop you, can I?' he said, going round to sit in the squeaking swivel chair opposite. He did not look particularly reassured.

'I wonder if you've seen the newspapers this morning, Mr Jennings?'

'Newspapers, sergeant? No, can't say as I have. Not much of a one for papers, except the *Sunday Sport*.'

'Perhaps you've heard people talking about the skeleton in the caves up on Long Moor?'

Ward saw calculation in the man's eyes as he tried to work out the implications of an admission.

'Yeah,' he said, his manner off-hand. 'Sure. So?'

'Bonnie Bryant. Does the name mean anything to you?'

Again there was that flicker of calculation in the dark, watchful eyes. 'Yeah. I knew her a bit. Barry's twin. Drowned when we was kids.'

'It seems possible that may not be true – that the skeleton in the cave may be hers.'

'Really? Nasty, that.'

Was it news to him? Ward couldn't tell. 'At this stage we're trying to get some background to the summer when she disappeared.'

The hostility was only barely veiled. 'Well, don't look at me. I've enough problems when you lot ask me about last Saturday night, never mind twenty years ago.'

'There was a group of you, I understand, a group Bonnie Bryant would have liked to belong to—'

He shrugged. 'If you say so.'

'It was Jay Darke's gang, wasn't it?'

'So? Kids have gangs – you got a problem with that?'

'What sort of things did you do?'

'Christ, I told you, didn't I? I can't remember. Kids' stuff, I suppose.'

'In the caves?'

He was still for a fraction too long, then he gave an unconvincing laugh. 'Look, mate, you tell me. I remember mucking about the place, and not a lot else. I'm not smart enough to have a good memory.'

'Yet you passed the eleven-plus.'

Jennings' eyes narrowed. 'Been doing your homework, have you, sergeant? Well, if you'd done it right you'd have found out they chucked me out after a year. Just as well – didn't get car maintenance at the Grammar, did you, and poncey stuff like Latin's not a lot of use when you've an exhaust to fix. Any road, I just don't remember. OK?'

Ward got up. This was a waste of time. 'So you can't think of any reason why Bonnie should have been in the caves?'

He felt, rather than saw, Jennings relax. 'Not a clue.'

At the door, Ward turned. 'And you don't know anything about a jackal-headed god and the bones of a lot of small animals?'

Jennings couldn't control the gasp, the flicker of what might almost be fear in his eyes. 'I – I don't know what you mean,' he said, clearing his throat.

'Don't you?' said Ward, and went out.

Chapter Eight

Harry Cartwright glanced impatiently at the gold Rolex on his wrist for about the tenth time. It was part of his carefully cultivated image that he didn't do waiting. Harry Cartwright was the one people waited for. People who waited were erks, and even when his inconvenience was caused by sluggish baggage handlers at Heathrow Airport, it was hard not to take it as a personal affront. It made him feel insecure, as if perhaps under all the trappings of success he was still just little Harry Cartwright the miner's son.

He took a couple of impatient paces, bumping into an inoffensive middle-aged lady who apologised when he glared at her. Behind him someone said, 'Excuse me,' but he pretended not to hear, and as the laden luggage-trolley, erratically steered with one hand by a harassed-looking man holding a toddler with the other, weaved its way awkwardly round him, Harry glared at him too. This was intolerable!

He looked at his watch again. Five fourteen. The Paris plane had touched down half an hour ago, for chrissake. How long could it take able-bodied men to shovel suitcases on to a truck then dump them on a conveyor belt? What were they doing – opening the cases to try on the women's dresses? Southern poofters!

Five sixteen. Flabby management, that was what it was all about. Give him a couple of days with hire-and-fire power, and he'd show them what they meant by work in the Midlands.

Five seventeen. He couldn't remember the last time he'd come to meet someone off a plane. He had people to do that sort of thing for him, but ever since his daughter's phonecall from France he'd been in a state of protective fury that anyone, least of all a little nerd like Darke, had had the gall to treat Harry Cartwright's daughter like that.

He'd decided to drive her straight over there to have it out with him – always supposing they ever let her out of the International Arrivals area – because that was what Juliette had decided she must do and they might as well get it over with as soon as possible.

When Harry had told Joe Rickman, his lawyer, what the plan was, he had shaken his head and sucked his yellowing teeth. Joe was no oil painting, but he was the sharpest operator in the legal business. If he wasn't, he wouldn't be working for Harry, would he?

'Don't advise it,' he said, his lugubrious face set in lines even more pessimistic than usual.

But Juliette, when she chose, could be as stubborn as her old man himself, he told Joe with a certain pride. 'That's my way of doing it – straight out, no messing. Takes guts – but after all, she's Harry Cartwright's daughter. And I'll be right there behind her to see that he doesn't try anything cute.'

'Don't try anything cute yourself, Harry,' Rickman warned him. 'Play this one straight, all legal and above board, and we'll screw him with the divorce settlement. We can make it hurt – trust me.'

'Have I ever done anything else, my son?' Harry had slapped him on the shoulder, promising superhuman patience even if what he really wanted to do was shove Jay Darke's teeth through the back of his skull. Well, he had people who could do that for him too, if Darke started playing rough games.

Five twenty. His supplies of superhuman patience, limited at the best of times, were all getting used up just standing here waiting for some moron to work out which button you pressed to start the conveyor belt.

He'd booked them into the Hilton tonight, so the sooner

they dealt with Darke, the better. He wouldn't get any sense out of Juliette with the confrontation hanging over her, and he wanted to start making plans for her future. It would be good to chat to his own daughter over dinner without a sarcastic, sneering presence at her side. There was a lot he hadn't said in the past that wanted saying, and he was looking forward to his evening.

Juliette would just have to come back to Burlow meantime. Well, she was homeless and penniless for the moment, and what she needed was a bit of a break to sort herself out. A nice PA job in Sheffield, for instance – that could be just the thing, and he knew exactly which strings to pull.

Of course, Debbie wasn't over the moon at the prospect of having Juliette living at home – why didn't he just get her a flat in London, she'd said – but he wasn't having any of that until she got her head together. Debbie was always awkward round Juliette, but she'd do her best when it came to it. She'd a good heart, had Debbie.

Five twenty-six – and there she was at last, coming through the barrier, a slight figure in jeans and a plain white T-shirt. Seeing her at a distance before she saw him, he was suddenly struck by her likeness to her dead mother.

He felt a brief, nostalgic pang for the French girl who had been so totally unsuitable as a wife for him. This was exactly as he remembered her – slim and dark, with that look of elegance you couldn't quite explain. Debbie spent a fortune on clothes and grooming without coming close.

Then Juliette caught sight of him. Her sombre expression lifted and she waved, making her way through the crowd towards him. He held out his arms and she set down her luggage and threw herself into them with an abandon she hadn't shown since she was eight years old. 'Oh Dad!' she said.

He felt a sentimental lump in his throat, and when she lifted her face to kiss him he saw tears in the deep blue eyes which were so like his own.

He held her away from him, giving her a gentle shake. 'Come on, my girl, this won't do,' he said gruffly. 'You're safe now with your old dad to look out for you. Everything'll be all right now – trust Harry Cartwright to see to that.'

He picked up her suitcase, put his other arm round her shoulders to draw her to his side, and they set off together for the car park.

'If you're really telling me you can't bring yourself to collect what's your own property from the house, then you'll just have to make an inventory and we'll send someone in. Or else Joe Rickman can arrange a valuation and stick him with the bill, but I'm damned if I'm leaving Darke with a house fitted out at my expense.'

With her head turned to look out of the tinted window of her father's Jaguar XK8 at the stationary rush-hour traffic, Juliette stifled a sigh. What was it with the child–parent relationship? Half an hour ago, she had shed tears of love, yet already she had reached the stage of wanting to scream.

She had told him what she intended to do, not stated a basis for negotiation. The problem here was that her father simply could not understand that to her money was just something you needed to buy food, clothes and shelter, and, if you were lucky, the occasional luxury. To him money was power, or leverage, or as in this case, revenge.

She had been quite childishly thankful to see him waiting for her at the airport, his solid frame a reassuring bulwark against the world. She knew she could rely on him for whatever protection was within his power, from the very best legal advice right down to the defence of his powerful fists if things got physical. It gave her the comforting illusion of complete security.

But at what cost? His definition of protective paternal love came perilously close to possessiveness and outright domination. Much like Jay, in fact. Indeed, the thought struck her, how much had her own acceptance of that relationship been conditioned by her father's attitude? How outraged Harry would be at the suggestion of any comparison between the two!

She must be vigilant, or having escaped one emotional

prison she could hideously easily find herself in another.

The notion that Juliette should leave Jay in possession of everything she had left behind in the marital home – the sentimental odds and ends from her girlhood, the wedding presents Harry's friends had lavished on her, the canteen of solid silver cutlery which had been his own gift – had been to Harry simply incomprehensible.

She had tried to convey to him the futility of haggling over possessions now irrevocably tainted with Jay's cruelty and her own miserable helplessness.

'Things aren't that important to me,' she said lamely. 'I – I just want to forget about that part of my life, close the door behind me and walk away.'

Harry glanced at her disapprovingly. 'You just watch out that running away doesn't get to be a habit with you, my lass. It doesn't solve anything – tried it once before, didn't you, and look what happened.'

Juliette bit her lip. 'I know. That was cruel and cowardly, which is why despite what Jay's done I owe it to him this time to tell him face to face. But that isn't what I'm talking about when I say I don't want a "whose-is-what" squabble. The point is that there's nothing I left behind that's worth it – nothing that isn't spoiled for me now.'

That was when Harry made the remark about the inventory. She didn't argue. She might, later, though she'd probably lose.

Just at the moment, anyway, she had no energy to spare. She needed it to summon up every scrap of courage and resolve for the interview which lay ahead.

As Harry manoeuvred the big car through the narrow entrance to the mews her heart was racing and she found she was taking short, shallow breaths. She dug her nails into her sweating palms to steel herself as she got out of the car. Harry closed the door after her and gave her shoulders a quick squeeze.

'Just remember I'm right behind you, sweetheart,' he said, and she managed a wavering smile.

'But you're going to let me do the talking, Dad,' she reminded him.

'Promise I'll do my best. Don't promise I'll succeed.' He gave her his most disarming grin.

She walked across the worn cobblestones, past the other smart little houses with their window-boxes and brightly painted doors. One of the neighbours was outside polishing his car and he raised his hand in greeting as they passed. Venables, that was his name; it was all so normal, so familiar, and yet it felt as if she had been absent for years not days.

And here was their own house, with its cheerful yellow door and brass dolphin knocker. The brass was dull, and she registered automatically that the flowers in the window-box were wilting badly. Jay must have stopped watering them. She raised the dolphin's smiling head and tapped.

When the door swung open, Jay's expressionless face gave no hint of surprise at seeing them there. His green-brown eyes were dead-looking, opaque. He stood in the doorway without speaking, his hands shoved into the pockets of his black jeans.

He didn't look unkempt or marked by distress at her desertion. Nor did he, as she had feared he might, catch her eyes with that look which had always said that, come what might, she was his, predestined for him since the beginning of the world. He just stood there as if he was bored, as if he had all the time in the world to wait for her to select her opening gambit.

It was easier if he was going to play games. 'May we come in?' Juliette suggested quietly. 'I shouldn't have thought you would particularly want to have Mr Venables in on this discussion.'

Jay glanced beyond them to the man who had stopped polishing his car to gape, shrugged, then stood aside to let them in.

She'd forgotten how dark the house was. Outside, it was a golden summer evening, but inside the lamps were on and the screens of Jay's computers at the back glowed with an unearthly light. His swivel chair was pushed back as if he had got up from working there to answer the door.

She glanced up at the corner of the room, where the red eye of a security camera had always flashed, but the lens was blank and dead now that she wasn't there to spy on.

'Jay—' She faltered; she hadn't realised quite how hard it

would be to form the words which would finish their marriage. 'I'm – I'm never coming back to you,' she managed at last.

'Now, however did I guess that was what you and your minder had come to say?'

His tone was flippant, insulting. Beside her Harry tensed, took a step forward.

'Jay, you don't love me, do you?' She looked up into his cold eyes, trying to connect, trying to coerce him to some sort of emotional truth. 'Be honest! Please, please be honest! It's been impossible for you to forgive me for running away from you in the first place, hasn't it? Believe me, I understand that. It was cruel of me, dishonest, cowardly.'

He was still staring at her, unblinking. She took a deep breath and went on, 'You should have told me how hurt and angry you were when you found me again. But you didn't, did you? You smiled, you pretended, you planned a cruel, long-drawn-out revenge. How far would you have gone, Jay? How was the torture meant to end?' Her voice broke on the words.

Her father stepped forward to put a hand on her shoulder; it steadied her, and she controlled herself with an effort. 'I'm sorry, Jay, I'm sorry – please believe that. But I know you hate me, I know you want to punish me and I'm not coming back to give you that pleasure again. I can't love someone who hates me – I'm not prepared even to try any more. This is the end. Finish.' She bowed her head.

Jay had listened in silence; he stood silent for a moment longer. Then he said, 'Are you sure there's nothing that can make you change your mind?' Juliette looked up as he went over to a shelf and picked up, apparently idly, an ornament which stood there. It was a polished basalt figurine of a human body with a jackal's head. He fingered its smooth curves. 'Are you absolutely sure?' he said.

Had she imagined that the room grew darker still, and very cold? She shivered, but she spoke steadily.

'I'm very sure. Don't go trying that on me, Jay. I grew out of it a very long time ago. Anubis has no power over me any longer.'

He smiled, a chilling, brilliant, mirthless smile which made his eyes glitter in the lamplight. 'Ah, you know that. But does he?'

Harry looked from one to the other, uncomprehending but suspicious, as if like a dog he could scent danger without knowing what it was. 'Hey, what's going on?' he demanded roughly. 'What's this about—'

'No, Dad, don't get involved. You promised.' The step that took her nearer to his protective bulk was unconscious. 'It's meaningless, just a silly childish game.'

Jay stopped smiling. 'If you say so,' he said, and set the figurine back in its place.

'I wish it had been different.' Juliette was aware that she was speaking the epitaph for their marriage. 'I thought there was love between us, Jay, but all the time you were somewhere else, somewhere dark and ugly. There's no way back.'

She paused to let him have his say; when he said nothing, she went on, her voice flat now. 'I'm starting proceedings for divorce.'

Harry shifted impatiently. 'Well, that's it, then. Nothing more to be said, is there? You'll be hearing from my solicitors in due course. But don't kid yourself you've got away with it—'

'Dad!' Juliette warned him again. She grasped his sleeve, pulling him towards the door.

'And you think, poor fool, that you have?' Jay's voice, behind them, was a low snarl, and Juliette had to grab Harry's arm with the full force of her weight behind it, as he bunched his fists and advanced belligerently on his son-in-law.

'Don't let him trap you,' she begged. 'That's what he wants – he's trying to wind you up. Let's go. I've said what I had to say.'

Reluctantly recognising the wisdom of her words, Harry allowed himself to be edged out of the door ahead of her.

She looked back. 'Goodbye, Jay.'

He met her eyes with the look she had dreaded earlier. He said, slowly and bleakly, 'And so it is fulfilled: "I am One, who becomes Two, who becomes Four, who becomes Eight, and then I am One again."'

She found she was unable to move, staring back into those moss-agate eyes as if she were mesmerised. Harry, who had gone out, stepped back into the house again irritably.

'Juliette! Juliette, what's keeping you? There's a drink with my name on it waiting at the Hilton. Let's get out of here.'

She started as if a spell had been broken. As she turned and walked out without looking back, she heard Jay close the door.

Under the interested gaze of her one-time neighbour, they went back to the car. As Harry held the door open for her, she heard from the house the strains of the *Isis and Osiris* aria, played much too loudly.

When they had gone, Jay Darke stood motionless in the sitting room, letting Mozart's waves of sound wash over him, staring towards the sculpture of the jackal-headed god with unseeing eyes. He stood until the aria was finished, then clicked the control he was holding for silence.

In front of him, the shelves above the stereo system held his collection of Egyptian treasures − scarabs, cloudy ancient glass, pottery, jewellery made from gold wire and *lapis lazuli* − elegantly displayed and cleverly lit, purchased over the years from specialist dealers in a dozen capital cities. There was the Anubis figure too, of course, and two small clay pots with lids sculpted like animal heads.

Suddenly his face contorted in violent emotion: rage perhaps, or grief. With sweeping movements he cleared the shelves, pitching the precious, fragile artefacts which had survived more than a thousand years to destruction on the polished wooden floor.

The moment passed and he was in control again, looking down impassively at the shards of history. Deliberately he trod across them, pulverising glass and clay to dust and trampling gold wire, then went back to sit at his computer desk, his nerve centre.

With this small machine he could conjure up all knowledge, could extend his control wherever he chose. He nudged the mouse impatiently to re-activate the screen.

He had barely slept, the last couple of days, working and planning, not being sure when he would want to activate his plans. The time had come. He stretched in his chair, then got to his feet.

On the floor, the splinters of glass and silver glittered in the artificial light. In the debris the Anubis figure was lying on its back, undamaged.

He hesitated, then with an odd smile twisting his lips went over to pick it up and set it in solitary grandeur in its old position, the middle of the middle shelf. The backlighting gave it theatrical definition.

He selected the *Isis and Osiris* aria once more, listening intently as the velvet voice of the bass caressed the challenging lowest notes. As it came to the end of the heathen prayer to those ancient gods, Jay Darke closed his eyes.

Once the last note had died away, he opened his eyes again. He met the blank, sightless stare of the jackal-headed idol, bowed his head in a salute that was only part-mocking, then turned away.

The door to the Criterion bar was open tonight, and a few of its patrons were standing outside with their drinks in the evening sunshine. Inside it was dark, noisy, smoky, and fetid with the press of bodies.

Tom Ward eyed it with distaste. If he went home he could stroll down to the beer-garden at the Bell, a much more appealing prospect. But the Cri was the Flitchford police station's local; Alex Denholm was usually to be found there for half an hour after he knocked off, and Ward wanted to talk to him.

His meeting with Broughton had been short and purposeful. The Super had been pleased with what he'd extracted from Maxton, but as Ward had foreseen, with ID all but confirmed and Press interest fading fast, the investigation was being downgraded. The chances of a successful prosecution at this distance in time were, to say the least of it, slim, and there were as always pressing demands on police time.

Ward was to follow up the leads he'd got from Maxton, of course, and anything developing from them, but no further resources would be allocated. The Bryant murder would just form part of his normal case-load, taking its turn with everything else, like the complaint about stolen farm machinery that he'd been detailed to check out tomorrow on the way to see Abbie Bettison.

That was the down side. The up side was that it would be, in fact if not in theory, his own case to pursue as and when he could.

So he was keen to catch Alex and find out what, if anything, his visit to Burlow had turned up. He'd be interested to hear about Bella Bryant, for a start.

Blinking in the sudden darkness he went into the crowded room and insinuated his way towards the bar. He was in luck; at the far end he could see Alex's broad back as he stood with DC Barclay and another off-duty officer whom Ward knew slightly. Alex was holding the floor.

'And then, after all that, the old witch suddenly grabbed my arm,' he was saying, then as Ward came up behind him and suited the action to the words, he gave a start which slopped half the beer in his glass onto the bar.

'Bloody hell, Tom, you can buy me another for that,' he sputtered as his companions chortled.

'Pint of draught bitter, please, love.' Ward, grinning broadly, managed to attract the barmaid's attention. 'And you'd better set up another for him – he's got the shakes. Anyone else?'

As the two other men shook their heads he went on, 'So, you had an interesting afternoon, did you, Alex?'

Placated, Denholm returned to his interrupted tale. 'You'd better believe it! Off her trolley, that Bryant woman. Ought to be in a straitjacket—'

'Start at the beginning,' Ward suggested.

Barclay groaned. 'That's where I came in,' he said, emptying his glass. 'Anyway, I promised the wife I'd babysit to let her out for her aerobics class.'

The other man followed suit, claiming a church meeting. Denholm finished off what was left in his glass and picked up his second pint.

'Do you ever ask yourself what it is about you that makes people leave whenever you arrive?'

'Seizing their chance to escape, that's all. It's the way you tell them.' A bar stool became vacant and Ward perched himself on it, ready to listen.

They had taken statements that day from Perce Willis, Jim and Doreen Archer at the Three Tuns, and Annie Stephens. According to Denholm she'd been off work, to Doreen's voluble disgust, and was sitting at home with a permanent fag in her face, twitching. She'd been able, under persuasion, to come up with the name of the firm of dentists where Bonnie had her teeth done, so the chart could be sent direct from the labs, but apart from that the statements had been confirmatory rather than instructive.

It was, however, an account of the interview with Bella Bryant with which Denholm had been regaling his colleagues. He began now, with the air of one who has saved the best till last.

'Just for a start, she's repellent. Gross, if you can remember what that meant before American kids took it over. Just sits like a white slug in her chair in the lounge of the home, watching whatever's on TV. She's got this great puffy face with these funny dark eyes and the way she looks at you, you keep checking to make sure she hasn't turned you into a frog.'

'A nasty lady at the best of times, according to my source.'

'And this, let me tell you, isn't the best of times. Well, the matron was there and I had Jenny with me to provide the feminine touch, and she did her stuff – breaking the news gently, not too much detail, text-book performance. And as far as you could tell, it just didn't connect. She didn't speak, didn't move, just sat there staring.'

'Puts you off, doesn't it, when they don't say anything.'

'That's right. So I tried a few questions, but that didn't get us anywhere. The matron tried to sort of jolly her along – you know, "Not feeling very chatty today, Bella, are we?" Sort of thing that would make any normal person take a swing at her, but they seem to think the crumblies like it.

'But that wasn't any better, so we got up to leave. And suddenly she rose like a rocket and came at me. I'd have been ready to swear it was impossible, but she moved like a striking snake.

'She was trying to claw at my face. "You did it, you bastard, you killed her! I knew it, you were stalking her, lusting after her. I knew it!" She was screaming all this stuff at the top of her voice, and there's me trying to hold her off while all the old biddies are acting as if I'm going to set about raping the lot of them. You can't imagine what it was like.

'Oh yes,' he said with some bitterness, as Ward began to laugh, 'bloody funny, if it wasn't you. But anyway, Jenny was trying to get hold of her and then a male nurse came running and pinioned her arms from behind and got her back in her chair. So she just slumps back and sits there as if nothing had happened.'

Ward was fascinated. 'Who did she think you were?'

Denholm was not going to be hurried. 'Wouldn't tell me, would she? I asked, of course, but she only said, "You know who you are," and let loose with a flood of the sort of obscenities I'd like to think old ladies like her didn't know.'

'So did you find out?'

'Jenny got it out of her – bright girl, Jenny. She pointed at me and said, "Who's that man, Bella? I don't like the look of him." And then, pat as you like, guess what she says?'

'Frankenstein? Lord Lucan?'

'Weirder than that. "Harry Cartwright."'

'*Harry Cartwright?*'

Satisfied with the effect he had achieved, Denholm beamed. 'Thought you'd like that. The Chief Constable won't, though.'

'No he won't, will he?' Ward whistled thoughtfully. 'You really don't want one of your cronies at the Golf Club—'

'– and one of the biggest donors to the police benevolent fund—'

'– and one of the major employers in the area—'

'– to be dragged into an investigation into allegations of murder. And worse.'

'Particularly when the allegations have been made by someone who is, taking the case at its highest, several buns short of an old folks' treat.'

They were silent for a moment, contemplating the ramifications, then Ward said, 'Well, anyway, what happened after that?'

'Oh, Matron went purple and shushed her and the nurse pointed out, in case we hadn't noticed, that she was batty, and we went to go out.

'Then just as I passed her chair she grabbed my arm, and you wouldn't believe what a powerful grip she's got. I'd have had to hurt her to get free, so all I could do was stand there while she hissed about me being made to pay, and treating her like dirt, all that sort of stuff.

'Then just as suddenly, she lets me go and sits back, and then she's saying, "Isn't it time for me tea yet?" calm as you like.'

'Extraordinary,' Ward said. 'The son wasn't there, was he? Barry – headmaster of Burlow Primary. He was meant to be away till Wednesday on a school trip to York.'

Denholm shook his head. 'Didn't come back. He'd phoned Matron last night, she said, but he'd a problem because the only other adults there are two mums who are helping out with the girls. If he left they'd have to come home and spoil the kids' holiday, so he's to phone tonight and see if she's upset and needs him. But according to Matron, she barely recognises him anyway, so I should think he'll be advised not to hurry home.'

'Right. I've plenty to keep me busy till then. Still, interesting times! What did Broughton say when you told him about Cartwright? He didn't mention it to me.'

'Ah.' Denholm looked awkward. 'Well, I had to check in with Little when we got back, and when he heard that he went into a sort of hand-washing ritual – said the case was being downgraded, you were dealing with it and it was nothing to do with him. He told me to leave a note on your desk so you could tell the Super in the morning.'

'Cheers!' Ward said grimly. 'I'm looking forward to it already. So no doubt I'll be the one who ends up putting the awkward questions to Harry Cartwright – that's the Harry Cartwright who nibbles people who get in his way instead of crisps with his triple Chivas Regal before dinner.

'And we can hardly brush it under the carpet, can we, even if Bonnie hardly looks our Harry's type and her mother, according to Arthur Maxton, was famous for purveying malicious and unreliable gossip.'

'Not after she's said that to us in front of witnesses, you can't, unless you fancy a starring role in a police corruption inquiry. Oh well, you were the one who was keen to be at the sharp end, weren't you? As the saying goes, be very careful what you want because you just might get it.'

'Mmm.' Ward was deep in thought. 'Er – there couldn't possibly be any truth in what she said, could there, Alex?'

Denholm considered the question. 'Well, she certainly sounded pretty convinced about it, for what that's worth.'

'Yes.' He sighed. 'But then, as my friend Arthur pointed out to me this morning, people who believe in the truth of their fantasies are the most dangerous ones of all.'

For the second time that day, Harry Cartwright was seriously put out. He was sitting by himself in the cocktail bar with a large Scotch – not his first – in front of him, brooding like some latter-day Lear on filial ingratitude.

He'd given up time to his daughter, and Harry Cartwright's time was valuable. But had he grudged it? No. He'd been a good father, 'been there' for his daughter, as they called it nowadays. And not only had he caused someone to arrange her flight, and paid for it, he'd actually played chauffeur himself, played the heavy, even played dumb at her request, which went right against the grain. Surely, after all that, the company of his daughter at dinner in what was one of London's top hotels – the sort he wouldn't have dreamed of being able to set foot in, when he was her age – wasn't much to ask?

OK, so she was feeling a bit low. He'd respected that, left her alone and pretended not to notice her dabbing her eyes in the car on the way here. Hell, he could remember the feeling when Marguérite took herself off. Despite getting custody of his daughter, he'd felt down himself for a bit.

So he knew just what Juliette needed – to be taken out of herself, a couple of glasses of champagne, a good dinner, and lots of sound positive suggestions about her future to give her something else to think about. Not that he was planning to dictate to her, naturally. There were half a dozen schemes he had in mind for her to choose from.

But what had she done? Gone straight to her room when they'd checked in, and when he phoned half an hour later to suggest a drink, she'd told him flatly that she didn't want a drink, or dinner. She'd a headache, she claimed, and all she wanted was an early night. He might just as well have booked them into a B&B on the North Circular and saved his money.

He'd been stood up, as good as, and that was something else Harry Cartwright wasn't used to. He wished now he'd brought Debbie with him after all; she'd offered, in case Juliette might need female support but she hadn't been keen and anyway he'd fancied parading his pretty daughter. And the result? Here he was, on his tod, with the evening stretching ahead of him.

Moodily, he finished his Scotch. A hovering waiter came across and said, 'Your table's ready now, sir, if you'd care to go through.'

Harry grunted, and got up to follow him. He disliked eating alone, however good the chef was; he'd ordered a plain steak and chips, and a bottle of claret because a half-bottle wasn't enough. The bottle was more than he wanted, really, but – waste not, want not – he drank it anyway, too quickly to give the wine the respect its price deserved. If Juliette had been there, she'd have drunk a couple of glasses and they'd have lingered over it. His sense of injustice grew.

He refused pudding and the cheeseboard; they brought him

a cigar and he sat puffing at it along with his coffee and another Chivas Regal.

Responsibility for the failure of his evening lay squarely at Darke's door. Weird bastard, he was; he'd always had some sort of strange hold on Juliette, had even been trying to exert it this evening under Harry's very nose. She hadn't fallen for it, thank God, but he'd have to see to it that Darke didn't get another chance. He'd been naïve enough to think once before that Juliette had come to her senses, and look what had happened then. He couldn't understand the girl, but then he'd never understood her mother and it was his theory that if you were studying racing form you looked to the dam for the temperament.

Well, he'd just have to put in a bit of serious training on his filly. He could see to it that Darke didn't come after her again, but there was no doubt about it, she'd have to get her feet set firmly back on good Derbyshire soil.

He ground out his cigar and leaving the restaurant consulted his watch. Quarter to ten – what sort of stupid time was that? Too early to turn in, that was for sure.

On a sudden impulse he went down to the hotel foyer and crossed over to the reception desk. He handed in his key.

'I want a taxi,' he said to the impeccably suited young man who came forward.

'Of course, sir. Our doorman will be happy to call one for you – over there.'

Harry had drunk enough to be spoiling for a fight. 'I didn't tell your doorman to get me a taxi, damn you. I told you. When I ask for service I expect to get it.'

The young man coloured, but said steadily, 'Certainly, sir, if that's what you want.'

Cheated of an excuse to lose his temper, Harry followed him to the entrance where half a dozen taxis stood waiting. The surprised doorman, in response to a signal from the reception clerk, stood aside.

As the cab rolled forward, the young man opened the door while Harry, without acknowledgement, climbed in.

'What address shall I give the driver, sir?'

'I've got a tongue in my head. Shut the door, will you?'

Expressionlessly, the clerk obeyed and stood back as the taxi moved off.

'What's his problem, then?' the doorman, a six foot British Nigerian, asked.

'Who knows?' The other man shrugged. 'Just rich white trash, I would say.'

With a wink to the doorman he went back to his post.

Chapter Nine

At seven fifteen precisely, Adrian Venables let himself out of his immaculate mews flat, glancing at his thin gold watch to be re-assured that he was, as usual, on time. He always liked to get to the office early to make a cup of his strong espresso coffee from the little machine he kept there and sip it while he prepared himself for the day ahead. Anyway, travel in rush hour with other people's sweaty, smelly bodies invading your space was just *so* distasteful, and arriving all flustered and dishevelled simply wasn't his style.

He set the burglar alarm, then locked the door carefully behind him, wiggling the handle just to make sure. In the bright blue tub to the right of his doorstep, a pink geranium flower which was past its best caught his eye and he bent to snap it off. It was then he heard the car engine running.

He straightened up and looked about him, frowning. The little mews was empty of cars; it was quite a cramped space and the Residents' Association was positively *fierce* about cars being garaged when not in use. None of the garage doors was open. Where—?

That was when he caught the dusty, choking smell of a car's exhaust, and looking in the direction of the sound saw the fumes seeping out of his neighbour's garage, misty blue and deadly, before they dissipated in the morning air.

It just couldn't be— Disbelieving, he stared for a moment, then hurried over.

The bright yellow, panelled door had no handle, no keyhole. Electronically controlled, of course, but he pushed against it and banged and shouted. The fumes caught at his throat; he started to cough, and his eyes were watering. A door opened further up the mews, but from within there came no sound except the idling engine.

'Something wrong?' the woman who had come out called anxiously from her doorstep, and he shouted back, conscious even as he spoke of something satisfying in the melodrama of the statement, 'Police! I'm going to call the police!'

Made clumsy by shock and a little dizzy from the smoke, he stumbled back to his own house and let himself in, but it took him two attempts at the code before he managed to de-activate his security alarm and grab the phone. He dialled 999.

Harry Cartwright woke at quarter to eight with a hangover like a personal intimation of the wrath of God. His mouth felt like the Sahara after a couple of camel caravans has passed non-chalantly through and the percussion section of a brass band had taken up residence in his skull. His stomach – well, the less he thought about his stomach the better.

He never went anywhere without the pills his doctor pre-scribed for him privately for just such emergencies, but they were in the bathroom, away across all those acres of moss-coloured velvet pile carpet. Once more, he found himself wishing he had contented himself with more modest accommodation.

Harry closed his eyes again, more in hope than in expecta-tion of sleeping it off. But it was no use. He would have to get those pills. Groaning, he raised himself and groped his way to the bathroom, eyes half shut. He swallowed the pills without looking at himself in the mercilessly illuminated mirror over the basin, then crawled back to bed.

As the discomfort began at last to lessen, he dropped back to sleep. It was half-past nine when the ringing of the phone dragged him unwillingly to the surface.

He swore, sitting up gingerly and blinking blearily about him at the tangled sheets, at the clothes he had discarded on the floor last night in a trail from the door to the bed.

Well, at least the edge seemed to have been taken off his hangover. He ran his hands through his hair, shook his head to clear it and picked up the phone on the fourth ring.

'Harry! Oh, thank God I've got you! I was just going to try your mobile.'

'Debbie!' His voice cracked; he coughed to clear it, then said, 'Debbie?' again, as a question this time.

'Oh Harry, it's awful, just awful. I've had the police at the door—'

Suddenly he was wide awake, his physical ills forgotten, his mind racing. 'The police? What the hell did they want, then? And what do they think they're bloody doing, calling at the house and upsetting my wife? Have you phoned Joe? I'll—'

'No, no, Harry, it's nothing like that. They'd had the police in London on to them, trying to trace Juliette – they'd found our phone number in the house. Jay's committed suicide, Harry! Isn't it *awful*!'

'*Suicide?*' Harry was sitting bolt upright now. 'But he was – last night he was—'

'They were called round there early this morning. In his car, they found him – put a hosepipe from the exhaust in through the window. Oh Harry, how are you going to tell Juliette?'

Debbie was in tears. Harry's eyes narrowed as rage superseded shock. 'The bastard!' he exclaimed. 'He's done that deliberately!'

There was a fractional, shocked silence at the other end of the line, then Debbie said hesitantly, 'Well – yes, I told you, he killed himself—'

Harry went on as if she hadn't spoken. 'He's done it to get at Juliette, to get at me – that's the only possible reason, and there's not a thing I can do to get back at the little sod.'

'Well – he is *dead*, Harry.' Debbie, giving up on a conversation she couldn't really get a handle on, changed the subject. 'The police gave me a London number you're to call. Shall I give it to you now?'

As Harry fumbled for the bedside notepad and pen, she went

on, 'Do you want me to come down, to be there for Juliette? I could be on the ten-thirty train.'

'I'll get back to you.' He jotted down the number then rang off, leaning back against his pillows while he tried to collect his thoughts.

Juliette had warned him that Jay would be hell-bent on revenge, but he'd thought of it in financial terms, or even physical, though that seemed unlikely. But suicide! In terms of making Juliette feel guilty, it was a psychological nuclear strike. Surely he couldn't have – but then he always was a sadistic bastard!

Harry Cartwright was shrewd, but he wasn't subtle. The activities which he had for a moment feared had attracted un-welcome police attention might be flirting with illegality, relying on Joe Rickman's acumen to ensure they were on the right side of the law, if only just. But they were straightforward enough.

He'd always flattered himself that he'd known since he was in his teens how to handle himself in any situation, but this was different. He couldn't understand a kind of depraved cruelty that might reach from beyond the grave itself to inflict torture, and for the first time in his adult life he felt he was out of his depth.

Just how far out, he did not as yet realise.

Juliette felt almost as bad as her father when she woke in the morning, though her wildest excess had been a second bottle of water from the mini-bar. Her head was aching and her eyes were sticky from the tears she had shed for her marriage, for the death of love, before sleep came at last in the early hours of the morning. She seemed to have slept curled into a tight ball, like a wretched animal.

She turned over, stretching across the huge bed to ease her cramped muscles, then lay back against the down pillows. She felt – drained, or purged, perhaps that was the word, and possessed now by a curious calm. It felt rather as if she had been through an illness and the crisis was safely past, even if a long convalescence lay ahead.

Well, she had done it. She had found the courage to face Jay and the will to defy him. She had been haunted – needlessly – by the fear that when he fixed his eyes on her she would be helpless to resist. His tyrant's reign was over. He had lost his power.

But there was no denying that she had been very shaken by his unnerving invocation of Anubis. They hadn't talked directly in those terms since the terrible day of Bonnie Bryant's disappearance; Juliette had always told herself that however uncomfortable she might be with it, Jay's adult fascination with Ancient Egypt was purely cultural.

And yet, and yet, the old childish game – for that, surely, was all it had been – had somehow lurked there at the edges of their relationship, like something you caught a glimpse of out of the corner of your eye which was gone when you turned your head.

He had shown last night that for him it was more, much more than a game. Perhaps she had always suspected he had dark superstitions, but it was only then, when he stood with the figurine in his hands, that he had declared himself. At some level, he believed that this heathen idol, this meaningless man-made figure, had power.

And she didn't? Well, in daylight and with her father at her elbow, she didn't, no.

Thank God for Harry; it was impossible to imagine the supernatural and Harry co-existing. You couldn't see it, hear it, touch it, taste it or smell it? Then it wasn't bloody there, was it? If you thought it was, you were the victim either of a delusion or a conjuring trick.

Harry would be on hand to protect her from whatever vengeance Jay was doubtless devising even now. She wouldn't even have to read his letters – Joe Rickman could do that – and having so carefully isolated her from her friends Jay would find it much harder than he had the last time to find her again. Especially if she went to France – he had no idea where Grandmère lived.

She'd go back to Burlow for a bit to start with, anyway. That was what Harry wanted, and she owed him. In any case, it wouldn't do her any harm to take time to sort herself out. She could do her translations anywhere with a computer link-up, so she wouldn't have the humiliation of taking an allowance from him while she was working out what to do with the rest of her life.

Juliette was feeling better all the time. She got up, opened the curtains on to a sunny morning and a spectacular view of Park Lane, and stood enjoying it for a moment before she glanced at her watch.

Was that really half-past nine? She'd been late going to sleep, of course. And now she came to think of it, she hadn't eaten last night and she was starving.

A shower first, then she'd phone room service. Harry had no doubt breakfasted already; it was kind of him, not to say uncharacteristic, not to call her when he woke.

Juliette stood under the powerful spray, relishing the therapeutic pounding of water on her head and shoulders, feeling the aches and weariness gradually dissipating.

She got out at last, splashed her face with cold water and blow-dried her hair. Then, to please her father who would no doubt want to spend a bit of time in town before they headed north, she put on the smart suit Harry had bought her last year.

She was almost faint with hunger now. She had just picked up the room service menu and the phone when she heard Harry's knock on the door.

'Juliette! Are you in there?'

She put them down and went to let him in, ready with a smile and a cheerful remark about how much better she was feeling today. Dad always liked cheerful.

But he wasn't looking cheerful himself. At the sight of his face, her insides twisted into a nervous knot.

'Dad! What is it? What's happened?'

He came in and as she closed the door behind him went to sit down heavily on the bed. He patted it. 'Come here and sit down.'

She could feel the blood drain from her face as she obeyed him.

He told her, simply. It took a moment before she could make sense of what he had said.

'Jay?' she said. 'Jay killed himself?'

I am One, who becomes Two, who becomes Four, who becomes Eight, and then I am One again.

The words rang inside her head, which had become huge and very light, like a great balloon which might drift away. She got up unsteadily, went to the sealed window as if for air. Below her were tiny people and tiny cars, swarming about their ant-heap as she looked down from far far above them in some other world.

'So Osiris is dead,' she said in a strange, high-pitched voice, 'and Osiris will come back from the dead, when Isis collects the pieces and brings them together again. But I can't, I can't!'

Her legs wouldn't hold her any more. She saw, with an odd detatchment, her father leap up to catch her before everything went black.

'Harry Cartwright?'

Superintendent Broughton's bushy eyebrows almost met his slightly receding hairline when Tom Ward told him about Mrs Bryant's accusation.

There was a long pause, then he said, 'I see,' like a man who does but wishes that he didn't. Then he sighed. 'Well, we're clearly going to have to look into the wretched woman's allegations, even if she has lost most of her marbles. It's going to be a bit awkward, to say the least.'

'Yes, sir.' Ward's agreement was heartfelt.

'Leave it with me meantime. I think the Chief Constable would probably like to be informed. Harry's always been such a great supporter of the police.'

'Yes, sir.' This time, Ward's agreement was less wholehearted. Down in the lower echelons, the feeling was that Harry was there or thereabouts in a few deals which, if not actually shady, wouldn't look good under the spotlight of absolute probity. Still, he was happy to let the Super sort it out.

He was planning his own next steps in the inquiry as he went along to the CID room to shift a bit of paperwork. Once he had that out of the way, he could check that Kate Cosgrove would be in her office if he drove up to Sheffield, then hope to speak to the farmer with the stolen tractor problem as well as Abbie Bettison on his way home. That ought to leave him time enough to catch Barry Bryant whenever he got back this afternoon from his school trip.

The big question was whether he'd be able to swing permission to go up to London to interview Jay and Juliette Darke. With everyone so cost-conscious these days someone was bound to suggest they give a man from the Met a list of questions instead.

The trouble was, he wouldn't know what questions to ask until he heard what they said, and anyway the Met would hardly give it top priority, so the inquiry would lose what momentum it still had. Well, he'd just have to fight his corner with Broughton, that was all. And if the Chief Constable was keen to clear Harry Cartwright – and sufficiently confident that this was what a completed inquiry would do – then that ought to help as well.

When he got back to the CID room, Alex Denholm was working at his desk. 'Ah, Tom, there you are!' he said, grinning. 'Little wants you to pop along to see him. He's got a lovely surprise for you.' In retaliation for Tom's irritating secretiveness yesterday, Denholm declined to relieve his friend's suspense.

There was no mistaking the malicious pleasure with which Little greeted Ward, handing him a report from the police in Buxton. Acting on a tip-off, they had gone to a house in their area and found their suspect surrounded by stolen goods, some of which, it seemed likely, had come from a Flitchford house-breaking last month. There was now an Aladdin's cave of other people's property in one of their cells and they were anxious to get it sorted out as soon as possible.

'Get on over there this morning, check that it looks like the stuff that was lifted then sit in on the questioning and see if you can manage to tie Chummy in with the case. Then all being well you could contact Mr Mowbray to come and identify his belongings formally. He'll appreciate the personal attention of the officer in charge of the case – he's constantly on the phone complaining about police inefficiency.'

'Yes, sir, I do know that.' Ward had fielded most of the calls from the householder, a civil servant (*that* was a joke), and finding his property wouldn't convert him into a satisfied customer. This little project would take up most of his morning, and his reward would be abuse for not solving the case sooner.

'So you'll just have to muck in with some ordinary police-work today, like the rest of us, instead of fairying around playing boy detective, won't you?' Little made no attempt to hide his satisfaction, easing his bulk back in his chair and smiling unpleasantly.

Fighting the temptation to push him over backwards through the window behind him, Ward said, 'I'll get on to it right away,' through gritted teeth and went to obey his orders with a bad grace.

It was lunch time before Ward got rid of his incubus, by which time he was suffering psychological indigestion from the insults he had been forced to swallow. It was too late to go to Sheffield now; he'd have to settle for Abbie Bettison – and the aggrieved farmer, though that shouldn't take long – and Barry Bryant.

He phoned ahead to the Bettisons'. Yes, a nervous voice assured him, she would be happy to speak to him and help in any way she could.

She didn't sound happy, but then how many perfectly innocent people enjoyed talking to the police? In his depressed moments Ward sometimes felt he should go round with a bell and clappers shouting, 'Unclean, unclean!'

He stopped at the burgled farm, listened sympathetically to the farmer's complaints, made the usual notes and soothing noises and empty promises, and was on his way again in twenty minutes. He was almost at Burlow on the way to the Bettison farm when he noticed that the warning light on the petrol gauge had come on. Damn! He'd meant to fill up before he left. Oh well, he'd just have to put a bit of custom in the way of the unsavoury Mr Jennings and get it there. Probably it was safe to assume that he couldn't have got the petrol off the back of a lorry.

★

'Chips? We don't do *chips!*'

Doreen Archer's reaction to the boy's hopeful request neatly combined outrage and contempt in equal measure, as if he had strolled into the Ritz and demanded that they rustle up pie and beans.

'The special's roast lamb, cabbage and mash. There, see – it says on the menu. Or you could have shepherd's pie. Proper home cooking.'

Judging by the grease stains, the menu card which featured these two items and a list of sandwiches – cheese, cheese and chutney, cheese and ham, ham – didn't change very frequently.

The little family group, driven into the Three Tuns by a sudden downpour, studied it bleakly.

'He – he doesn't really like any of that,' the mother, a thin, anxious-looking woman in a beige padded jacket, said apologetically, indicating the nine-year-old, whose mouth had turned down in an ominous line.

'I want chips, Mum!' he whined again.

Doreen, imposing today in hand-knitted magenta which matched her flushed cheeks almost exactly, sniffed. Her sniffs were always eloquent: this one forecast chips today, mainlining heroin tomorrow. She indicated the dog-eared card once more.

'That's what there is. Let me know when you've decided.' As they went into a huddle, she stalked back to stand, arms folded, beside her husband on the other side of the bar, radiating suppressed irritation.

Jim Archer sighed quietly, his customary expression of settled gloom darkening to moroseness. Annie hadn't come in again today, and Doreen was feeling martyred. It was never good for business to have Doreen out front, especially in one of her Moods; she didn't really have a touch with customers. Admittedly, Annie wasn't wonderful either, but at least she didn't insult them.

Come to that, Doreen wasn't any great shakes with the cooking either, for all she gave herself airs, but then their casual clientele didn't discover what the reheated, stringy lamb with its glutinous gravy was like until it was on the table in front of them, and fortunately most people didn't like to make a fuss.

Oh, he'd tried suggesting they get a microwave, have a bit more variety with food in freezer packs, even – chancing his arm – oven chips, but it hadn't gone down well, not well at all.

'If My Sainted Mother –' Doreen always accorded vocal capitals to this description, which was hard for Jim to reconcile with the ill-tempered old battleaxe of his own recollection '– could see her daughter reduced to serving *portioned* food instead of wholesome home cooking, she'd turn in her grave.'

And if indeed she did, for the huge variety of reasons her daughter was inclined to suggest she might, the old bat would be bloody well dizzy by now, Jim sometimes reflected rebelliously.

After their whispered conclave, the little party got up and shuffled out self-consciously.

'Good riddance,' Doreen said, loud enough to be heard before they shut the door, then withdrew to the kitchen with the air of one who has successfully repelled boarders. Jim sighed again, and her dog, a lethargic brown spaniel which had been lying almost invisibly on a brown shag-pile rug in front of the coal-effect fire, suddenly came to life and waddled hopefully through behind her. The pickings should be good today.

Perce Willis, resplendent in a brand-new polyester blazer with plastic brass-style military buttons, an almost white shirt and a quasi-regimental tie, cackled from his usual corner. 'Small wonder that cur has a serious problem with *avoirdupois*. He's had more hot dinners than I've had pints. Talking of which, landlord, if you would be so good—' He slid his empty glass along the bar.

Jim fielded it with a surliness he saw no reason to conceal. Perce had been boasting and splashing it about ever since his five minutes of glory in the papers, which might be good for the takings but certainly got right up your nose.

They'd been quite busy today, with people coming in out of the rain. If the weather was good, they tended to stroll along and discover the Cavendish Arms, after which there was no contest. Today there had been the usual regulars who dropped in for a quick one on their way to lunch – they knew better than to eat at the Three Tuns – but they'd done a few lunches as well. The last of them, a couple at the table in the corner who'd eaten their shepherd's pie without complaint, had finished now; Jim had just gone to take away their plates when Eddie Jennings came in.

Behind him, the rain looked as if it was falling in a solid sheet. His close-cropped hair was slicked to his head and his denim jacket had dark sodden patches all across the arms and shoulders. When he struggled out of it, his V-necked T-shirt was soaked too. His face was black with temper.

Jim's heart sank. That was all he needed! You never knew with Eddie, all glad-handing and back-slapping one day, ready to take offence at someone breathing quietly in the far corner the next. He was a good customer, though, one of the best, in at least once a day and often twice. When he'd had one of his regular barneys with his Missus, he could be in all evening.

'Your usual, Eddie?' Jim went back behind the bar to serve him as Eddie pointedly took a bar stool as far away from Perce as possible. It was to be hoped that Perce would get the message and leave him be, but with Perce above himself like he was just now that was probably too much to hope for.

Jennings grunted. He was looking really rough today, his colour poor and his eyes bloodshot and red-rimmed, as if he hadn't had much sleep. As Jim drew the pint of draught lager, Perce's voice piped up, offensively cheerful.

'Not at our bright-eyed and bushy-tailed best, then, Eddie? A heavy night, was it?'

From under knotted black brows, Eddie gave him a dangerous look. 'You could say. If that's any of your business.'

'Oooh!' Perce was undaunted by this response. 'Well, take my advice, lad, and have mine host here fix you up with a Bloody Mary – everyone swore by that in the Officers' Mess.'

'And how would you know?' Jim interrupted rudely, and Eddie snarled, 'Who said I'd a hangover? Butt out, old man – living on borrowed time, you are.' He took a drink, then lit up a cigarette and relapsed into what looked like a state of simmering fury.

Casting a warning glare at Willis, Jim cleared his throat. 'Er

– busy morning, then, Eddie?' It was the landlord's standard opening gambit, the undemanding question which could open up a conversation if that was wanted, but otherwise needed no more than a grunt in reply. He'd have put money on the grunt option, but he'd have lost it; Eddie, it appeared, was a positive volcano of grievance just looking for a chance to erupt.

'Oh, I've had a great morning, me! The sodding computer's only crashed, hasn't it? That's a morning's work on invoices down the drain.'

Jim's sympathy was genuine. It was his hope that he could make it to retirement without ever being forced to touch one of the damned things. 'That's bad, Eddie.'

'Bad? Is that all you can say? Frigging useless load of junk. And it gets right up my nose the way it asks bloody silly questions – like I type "Dear—" and what happens? Up comes a message saying, "Looks like you're writing a letter. Do you want help?" Help? I'll give it help – a brick through the screen, it wants. I can't abide a machine as sets up to be cleverer than me.'

'Like a washing-machine, say?' Perce chuckled, delighted at his own gadfly wit.

Eddie swung round on his seat and leaned down the bar on heavily muscled arms, his eyes bulging with rage.

'Shut your stupid mouth, Perce Willis, or do I have to come across and shut it for you?'

He had raised his voice. The couple at the corner table who had been studying the sweet menu – rhubarb pie and custard, fruit jelly or vanilla ice-cream – put it down and exchanged anxious glances.

'OK, OK. Take it easy,' Jim said nervously. 'Sorry, Eddie, sorry.' As Eddie, with a final glare, sat back again, he turned on Perce. 'And you – you can drink that up and get out. I'm not having you start a fight in my pub.'

Perce raised his brows. 'I, my good man?' he said haughtily, but as Jim showed signs of exercising a landlord's privilege to exclude and made a move on his pint, he grabbed it with more haste than dignity and subsided.

The couple, who had abandoned the menu, hurriedly gathered

their belongings together, paid and left. Eddie lapsed into brooding silence again. Perce sipped his drink, looking brightly about him as if still hopeful of further entertainment. Jim rinsed out a cloth in the sink behind the bar and went to do Annie's job of wiping tables.

It was almost two o'clock when the door opened suddenly and on the threshold appeared a stout matron, battling to fold down an umbrella from which rain was streaming on to the doormat.

It was an unexpected sight. Muriel Pook was one of Doreen's cronies, a formidable group of ladies who saw themselves as the Burlow élite. None, under normal circumstances, would have entertained the notion of entering a public bar unescorted by a husband to shield her from whatever scandalous male excess might be in progress.

'Muriel!' Jim went to help her, grabbing the door as a gust of wind took it and managing to shut it behind her. 'What can I do—'

She cut him short, breathless, it seemed from more than just her recent struggle with the umbrella. 'Where's Doreen? I want to speak to Doreen—'

On cue, Doreen appeared from the kitchen, looking surprised and not altogether pleased at this departure from established etiquette. 'Well, Muriel, what do we owe this to?'

Muriel flushed, as if suddenly recognising the eccentricity of her behaviour, nodding jerkily in recognition to the two men sitting at the bar.

'Sorry – I wouldn't usually, of course, but, well, Doreen, I just thought you would want to know—'

'Oh!' Doreen's voice changed at this unmistakable signal that some more than usually tasty item of scandal was about to be dished. 'Do you want to come through the back?' She probably wasn't aware of licking her lips.

But Muriel, big with news, could brook no further delay. 'I've just seen Betty – you know she obliges for the Cartwrights? Well, Debbie's in ever such a state, you wouldn't believe – didn't open her shop today or anything! That Jay Darke, you know, married Harry's daughter — killed himself in London last night!'

'Killed himself!' Doreen's narrow eyes opened almost wide. 'Well, I never! Whatever would he go and do that for? Doing well for himself, is what I heard.'

Muriel could only shake her head regretfully. 'Well, I asked Betty that, of course, but she really couldn't say. That was all she got from Debbie — gassed himself in his car, she said.'

Doreen pursed her lips as she savoured this further scrap of information. 'Well, he were always so sharp he were going to cut himself, if you ask me. You remember—'

She stopped, as if suddenly becoming aware that there were male intruders on this sacred female ceremony of speculative gossip. 'Come through the back, Muriel, and I'll make us a cup of tea,' she said, a high priestess ready to celebrate the next part of the ritual. Her acolyte followed meekly, shutting the door behind them.

Perce was the first to speak. 'Now there's a curious concatenation of circumstances,' he said, savouring the words. 'Funny it should happen so soon after the tragic revelations concerning poor little Bonnie.'

'Funny,' Jim echoed hollowly. Eddie said nothing.

'There might almost, one might surmise, be a connection between the two.' In a pantomime of thought, Perce propped his chin on his hand, one finger to his cheek. 'Maybe he did something he shouldn't have?' He paused, glancing provocatively at Eddie's unresponsive profile. 'Of course, the two of you were great chums, weren't you, Eddie? How much do you know? Maybe you can shed a light on our darkness — why would a likely lad like Jay want to go killing himself?'

Jim tensed, ready to get between them if he had to. Eddie rose, slowly and menacingly. He finished his pint, stubbed out his cigarette, and stalked towards the door. As he came level with Perce he spun round with sudden savagery on the balls of his feet, grabbed the old man's blazer and bent to thrust his face into his.

'Pity, if someone was to die, it weren't the right one. You're pushing your luck way past its limits.' He let go of the blazer with a push which set the bar stool rocking. 'Mind how you go, won't you?'

Perce clutched at the bar to stop himself from toppling. 'Only a joke, lad, only a joke—'

With a snort of contempt Jennings went to the door, crashing it to behind him.

Almost before the echoes of its slamming had died away, Perce, like a weeble man, was bouncing up again. Tenderly smoothing down the material of his blazer, he said, 'Very interesting, I call that, very interesting. Do you know, I think I feel another lucrative phonecall coming on?'

'You watch your step, Perce. You heard what he said, and you may have been joking, but he wasn't,' Jim warned him sourly. 'And you can't phone from here. I'm closed now, so you can drink up and get out.'

For once, Perce put up no resistance to finishing his drink.

Back in his dismal little office beside the shop, Eddie Jennings seized a grubby towel which was hanging by the sink in the corner to dry off his hair. He hung his wet jacket up on a peg on the back of the door, shivering in the thin T-shirt which wasn't dry either. He was cold and tired and depressed, and he looked with loathing at the computer squatting on his desk, its screen smugly blank. He lacked the immediate courage to switch it on and find out exactly what he had lost.

If it had only been the invoices, it would have been bad enough, but it was the list—

Perhaps he shouldn't have entrusted his little insurance policy to the computer at all, given how little he understood about the way it worked, but it wasn't the sort of information you wanted lying around on a piece of paper. He'd managed to work out how to protect it with a password and all, and it had been working well, up till today when he had another little bit to add to it. And somehow – he still didn't quite know how – he'd lost it. It had vanished off the screen along with his morning's work on VAT. No wonder he'd nearly killed Perce Willis – stupid old bastard.

There was a packet of Jaffa cakes lying on a tray; he hadn't had any lunch and he couldn't be bothered fetching his usual sandwich from the shop. He ate a couple, though they were stale and unappetising, then lit up another cigarette and went to stand by the dirty window which looked out over the garage forecourt.

A couple of cars had been filling up at the pumps; he watched sombrely as their owners came across to pay. A silver Ford Capri – K-reg, he noted automatically – pulled in behind them, and this time, as the man put the petrol nozzle back and turned towards him, he recognised him with a sickening lurch of the stomach – the CID man who had called in on Tuesday! Instinctively he shrank back out of sight, his mind racing.

He heard the bell on the shop door ring as the copper went in, waited in painful tension for the knock on the door. It didn't come; a minute later he heard the bell chime again, the man came out without a glance towards the office, got back into his car and drove off.

Well, whaddya know? Just needed petrol, like anyone else. It cheered him a little and he crushed out his cigarette and went back to his desk. The problem wasn't going to go away, and he might as well know the worst.

He switched the computer on, waiting impatiently until he could send the mouse pointer racing through the lists of files. Not there, not there, not there! He swore violently, crashing his clenched fist down on the desk with a force which made the mouse jump off its pad with all the agility of its live counterpart. He swore again. If he found himself up the proverbial now, he'd lost his paddle.

Oh, no doubt the information was there somewhere, locked away in its innards, where someone more knowledgeable than he could no doubt access it – someone like Jay, for instance. His mind swerved uneasily away from that thought.

Anyway, it wasn't exactly the sort of information you would

want anyone else retrieving for you. Maybe he could work something out for himself.

He was staring blackly at the screen in front of him when there was a knock on the door and the girl from the cash desk put her head round.

'Mr Robinson phoned when you was out. Wants to know, have you got the brake shoe for his Renault.'

'Stupid bastard! Told him I'd let him know, didn't I? Suppose I could see if they've e-mailed, but phone and tell him no, it bloody well isn't in.'

The girl withdrew, and with a sigh he turned to the computer again to check. It signalled that mail was waiting and he clicked to access it.

At first, he could make no sense of what he read. '*I am One who becomes Two who becomes Four who becomes Eight and then I am One again,*' it began. The colour leaving his face, he had to read it through twice, slowly, right down to the conclusion, '*Under the Curse of Anubis, a Neter to Death and Beyond.*'

He would not have described himself as a superstitious man, but at that moment a terror rooted in those childhood cere-monies took possession of him. In fumbling haste he clicked the icon to close the message down as if that could wipe it from his memory, then sat staring foolishly at the empty screen.

Chapter Ten

Something weird had happened to the clock this morning. It was a digital clock, glowing discreetly in the steel-grey frame of the seriously upmarket slimline television in one corner of the hotel room, and sometimes when Juliette looked at it after an hour had passed it only registered a few minutes. Then again, a few minutes later when she looked, it would be telling her an hour had gone by.

In the smart, impersonal room, people came and went as she sat, the still centre of all the activity, in a deep armchair by the window. They spoke in different sorts of voices and did different sorts of things: a doctor had come and taken her pulse and her blood pressure, waiters had brought coffee and sandwiches, policemen, no, policepersons because one of them was a woman, had come wearing ordinary clothes and asked her a lot of questions. They were quite simple questions but somehow she found it hard to answer them because the inside of her head felt as if it was full of clouds, all fluffy and misty.

And Harry was there too, making endless phonecalls and pacing to and fro, snarling like a caged tiger at anyone in his way. Then he would come over and take her hand and talk to her in an odd sort of hushed voice which was so unlike him as to be seriously disconcerting. She didn't take in much of what he said, but what came over to her was that he was entirely at a loss, and that made her feel cold and frightened.

He insisted she ate some of the sandwiches and drank the

coffee – the doctor had talked about low blood sugar – and after a bit she started to feel better, only that was worse because she could think more clearly.

They had found Jay in the garage, in his little VW Golf gti with the engine running and a length of hosepipe fed in through the window. ('But we only had that for watering the window-boxes!' Juliette had said foolishly.)

They hadn't told her how he looked, but she had a dreadful, vivid picture of him with his hands on the steering-wheel, head back against the leather head-rest, eyes wide-open, staring at the blank wall in front of him.

That would have been what he saw ahead of him – a blank wall. No way out.

It hadn't for a moment occurred to her that he might take his own life. Even with two police officers telling her he had, she still couldn't believe it. He had his revenge to live for, after all.

'Had you any idea that your husband might try to commit suicide, Mrs Darke?' 'Had your husband threatened suicide before, Mrs Darke?' 'Was your husband frequently depressed, Mrs Darke?' They kept asking her questions like that, and sometimes she said no, and sometimes she just shook her head.

She had been depressed. Jay hadn't. And why should he be? He had had everything in his control, just the way he liked it: a well-paid, interesting job which was also his favourite hobby, with Juliette as the ultimate in sophisticated playthings for his leisure hours.

But how would he have reacted when she wasn't available, to pet or torture as he chose? She hadn't considered, when she escaped his tyranny, what a tyrant might do when he no longer had a victim.

He would have been angry when he came home and found her gone, furiously angry. She had exercised her own free will, when he must have believed that by now she had none. He would have been bitter, counting this as her second betrayal. He would have been – yes, disbelieving.

'Yes!' she said suddenly out loud, and Harry, the only person in the room at the time, broke off from the conversation he was having over his mobile phone about a consignment of something to say, 'What?' She shook her head, and he returned to it.

Jay simply wouldn't have believed that she could leave him finally and for ever, because he knew with a certainty far beyond reason that they were bound together for eternity. It was an article of faith. He had told her that often enough, both as promise and threat.

So yesterday, when she had told him it was all over, he would have been shocked. Their marriage had proved to be not eternal but temporal, brief, indeed, and now at an end. In the empty little house, with only the virtual reality of the computer world to fill his life, he had seen nothing for it but to end it . . .

Had he? Had he, indeed? *Jay?*

It came back to her now, a conversation they had had once at university, in the tragic aftermath of a fellow student's suicide.

'He lost curiosity about what would happen tomorrow,' Jay had said. 'Didn't want to turn the next page.'

'Like Cleopatra,' she had agreed, through her tears. ' "There is nothing left remarkable Beneath the visiting moon." '

Jay's face swam up before her now, sharp and intelligent and zestful. Surely Jay hadn't so suddenly stopped wondering what would happen next.

The numbness she had felt was wearing off, as if it had been a novocaine injection. The pain, and, yes, the guilt was taking its place. Perhaps she had been unthinking, self-centred, even brutal—

The sun was coming through the window now and she was uncomfortably hot. Harry, sitting on the bed, was engaged in another interminable conversation; she got up, a little unsteadily, and went to put her forehead against the cold glass of the window pane.

Down below in the street, the little people were still scurrying importantly around their ant-heap, so terribly busy about their little lives. As if it mattered. As if, in the end, anything mattered. Restlessly she turned away.

If Jay had killed himself (why was she still saying if?) it wouldn't be for ordinary reasons like despair and loneliness. Jay despised the ordinary. Jay's reasons for doing things were never commonplace.

Perhaps – and the disquieting thought chilled her like an icy finger stroking her spine – he had indeed lost curiosity about life because he was more curious about death? Perhaps – perhaps he had even convinced himself that beyond death he could be Osiris once more.

As she would be Isis! Her hand flew to her throat as she gave a little gasp of terror. Perhaps he hadn't given up last night. Perhaps he had simply moved the game on.

Bewildered and shocked as she had been, she had sensed the hostility in the carefully neutral police voices. They knew nothing of the history of her marriage; come to that, no one did, except Harry. They saw only a woman who had deserted a man who loved her so much that he couldn't live without her. They hadn't said anything, of course, but she had felt it – they *blamed* her. A lot of people would.

How soon would she start blaming herself for what he had done? She'd started already, for heaven's sake, wondering if she'd been thoughtless and cruel—

Alive, he could have been banished from her life. Dead, he could haunt her for ever.

And how long had he reckoned it would be before she, too, began to lose interest in turning the next page?

'Well, she took that pretty coolly, didn't she?'

The policewoman edged her car carefully out into the stream of Park Lane traffic.

Beside her, the young detective constable nodded. 'Bit of a cold fish, maybe. But tasty, very tasty.' Collecting a quelling glance from his superior, he moved hastily on to a safer topic. 'I wouldn't trust her old man round the corner, though. He's almost a caricature of the rather dodgy entrepeneur.'

'Mmmm. That hit me too. Get them to run a check on him for me, will you? I wouldn't be surprised if he's got form and I like to know what I'm dealing with.'

As he dialled the number, he asked, 'Are we to go across to the locus now, sarge?'

She nodded. 'I'll just check they've taken him away, poor bastard, then I'll get the wife brought over. The guv'nor wants to see her there this afternoon. They'll need formal ID at the mortuary, of course, but her father can handle that. Not that I think she'd be overcome if she'd to do it herself.'

He lodged the request for a computer check on previous convictions, then went back to the conversation.

'To be fair, she could just be in shock,' he pointed out. 'And she'd walked out on him, after all, so it'd be a bit phoney if she went into the grieving widow routine.'

The sergeant, a sallow, unattractive woman with a long nose, a thin mouth and a heavy jawline, sniffed. 'Oh, no doubt there's another man lurking about somewhere. Her kind never let go of one meal ticket before they've got the next lined up.'

Glancing at her ringless hands the words 'Sour grapes?' came temptingly to his mind, but since he'd never seen much point in heroics, he opted for discretion.

'It might not be that. Maybe he beat her up,' he argued. 'You never know.'

She gave him a look of extreme exasperation. 'Men!' she snapped. 'All the same when it comes to a pretty woman.'

He thought of saying, 'And women aren't?' but once again chose valour's better part. Fortunately, at that moment the phone rang. He listened, then said, 'OK, thanks,' and switched it off.

'No previous, apparently.'

'Right.' She was thoughtful, drumming her fingers on the steering-wheel as she waited for a red light to change. 'There's something about him, though. Look, when you get back chase up his local nick, will you – see if they can give you any background.'

He raised his eyebrows. 'There's nothing fishy about this one, is there?'

'Not so far as I know. I just like to be in the picture, all right?'

'Sure, sarge, if that's what you want.'

He settled back in his seat reflectively. Her nickname was

'The Nose', and it wasn't just because the feature in question was long, prominent and slightly bulbous at the tip.

However reluctant Mrs Bettison might feel about talking to the police, there was nothing grudging about the reception Tom Ward got when he arrived at the substantial old house from which Bettisons had farmed their acres for a hundred years.

'Oh, call me Abbie!' she protested in response to his formal, 'Mrs Bettison?' 'Mrs Bettison's my mother-in-law, and whenever anyone says that I look over my shoulder.'

When Abbie smiled, engaging dimples appeared in her rounded cheeks. The word 'comely' could have been invented for her, Ward thought – she wasn't exactly pretty but she was a pleasure to look at, with an expression that seemed to invite confidences. She probably had a dreadful problem with talkative old ladies in railway carriages.

There was a solemn toddler at her side holding a yellow tractor; he surveyed Ward silently as he took the seat Abbie indicated at the kitchen table, where there were home-made biscuits laid out with the cups and saucers. While she made tea, a collie with a greying muzzle eyed him watchfully from a basket beside the Aga.

'That's a good place for him,' Ward said, pointing.

Abbie smiled. 'Her, actually. Flossie likes lying in the sunshine best, but there's not a lot of chance of that this afternoon.'

'Not very nice out, is it?'

'Well, you know what they say about Derbyshire – nine months of winter then three of bad weather.'

She put the teapot on the table and sat down opposite him. With her face creased in unnatural lines of anxiety she looked absurdly young and uncomfortable, like a schoolgirl expecting an awkward interview with her headmaster.

Ward chatted inconsequentially a little longer, hoping to get her more relaxed before they got down to business, but it was she who said, 'You're being very kind, sergeant, but to tell you the truth I'd rather just get this over with. What do you want to ask me?'

He met her direct look with matching frankness. 'I don't really know, that's the trouble. We're still just at the start of this investigation, and the trail's cold, so we can't do things by the book. This isn't a formal interview – I haven't brought a constable with me, and I'm not even going to take notes. I just want you to tell me whatever you can remember about the time leading up to Bonnie Bryant's disappearance.

'For instance, there was a gang at school, wasn't there? Would you like to start with that?'

Abbie swallowed convulsively, and her cheeks turned scarlet. She turned her head, as if to make sure that the child, now on his hands and knees pushing the tractor into a room leading off the kitchen, was out of hearing, though he couldn't be old enough to understand what she might say.

'You're asking me about the thing in my life I'm most ashamed of. I try not to think about it, because I can't bear to believe that I took the part I did in the things that happened.'

Astonished, Ward did his best to conceal his reaction. 'Yes?' he prompted gently.

'It was Jay – Jay Darke – who started it – the Egyptian Game.' She winced as she said his name. 'I still can't explain how we got caught up in it, Juliette and I. I never liked him – but somehow, somehow he could make you do whatever he wanted. Oh, not literally of course – I'm not trying to use that as an excuse, but—'

Her voice trailed off, Ward said nothing, and after a pause she went on. To start with, most of what she told him he had gathered already from talking to Arthur Maxton: the Egyptian craze, the names of the children in the gang, the calculated exclusion of others which caused so much trouble in the class, Jay Darke's obsession with Juliette. All that came out fairly fluently.

Then she faltered again. She got up to check on the child, put a video on for him to watch in the other room, poured more tea into their cups before reluctantly sitting back down.

With the idea of getting her started again, Ward produced from his pocket the plastic bag containing the figurine from the cave. He laid it down on the table between them, smoothing out the plastic to expose the flaking pinkish paint and snarling muzzle of the creature. 'We found this in a little crevice cave,' he said.

Once again he had difficulty in concealing his astonishment at her reaction.

She cringed away from it with a gasp. 'Oh God, that horrible, horrible thing! Put it away – please, please, put it away!'

She was shaking, and her eyes had filled with tears of shock. Ward swept it swiftly off the table and pocketed it again, annoyed at his own insensitivity. He was usually better than this at reading the subtext.

'I'm so sorry. I had no idea . . . Look, have some tea. That'll make you feel better.'

Abbie smiled wanly at the trite suggestion, but dutifully sipped at her cup, blinking hard until she got control of herself once more. She took a deep breath.

'Right. I'm going to do it now. Get it over. I think it'll be easier if you don't interrupt me.'

Without the faintest idea of what he was about to hear, he nodded agreement. With her hands clasped together in front of her, so tightly that the knuckles showed white, she began.

'That – that *thing* you showed me was Anubis, God of the Dead. Jay made him out of clay he found in the caves – that was where we held our meetings. And he has a jackal head because jackals prefer carrion to live meat, and— Well, you can fill in the rest for yourself, I dare say.

'We were called the Neters – they were animal gods, or something – and when you were made one there had to be a sacrifice to Anubis. A *live* sacrifice – something small, like a rabbit or a bird or even—' She choked, and didn't finish her sentence.

'I was to be Bastet, the cat-goddess. The goddess of joy and motherhood, which sounded nice. Quite appropriate, in fact, wasn't it?' She made a self-mocking gesture towards the homely room about them.

'I was the last to join them. They wouldn't have wanted me, really, if I hadn't been Juliette's friend.

'No one would tell me what was to happen – everything was always very secret, you see. Juliette took me to the caves, and then there was – oh, sort of chanting and dancing and stamping, and we had these flaring torches. It was, well, primitive, like savages probably. You felt different, somehow, excited and, and – just different.

'Then I was brought to the little cave – Anubis's temple. Where you found – it, I suppose. Sekhmet – that was Kate, the lioness goddess – came forward and cut my finger with a little knife, then everyone else's, and we walked round and mingled blood and marked each other's faces and swore an oath of loyalty and stuff. There was something about bowing, bowing eight times because there was some chant about One becoming Eight – I don't remember that bit very clearly. But I remember the next bit. I wish I didn't.'

She drank some of her tea, and Ward noticed that her hands were shaking and her face had turned pale and shiny with sweat. 'Are you all right? Do you want to take a break?' he asked with some anxiety, but she was going on, her voice flat.

'Jay was Osiris, the King of the Underworld and Juliette was Isis, his Queen. They had crowns they always put on, made of wire and gold paper and stuff, with a snake's head sort of rearing up – you know. Well, Jay came forward in his crown and Kate produced this – this kitten—

'I'm sorry, I think I'm going to be sick.'

Abbie leapt to her feet and stood at the kitchen sink, her head bent, taking deep uneven breaths. She wasn't sick; she ran the tap cold, filled a glass with water and came back sipping it. She set it down and wiped her face with her hankie.

'Look,' Ward said uneasily. 'I'm not at all happy about this. I think, perhaps—'

She shook her head fiercely. 'No, don't stop me. I couldn't bear to have to make a start to this all over again.

'It was a black kitten with bright yellow eyes. Very small. I don't know where it came from. Jay took it, stroked it, then very suddenly wrung its neck. Its head—' A violent shudder seized her.

'I screamed. I wanted to run away, but the others stopped me. Osiris said that now I was a Neter I could never leave, never escape, or Anubis would hunt me down. "A Neter to death and beyond" – that was what he said. And I know it's really silly,' she gave a unconvincing laugh, 'but I'm scared, even at this moment, about betraying the secrets.

'I should never have gone back, of course. I should have told my parents – my mother was worried about me anyway, because I started having dreadful nightmares.

'But at first I was too afraid, you see, and then, well, I suppose I got drawn into that horrible unhealthy excitement, just the way Juliette did, even though she's a lovely person – warm and funny and sweet. Only I was able to put it behind me, but Jay kept after her till she married him. I don't know how she could – though I think actually she's left him now.'

She stopped to drink some more water. Ward prompted tentatively, 'And Bonnie?'

'Ah.' She looked down as if she didn't want to meet his eyes. 'That's the worst part.

'I didn't like Bonnie. No one did. When I look back, even now I still think she was really nasty – cruel, spiteful, envious. She simply hated anyone having what she didn't, even if she didn't want it herself. She was always telling tales and her mother believed whatever she said and made trouble.

'The Neters really got to her, perhaps partly because Barry was one and she wasn't. That was probably why Jay picked him, come to think of it. That would be just like him.

'She would keep following us, trying to find out where we went and what we did. Losing her became part of the fun.'

Studying her intently, Ward was intrigued to catch a note of arrogant irritation in her voice, foreign, he would have imagined, to the woman herself. The soft contours of her face almost seemed to sharpen as he looked at her.

'I don't know how she found us at the caves that day. We'd been dancing to a drum that Set – Eddie Jennings – was beating, slow at first, then faster and faster.'

Her eyes were hard and bright with recollection. 'Then he

suddenly stopped for Isis to start the most sacred part of the dance. It was very beautiful – she's always been graceful, and we were all watching her by the light of the torches. There was darkness all round; it was terribly dramatic. I remember all the faces, golden in the flickering light—'

She sounded almost dreamy for a moment, then her voice turned harsh, and her eyes narrowed. 'It was Osiris who saw Bonnie first, spying on us from behind a rock. When he screamed, "Get her! Get her!" I wanted – I wanted *blood*!

'We hunted her, howling and shrieking, down the passages. I don't know how we lost her, but suddenly she wasn't there. I'm still not sure what we'd have done if we'd caught her. And then the flames of the torches began to go out, and someone switched on an electric torch and we began to feel cold and a bit silly.'

Abbie had been leaning forward eagerly with a strange light in her eyes. Now she sat back, her shoulders sagging as if she was returning to normal again.

'We started feeling – well, ashamed, I suppose. We split up very quickly and went off home by ourselves. I think mostly we were scared about what we'd done, because Bonnie would tell her mother, for sure.

'But then, when they found the bike up by the Quarry Lake—'

She broke off, biting her lip. 'I've told you most of the worst now, sergeant. But I have to be honest about one more thing.

'Discovering that Bonnie had been murdered was an amazing relief. I was afraid all this time that I'd helped to drive her to suicide, and hearing that someone had killed her deliberately – well, it cleared me, you see. I've felt as if a weight I've borne all my life had been taken off my shoulders. I know I ought to be horrified, but I wasn't the person who killed her, and it wasn't my fault.'

'So who did, and why?'

'I don't know. I've been racking my brains. Did someone go back to look for her? Who was last out of the caves? And why?

Well, you could be very scared about getting in trouble, couldn't you? Children sometimes just get things way out of proportion. But I don't know.

'The trouble is, I only remember snatches – the dancing in the cave, the sacrifice— It's all too long ago to remember clearly.'

Ward persisted. 'There wasn't anything you noticed on your way back? Some adult hanging about, for instance?'

Abbie shook her head. 'Believe me, I've thought of that. They asked us all if we'd noticed anything, seen Bonnie on her bike afterwards, but no one had of course. I couldn't claim to remember, but I would guess I might have remembered seeing a grown-up. Even ones you didn't know were authority figures in those days, and I would have felt guilt was written all over my face.'

'Yes, I take the point. Don't blame yourself too much, Abbie – children are a primitive species. Think of *Lord of the Flies* – and I disembowelled my sister's favourite doll and then beheaded it when I was angry with her once. She's never let me forget it.'

She laughed, shakily.

'Now,' he went on, 'I mustn't take up more of your time, but there's one question I want to ask before I leave you in peace.

'I spoke to Mr Maxton earlier, and he mentioned some problem over the eleven-plus that year. He wasn't very specific – do you remember anything about that?'

Her face, which had clouded at the mention of another question, cleared, and a reminiscent, even mischievous smile came over it.

'Gracious, I haven't thought of that for years! Oh, there was the most frightful fuss, actually. It did seem seriously wicked at the time, and all the Neters took a vow of silence. I suppose it was bad, but nowadays when we're all told that grammar schools were evil and socially divisive and all that stuff, it just seems rather funny, looking back.

'The thing was, Jay was determined the Neters shouldn't be separated at the end of the year. He was going to get into the Grammar School, obviously, but it was very tough – sometimes

Burlow only got one or two in. So he managed to find out that the exam papers were delivered three days before, and we all sneaked out of our houses when we were meant to be in bed and broke in.

'We turned over a few desks and spilt a bit of paint so it looked like vandalism, and then Eddie picked the padlock on Mr Maxton's cupboard. We opened the envelopes – very carefully, you know, so we could seal them up again – and copied down the questions. Then we put them back and padlocked the cupboard again.

'Jay coached us after school – he's seriously clever, you know – and made us all swot up the answers so we could get into Grammar School. Which they did – all except me!' She laughed. 'I was so dumb I couldn't get in, even knowing the questions! Anyway, I didn't much fancy Grammar School. I had a lovely time at the Convent – I made nice friends and did home economics which was a lot more use to me than Latin would have been.'

Ward frowned. That rang a bell, didn't it . . . But she was going on.

'There was a real sensation when the results came out. Rumours were flying and I think myself that Mr Maxton probably realised – but he wouldn't admit it, of course. I'm afraid I really don't feel bad about it, though I probably should.'

'Certainly not,' Ward said robustly. 'The old-style secondary modern was an abomination – my dad taught in a comprehensive and he used to say "Secondary Modern" as if it was a swearword.'

As Ward got back into his car, he saw a tractor turn the corner with a pleasant-looking young man at the wheel, who gave him a curious look as he drove it into the shed.

Was he wrong in guessing, from the expression on her face, that Abbie Bettison had hoped he would be gone before her husband, if that were he, came back and saw that she had a visitor? How much did he know of what his wife had said this afternoon?

She seemed a nice lady, with what looked like a nice happy

family, but he couldn't quite forget the change which had come over her face when she was describing the hunt in the cave.

It was almost as if still, at some level, that early indoctrination had left a deep and sinister mark. He was frowning thoughtfully as he drove away.

Chapter Eleven

'I'll have to drop you here, mate. Can't get turned in.' The taxi-driver drawing up outside the mews in Westbourne Grove turned to stare curiously at the vehicles blocking the small cobbled area. 'Something going on here, then?'

Paying him off, Harry Cartwright chose to treat this question as rhetorical. Ahead of him, Juliette stepped out to be accosted by a bashful youth in police uniform. When she gave her name, he became even more awkward.

'Oh – er – yes miss, er – madam. Er – my condolences. Very sorry – er—'

It would have been truly shocking to laugh at the way his blush spread to colour the tips of his fair large ears a brilliant vermilion, and anyway it probably wasn't as funny as all that. The hysterical giggle she was fighting to suppress didn't have anything to do with merriment. She swallowed hard, then murmured something suitable as she paused to wait for Harry.

He took control, as usual. 'Inspector Neale is expecting us,' he said and with patent relief the young man waved them through.

There was a number of officers about, both uniformed and, just as unmistakably, in plain clothes. As they walked past, Juliette saw their neighbour Adrian Venables standing on his doorstep in animated conversation with another of the mews' residents. She offered a small, tentative smile but got no corresponding acknowledgement from either of them; their conversation stopped and she heard it start up again once she and Harry were past.

The house door was standing open, as was the door to the garage. She glanced in that direction; the car was gone, and there was only an innocent, cavernous space. A policeman waved them into the house, and with a sense of unreality Juliette crossed the threshold of her former home.

Standing just inside was a tall, thin, dark man in a charcoal-grey suit which made him look even taller and thinner, and with him the policewoman who had come to the hotel that morning. Juliette hadn't taken to her; she couldn't help being plain, but you didn't get a sour, embittered expression by accident and her beady dark eyes were cold.

She stepped forward. 'This is Mrs Darke, sir, and Mr Cartwright, her father.' She turned to them. 'This is Detective Inspector Neale.'

The inspector acknowledged the introduction. He had eyes that gave nothing away, deeply hooded, watchful eyes. 'Thank you, Sergeant Dowdalls. Mrs Darke, let me say first how very sorry we are about the circumstances in which we meet today. This must all be very upsetting for you. Now, may I suggest we sit down?'

It was very polished, very controlled, in stark contrast to the awkwardness of the young Janus. Juliette couldn't help being impressed by the adroitness with which he had made his nod to the social conventions without suggesting that an estranged spouse was a widow in mourning.

Instead of the lamps, they had switched on the sitting-room overhead lights which she and Jay had almost never used. Under this harsher illumination it seemed unreal, somehow, insubstantial, almost like a stage-set. Someone had moved the furniture, too, and things weren't in their usual positions, making the familiar room look disconcertingly different.

At least the Victorian sofa, covered in red plush, was still in its old place along one wall, and Juliette went to sit on it. She was struck by a sudden painful memory of the day she and Jay had bought it in a little antique shop in a pretty Suffolk village, one happy, sunny day shortly after they were married.

Harry took his place beside her, and the two police officers sat down in chairs, one to the right and one to the left. Had they done that deliberately, chosen the sort of uncomfortable positioning which meant that you couldn't look at both at the same time?

Juliette sensed danger. It was strange; she had no reason for fear, yet some primitive instinct, stronger than reason, which she had not known she possessed, was telling her that somewhere outside the wolves were circling. With a conscious effort she clasped her hands loosely in her lap, then looked up enquiringly at the inspector.

As she did so, her eye was caught by the display shelves on the other side of the room, still with their lights on, illuminating the black, dramatic, solitary statuette of Anubis. Then her startled gaze travelled to the shattered remains of Jay's precious Egyptian collection lying on the floor, and a cry of dismay escaped her.

'Ah yes,' the DI said in tones of mild interest. 'Can you enlighten us as to what happened here, Mrs Darke?'

At her side, Harry stiffened. 'Look, inspector, my daughter doesn't know a thing about whatever went on after we left yesterday. And at that time it was all in perfect order.'

'So you're saying that this wasn't the result of some struggle – that Mr Darke must have done this himself? Destroyed a collection which, we are given to understand, was both rare and valuable?'

'Must have, mustn't he?'

The inspector's nod to DS Dowdalls was almost imperceptible, but she moved instantly into the next question.

'Was your meeting last night an amicable one, Mr Cartwright?'

Harry's jaw was jutting pugnaciously. 'What is this?' he demanded. 'My son-in-law committed suicide, right?'

'Not necessarily.' The sergeant's was a steely reply, but Neale intervened.

'I'm afraid we're not in any position to make official pronouncements before we have a full forensic report. It's just an unexplained death at the moment, though naturally in circumstances like these suicide does appear to be the most likely explanation.'

Harry relaxed, apparently reassured. 'Right. Just so long as we have that absolutely straight.'

'Was it an amicable meeting?' Dowdalls went back to her question like a terrier released from a 'Stay!' to go back to worrying some small mammal.

As Harry drew breath to reply, Juliette, who had not been reassured in the very slightest degree, put out her hand to stop him.

'No, not really,' she said steadily. 'But it wasn't a punch-up either. We had a perfectly civilised discussion.

'My husband didn't want me to leave him, sergeant, but I had been very unhappy for a long time and I'd made up my mind.'

'Did he plead with you? Try to get you to stay?'

There was an unpleasant hopefulness in her manner of asking the question. What she wanted, Juliette realised, was to surprise an admission that she had been callous, had taken deliberate pleasure in kicking him in the teeth.

'Only by invoking the Egyptian gods. He threatened me with the vengeance of Anubis – that figure there.'

The officers followed her pointing finger, then exchanged glances. Dowdalls' mouth turned down into an even sourer line, as if somehow Juliette had pulled a fast one. Neale cleared his throat.

'Are you saying he was – mentally disturbed?'

She hesitated. 'I wouldn't have said that, exactly. He was just – different. He was my husband, so of course I was used to his ways, but perhaps if you observed him clinically you might wonder – I don't know.' Juliette was finding her voice, becoming more confident. 'He was a brilliant obsessive – very charming when he chose to be, very clever indeed, but certainly not like ordinary people. Not like you and me. He didn't want to be. If you really want to know, sergeant, he despised us.'

She smiled, and didn't care that there was no answering smile from the other woman. 'The reason I left him was because he wanted complete control over my life. He cut me off from all my friends, he installed electronic surveillance, kept me without money. I was virtually his prisoner.'

The inspector, eyes narrowed, watched her without comment. Dowdalls interrupted shrilly.

'Oh yes? Then how come one of your neighbours says he saw you going out together all the time, happy as two lovebirds?'

Juliette coloured, but would not allow herself to be shaken. 'There is no reason why Mr Venables should know anything about the state of our marriage, but perhaps you could ask him if he ever saw me out alone? And I suspect if you check the security cameras you'll find the film Jay took of me day and night. You'll probably find that the phone is – or at least was – bugged. If you contact the bank, or the credit company, you'll find his signature on every cheque, every invoice. You can ask my friends – they'll tell you they've hardly seen me in the last two years, and never on my own since the day I got married.'

'So you can't exactly be upset that he's dead, then?' There was no mistaking Dowdalls' hostile tone.

Harry, who had listened to this with increasingly ill-controlled impatience, erupted, addressing himself to the senior officer. 'You're in charge – let her go on like that, and it's your head on the block when I make an official complaint.

'My daughter's in a state of shock. She fainted this morning when she heard the news, as this – this creature' – he gestured at Dowdalls, whose lips were compressed until they had almost disappeared – 'very well knows. Jay Darke, who was off his trolley, has despatched himself to Shangri-la or whatever he would have called it, and you've got the brass neck to give my daughter the third degree!

'Listen, laddie, I want the name of your Chief Constable. I shouldn't be surprised if he knows our man in Derbyshire, who's a good mate of mine, and I think perhaps the two of them should get together to sort things out.'

The DI leaned forward earnestly. 'Mr Cartwright, I can't apologise enough. We've obviously given entirely the wrong impression. It's just important that at this stage we don't overlook anything which might help us if there are questions that need to be answered later. Pat, here' – he indicated the impassive sergeant – 'is a good officer, but she does get a little bit carried away sometimes, don't you, Pat? She's watched too many episodes of *The Bill*.'

She smiled. At Pat Dowdalls' smile, the blood of hardened criminals had been known to turn to ice in their veins. 'Sorry, Mrs Darke,' she said.

Harry, mollified, subsided. Juliette, watching the inspector's shuttered face, felt his was the more chilling expression of the two.

'We won't keep you any longer,' Neale went on, getting to his feet. 'I'm sure Mrs Darke ought to go back and get some rest. There were just a couple of other little things we wanted to check. What was your husband's usual tipple, Mrs Darke?'

Juliette was taken by surprise. '*Tipple*? I'm sorry, I don't think I've ever thought of it like that. It depends what you mean. He liked vodka and cranberry juice, and wine, of course. Armagnac after dinner.'

'Ah, now that's interesting. There was a glass left in the kitchen which showed traces, they tell us, of vodka and cranberry juice, but also an over-the-counter sleeping draught in high concentration.'

'So?' Harry met his look of mild enquiry with belligerence.

'Well, there weren't any fingerprints on the glass, you see. A little curious, we thought.'

This time, Harry said nothing. Juliette found she was staring at the inspector as if she had been mesmerised.

'So, purely for the record, of course –' Neale smiled for the first time, showing crooked teeth with long incisors '– can you both just fill us in on where you were last night?'

After waiting a fraction of a second to allow Harry to go first if he wanted to, Juliette said, 'We were staying at the Hilton, as you know. I – I was feeling quite upset, so I went straight to my room and stayed there until my father came to break the news to me this morning, around half-past nine, I think.'

'Anyone vouch for that? Any phonecalls?' Dowdalls' questions were sharp.

'No. Oh, a maid did come in to turn down the bed – I don't know what time that was.'

'And you, sir?' That was Neale, his tone bland and level.

'Me? Oh, same story, really. Went down to the bar for a drink, had a bite of dinner in the restaurant, then decided on an early night. The bed had been turned down when I got back, so you could say I didn't have an alibi. Always supposing I needed one. Which I don't.'

He glared defiantly round at his questioners. With absolute horror Juliette realised that not one of them, including her, believed that he was telling the truth.

Neale broke the uncomfortable silence. 'The other thing, Mrs Darke – just a footnote, really. Your husband didn't leave anything to explain his intention to kill himself, and of course contrary to popular superstition people often don't. But I wondered if you had any views about it? He was clever, articulate, possibly aggrieved – just the type, I would have thought, to want to have the last word.'

With some difficulty, Juliette collected her thoughts. 'Yes – yes, I think I would agree. Have you checked his computer?'

'There's a password protecting access. Do you know what it was?'

Juliette was just about to speak when Harry, who had been sitting with his head bent, suddenly stood up. 'That's enough,' he said harshly. 'I'm not happy about what's going on here. Juliette, keep your mouth shut till we get legal advice. We're leaving now – unless you're planning to stop us, and I warn you I know just what you lot can and can't do.'

'I'm sure you do, Mr Cartwright. No, we've no wish to hold you back. Mrs Darke, just one last thing.

'We contacted the firm your husband works for, and they're anxious to take away their own computing equipment with the projects he was working on under contract to them. They have legal rights, but they need your permission for access. Is that all right?'

'Yes, of course,' Juliette agreed. 'Do you want me to be present?'

'That would certainly be helpful.'

'I can't waste any more time down here – I'll have to get back to Derbyshire. I've businesses there that won't run themselves.' Harry's was a flat statement, demanding acceptance, and Neale made no challenge.

'Indeed, sir. And by tomorrow we should have the forensic report and that may sort everything out.'

'For your sake, I certainly hope it does. I'm too busy to want to cause trouble just for the sake of it, but I will if I have to. And I would prefer to take my daughter home with me—'

'I've said I'll stay, Dad.' Juliette's interruption was quiet but firm. Harry shrugged, displeased.

'Shall we say ten o'clock, Mrs Darke?' Neale suggested.

'Ten o'clock.'

Juliette followed her father out. Harry marched straight through the mews, not looking to right or to left, or waiting for her. By the time she caught him up he had hailed a taxi which was drawing in to the kerb.

As he held the door open for her, she glanced up and saw that sweat was beading his upper lip. The sun was shining but it certainly wasn't as hot as all that.

Children were disembarking from a touring bus which was taking up most of the road outside Burlow Primary when Tom Ward drove up. They were jumping down the steps, pushing, jostling, shrieking to family and friends, bobbing about in the swell of waiting parents like corks in a choppy sea.

At the centre of the maelstrom, passing out suitcases and rucksacks as they were excavated from the bus's innards was a young man whom Ward recognised without difficulty as Barry Bryant, the school's headmaster and Bonnie's twin.

He had changed remarkably little from the lad in Maxton's Leavers' photograph; with his fair skin and crisp curling hair he looked boyish even now, in his early thirties, and he was wearing jeans and a T-shirt like many of his charges.

There were visible marks of strain about his shadowed eyes, though, and he looked drawn and tired, but he was dealing with queries, finding lost property, reassuring a fussing mother and still managing to smile, with at the very least a good imitation of sincerity, at the pupils who, prompted by the more punctilious parents, were coming up to say thank you.

At a little distance from the action, Ward was leaning against his car, hands in his pockets, thinking that for all he sometimes complained there were probably worse jobs than being a policeman, when two women came purposefully towards him.

He had noticed them getting off the bus with the children earlier, one tall and buxom with untidy blonde hair, the other short, plump and dark. They had looked rather jolly, joking with kids and other mums; now their demeanour, as they advanced on him, could best be described as menacing and unconsciously he stood up straight and took his hands out of his pockets.

'Excuse me!' The larger, more imposing lady accosted him as they came up, adding with chilling emphasis, 'Can we just Have a Word?'

Fighting an impulse to flee as they closed with him, Ward managed to smile. 'Yes, of course.'

The smaller woman, standing shoulder to elbow with her friend in solidarity, fixed him with a glare like a barbecue skewer.

'You're not hanging around wanting to talk to the Head, are you?'

'Er – yes, I was, in fact.'

'Well, he's tired,' the other woman said flatly. 'That's right, isn't it, Gina?'

Gina, who had emitted a small, indignant snort at his blatant admission, agreed. 'That's right, Maggie. Wore out. What he needs is a nice cuppa and a good sit down and a bit of peace, not to be bothered by the likes of you.'

'If you're wanting something as you can put in your rubbish paper, you can put as how teachers' salaries isn't the half of what they should be. And you can quote me.'

Maggie tossed her head, all but dusting her hands in satisfaction at having annihilated this lower form of life. Ward found he had taken a reflex step backwards, and began by apologising before he could stop himself.

'I'm sorry, ladies, but I'm afraid this is a misunderstanding. I'm not a journalist, I'm a policeman.'

'Oh—' They exchanged glances, momentarily at a disadvantage, then regrouped with a ruthless professionalism which would have put the Paras to shame.

'Supposing you are' — Maggie opened up a new front with the air of one casting doubt not only on his veracity but also on his motives and possibly even his parentage as well — 'he's still wanting a good rest. Up half the night we all was, with that Tracy Hunter eating so much chocolate she made herself sick, and trying to keep her from waking every other dratted kiddie in the place—'

'Oh dear.' Ward exuded sympathy. 'Not a very good end to the trip. Not that anyone could possibly guess that you'd both missed your beauty sleep.'

Blatant flattery was a high-risk strategy, and they might take exception to his cheek, but the disarming grin he produced had usually worked before.

It worked now. The women looked at each other, then giggled.

'Well, being mums we're used to it. But I never knew as they'd started sending you lot to charm school,' Maggie said, with just a hint of flirtatiousness.

'Not at all. It's part of our training to be absolutely truthful,' he said, straight-faced.

'Oooh, got to watch this one, don't we?' Gina winked at her friend, but even so she was not going to allow herself to be deflected. 'Anyway, you don't have to see poor Barry now, do you? By rights, he should have come home Monday but he wouldn't do it, seeing as the kids saved up for their trip and all.'

'I need to speak to him before I go back to Flitchford, to keep my boss off my back, but I promise I won't keep him long. He hasn't got a wife waiting for him, or anything?'

The two women exchanged glances, giggling a little. 'Well, he's young enough yet,' Gina said, and Maggie added, 'There's one of the young lady teachers he's taken out a couple of times, but it were a bit hard, with all the kids making jokes next morning. Can't do a thing here without everyone knows.'

Gina agreed. 'Have to be ever so careful, being a head like he is. And with all this talk about poor Bonnie – must be hard for him, that, too.'

'It's been a sad business. Were either of you living here at the time? Do you remember when it all happened?'

'Course we do. There's nothing much happened in Burlow since then, any road!' Maggie laughed, and Gina nodded in agreement.

'You was working over Buxton way, Maggie, remember, and I were doing secretarial.'

'That's right. Couldn't move for all the policemen, and everyone in a state. Poor Mrs Bryant – never got over it, did she?'

'Did you ever hear her say anything about anyone who might have been involved in Bonnie's disappearance?'

'Oh, Harry Cartwright, you mean?' Gina's response was matter-of-fact; Bella Bryant's accusations were clearly common knowledge. 'That were just her. Hated Harry, by all accounts, because they'd had a bit of a thing going when they was young, and then he dumped her.'

'Wouldn't think so to look at her,' Maggie chimed in, 'but my mum said she weren't so bad-looking before she put on weight. But then he took up with this French girl – I remember her, ever so pretty, she were – and that were it. And then he made his pile, gave himself airs—'

Gina sniffed. 'And that Debbie – thinks she's Lady Muck, she does.'

'So you think Mrs Bryant made up the accusation, just for spite?'

They both hesitated, then Gina shrugged. 'Well, could have done.'

Clearly the Harry Cartwright story had been accepted as myth for so long that the discovery of Bonnie's body, proving

Bella Bryant right all along in believing her daughter had been murdered, wasn't enough to shake settled opinion.

She went on, 'Anyway, it all sent her – well, funny, didn't it? Not the same, she weren't, after it happened. That's right, i'n't it, Maggie?'

'Sssh!' Maggie hissed, nudging her friend. 'Here's Barry!'

The crowd was thinning now, as parents collected up children and their belongings and drifted away. Two girls, who from their build and colouring looked as if they belonged to Maggie and Gina, were hovering impatiently nearby.

Bryant came up to the two women smiling, and put an arm round each. 'I don't know how to thank you, girls. Whatever would I have done without you?'

He planted a kiss on each cheek, and was hugged in return. Then he noticed Ward and looked at him enquiringly.

'He's a policeman, Barry,' Maggie explained. 'We've told him as how you're tired, and he's said he won't keep you.'

'He's quite nice,' Gina stage-whispered, with a roguish glance at Ward.

Bryant's smile faded, and a look of immense weariness took its place. 'Right,' he said heavily. 'I suppose it's as well to get it over with. I must go and see my mother too, very shortly, so I'm afraid I can't really give you very long today.'

'That's all right, sir. I appreciate your co-operation.'

Barry nodded, then picked up a rucksack and a gaping bag untidily stuffed with folders, books, brochures, papers and what looked like a lap-top computer. They were the only items of luggage left lying on the pavement beside the bus and Ward took the bag from him as Bryant slung the rucksack over his shoulder.

'Thanks. Now that's good – it's always something of a triumph when you get to this stage and you find you haven't got a child waiting and no bag for it, or a bag but no child.' He had a very attractive smile. 'We can go to my house – it's just next door. But I'll have to check the bus first.'

The women, calling farewells, gathered up their disgruntled offspring and departed. Ward waited below as Bryant went up and down the aisle of the bus, checking for litter and lost property then shaking hands warmly with the driver. How anyone had the patience for all that was beyond him, though if Maggie and Gina were typical, you did at least have the reward of satisfied customers, which wasn't something you could very often say in his own line of work.

The house, when Barry Bryant opened the brightly painted blue front door, had a dank, unaired smell, familiar to Ward from returning to his own empty house. Familiar, too, was the drift of letters and junk mail on the floor; Bryant scooped up the pile and dumped it on a table in the hall where an answer-phone was winking urgently. He ignored that too, leading the way into a room to the left of the front door.

It was a dark, narrow room, haphazardly furnished with wood-framed, upholstered chairs, a modern white coffee table and two or three ugly repro pieces which looked as if they might have been salvaged from the family home, incongruous beside the office-style desk with a personal computer and printer on it, and neatly labelled box-files piled up at one end. The shelves on one wall were crammed with books, mainly paperbacks, and an old-fashioned chrome electric fire was set in a flimsy painted panel blocking the fireplace. Bryant motioned Ward to take a seat then switched it on, holding out his hands to it as the bars turned first pink then red, as if he were chilled, though the room wasn't really cold.

Lack of sleep, Ward diagnosed; he looked absolutely shattered. He'd better make it snappy before the man keeled over.

'I'll keep this as brief as I can, sir. You've had a lot to cope with, and these trips must be pretty exhausting at the best of times.'

A ghost of a smile hovered round Bryant's lips. 'Tell me about it!'

With genuine curiosity, Ward asked, 'What made you go into teaching? My father was a teacher, and I could never understand how he could do it year after year with new kids and new problems.'

'It was always a burning ambition, right from when I was at school myself – well, my grandfather taught, so it was in the genes, maybe. And good teaching makes a difference, you know, so you can see you're doing something really worthwhile. Nowadays, when we can pick up learning problems early, we can actually transform a child's life. I get a real kick out of that. And I was seriously lucky to get a headship so soon, after only one teaching post down in Dorset.' Despite his weariness he spoke with impressive enthusiasm.

'You weren't tempted to stay there?'

Bryant shook his head. 'Quite simply, this is home. I love the work, mostly. And at least I don't have to take them on trips every day. Kids in the classroom are one thing, kids larking about at three in the morning are something else. How parents cope I don't know.'

'They don't usually have more than two or three to deal with at once. And of course the way children act is very different when they're in a group, isn't it?'

Ward hadn't intended to put emphasis on the last remark, but as he spoke its significance occurred to him, and Bryant was quick to pick up the tiny stress. He had been gazing at the glowing bars of the bleak electric fire as if they had been flickering flames, but he turned sharply to meet Ward's gaze. He had very clear blue eyes.

'You've heard about the Neters then, obviously.'

Not a stupid man. But perhaps a more subtle man would have given himself time, pretended to miss the implication? Ward said innocently, 'So were you one of them, sir?'

The violence of Bryant's reaction took him completely by surprise. He jumped to his feet, and colour came into his pale cheeks.

'I think we'd better stop right here, sergeant. You took care to give me the impression that we were just talking, trying to fill in a picture of what might have happened to my sister so that you can find out who killed her. Not unnaturally, it's a cause close to my heart. But you're not asking straight questions, are you? You're setting traps.

'I'm not a fool. Whoever told you about the Neters would hardly have failed to mention that I was one.' His voice was savage. '"Barry Bryant, who helped to hunt his sister – his *twin* sister – to her death" – isn't that what they said?

'God knows, I wish I'd never had anything to do with them. I don't know why Jay ever chose me—'

'Someone suggested it was to spite Bonnie.'

Bryant flinched, and his lips tightened. 'That's all too possible. But in any case, sergeant, I'm really too tired to go on in this spirit. If you want me to come to the police station to make a statement, I'd be more than happy to do that tomorrow, after I've seen my mother – about whom I am extremely anxious – and had a good night's sleep. What I'm not prepared to do at the moment is play games.'

Bryant must be a very effective headmaster. He certainly made Ward feel like a schoolboy who had got it seriously wrong. He was furious with himself for having arrogantly under-estimated the person he was dealing with, and now he had a stark choice – he could bluster or he could grovel. Blustering wasn't his style, and anyway Bryant wasn't the type to be impressed. He grovelled.

'I'm sorry, sir,' he said with the sort of sincerity he'd had a lot of practice in faking in his own distant schooldays. 'In my job, you get to the point where asking a straight question is more or less professional negligence. I hope you won't throw me out, partly for the progress of the investigation and partly, I confess, because screwing up an interview like this would hit my pride right where it hurts.'

Had it worked? He tried not to hold his breath as it hung in the balance.

Then Bryant smiled. It was a wary smile, as if he couldn't be sure that this wasn't just another calculated tactic – as indeed it was. But at least he sat down once more.

Given this second chance, Ward wasn't about to make the same mistake again. He had covered the Neters' background extensively with Abbie Bettison, and if need be he could take Bryant over it in a more formal interview later on. There was pressure on time, and he had plenty of fresh questions to ask.

'Can you remember what happened that day, before Bonnie disappeared? Was there anything special about it, anything different?'

Clearly, it wasn't the first time this question had been asked. Bryant smiled with weary resignation.

'We went through that so often that it was a set piece. I could probably, to this day, recite it in my sleep, and I should warn you that my actual memories are probably relatively hazy and what I am remembering is a construct of the narrative rather than a description of events. However, I'm happy to run through it again, if it will help.

'It was just an ordinary Saturday, like any other. We watched morning telly while our parents had a lie-in, then there was breakfast – sugar puffs for me, frosties for Bonnie, if you really want to know—'

'The questioning was pretty thorough, obviously.'

'Oh, it was thorough. Then we did our chores – I brought in the coal for the boiler and I think Bonnie had to help with making the beds. Then we were free to do as we liked.'

'What did your parents do?'

Bryant frowned. 'I don't remember. They probably didn't ask me that. Mum would have gone out shopping, I expect, then cooked lunch. Dad – washed the car, then went down the pub, maybe. But it was all perfectly normal – I know that.'

He stopped. That had obviously been the easy bit. 'And then?' Ward prompted.

Bryant had turned towards the fire again, fingers splayed towards the heat.

'I was meeting up with the Neters, of course.'

'And did you tell the police that at the time?'

His mouth twisted, and he shook his head. 'No. By then, everyone thought Bonnie was drowned. I'd like to think that if they'd been looking for her, I'd have told them –' he began to pick at his nails '– but I wonder, would I? It was all so strange, so different from anything else in my life. I wasn't myself – or at least, I wasn't what I like to believe I am.'

He fell silent. Ward waited a moment to see if he would continue, then said, 'Go on with what happened that morning. Did Bonnie follow you?'

He shook his head. 'She was hanging around, waiting to see what I was going to do, but I pretended I wasn't going out and eventually she gave up and went off on her bike.'

'Did she believe you were staying in?'

'I think so. There was something I did – oh God, yes, I'd forgotten this! I got out a model I was making, quite an elaborate one, a Spanish galleon I'd been working on for ages and pretended I was going to do that. So I think she believed me, yes.'

His voice faltered, 'I – I smashed it, afterwards.'

'Did you get on with your sister, Mr Bryant?' Ward put the question delicately, aware he was chancing his arm, afraid that Bryant might sense a trap here too. From everything he had heard, from Maxton and from Abbie, it was unlikely they had been close, and protestations of deep affection would be – interesting.

'No, sergeant, I didn't. We fought like cat and dog, as a matter of fact.'

Well, that was straight enough. 'Did you quarrel that morning?'

'Probably, though I don't remember specifically. We quarrelled every morning.'

'What about?'

'What about? You don't need to quarrel *about* anything with your sister – you can quarrel because she has the last slice of toast, or because you nudged her as you passed her chair, or because it's raining or because the sun's shining. We were good at it.'

There was a raw edge to his tone which made Ward say, unconsciously echoing Gina earlier, 'That's what brothers and sisters do.'

'Oh yes. But then, most brothers don't bring their sisters to their death. If it wasn't for me, she probably wouldn't have cared so much about the Neters—' He had picked a tag of skin loose round the edge of his thumbnail; he tore at it, and a bead of bright blood appeared.

Hastily, Ward said, 'Look, I don't want to upset you, but I need to know what you remember of the business in the caves. When Bonnie disappeared.'

A shudder took Bryant, and he shut his eyes. 'I can't – I can't—' Then, with an obvious effort he opened them again and sat up. 'Sorry. Sorry, of course I must. I can't think why it should be getting to me like this – it was all so long ago.

'But even at the time, it was all confused. I remember – chasing her, and the lights and the shouting. I didn't actually see Bonnie myself, it was Jay who shouted and we all just ran after him.

'I don't know how long he kept her in view – you'd have to ask him. But I don't think it was long before she vanished.'

'OK. And then?'

He frowned. 'It's terribly hazy. We were all very excited. Then I think someone said we should go home, or we just felt we should, or something. Anyway, we would have left separately because we always did – it was a rule, so no one would see lots of kids coming out.'

'Who was last?'

He shook his head. 'I haven't a clue. Jay, perhaps – he usually was, I think. But I couldn't possibly say I remember – it could have been anyone.' He ran his hand tiredly through his short crop, as if his head was aching.

'Do you remember—'

'Look, I'm really sorry, but I do have to go and see my mother before it gets too late. If there's more you want to ask me, do you think we could leave it till tomorrow? You never know, I might be clearer after a good night's sleep.'

'Of course.' Ward got to his feet immediately. 'Just one last thing.' That was standard practice.

Bryant, who had also risen, paused courteously.

'It seems to be common knowledge that your mother thinks Harry Cartwright had something to do with all this.'

The other man groaned. 'Oh, I know. I'm just profoundly grateful he hasn't sued her for slander.'

'The ladies seemed to suggest that she was confused.'

He sighed. 'Oh yes,' he said wearily. 'Bonnie was always the good child where my mother was concerned, and she found it very hard to believe that she would have been disobedient enough to go and play at the Quarry Lake – a child had once fallen in and drowned, and we were all absolutely forbidden to go anywhere near it. The shock – well, quite frankly, sergeant, she was never quite clear in her mind afterwards, and it got worse.'

'But why should she pick on Mr Cartwright?'

Bryant sighed again. 'She always held a grudge – it was a failed romance, I believe. I think, as she got more and more confused, the two things got mixed up in her poor old head. She's a sad soul now.'

'So you didn't see Mr Cartwright – or anyone else – hanging around the caves at the time it happened?'

'I'm sure if I had I'd have mentioned it at the time, but I couldn't possibly claim to remember. And now—'

It was time for bluntness. 'So who do you think killed your sister?'

Bryant was equally blunt. 'I can't buy into the passing stranger story. How would they know where she was, for a start?

'I don't want to think it was one of the Neters, one of my friends – a child, for heaven's sake – but . . .'

'Which one?'

His eyes narrowed, and the easily smiling mouth set in a hard, unforgiving line. 'If you won't quote me, Jay Darke,' he said. 'He's a clever, ruthless, deceitful bastard. He always was.'

It was difficult not to betray surprise at such directness. Bryant used the word as if it did not come readily to his lips; perhaps when you were the headmaster of a primary school in a small town you had to be careful about swearing.

'Well, right,' Ward said, going to the front door. 'I'll follow that up.'

Just as he stepped outside, Bryant, in the act of shutting the door behind his visitor, paused.

'Where – where was it you found her?'

'In a cave off a passage just near the little cave where we found the statue of Anubis.'

He nodded, but said nothing. Ward could see a muscle in his jaw twitching as he went back into the solitude of his bleak little house and closed the door.

Chapter Twelve

It had been a hot day in London, one of those oppressive days when the damp air smells metallic and shimmers with petrol fumes. Kate Cosgrove could feel the greasy film of dirt clinging to her skin as she alighted from the Paddington express at Heathrow Airport. Her hair was frizzing into sweaty ringlets on her forehead, and her citrus-yellow linen dress felt limp and more than fashionably crumpled. She had been in a meeting since eight-thirty this morning, and its outcome had not been entirely satisfactory. She could feel the tightening band of a tension headache as she pulled out the handle of her overnight case to trundle it along, shifting her briefcase to the other hand.

Heathrow was even more unpleasantly crowded than usual. The holiday season was in full swing, air traffic controllers in half a dozen different countries were working to rule, delays were causing other delays, and the place was full of distracted parents with their bored and disorderly children and their crying babies.

She swept on purposefully through the aimless crowds, calculating how long it would be before she could get into her shower – three hours, probably, at the most optimistic estimate. She was scowling when the voice hailed her.

'Kate! Kate Cosgrove!'

That was all she needed. For a brief moment she thought of powering on as if she hadn't heard, but after all, it might be a potential voter. She swung round, smoothing her face into a professional smile.

Kate didn't recognise the woman who was beaming at her. She was wearing a white T-shirt with heavy gold embroidery, white pedal-pushers and gold thong sandals. She had very short, fantasy-blonde hair, bright red lips, nails and toenails, and she was bedizened with gold jewellery – well, gold-ish, anyway.

Behind her stood a fleshy man in navy shorts and an orange T-shirt which clung unkindly to the contours of his beer belly. Playing on a dangerously overloaded luggage trolley beside him were two small, bickering children in day-glo colours.

'Goodness, Kate, you haven't changed a bit!'

At least that was a clue, of sorts, and surely that was a Midlands accent? Someone from schooldays, perhaps? The husband was certainly showing no sign of recognition – or indeed any other identifiably human emotion.

'Don't recognise me, do you?' The woman wasn't offended, anyway; her tone of mock-reproof was positively triumphant. 'Well, I'd have to admit I've changed quite a bit since Burlow Primary. Len here couldn't even pick me out when I showed him the photos!' She cast a complacent look at Len, who was studying the go-faster stripes on his trainers with glum indifference.

'Burlow! Of course. I'm sorry.' Peering behind the make-up and the peroxide, Kate suddenly recognised the features of the dreariest girl in her class at school, a mousy creature called – called . . .

'Sandra! Sandra Bates!'

Sandra looked positively disappointed that transformation had not rendered her wholly unrecognisable. 'That's right, only it's Sandi Norman now, Sandi with an "i".'

'Right, right.' Kate nodded, almost as if she actually cared. 'And what are you doing now?'

'Well, right now we're waiting for the effing plane, aren't we, Len? By rights we should be in Marbella by now, sitting round the pool. But we live in Milton Keynes – oh Len, watch Darren! He's going to hit Kev with that bag!'

'Kiddies!' she said with an indulgently rueful smile as Len went to separate the warring infants. 'Got any of your own? Oh,' as her eyes went to Kate's bare ring finger, 'not married yet, then? Not that that goes for anything nowadays, though, does it?' She tittered suggestively.

I think you are confusing me with someone who wishes to have a conversation with you, Kate managed to stop herself saying. Instead, moving stealthily backwards, she declared herself childfree and unattached. 'Well, it's been nice to see you, but I've got a plane to catch—'

Sandi ignored the broad hint with an ease suggesting considerable practice. 'Ever such a coincidence, seeing you. I've just this minute been reading about poor Jay Darke in the paper. Remember him from Burlow? Ever so clever, he was.'

'Jay Darke?' Kate raised her eyebrows. 'Has something happened to him?'

Len, who had returned to the group, said morosely, 'Only killed hisself, hasn't he? Gassed hisself in his garage.'

'It's here somewhere.' Sandi dived into a wicker bag decorated with shells and sequins and produced a crumpled copy of the London *Evening Standard*. 'It was left on a seat – nothing to do, had we, but read it,' she explained as one who apologises for a weakness. She smoothed it out, folded it over and pointed to a small paragraph in one corner of the page.

Kate took it from her, read it slowly, then handed it back. 'How very sad.'

'Ever so sad, that's right. Specially for Juliette. They got married, you know. I liked her, nice, she was. But he was always a moody sod.

'Funny, though, meeting you after reading that. Wonder what the third thing will be – they always go in threes, things like that, don't they?'

She obviously hadn't heard about Bonnie, and Kate certainly wasn't about to tell her. 'Mmm. Well—' She was taking another hopeful step backwards when one of the precariously balanced cases toppled off the trolley followed by one of the day-glo children, whose head came into sharp contact with the tiled floor. He screamed uninhibitedly.

'Oh Kevin! Len, I thought you were keeping an eye—'

Kate seized her chance. 'You've got your hands full – I'll leave you. Have a good holiday.'

She made her way to the check-in desk. At the entrance to the departure lounge there was a stand of complimentary copies of the paper; she took one, and sat down to read the article again.

Not that it said much. A man had been found in a mews garage, dead in his car with the engine running. It gave his name and age, and mentioned that police were investigating.

And what were those investigating police thinking? Would they know enough to link it with the bones of a child, found in Derbyshire? And if so, would they duly conclude that Jay had been, if not overcome with remorse at a wicked deed, then appalled at the thought that it might be discovered?

And where, then, would that leave Juliette – the golden girl, everybody's pet, the one who could do no wrong? Kate hadn't seen Juliette for years, but even now, thinking of her, envy twisted her mouth.

Kate had had to learn to be charming, but for Juliette it was as natural as breathing. Everyone liked Juliette, even that stupid, vulgar woman she'd just escaped from. Juliette had always been effortlessly popular.

Kate wasn't popular. She never had been, though now she was respected and even admired. But she was respected for being competent and good at her job, and she was admired for her appearance, meticulously maintained. If you were popular, it wasn't *for* anything, except just for being you. Sometimes she got tired of having to work for every single little thing.

But then again, that was how you got on, wasn't it? A pleasing personality hadn't set Juliette well on her way to a seat in the House of Commons. What you needed was self-discipline and a clear vision and ruthless determination, all of which Kate possessed in abundance. Instinctively she straightened her slim shoulders and tossed her hair back from her face, attracting an appreciative look from the businessman in the seat opposite.

They were calling the flight now. She left her paper on the seat and made her way to the queue for boarding.

'After you!' the businessman said, waving her in front of him with an exaggerated courtly gesture. She rewarded him with a smile, as she might have thrown a biscuit to a puppy who had satisfactorily performed a trick, and preceded him through the departure gate.

Why was it that, when you were under pressure, you always found yourself trapped on a twisting road behind some brain-dead idiot who was hugging the tail of the trundling delivery van in front without the least intention of overtaking it, thus preventing anyone who had engagements more pressing than a date at the Morons' Convention from capitalising on the occasional safe straight for getting past?

Tom Ward was not in a tolerant frame of mind. He checked his watch again, groaning. He'd be lucky to be back at his desk before five o'clock, he had some paperwork on the recovered property to do, and he ought to make notes on the Bryant and Abbie Bettison interviews, while the details were still fresh in his mind. And he'd promised himself that he would go out this evening, even if it was only along to the Bell for a jar or perhaps a bite of supper, just to prove to himself that he still had a life. His training schedule for the Marathon was getting badly behind, and if all he was doing at his age was getting up in the morning to go to work, getting home at night to crash out, and thinking about the case in between, that made him one seriously sad person.

Seeing Barry Bryant's dismal house had depressed him badly, because, if he were honest, it wasn't much different from his own. Barry's job was pretty much all he had, too, though there were undoubtedly human rewards you didn't find in the police force. When was the last time Ward had been embraced in a professional capacity with the warmth Maggie and Gina had shown for their children's headmaster?

Then he grinned, reluctantly. It had been a couple of weeks ago, actually, when he'd happened to be on the spot when the call came in to pick up Suzi off a street corner in Flitchford after yet another complaint about her persistent activities, which were popular only with a small, if very appreciative, minority of the town's inhabitants. She had planted a smacker on his cheek and told him that he was a lovely boy, to the intense if discreet amusement of his constable.

But that wasn't the point. The point was that he ought to have more in his life than work, like other interests. Which he did, of course he did. There was the Test Match, for instance, where England had been set a challenging 375 runs to beat. He found the commentary on the car radio and listened until they said, 'England 53 for 4', when he switched it off again. Well, possibly not cricket.

Perhaps he was just a wage-slave after all and had become a geek without noticing. The traffic in front was slowing down, stopping. He swore under his breath, and drummed his fingers on the steering-wheel.

There was that girl he'd taken out a couple of times – Sara. He could phone her, suggest a film or a meal at the weekend. But then again, she'd shown worrying signs of getting a bit too serious the last time, so perhaps it might be wiser not to. He wasn't ready for that sort of stuff.

They still weren't moving, and nothing was coming through the other way. One of the minor accidents, no doubt, which bedevilled these roads in the summer. They didn't get too many major ones – fat chance of building up to the sort of speeds that did the serious damage!

He sighed. He could be here for some time, and now his thoughts were sneaking back, with a sort of guilty relief, to the job in hand. Well, it beat contemplating his pathetic lack of a personal life.

There was no shortage of information to process. He'd got a fairly consistent picture from the people he'd talked to, and parts of the story were clear, even vivid. He could see Bonnie, fat little plain Bonnie, pedalling away on her spying mission on that long-ago summer morning. Then he could see the hunt in the caves, with the yelling and the smoking flares and the frenzy, before it all went blank again after the Neters dispersed and someone found Bonnie in the cave that was to be her tomb. It was like a mental home movie: jerky, disconnected actions without a narrative thread to link them.

It was extraordinary that the child should have found her way along that tortuous passage and across the terrifying expanse of the huge cavern. Brave too, he thought, remembering his own profound discomfort – and he had had lights and company. All she had had was a kiddie's torch—

A torch! He'd seen the photograph, pinned with other grimmer police photographs to the panel boarding in the Incident Room. A little, pencil torch which still showed traces of its blue metallic paint, though much of the casing had corroded away.

She wouldn't have had a torch with her when she went out that morning, unless she had known where she was going. She'd known that they were meeting in the caves, then, had perhaps watched and followed more than once?

The home movie took up again: Bonnie, scrambling up the rock steps, slipping a little, perhaps, in the sandals he had seen in another photograph, mouldy now and rotten with age, the once shiny buckles a fragile filigree of rust; Bonnie reaching the top, then hiding behind a rock; Jay's cry, 'Get her!'

Then it stopped. What had she done, in that moment of panic? Had she tried to run, in the shadowy darkness lit by the flickering light of her pursuers' torches? Or, more likely, had she found some crevice haven she could shrink into, while the hunt passed her by?

And in the black darkness, had someone seen her, said nothing to the rest? Had one of them come back afterwards, calling her, perhaps, saying sorry, offering rescue?

Or – his eyes narrowed as the thought came to him – had someone followed stealthily behind her, through the caves from the outside? She wouldn't have concealed herself from someone coming behind; indeed, against the light of the torches ahead she could have been silhouetted.

And that someone could have been an adult. He had problems with the child theory – not that there weren't sick and ruthless children, but Abbie's suggestion that someone had killed her to stop Bonnie 'telling' seemed unconvincing.

The film took up again in his head: the second figure, in still deeper shadow, watchful and unseen; the children, shamefaced now as the self-induced hysteria faded, separating quietly; the gathering silence and darkness again, and at last the noiseless walk to the hiding-place where Bonnie had felt for the moment secure. Then her screams, echoing and re-echoing unheard as a man's evil fantasy was acted out, until at the end the soft sickening thud of a rock crushing the back of her head produced silence once more—

An indignant hoot from the car behind recalled him to the present; the queue was starting to move now and he eased the car forward mechanically, still in furious thought.

Yes, that could work. And then there was the bike, too, the silver bike which had so mysteriously appeared up at Quarry Lake. Once everyone was gone, what could be easier than fetching a car up the track, where Ward himself had driven two days ago, to stow the bike away for secret transportation?

Harry Cartwright. Inevitably, his was the name that came to mind. Bella Bryant had been right about her daughter's death; had she equally been right about her daughter's murderer, a Cassandra cursed – and possibly even mentally destabilised – by the world's refusal to believe her truth?

They'd never prove it, of course. With all the resources of modern forensic science at their disposal, the lab hadn't even been able to say whether Bonnie had been assaulted or not, and any other evidence was long gone. This could turn out to be one of the many cases on police files where you weren't looking any more, but you wouldn't be able to close it with a conviction.

Unless, of course, you got a confession, and you could wait for that from Harry Cartwright until the year after hell froze. Even if you found an eyewitness who'd seen him do it but just somehow hadn't thought to mention it at the time. Ward winced at the thought of what a good brief could do with evidence which was twenty years old and based on the memories of a child.

No, if Cartwright was the bastard who had killed Bonnie he would probably just walk away, same as he had done before

when he left the child's body to darkness and damp air and
time—

The traffic was starting to move again. He drove decorously
behind the irritating car in front until it reached the outskirts of
Flitchford where it turned in at McDonald's, just where the 30
mph speed limit started.

It was gone half-past five when Ward hurried in to police headquarters. Still, he told himself, if he worked flat out on the report,
then got some peace to do his notes, he could be out, surely, by
seven – quarter past at the latest. He wouldn't have time to run
more than three or four miles, but at least it was drying up to a
reasonable evening and the Bell didn't stop serving meals until
nine. With any luck he'd be able to pick up a game of bar
billiards—

'Tom!' The desk sergeant's voice sandbagged him. 'The
Super wanted to see you whenever you came in. I got the idea
he thought you'd have been back sooner.'

'That's Traffic's fault,' Ward said unfairly. 'If they got their
act together and treated clearing the road as a priority, instead of
taking details so that two incompetents can claim off the insurance because one stopped too suddenly and the other wasn't
paying attention, I'd have been here half an hour ago. Do you
know what he wants?'

Someone else's problem, the man's shrug suggested. 'No
idea. But he's buzzed down a couple of times – seems a bit
twitchy.'

'Is Little around as well?'

'No, he went off duty at lunch time. Said he was going
fishing.'

'All right for some.'

Ward was feeling ill-used as he climbed the stairs to the
Superintendent's office. Oh, he should have known better than
to tempt fate by making happy little plans. Something told him
his supper, yet again, was going to turn out to be a microwaved
pizza eaten standing up in his kitchen before he fell into bed.

When he opened the door in answer to Broughton's impatient, 'Come!' he saw to his surprise that Alex Denholm was there as well. There were empty cups on the table; it looked as if they had been in discussion for some time.

'Ah, there you are at last, Ward! Is that you just back from Burlow?'

He started to explain about the accident, but Broughton cut him short.

'Just sit down, man. You're here now, anyway. We've got a tricky situation on our hands and I want to get through this as quickly as possible so we can all go home.'

You and me both, Ward was tempted to mutter sourly as he took his seat in the vacant chair.

'Fill him in, Denholm, if you would. I think that's the easiest way.'

Denholm, it transpired, had had a phonecall from a DC at the Met, making enquiries about Harry Cartwright.

'Harry Cartwright!' At this unexpected link to his musings in the car, Ward sat up sharply.

Misinterpreting the movement, Broughton said, 'Yes, well, I know we talked about him before, but this is in an entirely different connection. His son-in-law, Jay Darke, has been found dead at his home in London.'

'*Dead!*' Ward was aware of sounding like Little Miss Echo, but the exclamation was surprised out of him. 'And Harry Cartwright—'

'No, no!' Broughton interrupted hastily. 'No one's actually accusing him of anything, as I understand it – I've got that right, haven't I, Denholm?'

'Well, more or less, sir. The DC said Darke was found in his car with the engine running, which of course points to suicide, but his sergeant wanted him to check out Harry Cartwright anyway. They call her "The Nose", apparently, and she thought she smelled something fishy.'

'Denholm, of course,' Broughton added for Ward's benefit, 'was able to reassure him—'

'Yes, sir,' Denholm murmured with his eyes lowered.

'But obviously I had to tell the Chief Constable. I went over to see him and we had a chat about it.'

He cleared his throat, and shifted in his seat. Ward shot him a sharp look. Uncomfortable about something, then, was he?

'Clearly this is very delicate,' he began. 'Mr Cartwright is a prominent and respectable local citizen, well known for his generosity to charity, which of course includes police charities. Added to which, he and the Chief Constable move in the same social circles. This means, of course —'

Just for a moment, Ward wasn't at all sure where that sentence was going. 'The same social circles' he recognised as code for 'the same masonic lodge', and for all he knew he might be the one non-mason in the room — though surely Alex would have told him, and he couldn't imagine him in the apron anyhow.

But Broughton was going on, '— that he is extremely insistent we should be completely scrupulous and transparent in the way we handle this. There must be no hint of favours being done, or any lack of professionalism.

'Am I right in thinking, Tom, that like Alex here, you have no — er, previous direct personal contact with Mr Cartwright?'

The Super was definitely squirming. Ward wouldn't have put him down as the masonic type, but then he was an ambitious man. Perhaps Denholm and Ward were the only poor saps in the building who weren't smart enough to get themselves in with the in-crowd.

'That's right.' He played along with the fiction that this wasn't a loaded question. 'I met him at a function once, and I think I said, "Good evening, sir," and he just went on talking to whoever he was with.'

Broughton's laugh held relief at escaping explicit explanations. 'Oh, I think that would stand up to scrutiny, Tom. Good, good.

'The thing is, now that we've been dragged in, the Chief Constable feels it might be a good idea for a couple of officers to go down to liaise with the Met, just for the day. It would be a courtesy to them, and we might be able to get a line on their thinking. Of course, if it turns out to be nothing at all, and you can persuade this woman, whoever she is, not to make any more waves— Well, you'll know how to handle it. I have every confidence in you both.'

Ward avoided catching Denholm's eye. No favours, eh? Train fares to London, two sergeants' time . . . Wonderful thing, brotherly love.

'Thank you, sir.' The atmosphere was positively convivial now; what a pity he was going to have to spoil it with his next remark. 'Still, it does strike me that it's very curious, Darke's death.'

'Curious?' Broughton startled at the word, like a deer hearing the sinister snapping of a twig in the undergrowth. 'How do you mean, curious?'

'Well, coming right on top of this whole Bonnie Bryant business. It came up in the interviews today – Jay Darke was the leader of a somewhat weird gang of children who were involved in persecution of the child – they were hunting her through the caves shortly before she was killed.'

Broughton stared at him, appalled. 'You mean,' he said slowly, 'there could be some tie-up between the two events that would –' he swallowed '– directly link – er, people here to this death in London?'

'I would have to think it was possible – they'll certainly have to look into it, won't they? Of course, if it's suicide . . .'

'Oh, if it's definitely suicide, which I'm sure it will prove to be . . .' Broughton lapsed into gloomy silence, taking off his spectacles and polishing them with his handkerchief – as if this might help him see his way more clearly – then putting them back on. He sighed. 'Well, whatever, I think we'll just have to proceed in the same way. After all,' he made a heavy-handed attempt to lighten the atmosphere, 'having said you were to be let off the leash for the day I can hardly disappoint you, can I?'

They all laughed dutifully. Broughton got to his feet.

'Right, first thing in the morning, then. Perhaps you can write me a summary of the state of play in the Bryant case, Tom.

I'd like to have it to hand before you go tomorrow. Are there any other problems?'

Ward decided to chance his arm. 'Well, I was to have written up a report on some recovered stolen goods for DCI Little – he wanted it by tomorrow too. I've got my notes, of course, but it's a question of time—'

'Oh, that's not a problem. Leave them with my secretary, will you, and she can pass them through to the DCI tomorrow. Presumably they're clear enough for him to be able to write up whatever it is that he needs?'

Doing his best to sound responsible rather than childishly gleeful, Ward confirmed that indeed they were.

'What about you, Alex?'

'Free as a bird, sir.'

Broughton looked sternly at him over his spectacles. 'This is work, you know, sergeant. Not an Awayday for the two of you.'

'Yes sir,' they choroused, with perish-the-thought expressions, and he dismissed them.

As the door closed, Ward and Denholm looked at each other, but said nothing until they reached the foot of the stairs. Then Ward said, 'Well, that's the first time I've ever discovered that there was a benefit in not being a mason in the police force. I bet Little's in it too so they couldn't send him. He'll be fit to be tied.'

Simpering, Denholm tossed his head. 'Well, I could have been one, only I didn't have the legs for it.'

'And always having to roll up your trousers plays merry hell with the gent's natty suiting. Broughton's got the shoulders for *décolletage*, though, I reckon.'

'Shows a shapely calf too, I wouldn't wonder. What colour do you think Little's pinny is?'

Chortling ribaldly, they went back to the CID room to fix up their arrangements for the next day.

Chapter Thirteen

The post and the newspaper arrived early at the Bettison farm on Thursday morning. The men had only just gone back to the fields after breakfast when the postman came, and normally Abbie would have set letters and paper aside for *Teletubby* time.

Today, however, she dried her hands on a dish-towel and seized the newspaper, almost afraid to see what it said this morning. Her mother had phoned her yesterday evening, full of the upsetting news of Jay's death and Debbie Cartwright's cleaner's story that Harry was under suspicion.

It was strange enough just thinking of Jay being dead, when she had spoken to him only the day before. It was stranger still – indeed, so unlikely she couldn't believe it – to think that Juliette's father, whom Abbie had known all her life, could possibly be a murderer.

But then again, suicide! If that really was what had happened, Abbie could have been one of the last people to speak to Jay. And he'd talked about Juliette leaving him, been angry and very bitter, which might be important. Was she going to have to tell the police?

She shouldn't have been hesitating. Her moral duty was clear, and she would like to think she was both moral and dutiful. But oh, how little she wanted to become still more involved with this horrible business – horrible, and getting worse! It was a harsh punishment for childish nastiness and stupidity.

She had almost lied to Sam yesterday, when he had asked her

about her visitor. The police, she explained, were talking to people who had been in Bonnie's class at school, which was the truth but very far from the whole truth. His unquestioning acceptance made her feel terribly, terribly unhappy, almost sick with misery.

If she contacted the police again she would have to tell Sam all about it, and watch his dear face cloud not only at what she had done as a child, but at her present lack of openness.

Perhaps, one way or the other, the *Midland Star* would make it clearer what had happened. She spread it out on the table beside the remains of breakfast.

In fact, it was surprisingly unhelpful. There was a brief item on the 'Local News' pages, very factual, giving bald details of Jay's death and mentioning his relationship to 'prominent local businessman' Harry Cartwright, with the discreet conclusion: 'though Darke and his wife Juliette are believed to have separated'.

So Abbie still didn't know what she must do. On balance the article seemed to suggest suicide, in which case she should undoubtedly phone Sergeant Ward, who had been so under-standing before. On the other hand, there were rules about what you could put in newspapers, weren't there, whatever might actually have happened?

She folded it up again and sorted mechanically through the post, her mind still on her problem. Circulars for Sam, bills (always bills!), a letter from a girlfriend overseas which she would save to read with her morning cuppa. And a square, thin package with a printed label addressed to her.

It looked like one of those samples firms send you because your name is on a list somewhere. The label had a red border, but there was no logo or address on the outside, and she opened it with only moderate interest.

Inside, there was a clear plastic box holding what looked like a CD – a promotion of some kind, obviously. She looked at it incuriously. They didn't have a CD player; neither of them was musical, and it was hard enough finding leisure time just to catch *Emmerdale Farm*.

Then she noticed there was an imprint saying 'CD-Rom'.

She'd heard of those – something you used with a computer, and they didn't have a computer either. That was silly – what a waste!

Then she noticed the label, which had something hand-written on it. She turned it round to read it.

'*To Bastet. I am One, who becomes Two, who becomes Four, who becomes Eight, and then I am One again. From Osiris, greetings! With this knowledge, I make you powerful – you, who never wanted power. They are helpless in your claws. Play with them! Under the Curse of Anubis, a Neter to Death and Beyond.*'

She stared at it in helpless dismay. What horrible information could Jay have locked inside before he died? She almost thought she could smell the whiff of corruption from the innocent plastic in her hands, and when little Sammie caught her unawares, coming up to tug at her for attention, she yelled at him in her fright. His tears brought her to her senses, but as she cuddled him comfortingly in the old armchair, she was staring beyond his little warm burrowing body in a black abyss.

Ward and Denholm went straight from St Pancras to the house in Westbourne Grove where they had been told they would find DS Pat Dowdalls.

The taxi dropped them there just before eleven. It was a sunny morning and the mews, all picturesque cobbles and burgeoning window-boxes and brightly painted front doors, looked post-card pretty.

Denholm whistled. 'Must've been doing all right for himself. I hate to think what these houses must go for – I don't think I can count that far.'

'Got it wrong, didn't we? Do you know there are six hundred thousand jobs worldwide in the electronics industry they can't fill, while we play hunt and peck on our keyboards? If you'd just spent your teen years as a saddo in an anorak with virtual mates instead of real ones, you could be writing your own paycheck.'

They reached number 6, which had a yellow door with a brass dolphin knocker. The house looked quiet enough, though there were a couple of cars parked outside and the garage had a blue-striped police 'do not enter' tape stretched across the front.

The door was opened by a squat woman with a sallow complexion and a long nose, wearing a trouser suit in an uncharitable shade of tan. She looked them over with an expression which suggested that disapproval was her natural state.

They introduced themselves. She came out of the house, pulling the door to behind her as she stepped forward to shake hands.

'We've had instructions to co-operate with you,' she said, unsmiling. 'Mr Cartwright seems to have friends in high places.'

Taken aback by the bluntness of the attack, Ward found his face was unreasonably turning a complicitous shade of pink. Denholm shifted his feet. 'Er – we're under orders too.'

Dowdalls sniffed, clearly unappeased. 'What do you want to know, then?'

Ward's embarrassment gave way to irritation. 'If it wouldn't be putting you to *too* much trouble, perhaps you could fill us in on what's happening here, and then maybe we can help you with some information from our end.'

Her contemptuous look expressed, all too clearly, her opinion of two hicks from the sticks who were probably payrolled by the notorious Derbyshire branch of the *Cosa Nostra*.

'There's a Dr Abbott from the firm Darke worked for checking out Darke's computer – he's been going on about intellectual property which I suppose means something. The wife's given her permission. I've been detailed to wait and see if he comes up with anything.'

'Are you any further on with the cause of death?' Ward asked.

She shrugged. 'They did the PM yesterday, but they were about as helpful as they usually are. He was heavily sedated, but it's an over-the-counter antihistamine and there's nothing to say whether he took it himself or someone gave it him, or even at what time. But the glass he drank it from was wiped, which is suggestive, and the bottle they found in the dustbin was clean too.'

Denholm said thoughtfully, 'So if someone did dope him and then put him in the car, it would probably have meant being strong enough to lift him.'

Ward agreed. 'Someone of powerful build. Like, say, Harry Cartwright.'

Whatever else Pat Dowdalls might be, she wasn't a fool. She looked at him with quick understanding and slightly greater respect.

'Right. I see. Yes, just like Harry Cartwright.'

Ward could almost read the thought crossing her brain: *Perhaps they might be useful after all.* Well, he wasn't about to make it easy for her. If she wanted to find out, she could ask. Grovel, preferably. He smiled blandly.

After a moment she caved in. 'Er – do you have anything on him in Derbyshire that we should know?'

Denholm grimaced. 'Unfortunately not.'

'He's got a good lawyer,' Ward added. 'He's always just on the right side of the dividing line. But there's a bit of background to all this that you might find helpful.'

Filling her in on the Bonnie Bryant saga took some time, but she was a good listener and the only questions she asked were short and pertinent. At the end of it she sniffed, which, Ward noticed in fascination, made the bulbous tip of her nose quiver like a rabbit's.

'I see. Interesting.' It wasn't what you could call a fulsome response, but afterwards she suggested with comparative cordiality that once Dr Abbott had done what he wanted to do, they should come back to the Chestnut Road police station with her to talk to Inspector Neale.

She opened the front door and led the way inside.

The sitting room ran the full depth of the house with stairs to the upper floor rising at the back, and was dim in comparison to the brightness of the sun outside. Two lamps were burning in the front part, but Ward's eyes were drawn to the area fitted out as an office, brightly lit. A man – Dr Abbott, presumably – was working at one of the two computers; he was obviously immersed in what he was doing and didn't look up as they came in.

At first Ward was unaware of anyone else's presence, then as he turned to speak to Pat Dowdalls he saw the woman sitting quietly on a red plush sofa. On the table beside her, a big glass lamp with a creamy parchment shade cast its light on her shiny dark brown hair.

With a start of shock, Ward took an involuntary step forward, opening his mouth to speak. What on earth was Toinette – his best friend's wife, the woman who still had his heart – doing here, her neat head turned slightly away from him, her soft mouth drooping, her slim, tanned hands clasped in her lap?

Then, with her attention drawn by his movement, perhaps, she turned towards him and he realised his mistake just in time to avoid making a total fool of himself.

It wasn't Toinette, of course. The eyes of this woman were a dark, surprising blue instead of pansy brown and her face was thinner, with marks of the sort of strain he hoped Toinette would never have to experience. They were only a little more alike, when you looked closely, than any two slim young Frenchwomen would be – and someone had mentioned, hadn't they, that Juliette Darke's mother was French?

Still, the mistaken identity threw him. It made him feel as if he knew her already, and the smile he gave her was more personal than the distant acknowledgement of a stranger. She noticed that with a small frown of puzzlement, then she smiled back warmly, with what looked like gratitude. She was very pretty.

Denholm was asking Dowdalls how long she was expecting to stay here. They were booked on the six o'clock train back, and hanging around watching someone working at a computer didn't seem like the best use of time.

She glanced over her shoulder. 'Looks as if he could be there all day, doesn't he? I suppose . . .'

Just as she spoke, there was an exclamation from Abbott. He had been bent over, working at the computer screen; now he was sitting bolt upright, staring at it.

'Good God!' he said blankly. Then he looked round. 'Sergeant – I think you ought to see this.'

At the Hilton, the under-manager who had got the rough end of Harry Cartwright's tongue on Tuesday night, had been happy to make a statement that he had gone out just before ten o'clock. The night porter, roused from sleep, was able to add that a gentleman of Mr Cartwright's description had come in again at about half-past two.

Adrian Venables, the Darkes' neighbour at number 5, had testified to hearing the front door of number 6 open and shut a couple of times in the late evening, but reluctantly admitted he hadn't heard voices or any disturbance. He had been so absorbed in a documentary about Cecil Beaton that he hadn't even looked out to see who it was – it could just have been Jay himself coming and going, but he couldn't say.

There wasn't any very definite evidence there, except that Cartwright had clearly lied to the police about his movements, but when Pat Dowdalls phoned Neale to tell him about Abbott's discovery, he didn't hesitate.

'Bring the wife in. Cartwright's back in Derbyshire, I understand, but I'd like to find out what she knows first.'

'She's demanding to be told what Abbott found, sir. Do I have to let her see it?'

Neale paused. There were so many rules now, it was sometimes hard to know when someone could later cry foul.

'The lawyer's not there making a fuss, is he? Well, get a printout and bring her in now. I'll give it to her myself when I can watch her reaction.'

Barry Bryant woke late on Thursday morning, still feeling tired and headachy. He had gone straight to bed after visiting his mother and had slept heavily, aware of dreaming endless uncomfortable, complicated dreams which he was unable to recall.

The visit to his mother last night had been even more depressing than usual. Sometimes he wondered if he'd been a fool to come back, when there was a good career ahead of him in Dorset, where no ghosts of his past could come back to haunt him. She had shown no flicker of recognition, looking past him with lack-lustre eyes and saying nothing. He had talked to her, kneeling beside her chair and holding one of her pudgy hands in his.

Was he the only person who could remember her as she had been when he was small, her dark hair neatly waved, her face carefully made up and the thick lashes round her intriguingly tilted eyes brushed with mascara? She'd always been well-rounded, of course, but looking back on his childhood he seemed to remember that she'd only begun to get really fat after the rows had started with his father, rows when his father stamped out of the house and didn't come back for two or three days. Barry, as the remaining man in the house, had had a lot to put up with as the nearest representative of the male sex, but he'd never held that against her. Looking at her fat, pale, expression-less face with the pretty eyes obscured by folds of puffy flesh, and seeing what she had become still moved him painfully.

He hadn't mentioned Bonnie to her. The matron, a chatty, competent woman, had cautioned against it.

'Nothing to gain,' she'd said bluntly. 'After all, if she's capable of taking it in properly, she's been told already, and if she isn't – well, what's the point of upsetting her all over again? She was definitely disturbed when the police talked to her about it – not rational, of course, and really almost violent.'

Barry groaned. 'She didn't spout the usual nonsense about Harry Cartwright, did she? The police seemed to know about it, and I suppose there's a limit to how understanding he's prepared to be.'

'Well, she did, actually, yes. We said she'd always had this bee in her bonnet, so they knew the background.' But there was some-thing odd in the way she said it, and he looked at her quizzically.

She looked flustered. 'Oh, I know, I know, she's not quite – well, normal . . . But after all, she was right about Bonnie being murdered, wasn't she, and no one believed her.'

'You don't mean you really think *Harry Cartwright*—'

'No, no, of course not.' Her denial was less than wholly con-vincing. 'It's just a bit funny – you know his son-in-law was found dead, gassed in his car, just after Harry's daughter had walked out on him—'

'Jay Darke? Good grief, no, I didn't. He always adored her, of course, so I suppose— But what an awful thing, and what a dreadful burden for poor Juliette to bear!'

'Well, maybe.' The matron's tone was dry. 'But Betty Watson – you know her, works at the Cartwrights' and comes here to clean in the evenings – she says Debbie Cartwright was in a real state this afternoon because the police won't definitely say it's suicide. And where was Harry last night? In London with Juliette! What do you make of that?'

'We-ell – it's probably just a technical formality.' Barry gave the automatic response – damping down rampant rumour was something that came with the territory for a headmaster – but he could not hide his concern at what she had said. 'Are they definitely saying it *wasn't* suicide?'

'Not exactly. But – well, someone killed your sister, and if Jay knew it was Harry—'

'You could just as easily say it was Jay, and he killed himself from remorse when they found her,' Barry had suggested, but it was clear that Burlow would not readily abandon a story so pregnant with fascinating possibilities.

He had made his visit to his mother then had gone home, so tired and oppressed in spirit that he made no attempt to unpack anything more than his toothbrush before falling into bed.

In the morning he had to force himself to tackle the backlog, setting dirty clothes to wash, noting phone messages, most of them from the Press, and opening his post, most of it junk mail headed straight for the bin. There were a few letters he would need to reply to, so he made himself another mug of tea and settled down at his PC. He'd given up writing by hand long ago.

As a routine, he checked his e-mail, though during the holidays he didn't get much. There was only one message, and he clicked on the entry to access it.

'*I am One, who becomes Two, who becomes Four*—' For a second he looked at it blankly, then as he read the stark threat it contained, the shock of its trouble-making malice hit him.

Jay Darke was dead. Could his computer continue to stalk the living, a sort of vindictive electronic ghost?

★

Denholm went in the car with Pat Dowdalls and a pale and shaken Juliette Darke. Ward had offered to wait while Abbott did a brief search for any other obvious messages.

An untidy man in his forties with an exuberant grey beard, wearing baggy jeans and a V-necked slipover, Abbott was methodically and expertly running through files. 'There could be any amount of stuff stashed away, on other disks, for example.' He gestured to a stack of boxes filled with them. 'Checking all this properly will take months, and I doubt if there'll be anything there. After all, this one was very clearly tagged.'

He highlighted the file name – 'billpleaseread'.

'You're Bill?'

'That's right. We were working on interlocking projects, and we held each other's passwords for the work we were doing. So he'd assume if anything happened to him I'd be sent along to deal with it.

'The only reason I didn't pick up on it sooner was because I was anxious about a couple of major programs he was working on for the company, so I checked out those first. He'll be a serious loss, I can tell you that.'

'And there aren't any other files that look immediately suspicious?'

'Not that I can see, though as I said what I have here is the tip of the iceberg. And then of course there's his own personal computer too. Do you want me to take a look at that?'

Ward looked at the enigmatic, shifting display on the screen, flatfish drifting eerily with now and then a shark appearing among them. 'I'm not really up on the legal position on these things. We'd probably need a warrant if any of it was to be used as evidence. Can't say it isn't tempting, though.'

The other man grinned. 'Nothing to stop me having a look, though, is there? After all, there might be some of our research on this one as well. And if you happened to be looking over my shoulder—'

Ward laughed. 'Fair enough. And then we'd know whether it was worth all the hassle of getting a warrant, wouldn't we?'

'Exactly.' Abbott swivelled his chair to sit at the other

computer. A moment later he said, 'He's got a different password for this. I don't know what it is.'

Disappointed, Ward asked, 'Can't you get round it? Hack in, or something – I thought you experts were always browsing through the top-secret files in the Pentagon.'

'Sure we do. It's not my bag, but you'd be amazed at the places where Jay hung out. But it all takes time – much simpler if you can guess. I'll try "Juliette", shall I? I use my wife's name for mine.'

Ward thought that was unlikely, and it didn't work. Looking round for inspiration, his eye fell on the glass shelf with its one remaining ornament. 'Try Anubis,' he suggested.

Abbott raised his eyebrows, but complied, again without success.

'Osiris, then.'

This time it worked. As the files came up, Ward exclaimed.

'Look at those! Those are the names of Egyptian gods – Sekhmet, Set, Thoth— Can you click on one?'

'Sure.' Abbott clicked on the file marked 'Sekhmet', but as he did so a pattern began to form on the screen, a mushroom cloud with a warning underneath. TOUCH IT AND KISS YOUR ASS GOODBYE, it read crudely, and Abbott lifted his hands from the keyboard as if it was red-hot.

'He's booby-trapped it,' he said. 'Devious bastard!'

'What does that mean?'

'He's put in a virus – something that would scream through the whole system, destroying everything. He'd know how to bypass it, obviously, but I don't. If he's invented it himself – which he almost certainly has – then he'll have fixed it so our anti-virus software won't recognise it, and I wouldn't put it past him to have linked it into the company computer as well. I'm going to quit now, and I just hope to hell that isn't the trigger to set it off.'

Abbott clicked the mouse rather as a bomb-disposal expert might snip a wire. His relief was patent as the threatening image disappeared from the screen.

'I *think* that was all right.' He turned back to the other computer and accessed the files he had been working on earlier.

'Well, they seem intact, but I think I'll just take the whole system back to the office to check it out properly. The sooner we can take out what we need and junk the rest, the more comfortable I shall be.'

He logged off, then bent down to disconnect the company's sophisticated machinery.

Ward was thoughtful. 'What could he have had in those files that he was so determined no one else would find out?'

Abbott's shrug was non-committal, but Ward persisted. 'Look, you knew him. I never met him. Was he as weird and unpleasant as everyone seems to say?'

Abbott, who had been winding up the flex and filling boxes with disks, stopped.

'Is this entirely off the record?'

'If you like. You're not in the frame – unless of course it was you who came round the night before last and slipped him a Mickey Finn.'

'Well, I was the bouncer at my daughter's eighteenth birthday party that night so I have an alibi from about sixty pimpled youths and body-pierced young women, if any of them were sober enough to tell me from Santa Claus.

'Seriously, though— How much psychology do you know?'

'Not a lot. We covered a bit in training but it was all fairly basic.'

'I came to computers late, and my degrees are actually in psychology. And the first time I ever met Jay Darke I said to myself, "Borderline Asperger's, that's what he is." Ever heard of it?'

Ward shook his head.

'It's linked to autism, which you're probably familiar with – where the child is unable to form relationships and lives withdrawn in a world of its own.

'Asperger's Disorder, to state it very crudely, is a mild form of autism, and Jay seemed to me to have a mild form of Asperger's. It's much more common in men than women, and they're nearly always highly intelligent.'

Ward was intrigued. 'What was it about Jay that made you think of it?'

'His detachment. He went through the motions, made all the right noises, but in fact he was unable to relate to people in any easy or normal way. Almost inhuman. And he was totally obsessional about computers – well, all of us nerds would say we were, of course, but with him you felt he depended on them for some sort of validation of himself. He was clumsy, too – unexpectedly in someone so orderly, and that's a symptom as well.

'Then poor Juliette – lovely girl, but the relationship definitely wasn't healthy. He was completely fixated on her; they came to dinner occasionally, and he never let her have a conversation with anyone when it didn't include him. I'm afraid we didn't have them over very often. It made for a most uncomfortable evening.'

'Did he make friends in the office?'

'No. The rest of us – well, we're all good mates, muck about a bit and have a lot of laughs. When Jay came in on a Friday morning, the atmosphere changed. He'd say amusing things, but we all felt he was watching our reactions all the time. Creepy.

'But as I say, it was at worst only a borderline case, and it was only my opinion – I couldn't possibly substantiate it.'

'Right.' As Abbott dismantled the equipment, Ward mulled over what he had said. 'Would it make him cold-blooded, unfeeling towards other people?'

'Absolutely. Lack of empathy – that's a primary symptom.'

'Keen on control?'

'One of Gillberg's Criteria for diagnosis of the disorder.'

'That's brilliant. Just tell me one more thing. Give me a definitive answer to this and then we can all go home. Would he be more likely to leave a message like that if he thought he might be killed, or if he planned to kill himself?'

Abbott picked up the distribution box from its place on the floor, balanced a keyboard on top of it and looked about him elaborately. 'I can't find it,' he said.

'Find what?'

'The crystal ball you obviously think is part of the equipment. When it comes to questions like that, you're on your own, sunshine. But—' He paused.

215

'Yes?'

'If you wanted a speculative answer, I would say that suicide tends to be the result of overpowering emotion.'

'And you suggested that he was almost incapable of emotion?'

'Something like that. But I wouldn't like you to quote me.' He sighed. 'The last thing I want to do is make things tougher for poor Juliette. They won't be kind, will they?'

There was nothing Ward could say to reassure him.

Juliette sat alone in the bleak waiting-room where they had left her, trying to hold her hands steady enough to drink the grey tea they had brought and eat the two Marie biscuits which were soggy in the slop from the saucer. She was determined not to humiliate herself by fainting again.

She had suffered occasionally from night terrors as a child, scary episodes when you were awake and out of bed, yet the horrors of the dream-world persisted. She recognised now the same feeling of helpless, unspecific fear.

The policewoman had been almost swaggering as she ushered Juliette in here. The other policeman, the older one, had looked more sympathetic but said nothing, and the younger one, with the interesting face, who had smiled and looked at her as if she was a person, had stayed behind at the house with Bill Abbott.

What more would Bill discover when he searched Jay's computers? What was it, come to that, that he had found already – this message which had so galvanised them into threatening action?

Juliette didn't know Bill well. They had met at perhaps half a dozen dinner parties, but he had always been kind. He wouldn't, she was sure, deliberately cause trouble for her – but she couldn't expect him to conceal information from the police for her sake.

And anyway, what was there to conceal? Her conscience was clear. Whatever Jay's opinion of her, whatever he might have written, however spiteful and shocking it might be, they couldn't prove she had done anything wrong, because she hadn't. She tried to hold that thought.

But then, why had they brought her here? They hadn't

forced her to come; the woman was, she claimed, 'inviting' her, but the invitation was issued in such a way as to make it plain that even the politest refusal would offend.

She knew what Harry would say – that she must summon Joe Rickman and keep her mouth shut till he got here. But she loathed Joe, with his tobacco-stained teeth and his ridged yellow nails and his open-pored skin which was dirty-grey from cigarette smoke. He looked so seedy that she always felt that any client of his would be judged guilty by association.

So Juliette didn't make the call. She was, she told herself, an intelligent woman, and she was on her guard. All the same, pitting herself against Jay's talent for inspired malevolence was a terrifying thought.

Yet it seemed awful, too, to be talking about her dead husband in such a way. Was she cold and unnatural, that she wasn't grieving helplessly for the man she had believed she loved? Shock, her father had said, and perhaps he was right.

She shivered, and looked at her watch. She had been waiting for quarter of an hour now, with nothing to distract her from her distressing thoughts. It was only the suspicion that they were doing this deliberately to soften her up that stopped her from putting her head in her hands and sobbing like a frightened child.

The hopeful look on DS Dowdalls' face as she opened the door was all the confirmation Juliette needed. She made herself sit back in her chair, hands loosely clasped in her lap, and looked up with a social smile; the disappointed tightening of the policewoman's lips was her reward.

'Inspector Neale will see you now,' she said and Juliette rose obediently to follow her through the labyrinth of corridors, holding her head well up.

Behind his desk, Neale looked even more forbidding than he had at the mews the day before. He made a token gesture towards getting up as she came in, waving her to the chair opposite while DS Dowdalls went to stand behind him at the window, taking out a notebook. The grey-haired policeman who had come with them from the mews was sitting in the farther corner of the room, as if somehow detached.

'Thank you for agreeing to come and help us with our enquiries,' Neale said formally. Dowdalls scribbled a note.

Like I had a choice? Juliette wanted to say, but confined herself to a nod and a half-smile, adding 'I'd be very grateful if you could explain to me what all this is about.' She was pleased to find her voice sounded quite steady.

'Perhaps one or two questions first.' Neale was flicking the edge of a piece of paper, the print-out from Jay's computer, no doubt, and the notion that he was toying with her gave her the courage of anger.

'No, inspector, I don't think I'd be very comfortable with that. Before I say anything, I'll want to know the context.'

Dowdalls gave a sniff that was almost a snort, and Neale looked at her with cold eyes.

She met them squarely. 'You did *invite* me here, after all, didn't you?'

'Of course.' His eyes dropped to the paper again, then with the sudden change of tactics she had noticed him use before when dealing with her father, he looked up smiling. 'And of course we're very grateful to you for agreeing to help. So let me just show you this, which Dr Abbott found on your husband's computer this morning.'

It was annoying that her hand should shake as she took it, and she knew they had noticed. Bracing herself, she held it still enough to read.

'*Bill — since you're reading this, I assume I must be dead. Can I ask you, as a final favour, to check out what happened to me pretty carefully? I have a father-in-law with a temper and a relaxed attitude to the laws against violence to the person and if there's anything in the least dubious he'll be at the back of it somewhere. Stick the constabulary on to him, will you? I'd hate him to get away with it. It's been nice knowing you. Perhaps we'll meet up again sometime in the Afterlife.*'

Shock took her breath away as she read it; at the end she gasped for air with a sort of choking sob. She looked up to find them watching her intently.

'This — this is nonsense!' she cried wildly. 'This is just Jay being spiteful, trying to punish me by attacking my father—'

'Not much fun, doing that sort of thing if you're dead and not there to see it,' Neale said. 'You will appreciate that someone reading this without your privileged knowledge of your husband's character wouldn't immediately seize on that as the most obvious explanation.'

She read it through again, slowly. It didn't read demented or paranoid; it read calm, almost jaunty, as if the person who had written it didn't quite believe that his fears would ever be realised. Jay was clever, of course, very clever, but— Even in her own mind, it sowed another tiny seed of doubt.

'Yes, I see that,' she agreed unwillingly. 'But – but my father would never—'

'That's your opinion,' Dowdalls snapped. 'It wasn't your husband's, evidently.'

'Mrs Darke, can I ask you again about Tuesday night? Do you have any idea where your father was?'

'He was in the hotel. He – he told you.' But even at the time she had doubted Harry's account, and she couldn't make her voice carry conviction.

'Yes, so he said. But can you confirm this – give him some sort of alibi?'

How tempting it was, suddenly to recall a visit to his room, or even a phonecall! She couldn't do it, though, and as she shook her head she realised from their faces that this had been a trap. They knew something, and a lie from her would have brought her squarely within their sights.

'You see,' Neale went on smoothly, 'we have witnesses who can say that your father went out at ten, and that it was after two when he came back.'

Juliette felt as if he had punched her, but she managed not to flinch. 'He wasn't under house arrest. Presumably he was entitled to come and go as he pleased.'

'Certainly. But if he went out for totally innocent reasons, he was singularly unwise not to be frank.'

She bowed her head, afraid he would be able to read the doubts in her own eyes. 'I accept that.'

Scenting blood on the water, Dowdalls attacked. 'Mrs Darke,

we want to know all about the relationship between your husband and your father. There's no point in telling lies – we'll find out anyway.'

Thinking furiously, Juliette said nothing until Dowdalls repeated impatiently, 'Mrs Darke?'

With sudden decision, Juliette got up. 'I'm sorry, I'm really not prepared to say anything more without a lawyer to advise me. I presume I'm free to go?'

Neale didn't move. 'Surely you want your husband's killer brought to justice, Mrs Darke?'

Without hesitation, she said, 'If there was one, yes. Do you have any proof that he didn't kill himself?'

Neale got up now too, taking no pains to conceal his irritation. 'We're not about to go into that with you.'

'So I take it that means you haven't.' Juliette was getting angry in her turn. 'You'd have a warrant out for my father's arrest if you did, wouldn't you?

'I don't know the truth about Jay's death. I don't know whether my father killed him, or whether someone else did, or whether Jay killed himself. But just let me point out that neither do you. And from long experience of my husband, I can tell you that if he planned to kill himself his legacy wouldn't be a message of tenderness and reconciliation. He'd do something just like this, to cause as much pain and distress to the people he blamed as he possibly could.'

'May I remind you, yet again, that he's *dead*?' Neale's tone was as stinging as a whiplash.

She drew a shaking breath. 'Yes, inspector,' she said. 'He's dead, but he won't lie down.'

She got herself out of the room before they could see the tears which had started to spill down her cheeks. As she reached the corridor, she heard the policeman who had sat silent in the corner say, 'Well, you have to hand it to her. That was quite an exit line.'

Chapter Fourteen

'I'm sure you did your best, Kate,' the senior partner said patronisingly as she sat opposite, forcing a grateful smile.

Of course she bloody had, and if her best hadn't done the business, it was because it hadn't been there to be done. Certainly not by the senior partner who was only kept on because he owned rather more than half of the company.

She'd had a wasted day in London yesterday at that abortive meeting, and now he'd wasted half an hour of her morning. Smarting from his sympathy, she returned to her office to find that her secretary had gone home nursing a migraine. With a snarl, Kate refused the offer of a junior to help out, gave instructions that she wasn't to be disturbed, and slammed the door.

She eyed the piles of papers squatting on her desk with revulsion. Why was it the advent of the electronic office seemed to produce more paper, not less? If she had her way, she'd confiscate printers and force everybody to communicate through a keyboard and screen.

E-mail first, she decided. She could probably get quite a lot shifted directly and informally, which just might make her feel better about the day ahead. There were ten in-coming messages which had collected while she was away, the first five straightforward enough and the sixth a scurrilous memo about the senior partner from one of her allies in the firm. She smiled and mailed back an equally libellous reply. She was working well, and her spirits had begun to rise by the time she accessed the seventh message.

As it came up on screen she stared at it, frowning, '*I am One, who becomes Two, who becomes Four . . .*' What on earth—?

Then she saw the words '*Sekhmet, destroyer of men*', and her eyes widened. She read on, her face turning dark and ugly with anger and dismay. She had locked the stable door, but only, it seemed from this, long after the horse was gone.

After Jay's death, everything should have gone quiet. The circumstances spelled out suicide in capital letters, and even the police must surely deduce from it that he had killed Bonnie Bryant, panicked when her body was discovered, and killed himself? End of case, end of investigation.

The message made her blood run cold. Oh, she was merely contemptuous of the melodramatic 'Curse of Anubis' conclusion. She had renounced superstition for good after the insanity of the Egyptian Game, and Jay knew that. He'd certainly resented it enough at the time.

It was nothing supernatural she feared. But if the malicious bastard had carried out this threat of disclosure to some human agent before he died, then she certainly was afraid, very afraid indeed. This could, quite simply, screw everything she had worked for over the years, finish her.

Unconsciously she bit at her manicured thumbnail; the twinge of pain as it tore recalled her to herself and she looked down at it with startled displeasure. This wouldn't do!

She would have to think this through, try to follow the way his mind had been working. Make a few phonecalls, perhaps. Talk – carefully, of course – to the people who might be expected to know. But meantime – meantime she had to resist his attempt at psychological terrorism, and get on with normal life. Like this stuff on her desk which certainly wasn't going to go away. With grim determination Kate applied herself to it, though her concentration was less than perfect.

She was reading through a contract with knotted brows when the phone buzzed. She answered it irritably.

The receptionist, sounding scared, apologised for disturbing her. 'I know you gave instructions, Ms Cosgrove, but it's the police wanting to speak to you on a personal matter.'

Kate managed not to repeat, 'The police!' in tones of alarm, but it was hard to say, 'Oh, that's all right Mandy, put them through,' with a fair assumption of indifference. The hand which gripped the receiver was sweating and she took a tissue from her box to dab her forehead as she waited for the call to be transferred.

A simple request from a police secretary for an interview next day was what it turned out to be, and she made an afternoon appointment for DS Ward in her normal, businesslike manner, then rang off. She rubbed the palms of her hands with the balled-up tissue.

It was probably merest routine, she told herself. The chances were they were talking to everybody in Bonnie's class at school, and knew nothing about the Neters — provided everyone else had the sense to keep their mouths shut, and surely they would? No one could possibly want to get involved, and anyway, they had all taken the oath, on pain of the vengeance of Anubis—

Oh God! She couldn't believe that she had just, perfectly seriously, thought that.

Tom Ward was getting out of a taxi outside the Chestnut Road police station when he saw Juliette Darke, slim and neat in her white slacks and deep blue shirt, coming down the steps, out of the building. She was crying, tears pouring down her face; reaching the crowded pavement she blundered into a stout woman carrying a bag of groceries who gave her a startled look before averting her eyes and hurrying on.

As he waited for his receipt from the taxi-driver, he saw that Juliette had tucked herself into the angle of the building, her back to the street. Her shoulders were heaving and she seemed to be hunting in her pocket for a handkerchief, without success.

He felt anger welling up. What the hell did Dowdalls think she was playing at, bullying her into this state? Perhaps, as the spouse, Juliette was to some extent implicated, perhaps a female suspect had no more right to be treated with kid gloves than a male, but it didn't do the reputation of the police force any good to have young women coming out and having hysterics on their doorstep.

That, at least, was the reason he gave himself for going over to speak to her.

'Mrs Darke – can I help?' he said, and she spun round, trying to choke back her sobs and wiping ineffectually at her face with her hands, like a child.

When she saw who it was her expression hardened, but before she could speak he pulled out a large pocket-handkerchief and offered it to her.

'Here, take this. I promise it's clean, just a bit crumpled.'

She seemed to be considering a hostile refusal, but as he went on, 'I'm afraid ironing isn't one of my favourite occupations,' she accepted it, mopped her eyes and her cheeks and blew her nose.

'Thank you – you're very kind.' There was still the hiccup of a sob in her voice, but she spoke formally, taking a step back away from him.

'Look, I don't know what happened in there, but if they treated you badly I can only apologise.'

She looked up at him, the dark blue eyes he had noticed before red-rimmed and her face blotchy and puffy. 'Oh, I expect they were just doing their job,' she said bleakly. 'As you probably are now. What is it they call it – playing nice cop, nasty cop?'

Having base motives attributed to a kindly impulse is always galling. He said stiffly, 'Believe me, this was entirely unofficial. I didn't mean to intrude.'

He was half-way up the steps when Juliette called after him, and he turned.

'Your handkerchief,' she said awkwardly. 'Give me your address and I'll wash it and send it back to you.'

He shrugged, ready to tell her to keep it, when she added with what was almost a smile, 'I'll even iron it.'

Smiling in return, he came back down the steps. 'It doesn't matter about the handkerchief. I have an aunt who sends me half a dozen every Christmas and I either have to lose them, give them away or buy another chest of drawers. But I promise you, that was genuine sympathy. Even police officers have the occasional human emotion.'

'It was very rude of me. I'm sorry. It's only – well, I feel a bit bruised by what happened in there.'

'Bruised?' Ward was alarmed.

'Oh no, no, not like that. It was—' She broke off, her lips starting to quiver again.

'The message?'

She nodded. She looked very young, very vulnerable. Very like Toinette.

Perhaps that inspired the pity, the surge of protectiveness he felt. He glanced at his watch. He should really present himself to Neale, but Alex was there already, after all, and they wouldn't know how long he might have spent with Abbott.

'Can I buy you a cup of coffee?' he offered, then, as the wary look came back into her face, added, 'Everything strictly off the record. I swear this isn't some sort of devious trap. We needn't even talk about all this if you don't want to. But quite honestly, I think you ought to sit down before you fall down.'

She was shivering in the aftermath of her distress, but the level look she gave him suggested that it had not affected her ability to assess him quite shrewdly.

'All right, I'll trust you. You know I'm Juliette, but I don't know who you are.' She smiled suddenly, a smile which lit up her eyes and transformed her sombre expression.

Tom, unexpectedly receiving the full wattage, stumbled over his words as he shook the hand she held out. 'I'm – I'm Tom – Tom Ward. I'm a sergeant in the Flitchford CID.'

'Flitchford?' Her finely etched brows rose. 'From Derbyshire? What on earth are you doing here?'

As he began an expurgated explanation, they set off together, Tom adjusting his stride to her shorter steps. 'It's the Bonnie Bryant thing. It just seemed as if there might be some sort of link, so they sent us to chat to the people here in London.'

'*Bonnie Bryant?* You mean the girl who drowned when I was at school? What on earth does that have to do with this?'

'You haven't seen it in the papers? Wasn't your father talking about it?'

'I only came back from France on Tuesday, and all Dad and I talked about was my problem with Jay—'

They had reached a café where metal tables and chairs were set out on the pavement in the sunshine. Juliette sat down heavily, as if grateful to find something solid in a shifting world.

'Sergeant—'

'Tom. I've taken myself off duty.'

'Tom, then. Please tell me what all this is about. I feel as if either I've gone mad, or everyone else has.'

He ordered coffee, then told her as much as he felt he could. Her eyes fixed on his face, Juliette listened in silence. When he mentioned the Neters, she winced, but didn't interrupt.

The coffee arrived just as Tom finished. He had not mentioned Bella Bryant's accusation.

She said nothing while he poured it out, then gave a shuddering sigh. 'I always thought she'd fallen into Quarry Lake. It didn't even occur to me that she might have done it deliberately – not Bonnie. She was far too tough, far too fond of herself – it wouldn't have been like her at all.

'But I was shocked, of course – we all were. And it was as if suddenly we saw what we were really doing, without – well, without the glamour and excitement, you could say. It was sick and nasty – actually evil, I suppose.' She gulped. 'Did – did anyone tell you about the animals?'

He nodded, and she went on, 'I'm glad I don't have to. I can't believe now that I went along with it. Oh, children are little ghouls, of course, but looking back it wasn't in the least natural. It was almost as if we were possessed. Jay, of course—' She didn't finish her sentence.

Aware that he was on dangerous ground, Tom asked delicately, 'Did you ever think there was anything strange about your husband?'

'Anything strange about Jay?' She laughed, without humour. 'How long have you got?'

'Did you ever wonder if he might have a medical condition?'

She was puzzled. 'What do you mean?'

'Have you heard of Asperger's Disorder?'

She hadn't.

'I don't know a lot about it myself, only what Bill Abbott told me this morning.' He repeated what the psychologist had said, which wasn't, strictly speaking, according to the rule book, but he thought Bill wouldn't mind if it helped Juliette to understand what she had been living with, and feel a little better about the failure of their marriage.

She listened with almost painful attention. Then she said slowly, 'Do you mean – he couldn't help it?'

He hadn't anticipated that question. 'To a certain extent, I suppose that's true.'

'But how dreadful! If only I'd known, if only I'd recognised it as a mental disability—' She had been pale already, but now her olive skin was greenish and she clenched her hands together on the table until the knuckles showed white.

'Look, there's no point in thinking that way, Juliette.' Distressed at the outcome of his kindly impulse, Tom leaned forward, putting his hand over hers. 'Don't blame yourself. If it had been diagnosed, you'd probably never have married him in the first place. As it wasn't, what was there you could have done? There isn't a cure. It wasn't your fault.'

She gave him a brief, unconvinced smile, and he took his hand away.

'So – do you think I made him kill himself by leaving him?'

He was certainly paying now for professional indiscretion. What was he to say in reply to that – *Look on the bright side, your father might have murdered him*?

He said, 'If he killed himself, that was a choice he made. No one is responsible for a decision like that, except the person who makes it. Do you have reason to believe that's what he did?'

The police question slipped out before he could censor it, and he felt her immediate withdrawal.

'Not a reason, no. I just think perhaps he killed himself as a punishment for me – and if you really want to know, I wouldn't be surprised if he killed Bonnie as well.'

Did she believe what she was saying, or was it only what she wanted to be true? He wasn't sure.

She was going on now, defensively. 'And the message on the computer was exactly the sort of thing he would have done.' Then she faltered. 'Did – did Bill find anything else?'

'No,' Tom said, which was more or less true. He saw her relief, and felt a brute as he asked, 'Do you have a computer?'

'Yes. Oh—!' The thought of a message having been left there hadn't occurred to her, obviously, and now alarm flared in her eyes. 'I – I haven't used it, though, since I left. Will the police – will you—'

He noted the bracketing, realised with regret that she had, probably wisely, put the barriers firmly back in place.

'I'm sure they would like you to tell them if you found anything.'

She nodded, grateful for his oblique assurance that he wouldn't suggest investigating, but the shadow of officialdom had fallen on their conversation. She bent down to pick up her bag.

'What are you going to do now?' Tom asked.

'I'll pack a few things at the house and then I'm going back to Derbyshire tonight. I'll stay at home for a bit, until things get themselves sorted out. Thank you for the coffee.'

He got up as she did. 'I'll give you my own number,' he said, fishing in his pocket for a scrap of paper. 'If you need another cup of coffee, give me a ring. And I promise you nothing's been taken down to be used in evidence.'

Juliette flashed him a hard, brilliant smile. 'Well, I haven't really said anything useful, have I? I'm not that naïve.'

She was a bright, brave lady. He watched her, a little sadly, as without a backward glance she disappeared into the tide of humanity flowing past.

In his squalid office, Eddie Jennings was for the umpteenth time accessing the e-mail from a dead man, as if this time it might say something different, something that would mean he'd been doing his head in needlessly.

It didn't, of course. Half of it he couldn't understand, the other half he understood only too well, and he wasn't sure which scared him most.

He hadn't felt this stupid and useless and helpless for years, hadn't felt this bad, in fact, since he was a kid going down for the third time in the bloody Grammar School, and that had been Jay Darke's fault too. Looking back, he couldn't figure out why he'd let the cocky little bastard persuade him to con his way in, for no reason but to be his stooge all over again. He'd spent the most miserable months of his life there, and that was God's truth, even if you compared it with his stretches inside. Sussing out the system in the nick hadn't taken him long, but the Grammar School had him beat, with teachers who made him into the class butt and kids who sneered and called him Apeman.

But in the real world, the tough world outside, Eddie knew he was no fool. Oh sure, he'd made a few mistakes, but he'd turned some tidy profits as well. And if he took risks with people he didn't trust nowadays, he was smart enough to take precautions, like keeping a list with dates and places and names and car numbers – the list he had managed to lose yesterday morning—

The list which had inexplicably turned up on his screen in the middle of the garbage Jay had sent him before he died.

The good news was, he had his protection back. The bad news was, he didn't know who it was Jay might have sent it to, and in the wrong hands— There were people from both sides of the fence who, if they got hold of it, would come after him, and on the whole he'd prefer it was the pigs.

He scowled at the screen, his black brows coming together in a straight, angry line.

Blackmail he understood. Hell, he'd used it to some effect a couple of times himself, and what else could you call the list that was his insurance policy? He had no problem with blackmail – you just came out with your hands up and did what the man holding the big gun told you to do.

This time, he couldn't work out the pay-off. It hadn't been spelled out in any terms Eddie could understand, and anyway, even if Jay had had him by the short and curlies, why should he care, once he was dead? Unless it was just for the kick of doing something nasty – that would figure.

Eddie read it again, the mumbo-jumbo bit he didn't understand. Maybe once he'd known what it all meant, but at least one thing he'd said to the pig who'd questioned him the other day was true – he didn't remember a lot about it. He only knew it still had the power to scare him.

'*Osiris, all-knowing, knows Set's secrets, but not Osiris alone. Ah, god of deserts, would you be safe? Then follow the tracks in the desert that is your mind. Fail, and you pay the price. Remember it is your nature to be ruthless, a destroyer. Under the Curse of Anubis—*'

Eddie remembered Anubis, the jackal God of the Dead. He remembered sacrifices and ceremonies and— He didn't want to remember anything more.

He didn't want to think that Jay had powers which could continue after his physical death. He didn't want to find himself hearing sounds that weren't there and constantly looking over his shoulder in an empty room.

Jay Darke was dead. He couldn't do anything more – that was common sense. And if what he was saying was that someone else, to whom he had given dangerous knowledge, was stalking Eddie, then they would just have to be stopped, wouldn't they?

For once, this Thursday lunch time, Jim Archer's expression of settled gloom had lightened into what someone who knew him well might have recognised as an almost cheerful expression.

Perce Willis wasn't ensconced in his usual corner (being wined and lunched by one of the suckers from the Press, apparently) and the pub was doing good business. Feeling was running high against Harry Cartwright, and around the bar and at the tables there was a lot of head-shaking and lowering of voices.

Doreen was safely back in the kitchen; Annie had come back to her waiting duties, and even when her nephew Barry came in didn't burst into tears or collapse. No wonder Jim was nearly smiling.

They didn't see Barry in the pub at lunch time too often. It wouldn't be quite the thing for a headmaster during term time, of course, but in the evening he regularly dropped in for his pint of Boddington's. Jim took that kindly; as a professional man, Barry might have given himself airs and gone off to the Cavendish instead.

'Your usual, Barry?' Jim got down a pint mug from the rack overhead.

'Thanks, Jim.' Barry found a vacant stool at the bar and sat down, acknowledging the greetings of the men on either side. Like everyone else in the pub, they'd been talking about the Harry Cartwright business but when Barry appeared that conversation died, and another one, about football, rather unconvincingly started. Barry, Jim noticed, didn't join in.

That wasn't like Barry. He looked at him more closely as he handed over the pint and took the money. Not looking very sharp, was he – pale and a bit shadowy round the eyes, as if he'd a lot on his mind. Well, he would, wouldn't he? Couldn't be easy for him, all this.

And he was twitchy too, looking up every time the door opened as if he was expecting someone, then looking away again as if they hadn't arrived. He was replying politely enough if anyone spoke to him, but there was no doubt about it, Jim decided – he wasn't himself.

When Eddie Jennings came in, Barry's head came up sharply, as if that was what he'd been waiting for. Now there was a funny thing. Barry and Eddie, for all they'd been at school together, weren't exactly mates. Chalk and cheese, you could say, and though they might exchange a civil word, that was all.

Barry didn't get up, or go to speak to Eddie, who'd settled himself further along the bar. But he'd stopped watching the door.

Eddie didn't look cheerful either. Yesterday's bad mood was obviously lingering – perhaps his computer was still acting up. Jim could only be thankful that Perce wasn't there to goad him into some further outburst.

Jim offered one of his usual bland remarks but today Eddie

definitely didn't want to talk. He paid for his drink, grunted, then sat staring into empty space. He finished one pint, bought another.

Gradually the pub began to empty. Annie, having cleared the tables, went through to help Doreen with the washing-up, though there hadn't been all that many lunches sold – too many locals knew what they were like.

A little to Jim's surprise Barry was still there. He even ordered another half, and as the other seats round the bar became vacant he moved round to sit beside Eddie who looked up, surprised and unwelcoming.

'Haven't seen you in a while, Eddie,' he said. 'How's business?'

'Good enough.'

It wasn't what you could call encouragement, but Barry persisted. 'You must get quite a lot of trade from tourists, this weather?'

Eddie grunted. Intrigued at this one-sided conversation, Jim gathered the glasses from round the bar and ran water into the sink up at the far end where Barry and Eddie were sitting.

'Oh Jim,' Barry said suddenly, 'do you have any salt and vinegar crisps? I don't see any in here.'

Jim peered into the basket on the bar where packets of crisps were kept. 'No, don't seem to be any, right enough.'

'Got any through the back? I could really fancy some.'

Reluctantly, Jim dried his hands and went to the door into the back of the pub. There was definitely something unnatural in the way Barry had said that, something that made him suspect he was being got out of the way. Feeling just a little ashamed, he stepped through the doorway out of sight, then paused to listen.

Barry's voice said grimly, 'Is there something we ought to talk about, Eddie?'

There was a long silence. Then Eddie's voice said, 'Could be.'

'Tomorrow, sometime? I'll drop round.' Then Barry's voice changed and he called, 'What are you doing out there, Jim? Frying the crisps yourself?'

Starting guiltily, Jim called back, 'Just coming,' found the box and brought through a handful of packets.

He did notice that, though Barry thanked him effusively, he barely ate half and left the rest of the packet when he went five minutes later.

Tom Ward and Alex Denholm edged their way past the rows of standing passengers to find, amid envious glances, the seats which had been booked for them. They were on one side of a table for four; to get in they had to contort themselves into an S-shape and once they had collapsed thankfully, found themselves inadvertently playing kneesie with the two middle-aged women opposite who broke off their high-decibel conversation to glare at this unwarranted intrusion on their personal space.

'How do people live like this?' Denholm, penned into the seat by the window, wondered aloud as the train pulled out. 'I'm hot, filthy, exhausted, and I reckon on the tube I was subjected to at least half a dozen assaults on the person by males and females alike.'

'At one point I had to say to this large, rather florid woman, "Excuse me, *this* is my foot, *that* is the floor," since she didn't seem to have grasped the difference.'

Becoming aware of the large, rather florid woman opposite eyeing him dangerously, Ward subsided into silence.

As the train reached the outer limits of commuter-land, it gradually became quieter. The two matrons, festooned with glossy carrier bags, left the carriage and the men, with considerable relief, stretched out their legs.

Ward volunteered to fetch sandwiches and beer from the buffet car. When he got back he took the seat opposite Denholm and slid across one of the small brown carrier bags. 'Lucky we can claim for the sandwiches. I might just manage to pay for the beer with a substantial personal loan; if I'd been paying for the lot I'd have had to remortgage the house.'

'What's this?' Denholm peered at his sandwich suspiciously.

'Don't ask, Alex. It was all that was left apart from tuna.'

They flipped open their beer-cans almost in unison. 'Right,' Ward said, settling back in his seat. 'Did he or didn't he?'

'Did Harry, or did Darke?'

'Comes to the same thing, doesn't it, only the other way round.'

Ward outlined Abbott's Asperger's Disorder theory, and Denholm was interested if not wholly convinced.

'Shrinks always want people to be potty. It's their livelihood, isn't it? And anyway they're mostly potty themselves.'

'Abbott was sane enough to get out of it and into computing, where the money is,' Ward pointed out.

'OK, so suppose he's right. Suppose Darke wouldn't have killed himself. What does that leave us with? Harry?'

'Not necessarily. Once Bonnie's body was discovered, all sorts of things could come creeping out of the woodwork. Darke might have realised the significance of something he'd seen, threatened the person—'

'Or else someone might have worked out that Jay killed her, and killed him in revenge.' Denholm was pleased with his theory. 'That would have to be the brother, right?'

'Barry? Yes, I suppose it would.' Ward thought about it, crumpling up his sandwich pack and stuffing it into the bag. 'He certainly thought Jay might have done it – was quite fierce when he spoke about him. And he's on a guilt trip about Bonnie's death – they fought a lot, and he's not comfortable with that now.'

'What's he like?'

Ward considered. 'It's hard to say, actually. The pleasant kind, popular with everyone, but doesn't necessarily show what's inside. Still waters running deep stuff. I certainly wouldn't rule him out.'

'And apart from that, there's Harry. He's got two motives, after all.'

Ward shook his head. 'Don't like two motives. Having two motives for murder is less than half as plausible as having one.'

'No, hang on, Tom. They're separate – it's an either/or. *Either* Harry murdered Bonnie, probably having raped her first, Darke somehow cottoned on, so Harry had to shut him up, *or* Harry wanted to take him out because of some row over his daughter. That's what Neale and Co think.'

'I don't buy that. If Harry wanted Darke taken out, with his contacts he could set it up when he and his daughter were attending a civic function with the Lord Lieutenant and the Chief Constable. He's not a fool.'

'So who's your front runner?'

'Well, I suppose Harry can't be completely ruled out. But on the face of it, I could believe Barry might feel he could purge his own guilt by killing his sister's killer. And then, of course, there are the other Neters. Any of them could have killed Bonnie – almost accidentally, maybe, got so worked up they couldn't stop. Eddie Jennings, now – he's got form. Abbie Bettison – nice lady, but you'd be surprised how she looked when she was talking about hunting Bonnie in the caves. Kate Cosgrove – she's the dark horse I haven't managed to see. And there was one who emigrated, can't remember the name . . .'

'Count him out meantime. Then there's the wife,' Denholm pointed out. 'Motive, means and opportunity, and it's a good rule of thumb to assume it's the spouse until someone proves otherwise.'

Ward seemed curiously reluctant to pursue that line of reasoning. 'She doesn't look the type,' he said.

'Oh ho!' Denholm was not slow to pick up on his intonation. 'Pretty Miss Butter-wouldn't-melt! You should have too many years of service by now to fall for that.'

'I'm not falling for anything.' Ward was immediately defensive, then recognising that as a mistake, went on, 'Actually, I'll tell you what it is, Alex – do you remember me telling you once about Toinette – the French girl who married my best mate at university?'

Denholm stifled a smile. 'Oh yes, vaguely,' he said diplomatically. Whenever Tom had had a little too much to drink, he was apt to confide the story of his broken heart.

'Well, this girl's a dead ringer for her. It sort of threw me, you see. I feel as if I know her – which, of course, I don't. I'm quite clear about that, so you don't have to do your Dutch uncle bit, Alex. It's just, like I said, she doesn't look the type.'

Alex looked at his friend with sudden concern. He was an

attractive fellow, Tom, slim and athletic-looking with the sort of lively, intelligent face that women went for. He was amusing company too, and given the shortage of personable males who were straight, unattached and thirty-something – well, put it this way, it wasn't the first time Denholm had felt it his duty to try to save Tom from naïve entanglement with some predatory young woman who was viewing him with much the same affection as a buzzard reserves for a plump and oblivious rabbit. This, however, seemed an even more alarming prospective entanglement than most, and something warned him, too, that Tom wasn't being totally upfront.

'Come on, tell me the full story, Tom,' he urged, then grinned as Tom glared at him.

'Sometimes, Alex, you seem to forget you're not my bloody mother. Or my wife either. Nor am I under oath. I've told you all I need to tell you, that I've got this under perfect control. OK?'

Denholm groaned inwardly. As bad as that, was it? 'You could try writing on a card: "This woman is a suspect in a murder case, and I am an investigating officer," ' he suggested. 'Then you could pin it to your shaving mirror, just so you wouldn't forget.'

'Sure, sure.' Ward spoke so airily that Denholm eyed him with deep misgiving. If Tom was indulging in some form of emotional transference—

'Tom,' he began warningly, but Ward brushed him aside.

'Whoever it may be,' he said, changing the subject firmly, 'we're going to have our work cut out to nail anyone on the evidence so far.'

Denholm shook his head. That was the trouble with Tom; if he didn't want to talk about something, he was like a child putting his fingers in his ears and saying 'Waaaaaah!' to drown out the sound of reasoned argument, until you decided that you might as well save your breath. He realised that point had come, sighed, and joined in contemplation of what they had learned from the Met that afternoon.

Apart from the wiped glass and the sedative bottle, they had almost nothing. The hosepipe was ridged and didn't take prints.

Its metal connection ring had only one clear print, which was Darke's, but that could have got there when he was watering the flower tubs. The car and its door-handles were a mass of smudges.

Even Darke's message on the computer wasn't evidence of anything except the fact that he didn't trust his father-in-law. And, as Pat 'The Nose' Dowdalls had pointed out bitterly, even if they found Cartwright's prints in the house, there was an entirely legitimate reason for them to be there.

'Added to that, what have we got on Bonnie's killer?' Ward went on gloomily. 'It's all so long ago, any direct evidence has vanished and no one remembers anything clearly. If we were going to put money on it, I'd back whoever killed Jay Darke – which may be one and the same person, or may not – to walk away from it without a stain on his character.'

'Unless Darke killed Bonnie, then topped himself,' Denholm suggested brightly.

'Oh, don't! This is where we came in. But from all anyone's said about Darke, remorse seems an unlikely motive. And if Abbott's right, if you don't have real emotions you don't feel the sort of despair that drives people to suicide—'

'His wife thinks he did it from spite.'

'Well, it's a theory, but it sounds a bit flimsy to me.'

'Neale was quite short with her – pointed out it wasn't much fun unless you were there to see the results.'

'He's got a point.'

'Maybe Harry will confess when we go to see him tomorrow.'

'Oh, that'll be right, Alex. Neale obviously suggested we should do it because he recognised the sophistication of our technique for putting people who've spent a lifetime working on being the archetypal wide boy under so much psychological pressure that they crack.'

'Well, you never know. He might let something slip.'

Ward looked pityingly at his companion. 'Oh yes? This is Harry Cartwright we're talking about, is it? Two gets you four if Harry doesn't have greasy Joe Rickman riding shotgun.'

Denholm made no attempt to accept the bet.

'No,' Tom went on, 'you mark my words. It'll all just get less and less conclusive, and quieter and quieter until it all just fizzles out.'

He was to look back on those words later, and think how fortunate it was that he didn't have to make his living in any profession where predicting trends was an important skill.

Chapter Fifteen

It was a strange, not altogether comfortable feeling, walking out of the sprawling ranch-style house on the slope of the hill above Burlow, down the drive and on to the road for the half-mile walk into the town. How often Juliette had done just that as a child, past the verges with their cow parsley and buttercups and dandelion clocks, by herself or with Abbie or in a little group of her school friends! She could almost believe now that if she turned her head she would see them, the ghosts of Childhood Past.

The most unnerving thing was how little Burlow had changed while she herself had changed so much. There was a smart new deli and the Cavendish Arms had gone upmarket in a frenzy of petunias and extravagantly rustic benches, but she would swear that the display, if you could call it that, in the newsagent's window was the same as it had been when she left. The woman crossing the road had taught Juliette in Sunday School when she was six; she hadn't changed, either. Juliette waved, but she didn't see her.

Passing Debbie's gift shop – her plaything – she saw her stepmother leaning precariously into the shop window, applying a feather-duster to a buck-toothed plaster bunny with blue dungarees and a ladybird perched improbably on one ear. They nodded and smiled to one another.

Debbie was a good soul with a kind heart, and Juliette could see that she was the perfect wife for her father. She and Debbie both tried hard, but they had yet to find common ground and living under the same roof was stressful. Juliette had no intention of staying longer than she must, but when she had tried to reassure her stepmother on this point, Debbie had only looked alarmed and said she was sure Harry would take care of everything.

That was only one of the things tormenting Juliette. This morning, for instance, when she had said she was coming into town to buy stamps and tights and toothpaste, Harry had instructed her to take the car and not to hang about, because Joe Rickman was coming at ten and might want to tidy up her story before the police came.

Walking instead was childish; she accepted that. The terrible thing about parents was that when you were with them you found yourself coming over all adolescent rebel again. She couldn't actually defy him if he wanted her to talk to Rickman, but she had told Harry firmly that he needn't suggest any fancy footwork, that she would simply tell the truth – had told it already, in fact, so there wasn't any point in discussion.

Harry hadn't liked that. Harry was edgy, very edgy, which was another of the things that was worrying her. He should have been merely contemptuous of any police attempt to implicate him, but he most certainly wasn't.

She had been struggling, too, to come to terms with the sergeant's well-meant but unhelpful suggestion that Jay had been somehow emotionally handicapped. What sort of a person did it make her, that she had failed to recognise that, failed to make allowances for what he couldn't help? After a night of guilt and self-loathing, it had been difficult even to get herself out of bed to face the world this morning, let alone deal with her father and his problems. She was trying to convince herself that the exercise of walking was doing her good.

Juliette had just reached the Spar mini-mart and sub post-office when she noticed two girls she had gone to school with on the opposite pavement, one of them with a child in a pushchair. 'Jane! Patty! Hello!' she called, but they were deep in conversation and a car was going past; they did not hear her. She opened the shop door, with its familiar jangling bell, and went inside.

Mrs Archer from the Three Tuns, wearing a cable-twist twin-set in sunrise orange, was at the checkout with a basket of groceries. The woman operating the till, whom Juliette didn't know, looked up with a smile when Juliette said good morning, but Doreen Archer turned, raked her up and down with a hostile stare, then turned back.

Her face flaming, Juliette ducked down one of the aisles. She'd never been cut directly before, and now she knew why you called it being 'cut'; she felt as if the other woman had slashed her across the face. Now she thought about it, too, perhaps Patty and Jane had only pretended not to hear her. And her old Sunday School teacher – had she deliberately crossed the road to avoid speaking to Juliette?

What the hell was going on?

She went to the post-office counter at the back of the shop, over which Mr Roberts had benevolently presided since she was cashing birthday postal orders. He served her politely, but without making the normal kindly enquiries.

Picking up the things she needed, Juliette made her way to the checkout, looking neither to right nor to left, paid, and set out to walk home. What was it all about? Did they think that, as a new widow, she should have been at home with the blinds down? But no, that didn't fit with the unanimity of their response. Perhaps they were all blaming her for Jay's death, as she was beginning to blame herself?

It surprised her, though, as well as wounding her. She wouldn't have thought that there would have been so much feeling about Jay; he hadn't been popular, and his parents weren't local – his mother, whom Jay never visited, was living in Wiltshire now.

Another woman Juliette had known all her life crossed the road to avoid her. Juliette bit her lip.

Of course – Debbie would know what they were saying about her. She might try to be tactful, but Juliette would just have to make her tell her the worst.

The smell of pot-pourri hit her as she opened the door of the shop, a sickly mixture of cheap scents. There were no customers.

Debbie, whose face had been drooping when her stepdaughter came in, looked up with a bright, artificial smile.

'Hello, love, nice to see you. Come to have a chat?'

Juliette went straight to the point. 'Debbie, you have to tell me. What are they saying about me in the town? No one will speak to me, or even look me in the face.'

The smile evaporated and tears welled up in Debbie's big, china-blue eyes. 'Oh Juliette,' she said tragically, 'it's not you! It's Harry – they're saying the most terrible things about Harry, and I don't know what to do.'

Juliette listened with growing dismay as Debbie recounted the rumours: that Harry had followed Bonnie into the cave, assaulted her then murdered her, and now had killed his son-in-law because Jay had realised when the body was found what Harry had done . . .

'Oh Debbie!' She held out her arms. Debbie stumbled into them and they hugged, for once at ease with one another in their shared distress.

'Why don't you shut up shop and come home?' Juliette urged her. 'You're upset, and it's not likely you'll do much business anyway, as things are.'

Her stepmother allowed herself to be persuaded, and Juliette was quite relieved to be able to get into the powder-blue Mercedes coupé and be whisked past another couple who were studiously not noticing them.

Joe Rickman's silver Rolls-Royce was parked by the front door when they got back. Debbie drove straight into the double garage built onto the side of the house.

'We can just go in by the kitchen door and not disturb them,' was all she said, but her expression suggested that she didn't like Rickman either.

'He's a seriously smart lawyer, though,' Juliette said in tacit acknowledgement, and Debbie, sighing, agreed.

Betty, who 'obliged' for the Cartwrights, was working in the kitchen. She eyed them with sharp curiosity.

'You feeling all right, then, Debbie?' There was an un-attractive eagerness about the question, and Debbie didn't look at her, going over to fiddle with some papers by the phone.

'Oh, I'm fine, thanks, Betty,' she said over her shoulder. 'It's just it was a bit quiet in the shop today and I thought I'd get on with some of the bookwork back here instead.'

'I'll make a nice cup of coffee, then, shall I?' The offer sounded kindly enough, but Juliette suspected her motives; how many confidences had been poured out along with the coffee in the past, only to be passed on as gossip?

She said flatly, 'I'll just take these things up to my room and then come down and have some coffee too,' and thought she caught a flicker of disappointment on the woman's face.

But she only said, 'Right, then, Juliette – oh, and I've done that gent's hankie you put down for washing. It's on the table there.'

'Thanks very much, Betty. I was going to do it myself later, but that's great.' She picked it up. If Tom Ward turned out to be the policeman who came today she could give it to him and tell him at the same time that there had been no untoward messages on her lap-top. He'd be obliged to check that some-time, after all.

She was on her way out when Debbie called, 'Oh, Juliette, this came for you. I forgot to give it to you last night.' She held out a slim package.

Juliette went across to take it from her. 'I wonder who would be sending me something here? I didn't think anyone knew I was coming back.'

'There were a couple of phonecalls too, asking if you were here, only no one left a message,' Debbie was saying as Juliette glanced at the parcel curiously, but she hardly heard her. She knew this label, with its red border; it was the type Jay always used.

'Be down in a minute,' she managed to say, and got herself out of the kitchen and upstairs to the privacy of her bedroom.

She eyed the innocent parcel with loathing, and had to force herself to open it. Inside was a CD-Rom, sitting in its plastic case on which there was a label inscribed in Jay's bold, black script.

'*This is how it was. Watch it, and weep. Under the Curse of Anubis, a Neter to death and beyond.*'

Horror took her, as if she had felt the spectral hand of her dead husband on her shoulder, his chill, charnel-house breath on her cheek.

'My client has given me a statement which he wishes me to read to you on his behalf.'

Joe Rickman ground out a cigarette among the other stubs in the heavy crystal ashtray on Harry Cartwright's massive maple desk, and picked up a couple of sheets of paper from the blotter. At his side, Cartwright was silent and brooding, his chin propped in one hand and his brows drawn together.

Opposite them, Superintendent Chris Broughton sat in one of the maplewood and black leather chairs, looking acutely uncomfortable. The Chief Constable had intimated that he felt it would be a courtesy, and he was a man known to have a will of iron. Beside him, DS Tom Ward sat awkwardly forward on the edge of the other chair. He pulled out a notebook.

'Put it away, laddie,' Rickman drawled. 'My time's too expensive to waste, giving you this at dictation speed with pauses while you lick your pencil. You can have photocopies in triplicate afterwards if you want them.'

Ward glanced at Broughton, and at his slight nod set down the pad.

'"On the night of Tuesday eleventh July I was staying at the Hilton Hotel,"' Rickman read expressionlessly.

Harry's story was that his daughter had retired to her room and, being alone, after dinner at the Hilton he had taken a taxi to Soho, gone to a couple of strip clubs, drunk a considerable amount then taken a taxi back to the Hilton in the early hours of the morning. He was at present unable to recollect the names of the clubs, but hoped that by returning to the area he would be able to identify them, and that subsequently witnesses might be found to testify to his presence there.

I'll bet they will, Ward thought sourly, but didn't speak.

'My client,' Rickman went on, 'accepts that he was unwise to be less than wholly open with the London police, but he asks you to understand that it would be a difficult admission for a father to make with his daughter in the room. His conscience being clear, he had no reason to suppose this would be seen as a suspicious act. He was, naturally, anxious to set the record straight immediately, but on my advice waited until he could make this statement in the presence of his legal representative, as he is perfectly entitled to do. I would also remind you that his previous response was neither a formal statement, nor delivered under oath.'

Rickman laid the handwritten sheets down on the desk and spread his hands wide in a gesture of appeal.

'So there you have it, boys. Nothing sinister, nothing we're trying to keep from you. Just a bit of laddishness best kept from the ladies. All right?' He smiled, exposing glints of gold among his yellowing molars.

Wasn't there a saying, 'common as a rat with a gold tooth?' Ward waited decorously for his senior officer's response.

Broughton cleared his throat. 'Well, naturally I appreciate your position, Harry, but you will also understand that in circumstances like these it isn't possible just to take your word.'

Cartwright scowled. 'You've known me long enough—' he began, but Rickman interrupted smoothly, 'Of course, of course. It goes without saying we'll be doing everything we can to hand you the proof on a plate –'

What, Ward wondered, was the going rate these days for a spot of perjury?

'– which will save the taxpayers' money and let you lads get on with the real job of ferreting out the truth.

'Harry here has them working on it already. We've got someone talking to taxi-drivers now, and later today he's going up to London to try to pin down the clubs. But I'll be escorting him this time, seeing he doesn't get into mischief.'

Rickman seemed entirely unfazed by the fact that he was the only one who laughed.

His, 'Now, were there any other questions?' clearly indicated that the audience was at an end.

'Just at present, until there's a bit more information, I don't think—' Broughton paused, looking at Ward and raising his eyebrows.

'There is one other thing, sir, if you wouldn't mind. It might save us both time later if we dealt with it now.'

Ward's tone was carefully deferential, but Rickman's smile vanished. 'Well?' he snapped.

'As you probably know, we are currently investigating the murder of Bonnie Bryant in nineteen eighty.' Out of the corner of his eye he saw Broughton turn his head to look at him sharply; this was not something they had discussed at their early morning meeting, and though Ward hadn't exactly decided not to mention it, when it didn't come up he hadn't been altogether displeased. And at least Broughton wasn't trying to shut him up now.

'Perhaps you could help us by answering one or two questions. Then we mightn't have to trouble you again.'

Cartwright's face darkened, but before he could say anything Rickman once more intervened.

'It goes without saying that my client is anxious to assist in any way possible, but I may advise him against rashly answering questions on a subject of which he can at best have only a very partial recollection.'

His eyes slid hopefully towards Broughton. 'Perhaps, Superintendent, I could suggest that it would be more constructive to give us advance notice of the questions you intend putting to him, to give him time to search his memory—'

Ward tensed. Surprise was their only hope of good quality evidence – was Broughton about to let his fellow-mason off the hook?

It was an unworthy thought. Broughton's voice was firm as he said, 'No, Mr Rickman, I see no reason why it should prove a problem. Certainly, it was a long time ago, but we will make allowances for any difficulties there may be on that score.'

Rickman's expression, as he said, 'Very well, then,' was something approaching a snarl, and Ward thought yet again of a rat, cornered and ready to come out fighting.

'Did you know Bonnie Bryant, Mr Cartwright?' he asked.

Cartwright shifted in his seat. 'What do you mean, know? I

knew who she was, if that's what you're asking me. She was in my daughter's class at school.'

'Did she ever come to the house?'

'How the hell should I know? Juliette had friends around all the time. I shouldn't have thought so – I don't think she ever liked her much.'

'And you had no other contact with her?'

Was there just a tiny hesitation before he said, 'No'? Ward might have thought he had imagined it, if Rickman, who had put another cigarette in his mouth, hadn't paused for a fraction of a second before he snapped on his lighter. Above its flame, his goat's eyes were very watchful.

'Are you sure about that?' Ward pressed.

'He told you, sergeant,' Rickman interrupted sharply. 'I won't have my client badgered. And I should point out you are demanding categorical statements relating to events which took place twenty years ago, so if you're going to spring evidence that he once patted her on the head at a Sunday School picnic and call him a liar, we're not playing along. Mr Cartwright withdraws his previous answer to that question. You simply don't remember, isn't that right, Harry?'

'That's right,' Cartwright said obediently.

So they had stumbled on something. Ward made a note, and saw Cartwright's eyes flicker uneasily. 'Fine. Let's move on.'

'Do you remember what you were doing on the day Bonnie Bryant disappeared?'

This time, Rickman couldn't get in fast enough to stop him. Releasing his pent-up frustration, Cartwright bellowed, 'Remember? Are you seriously asking me to account for my movements twenty years ago? Don't be bloody ridiculous!'

'Harry, Harry!' Rickman's voice was mild, but the hand which shot out to grasp his client's wrist did so with such force that the man winced.

'I appreciate that, naturally, sir. But there was a great deal of publicity at the time, and sometimes that's enough to fix other things in your mind. Can you, for instance, recall whether you were involved in the search for Bonnie?'

'I – I—' Cartwright's high colour had faded; he paused, looking at Rickman, but Rickman, feeling perhaps his interventions had not been altogether successful, said nothing.

Was he wondering what other people might have said? Ward watched with interest as Cartwright licked his lips, as if they were dry.

'I – I think I joined in later in the afternoon. Yes, that's right – John Fenner phoned to tell me, and then picked me up.' His voice grew stronger, more confident. 'Yes, you can check up with him, if you like. We both went to the school where they were organising the search, and they sent us to the woods on the far side of Burlow. There were a couple of other men—'

'And you don't remember what you were doing before that, in the morning?'

Cartwright glared at him. 'I'm telling you what I remember, sergeant, and this is it.'

'Thank you, sir. Just one more thing—'

'Make it snappy, sergeant,' Rickman cut in. 'My client is a very busy man, and he has a great deal to do before he goes to London to waste his time in clearing his name – all thanks to your colleagues, I may say.'

'I'll be as brief as I can, sir. Mr Cartwright, you must be aware that Mrs Bryant has been making allegations against you—'

'Bella Bryant—' Cartwright's voice had risen again, and there was a pulse visibly beating in his temple. This time Rickman barked, 'Shut up, Harry,' and he subsided.

Rickman gave a wintry smile. 'As you can see, my client is most unhappy about this situation, and understandably intemperate. He has already asked me to look into it. Clearly, Mrs Bryant has been uttering these slanders for many years now, but in view of her mental state Mr Cartwright has been generous enough to overlook it. It seems, however, that in the light of recent events they have been gaining currency and a part of our discussion this morning concerned the feasibility of taking legal action against anyone repeating them. I trust that you are treating this with the contempt it deserves.'

Unexpectedly, Broughton said, 'Can I take it, then, that this is a categorical denial?'

'You certainly can,' Cartwright snapped. 'And if the woman wasn't barmy I'd sue her for every penny she has.'

'May I ask whether it's true that you and she at some stage had a relationship?'

As he spoke, Ward felt the astonished eyes of both Broughton and Rickman swivel towards him. Cartwright's face went a deep, dark crimson.

'Well – in a way, I suppose. We were very young – and – and she wasn't fat in those days!' he finished wildly.

'I think my client—' Rickman said at the same moment as Ward got to his feet. 'That's all I needed for the moment, sir. Thank you for your co-operation.'

Broughton led the way out, and the front door was shut behind them in a marked manner. Ward followed his superior with some trepidation, joining him as he stood on the gravel drive between their respective cars.

'That was an interesting line of questioning, Tom.' His tone was dry. 'Came to you as a sudden inspiration, did it?'

Ward fidgeted with his notebook. 'Well, sir, it just seemed a good opportunity – save another visit, you know.'

'Yes. Might have been an idea to clear it with me first, don't you think? In the circumstances.' Then – he was a fair-minded man – he smiled wryly. 'But I daresay you feel that you didn't join the Force to play politics. I thought that too when I was your age.'

There was no wise reply to that.

Broughton went on soberly, 'Do you really think he's implicated in that child's murder?'

Ward hesitated, weighing his words. 'I'm not sure,' he said at last. 'Truth to tell, I was a bit thrown when he twitched about contact. I think there's certainly something.'

'Yes, I noticed that too. So did Rickman.' Broughton sighed.

'Well, we'll just have to see what develops. You're off to Sheffield now, is that right? Good hunting.'

He got into his car and drove off. As Ward turned to get into his own car, he saw Juliette Darke. She was hovering uncertainly, but catching his eye she waved and came over.

'I spotted you from the kitchen window. Here – let me return this with thanks.' She handed him the neatly laundered handkerchief.

He looked down at it. 'You'll have given it ideas above its station,' he said. 'It hasn't had treatment like this since it emerged from its Cellophane.'

Juliette laughed. 'Betty's ministrations, not mine, I'm afraid. She got to it first. Well, I was very grateful for it, and for the coffee.'

She was turning to go. To detain her, he said quickly, 'How are things?' and saw her smile fade. Looking at her more closely he saw that under her careful make-up she was very pale and there were blue shadows under her eyes almost as dark as the eyes themselves.

'Oh – not brilliant,' she said, shrugging. 'You probably know – all the crazy rumours going round the village.'

'I'm afraid so. But there isn't a lot to be done, really, is there, except hope your father can prove them wrong.'

'And if he can't?' Juliette burst out. 'If no one can ever prove what happened, what then? The people here won't forget. They always looked sideways at Dad anyway, because he worked hard and made money and pulled himself up. He and Debbie – this could ruin their lives.'

'And yours?' he suggested.

Juliette shook her head. 'I can walk away, can't I? I wouldn't live here, even if every one of the bloody inhabitants cheered whenever they saw me. But for Dad, it's home.'

'Where will you go?'

She shrugged again. 'Back to London, maybe. Or France – I love France. My grandmother Daubigny lives in Ambys, near Limoges, so I may look for something there, near the family.'

'Daubigny – no relation to the artist, I suppose? Pity! But

France tempts me too, I must say. I spent a year there at university and I think it's the most civilised country in the world.'

'So you speak French?' She was interested.

'I don't wish to boast, but people have been kind enough to say I speak like a native.'

'*De Gascogne, peut-être?*' she suggested mockingly, and he laughed.

He switched to French himself. 'Unkind! Gascony may be famed for its boasters, but hardly its accent. *My* accent, I assure you, is purest Parisian.'

Her *moue* of appreciation was totally French, and yet again Ward was reminded of Toinette.

'OK,' she said, returning to English, 'you weren't boasting. Or at least, you were, but you were boasting accurately.'

'*Touché,*' he said, and she said, 'Oh, for goodness sake don't start showing off again,' and then they both laughed, just as if she hadn't been a suspect in what might be two cases of murder, and he wasn't one of the investigating officers.

An awkward silence fell. She took a couple of steps backwards, away from him, the animation in her face dying. 'Well, I'll – I'll probably see you around.'

The probable reason for a return visit from him hung in the air like a pall of smoke. Ward didn't want to ask the next question, but he knew he must.

'Oh, by the way! No uncomfortable messages on your computer, were there?'

Watching her closely, he saw her jaw tighten. 'No, fortunately there weren't,' Juliette said firmly, and he believed that was the truth. But from her body language – arms suddenly crossed, hugging herself – he was sure that it wasn't the whole truth. She was concealing something, and as a policeman, with his nose almost twitching, he ought to follow it up at once.

He said lightly, 'Oh, that's good. Well—'

'Well—' She backed away; he got into the car and slammed the door. With the briefest of waves, she disappeared through a door from the garage into the house.

As he turned on to the road which led into Burlow and out

beyond towards the main Sheffield road, Ward reflected uncomfortably on his behaviour.

He really shouldn't have any more professional dealings with
the attractive Mrs Darke. Not only was she Cartwright's
daughter but, objectively, she didn't have an alibi for the night
of her husband's death any more than her father did. He knew
that when Bonnie Bryant died, she had been right there at the
scene of the crime. He was quite sure that she was hiding something.

He also knew he wasn't about to suggest this to anyone
else and have them put pressure on Juliette who was so vulnerable and, he was convinced, innocent. And finally, he knew there
was no chance he would take himself out of the frame where
she was concerned.

He didn't want to think what that said about him as a police
officer. This was no time to air, even to himself, his continuing
doubts about his career.

Instead, he forced himself to focus on the meeting ahead.
Kate Cosgrove: successful lawyer, aspiring parliamentary candidate, a favourite with the Press. He'd seen her picture a few times
in the newspapers, but the image which stuck was that of the
child in Maxton's school photo – not pretty, but interesting, with
that Mona Lisa smile.

What part had that child played at the time of Bonnie's death?
She'd been there, certainly; Abbie Bettison had mentioned her.
She'd used her Neter name as well. What was it, now?

Try as he would, he couldn't remember. That was annoying;
as a lawyer, Cosgrove would be very much on her guard and it
might take something unexpected to surprise an unconsidered
answer.

Intermittently he cudgelled his brains while he drove to
Sheffield and then had lunch in a pleasant city pub, but his mind
remained obstinately blank. At last, admitting defeat, he decided
to phone Abbie Bettison. He had her number somewhere . . .

'Could I speak to Mrs Bettison, please?' he asked when a
middle-aged woman's voice answered the phone.

'Speaking.'

'Er—' He was confused. 'I was hoping to speak to Mrs Abbie Bettison—'

The laughter at the other end was rich, good-humoured. 'Oh, *Abbie!* You mean my daughter-in-law. I'm afraid she isn't here. I'm baby-sitting this afternoon so she can do some shopping in Flitchford in peace. Can I take a message?'

'Thank you, but don't bother. It doesn't matter.'

Ward switched off his mobile phone. It was probably ridiculous to imagine that Kate Cosgrove, a likely future member of the parliament of this realm, was likely to be anything other than entirely open and fully co-operative.

Chapter Sixteen

Abbie Bettison parked her car in the multi-storey in Flitchford. Usually a free afternoon, with Sammie being ridiculously over-indulged by a doting granny, was her highest treat, but today all she felt was a mixture of misery and resentment that Jay Darke, even dead, could so poison her contentment. She locked the car, checking to see that the dreadful package was still in her handbag. She had tried ignoring it, but failed; it had got to the point where she truly believed that whatever was in it couldn't possibly be worse than her fevered imaginings.

The opening of a cyber-café in Flitchford had attracted a lot of attention, and Abbie had passed it two or three times, peering curiously in at the machines and the clientele. She had never seen anyone remotely like herself inside, but how else could she discover Jay's cruel legacy?

She had put on jeans and a shirt instead of the smart summer dress she would normally have worn for a visit to town; Pam Bettison had obviously thought it strange, but was tactful enough not to comment.

It took a lot of courage to open the door, but the place was quiet; only three computers were in use, and everyone was so absorbed that not a single head turned as Abbie came in.

There was a young man behind the counter where there were coffee machines and the normal sort of biscuits and cakes, which was obscurely reassuring. The young man had a quarter-inch fuzz of black hair which barely veiled his skull, a set of steel pins in one ear and a snake tattooed round his neck, but his smile as Abbie approached was friendly and open.

'Yo!' he said.

Abbie smiled tentatively back. 'I wonder if you can help me? I don't know the first thing about computers, but someone's sent me one of these –' she fished in her bag for the disc '– and I need to know what's on it.'

'Well, friend, you've come to the right place. Cyber heaven, this is, and it's a doddle. Want a coffee or something? I'll get that, then get you up to speed. You'll be surfing the Net like a pro before you're through.'

It was surprisingly easy. With a mug of coffee at her elbow, Abbie found herself in front of a screen and keyboard, while the young man initiated her in the workings of the thing he called a mouse, put in the CD, and brought up a graphic, a black jackal's head on red.

'OK,' her instructor said. 'Just scroll on now, like I showed you. Give me a yell if there's a problem.'

Unable to speak, she nodded. He hovered incuriously for a moment to make sure she was coping before going back behind the counter. No one else was paying any attention at all.

Abbie's hands were shaking as she looked at what was on the screen. 'Thoth' was the first heading, and she began to read.

As she scrolled down, the way she had been taught, through the other headings her eyes grew wider and wider in disbelief at first, and then in dismay. The last was the worst – the pictures were so horrible that she couldn't look at them all, fumbling to find the setting which would eliminate them. She found it at last, but she knew what she had already seen would haunt her.

Was it all true? Or was some, or all of it even, evil invention? If it was true, how could Jay have collected it, and why? He had inflicted on her a moral dilemma which should have been none of her business. As he had said, she had never wanted power; that he had forced it upon her was truly the curse of Anubis.

What a bastard, Abbie found herself thinking, she who never swore – what a rotten, diseased, perverted bastard. Even if she destroyed the disc now it had tainted her, because if what was on it really were true she couldn't, in conscience, do nothing. But then, if she did start asking questions to find out whether it was true or not—

Quite suddenly, she realised how very, very dangerous this knowledge could be.

From her bedroom, Juliette could hear the sounds of her father preparing for departure to London. He hadn't said precisely why, but she had gathered it was something to do with an alibi.

Lunch had been a trying meal. Harry had been almost totally silent, while Rickman chatted with inappropriate joviality, and she and Debbie vied with one another for the chance to fetch food or clear plates. Refusing coffee, Juliette had escaped upstairs as soon as she decently could.

It was strange how fear drove other emotions from your mind. Last night, she had paced the floor of her bedroom, racked with guilt about her treatment of Jay. Today, this fresh evidence of his cruelty had in some sense absolved her, replacing guilt with something approaching terror over what she might be about to learn. *How delighted all this would have made him*, she thought bitterly.

At last she heard Debbie's voice calling, 'Right, love, see you tomorrow, then,' and the front door being closed. Glancing out of the window, she saw her father's Jaguar following Rickman's Rolls out of the drive. She heard Debbie greet Betty who had returned from her lunch break, then another door shut, and silence.

Juliette drew a deep, shuddering breath. Her lap-top didn't take CD-Roms, but downstairs in her father's now-vacant office there was a machine which did.

She had gone over it and over it. She could destroy the thing unseen; Jay was dead, and if he had indeed had any knowledge it must have died with him. But could she be sure of that? Perhaps even now Bill Abbott was finding a copy in Jay's boxes . . .

And anyway, could she bear not to know? What if it was hard evidence which, however she felt, she would have no right to suppress?

She knew, really, that there was no alternative to viewing it. And now there was no excuse, either, for delay. She picked up the perspex box from the table where it lay and ran quietly downstairs.

Without Harry's presence, his study seemed cold and curiously dead. There were no papers in the wooden trays on his desk, nothing on the blotter, and the light on the telephone showed that it had been switched through to the Flitchford office. The computer was on a table at right angles to the desk, its screen blank.

She switched it on, waiting impatiently as it ran through its starting-up procedures. At last it was ready; she laid the CD-Rom in place, then slotted it in.

She had no idea what to expect. What came up first was a familiar logo: a black outline of an Anubis head on a red screen, the logo Jay always used for his private work.

Then the animation started.

It was crude, sketchy, obviously done in a hurry. It had the appearance of a preliminary draft for one of the computer-games Jay had so successfully designed, almost as a hobby, but the action was clear enough.

There were the caves, a dark, undetailed, menacing background, through which a group jerkily advanced, led by two children hand-in-hand, with crowns on their heads surmounted by rearing snakes.

Herself and Jay – Isis and Osiris. The Egyptian Game. Juliette sat down heavily in the chair in front of the screen.

Walking behind them in procession came other figures, six of them, children's bodies wearing shorts and T-shirts, with animals' heads on their shoulders – a lion, a cat, an ibis, a crocodile, a ram, a curious hybrid. The sacred eight – the number Jay had chosen because of the 'I Am One' text which was so old that no one had ever quite known where or when it had originated.

Then a huge shadow fell over them, a shadow with a sharp snout and pointed ears, and in the shadow they danced. There was no sound, but she could almost hear the rising frenzy of their cries and chants.

Another figure appeared; a fat child in a summer dress and sandals, creeping from rock to rock, looking slyly about her. Bonnie.

Juliette watched, mesmerised, as the silent revellers spotted the intruder, chased her with a robotic pantomime of threatening gestures. Bonnie vanished from the screen, and after a moment, so did they.

Then there was nothing, and Juliette found that she had been holding her breath. She let it out in a sort of gasp. It had been shocking to see it acted out, but pointless in a way, and by no means as terrible as her feverish imaginings. She was leaning forward to eject the disk when she saw that it wasn't finished.

The screen was brightening again, and in the circumscribed pool of colour which suggested the light of a torch, another figure was stealthily approaching, a bulky, thick-set man Juliette had no difficulty in recognising as representing her father.

He approached a rock face, shone the torch towards it, looked furtively about him and went through it.

Again, the screen went dark. Her mouth dry, Juliette did not this time delude herself that it had come to an end, and moments later the torchlight reappeared.

He came out of the cave, a rock in his hand which he tossed down contemptuously. Then he turned, lewdly and horribly adjusting his clothing, and his face – Harry's face, in broad caricature – swam up to fill the whole screen, his eyes glittering and a sated smile of the foulest depravity distorting the mouth. The shadow of the jackal fell over that too, and then the screen went black.

There was a washroom leading off Harry's study; Juliette only just reached it before she was violently sick.

At last the paroxysms stopped. She cleaned up, washed her hands and face, tried to fill a tumbler but gave up because she was trembling so much that she feared she would break it. She put her mouth to the tap and gulped the cold, fresh water instead, then buried her face in one of the thick white towels.

Eventually she went back into the study, took the disk from its slot, put it in the pocket of her jeans and switched off the computer.

She didn't know what to do. She couldn't think straight; she was in shock, she told herself. Her one instinct was to flee back to the sanctuary of her room, hoping she wouldn't meet Debbie or, worse, Betty, on the way. She let herself out into the hall cautiously.

Juliette was hurrying up the stairs when the kitchen door opened and Debbie came out. She was sobbing, in no condition to notice her stepdaughter's pallor.

'Debbie!' Juliette exclaimed, coming back down. 'Whatever's wrong?'

The other woman turned. 'Oh Juliette, Juliette! It's so – so awful—'

Juliette could hear Betty in the kitchen. 'Come in here,' she said, and led Debbie into the lounge which ran across half the frontage of the house. She almost pushed her on to one of the cream leather sofas, went over to shut the door, then came back to sit beside her, taking her hand.

'Now Debbie, try to stop crying so you can tell me what's happened.'

Debbie choked back her sobs. 'Betty – she says she can't work here any more. She's leaving!'

'For heaven's sake, is that all?' Juliette, prepared for so much worse, had to work hard to suppress her irritation. 'Don't cry, Debbie. I know it's a big house, but I'm at home to help just now, and you'll soon find somebody else—'

Debbie shook her head vehemently. 'No, no, you don't understand. That doesn't matter, of course it doesn't. It's—'

Then she stopped and looked at Juliette piteously, the tears still coursing down her cheeks. Her mascara had smudged and run so that she looked like a sad clown.

'I – I can't say it.'

Juliette went very still. 'You can, Debbie. You have to,' she said grimly.

The other woman dropped her eyes. 'Betty said they're saying now that – that your mother knew what he had done to Bonnie, and that was why she left him and went back to France.'

Juliette heard her own voice saying scornfully, 'That's ridiculous! How could Betty, or anyone else for that matter, possibly know any such thing?'

But all the time it was Grandmère's voice that was ringing in her ears. *'Ils sont tous des assassins, ces Anglais. Comme ton père.'* They are all murderers, these English. Like your father.

The teenager, a wan-looking child with an abbreviated cotton top, an abbreviated lycra skirt and incongruously huge black boots at the end of her skinny bare legs, who showed Tom Ward into Kate Cosgrove's office was scared of her boss, he noticed. She tapped on the door as if she were alarmed by the noise it made, blundered into it as she stood aside to let him through and stammered as she announced him. Once she had done her duty she departed like a rabbit which has, against all the odds, regained the safety of its burrow after an encounter with a stoat.

Kate Cosgrove, elegant in bronze jacket and beige skirt, stood up from behind the desk where she had been working and came to greet him, holding out a slim, well-manicured hand.

'Sergeant Ward. Do come in and sit down. I apologise for Sharon; my PA is off sick.'

She led the way to the corner of the office where there was a charcoal-grey sofa, a chair and a low black table on which a small collection of ornate Arab silver boxes was displayed.

'I'm almost afraid to ask Sharon to bring coffee in case she drops it all over us, but we'll risk it, shall we?'

Her smile, inviting him to share in her amusement at the skinny child's inadequacies, was charming. As she went through to the outside office, Ward glanced round the room, noting the neatness of her desk, the serried ranks of reference books, the absence of photographs or personal mementoes.

There was only one picture on the smoke-grey walls, a clever semi-abstract which looked like a pattern of golds and yellows and browns until you suddenly saw the snarling mask of a lioness, crouched as if ready to spring, among tall, sun-dried grasses.

Of course! Sekhmet! The name of the lioness goddess he had been hunting all day popped into his head. So she didn't mind being reminded? Particularly in view of Abbie's revulsion to cats, that was interesting.

Kate came back into the room. 'Fingers crossed,' she said, laughing and dropping gracefully into the low chair beside the sofa where Ward was sitting, pushing back her mane of streaked blonde hair. The bronze varnish on her immaculate fingernails exactly matched the colour of her jacket.

'Now, sergeant, tell me how I can help you. I assume it's this sad business about poor little Bonnie Bryant?'

The golden-brown eyes were wide with innocent concern, which could not quite mask their cool calculation.

'That's right,' Ward said easily. 'We've been talking to a few of you who knew her.'

She sighed. 'Oh dear, it's all so long ago! And I'm afraid I'm not one of these people who can remember every ghastly detail of their childhood. I came into my own later in life, and I think I probably did my best to forget about it as quickly as possible!'

She laughed again, and he smiled. She would, he thought, read that as an appreciative smile, which in a way it was. He had recognised her speech as a pre-emptive strike, and he had never, in a long career of observing fluent liars exercising their skill, seen lying done quite so prettily.

'So you don't remember much about the summer when Bonnie disappeared?' She was shaking her head in charming regret when he added, 'Or the Neters?'

To Ward's intense annoyance, just as he said the word, Sharon made an ungraceful entry with a tray. It was entirely natural that Ms Cosgrove should jump up to go and take it from her.

By the time she had sat down again and begun to pour out the coffee, she was entirely in control.

'Neters,' she repeated thoughtfully. 'Actually, I have to say that does ring a faint bell. A club, was it – something like that?'

'Something like that,' he said drily. Oh, she was class, no doubt about it. But was this determined lack of recollection merely a politician's trick to avoid something that might turn into an unsavoury scandal, or had she some darker, more personal reason?

Deliberately, he set out to shock her with the details he had gleaned, and shocked she certainly appeared to be.

'God, was I really involved in that? How ghastly! No wonder I've done my best to blot it out of my memory. I can only apologise for the vileness of my childhood self.'

She had looked down, apparently in confusion and embarrassment, but when she raised her head she gave him for the first time a directly challenging look. 'But – correct me if I'm wrong – didn't I understand from the newspapers that the child was actually murdered, not hounded to her death by other children?'

'Yes, it was undoubtedly a direct act of violence. But that isn't to say that it couldn't have been the act of a child – perhaps, even, an act without a full understanding of the consequences.'

'That's an appalling thought!' The sincerity in her voice rang like a dud coin. 'So I suppose that makes me a suspect!'

Recrossing her long, elegant legs she looked across at him with a faint smile, inviting him to share her amusement at the absurdity of such a thought.

He didn't smile back. Instead, Ward took her meticulously through a compilation of the questions he had asked of the others.

It took a long time, but she did not waver. Her answers were all variations on the theme of polite regret over her inability to recall. Take away the finesse, and it could have been Eddie Jennings speaking.

Finally, Ward said, 'Well, here's a question you will be able to answer. Where were you on Tuesday night?'

Kate's brows came together and he suddenly realised that she was not, after all, a handsome woman. It was an illusion created by perfect grooming and clever make-up, but the proportions of her face were ugly and her mouth thin and mean.

'This Tuesday? Why, may I ask?' She rapped out the defensive question as if she were facing him across a courtroom.

'Perhaps you could just answer the question for me,' he said mildly, and he saw her colour with annoyance at her own lack of control.

'I'm so sorry, you took me by surprise. Yes, of course.' The smile, revealing teeth so white and even they could only be capped, was once more direct and friendly. 'I was away in London overnight, working on a business project.'

'I see. Thank you, Ms Cosgrove. I've taken up enough of your time.'

Kate got up as he did, standing a little too close to him and looking up at him under her lashes. 'And now I've told you what you asked, won't you tell me why you wanted to know? Or is that some big police secret?'

She really did have a very low opinion of men. It was the contempt behind the girlish performance which nettled him. 'Something like that,' he said curtly, wandering across apparently on impulse to study the picture of the lioness.

'This is very fine,' he said.

Kate smiled graciously. 'I like it. He's a very talented young artist. It may turn out to be a good investment too, I think.'

'I'm sure it will. But it's strange, isn't it, that when you were so appalled by the Neters and your charming little rituals that you blotted them out of your memory, you should keep a painting of a lioness which can only remind you of your old persona as Sekhmet?'

For the first time, the reaction he got was totally genuine. The tawny eyes blazed and she snarled, 'Who told you that?'

'That's another of our big police secrets,' he said and walked past her out of the room. He glanced back over his shoulder; she was staring after him, her face a mask of fury.

Kate was so angry with herself that she wasn't yet afraid. She rarely made miscalculations about men, but policemen were notoriously stupid; this one was young and quite attractive, the type who usually responded to some feminine charm. A gift, she had thought when he came in.

But it was he who had strung her along; she had totally underestimated the devious sod, and at the end he had made it scornfully plain that not only had her charm failed to have its usual effect but he had known she was lying all along. Which was extremely dangerous, if Jay had done what he had claimed to do.

She had been planning to go down to Burlow for the weekend, to see what she could ferret out, but now it was a matter of urgency. And there was remarkably little point in hanging about here pretending to work.

She vented her frustration on the way out by explaining clinically to the demoralised Sharon how clumsy, disorganised, stupid and wholly useless she was before she swept out of the office and down to the car park where her silver-grey Audi was waiting.

Barry Bryant, walking back from the school after checking on some plumbing repairs they were doing during the holidays, saw Kate Cosgrove flash past in her Audi and raised his hand in a half-hearted attempt to hail her. It could be useful to have a word with Kate too about what was going on, but then again . . . He hesitated.

He'd never been sure where he was with Kate. She was very civil when they met these days, but he'd no reason to believe she was any less hard and ruthless than she'd been as a child. It was no accident that Jay had named her Sekhmet, destroyer of men.

Or— He stopped walking, struck by the thought, then went on slowly to his house. Was it possible that it was *because* of Jay that her character became fixed?

He had named Barry Thoth, the god who brought knowledge, teaching man to write and count. Was it Jay who had instilled the notion that this was his destiny? Had Jay done it to all of them?

Barry let himself back into his silent, empty house. If he'd had some ordinary local job here in Burlow, maybe he'd have a wife and kids by now . . .

He caught himself up. He couldn't afford to torment himself by thinking like this. He went to his computer and set himself to work on some spreadsheets.

★

As Kate Cosgrove turned in at the driveway of the neat cottage, much gentrified, where she had grown up, Abbie Bettison was just arriving back home at the farm, hoping that her inner torment would not be obvious to the shrewd and kindly eyes of her mother-in-law. Juliette Darke was lying in a bath with her eyes closed, trying not to think about the prospect of the evening ahead in the company of the distraught Debbie. Eddie Jennings, whose wife Sue had had enough and taken the children to stay with her mother, was along at the Three Tuns which had just opened its doors, trying to forget the nagging worry which was no better after finding out that Barry knew no more than he did and was pretty much in the same boat. Barry was working grimly on at his lists.

So, with the exception of poor dead Dick Stevens and Brian Thorburn, now comfortably asleep in his bed in distant Vancouver, here they all were back around Burlow again – Sekhmet, Bastet, Thoth, Set and Isis herself. All Osiris's puppets, gathered to play out a drama of his creation. The Eight had become One, and that One was gone, but the evil he had implanted was growing and stirring.

Chapter Seventeen

Abbie found herself positively relieved when the phonecall came. Hers was a problem that couldn't be ignored indefinitely, and this was at least a first step in dealing with it.

Last night she had had such hideous nightmares that she had twice been shaken gently awake by Sam, wakened himself by her cries of terror. After the second time, at about five, she was too much afraid of a repetition to go back to sleep and crept downstairs to huddle by the Aga with a mug of tea and a drowsy Floss for company.

She had to face it: she must tell Sam the whole shameful story. He had noticed yesterday that she was looking tired and after last night he would know something was wrong. She couldn't lie to him directly, and anyway she was badly in need of his calm common sense.

Of course he loved her and she knew, in her heart of hearts, that he always would. But he'd be disappointed in her, not so much because of what she had done as a child – though she cringed from the thought of telling him – but because she had concealed all this for days now, deceiving him by omission at the very least. She still hated the thought of his disappointment, but she would just have to accept that as her punishment.

There wouldn't be a hope of talking properly during the working day, particularly since it looked like being one of the rare, fine, settled days of this dismal summer. She'd tell him tonight.

On Saturday nights they had an arrangement with one of the farm-workers' wives to babysit and let them have an evening out, but she could cancel that when she left Sammie there in the morning as she always did when she went to do the weekly shop in Flitchford. She'd buy a couple of nice steaks and a bottle of wine and they'd have a barbecue on the terrace if it was a nice evening, and look out on the garden and just talk. They didn't often take time to talk these days except about Sammie and the farm and the family.

Depression was not a natural state for Abbie. At the thought of sharing her dreadful burden with Sam, who always gave wise, down-to-earth advice, her spirits rose. It wouldn't be easy, but this time tomorrow the worst would be over. What an idiot she'd been not to confess sooner!

So when her husband came down at six-thirty as usual, his pleasant, cheerful face creased into lines of concern for her, Abbie greeted him with a smile, a kiss, a mug of tea and a rack of warm toast.

'I'm fine, honestly,' she said in answer to his anxious query. 'Don't worry about me. But there is something I'd really like to talk to you about – perhaps we could stay in tonight instead of going out, have a steak and a bottle of wine?'

'Sounds good to me.' He was happy to be reassured, pre-occupied already with the day ahead. He took a few gulps at his tea, spread a couple of slices of toast and picked them up. 'I'll take these with me. Can't afford to miss a minute of this weather.'

On his way to the door he paused to put his arm round her and dropped a kiss on her cheek. 'And afterwards, what do you say to an early night?' He leered at her suggestively, and she was laughing when he went out.

It was just as she was clearing up after eight o'clock breakfast that the phone rang.

She readily agreed to the arrangements, and was happy to give the assurance that she hadn't allowed herself to be so manipu-lated by Jay that she'd gone round telling people what he'd said. She was glad to think that at least part of it could be proved to be total fabrication, and if part, then why not all? If she could be convinced of that, then perhaps she needn't do anything except throw the horrid thing away. Though she would tell Sam anyway, because she'd learned how miserable it made her to keep secrets from him.

Oh, she wasn't stupid; if there had been any suggestion of meeting in some remote and unfrequented spot, she'd have said no, of course, but the multi-storey car park in Flitchford was safely public. Even so, feeling a little foolish, she had suggested the second-top rather than the top, open-air floor. It was a long way down from there to the ground – but that, surely was a needlessly melodramatic thought. Nor would she, she decided after she had rung off, take Jay's disc with her, as requested. In the first place, it held highly confidential information about other people, and in the second place it would be a sort of insurance policy – though again, she found it hard to convince herself that such a thing could possibly be necessary.

As she hastily finished the routine chores and ran over to the cottage to leave Sammie to be looked after, she all but talked herself into believing that this was nothing more than wicked trouble-making plotted by Jay. Now that she knew she wasn't the only person to have had an upsetting message, she thought it would be just like him to amuse himself by making people unhappy. Well, now he wasn't there any more to keep stirring things, she could see to it that his nasty lies died with him. She would have to be convinced, of course, but she was certainly going to this rendezvous in a receptive frame of mind.

It was half-past ten when Abbie got to the car park. It looked quite busy, though there was still a green 'Spaces' sign showing. She went up and up the spiral ramp until she reached the second-top floor, then turned in.

It wasn't absolutely full, though there were a lot of cars there already. She backed her elderly Vauxhall into a space beside a people-carrier from which children were spilling, jumping about and chattering to two adults. There were balloons in the back, and some gift-wrapped parcels; a birthday outing to the swimming pool or the bowling alley, with McDonalds' afterwards, Abbie guessed, smiling at them as she got out of her own car.

She couldn't see anyone else. A car parked, a man got out, locked it, and vanished. Another car came up the ramp but went on to the top deck. Abbie locked her car and looked around again.

She went over to look down the spirals of the ramp, but there wasn't even anyone on the way up. You could always hear the cars' engines labouring in low gear as they negotiated the tight turns of the spiral.

She sighed, and went back to her own car. Obviously she was going to have to wait, and she might as well wait sitting down in comfort.

Abbie had just opened the door when the blow came from behind. It caught her on the back of the head, just above the left ear; there was no pain, only shock, then blackness swept in and she crumpled to the ground.

It was Tom Ward's day off. He slept in, waking only when the sun blinked through a gap in the curtains. For once, it was a glorious morning for a run and he wasn't even tempted to turn over and go back to sleep.

The curlews were calling across the moor as he pounded up the steep path behind his cottage, and the sky was a clear soft blue with only a few fine lines of clouds suspended above the smoke-grey of the Peaks in the near distance.

He had been missing the exercise. For the last couple of days he had felt sluggish both in body and mind, and already as his lungs began to labour his head was beginning to clear.

He needed a clear head. He had been bombarded with so much information in the past week, so many apparently un-related facts, that it felt as if they were jumbled together in a random heap in his mind.

Inconsequentially Tom found himself reminded of his mother doing her embroidery. From the dazzling rainbow of shades in her work-box, she would select the appropriate colours, drawing a fine strand from each skein and threading a series of needles which she would set in order in a pincushion ready for use. He had always liked watching the process.

That was what he needed to do: order the strands.

Juliette Darke was the problem uppermost in his mind. He hadn't needed Alex to point out to him that he should have been in police service too long to behave unprofessionally towards a pretty suspect. He knew that. He also knew that if he was shown a video of her hitting Bonnie over the head with a rock, or dragging her unconscious husband to the car and fixing a hosepipe to the exhaust, he would persist in believing there must be some innocent explanation, and you didn't get a lot more unprofessional than that.

And on the other side, it was absurd to feel hurt that she hadn't confided her present anxiety. Tom was, after all, part of the system which had inflicted on her the agonising suspicion that her father might have killed her husband. Hell, he himself had asked the probing question which had revealed that she was hiding something. Why should she trust him?

Why indeed, he reflected grimly, as he tried to sort out what he actually thought about Harry.

Tom was certainly cynical about Rickman's methods, and would be astonished if a rock-solid alibi were not, surprise surprise, the outcome of the visit to London. But – well, if Jay had been murdered, it was such a neat, well-planned crime, with the wiped glass and bottle the only mistakes. Could he really see Harry doing it that way, instead of hiring a heavy?

Then again, he'd definitely been concealing something when asked about Bonnie. But to play devil's advocate, there were two reasons for concealment: one was guilt, and the other fear that a minor admission might leave you unjustly suspect.

It was possible, too, that Juliette's defensive reaction came of putting two and two together and coming up with five. She was deeply uneasy about her father, but was there a concrete reason for that unease? It would be good to think that if she *knew* he had blood on his hands she couldn't keep silent, and that she was – very naturally – giving him the benefit of the doubt because she had no actual evidence against him.

Perhaps he was kidding himself. Perhaps they were in it

together, laughing behind his back at how easily they had put one over on him. Perhaps Darke was heavily insured in his wife's favour . . .

He didn't believe that, either. Pig-headed, or what?

This was the part of the run he most enjoyed, high along the ridge of the hill, well into his stride, head up, arms and legs pumping. He could smell crushed grass under his feet, and high above larks were singing. It seemed as if all senses were heightened, colours sharper and the air pure and clean and cool in his mouth. This was when he always felt as if time had stopped, as if he could go on for ever, as if he were immortal and omnipotent and omniscient. One of the gods.

And in his clear, endorphin-enhanced judgement, Juliette was totally innocent. So that was that.

Which led him on to the other interview he had conducted yesterday. That was something else.

Kate Cosgrove wasn't a nice lady. In the French phrase, he judged her *capable de tout*, but then ruthlessness was more or less part of a politician's job description these days.

You didn't have to enjoy it, though, and something about Cosgrove – her attitude to the hapless Sharon, possibly – suggested she might even get a kick out of others' suffering. And if Jay Darke knew something – had seen her, say, following Bonnie after the Neters dispersed, Tom could see Cosgrove coolly deciding to stop his mouth and doing it not only clinically but with relish. She'd been in London that night, too.

That was all neat enough. But it was hard to imagine what possible motive the self-contained child in the school photograph could have for violence of any sort, let alone murder.

Barry, as next of kin, was a lot more likely. On his own admission he and his twin hadn't got on, and in families— Well, you might consider incest, but on the evidence of Maxton's photograph, Barry's childish stature and soft features suggested puberty was still some way off. And of course, Tom suddenly remembered, last Tuesday night Barry was definitely in York with his pupils, spending half the night ministering to some ailing child.

Eddie Jennings, certainly, was no stranger to violence, as his record showed, and was the possessor of a black temper. Could he have matured early, tried something on with Bonnie and then – whether or not he succeeded – flown into a rage and killed her? That was an angle they hadn't thought of; it might be an idea to pull him in for formal questioning then lean on him. Check up on his movements on Tuesday night too.

In principle he should also establish formally where Abbie Bettison had been on Tuesday night, though he would be astonished if the answer wasn't that she was at home. And if she was a killer, then he had totally lost all powers of judgement.

He had reached the end of the ridge now and the ground was sloping downwards – easier on the lungs but tougher on the calf-muscles. He started down rather too fast and almost stumbled; that was lack of concentration.

But there were so many other things to think about, all the odd little jigsaw pieces which might be part of the picture or might be part of another puzzle altogether. That business over the eleven-plus – was that relevant, or merest coincidence? And Bella Bryant's confused allegations, and Darke's message about his father-in-law, and Kate Cosgrove's amnesia and her lioness painting? Was it significant that one of the people in the frame had a lengthy criminal record? Then there was Bonnie's bike; how had it been transported to the Quarry? And someone had wiped the sedative bottle and glass at the mews flat – who?

The cottage came into sight down below. He increased his speed, pleased that despite the distance and his recent lack of practice he still had a sprint left in him.

Slowing down as he neared the gate, he thought, *Of course, if you applied Occam's Razor—*

It was a concept he liked, and which he had found useful in policework in the past: the proposition of the philosopher William of Occam which suggested slicing away complication since the simplest solution was usually the right one.

The simplest solution was that Darke had killed both Bonnie and himself. That was certainly what Juliette believed. Or said she believed – but could Tom believe her?

So here he was, back full circle, despite the exhilaration of the fresh air and the exercise-induced euphoria. He stood in the hall, sweat running down his face, his head slumped forward and his arms hanging loose as he panted in an effort to get his breath back, the feeling of supreme well-being draining away.

He was really no further forward in his reasoning – and was it fanciful to feel they were all being manipulated, that somewhere out there a mind was playing games?

Still, this was his day off. As a treat, he decided on a long, hot bath instead of his usual shower. He heard the phone ring while he was soaking, but the answer-phone was still switched on and he left it.

It was half-past eleven when Tom came downstairs again, bathed, shaved and dressed in shorts and a T-shirt. He'd have breakfast outside, and afterwards he might even cut the grass which seemed, with the wet weather, to have developed ambitions more appropriate to a tropical rain forest.

The answer-phone was winking at him as he passed. Tom was tempted to ignore it, at least until after breakfast, in case it was a summons which would put paid to his long, leisurely day, but conscience got the better of him. He pressed the 'Play' button.

That was how he heard about Abbie Bettison.

Harry Cartwright returned home shortly after half-past eleven, looking much more like his old self.

Juliette was having what felt like her hundredth cup of coffee with Debbie, who seemed unable to stop picking at her worries, like a child with a scab on its knee. How long would it be, Juliette wondered, before she would crack and yell at her stepmother. 'So you think you've got problems *now*?'

Then the door opened and Harry breezed in. 'Well, girls, what's all this? Am I expected to keep my wife and daughter in idleness when there are tourists out there with money to burn and a passion for buying the sort of souvenir mugs only a mug would buy?'

'Oh Harry!' Debbie got up to kiss him, her woebegone expression lightening. 'Have you—'

'Taken care of it, haven't I?' Harry poured himself coffee, then propped himself against the dresser to drink it. 'Got half a dozen people who'll speak to my whereabouts on Tuesday night, which should get the rozzers off my back. So cheer up.'

Debbie smiled obediently. 'That's good, love. But what about the rumours—?'

Plainly upset at this reminder, he scowled. 'I told you I've taken care of things, all right? There's a law against slander, and since there isn't a word of truth in what the lying bastards are saying, I'd prefer my wife to show a bit more trust.'

'Of course I trust you, Harry.' Debbie's attempt at cheerfulness was valiant, but the temperature in the room seemed to have dropped a degree or two.

'Suit yourself.' Harry, still irritated, put down his cup. 'I'm going to the office to check the post and the messages,' he said, and went out. The two women looked at each other.

'There you are!' Juliette did her best to sound cheerfully confident. 'He's shown the police how wrong they were to think he'd anything to do with Jay's death, and now Joe will make people stop saying these awful things. Then they'll forget about it. You know Burlow – there'll be another scandal along in a minute.'

'I just hope you're right,' Debbie said tremulously. 'I haven't told him what Betty said—'

'I shouldn't, if I were you,' Juliette said crisply. Unable to bear another interminable analysis of the situation she excused herself on the pretext of having to do some preparation for e-mailing the translation agencies on Monday.

Being less cynical about alibis than the police have every reason to be, she took comfort as she went upstairs from knowing Harry had, indeed, had nothing to do with Jay's death.

But then, though Juliette had been shaken she had never, in her heart of hearts, believed he had. She had always suspected that Jay, for his own bizarre reasons, might have decided to take his life in such a way as to make her own life hell on earth.

She only wished she could be as confident about what had happened to Bonnie Bryant. An alibi for Tuesday night had nothing whatsoever to do with that.

By half-past eleven, Abbie Bettison was fighting for her life in intensive care, and Flitchford town centre was swarming with police cars and officers both in uniform and plain clothes.

Another parking motorist had found Abbie, lying in a gathering pool of blood which was trickling darkly from a depressed wound in the back of her head. The door of the Vauxhall was open and the contents of glove-box and side-pockets were strewn across the seats, as if the interior had been subjected to a hasty search. Her handbag was lying open and empty beside her, its contents dumped on the concrete. A tyre lever, one end sticky with blood and hair, was thrown down beside it.

Her breathing was so shallow as to be imperceptible to the horrified man who discovered her, but the paramedics who arrived with commendable promptness discovered a thready pulse and were relieved to be able to deliver her alive, if only just, to the hospital.

The outlook, however, was grim, and in the expectation of a murder inquiry police were immediately being called in from days off and seconded from outlying towns.

They were questioning shocked motorists as they returned to their cars, but though the birthday party from the now-impounded people-carrier next to the Vauxhall remembered Abbie, no one had noticed anything unusual or anyone hanging about.

There were so many places in a car park where a mugger could lurk – behind a car, behind a pillar, inside another car – that it wouldn't be difficult to hide. It would be simplicity itself to wait for a lull in the approach of cars up the spiral ramp to carry out what was the work of only a minute or two.

DCI Brian Little refused to entertain DS Tom Ward's suggestion that this could have its origins in the Bryant–Darke business.

'Mugged,' he said flatly. 'That's what she was. It's what happens nowadays because they don't give us money to get on with the job and tie our hands when we catch the little toerags. This sort of thing didn't happen in Flitchford before we had human rights and cost control.'

Ward stood his ground. 'But sir, apparently her purse was still there, intact.'

Little's eyes bulged with fury. 'Disturbed, wasn't he, before he had a chance—'

'He had time to rifle through the car—'

'Ward!' Little barked the word. 'That's just typical of you, typical! One way or another, you always have to be centre stage, don't you? I was saying to the Super only yesterday what a mistake it was to pander to your self-importance by giving you a special brief.

'Well, today you've got a proper job to do, the sort of standard, boring policework that gets results, instead of poncing about with fancy theories, so get on with it, and stop wasting my valuable time. I've given you an order, Ward — jump to it!'

Ward didn't bother to say, 'Yes, sir,' as he turned on his heel. He was upset and he was angry, and only a small part of his anger was directed at the pompous prat who'd been yelling at him. He was upset about Abbie, and he was angry above all with himself, because for all his good brain and his bright ideas he hadn't managed to stop this tragedy befalling a decent young husband and a little boy with solemn eyes and a yellow toy tractor.

All that was certain now was that, no matter what else he might have done, it certainly wasn't Darke who had fractured Abbie Bettison's skull – whatever implications that might have.

As Ward made his way, black-visaged, to report for his orders, he saw the Super coming along the corridor towards him, looking grave and preoccupied.

'Sir—' he hailed him, but Broughton shook his head.

'I know what you're about to say, Tom, and perhaps we might discuss it at a more appropriate time. For the moment there's straightforward police procedure to follow, so just get on with it. All right?' Without waiting for an answer, he walked on.

'Sir,' Ward muttered, and went on to be briefed.

Fingertip searching wasn't really a detective sergeant's job, and Ward knew Little had specified that detail deliberately. That was the sort of pettiness that made him want to chuck it; OK, so he was a know-it-all sod who sometimes got it wrong and didn't try not to get up Little's nose, but he did have skills which would be more usefully employed in devising lines of questioning than in crawling on hands and knees over an oil-stained concrete floor.

It was filthy, smelly, unrewarding work. They found quantities of indiscriminate litter – discarded burger wrappings, polystyrene take-away trays, the contents of a couple of car ashtrays charmingly dumped onto the floor, even (with some excitement) a small penknife – but nothing to say that any of this related to the assault.

What was especially frustrating was that if he'd been interviewing people he could have slotted in his own questions. Like, had anyone seen Kate Cosgrove – a well-known local figure – or anyone answering to the descriptions of Cartwright, Jennings or Bryant? But by the time they finished up here, all the morning shoppers would be back in their homes discussing events in hushed tones which would not altogether disguise their macabre enjoyment of sensation.

It was quarter to two by the time they were stood down. Ward did try putting his queries to the cashier at the barrier, but from the man's blank look it was evident that taking money and giving change consecutively strained his mental capacity to its uttermost limits, leaving not a brain cell free for observation.

He badly needed a shower and a change of clothes, but he wouldn't have time to go home. He could get a shower at least at headquarters, and perhaps even have time to grab a pie in the canteen before discovering what humiliation Little had planned for him in the afternoon. He was heading back that way when his mobile phone rang.

'Got anything for me, Tommy?' said Kay Grattan's familiar, gravelly voice.

'You never miss a trick, do you? I should think you've got most of the facts already. But it's a tragedy – she was a really nice lady.'

'You knew her?' She was quick to pick up the implication.

'Yes, I did.' Suddenly, he saw how to angle it. 'That's right. I interviewed her because she was a classmate of Bonnie Bryant—'

'The skeleton-in-the-cave kid?'

'Just so. And of course, Jay Darke who was found dead in London last week was another one.'

'My God!' Scenting a scoop, her exclamation was positively reverent. 'That's quite a story. And Cartwright was implicated in that somehow, wasn't he?'

'He'll have an alibi, so be very careful what you say. But Kay, I'm looking for a *quid pro quo*'.

'You always are, Tommy.' Her groan was no more than a ritual protest.

'I want you to dig for all the background you can come up with on Barry Bryant, Kate Cosgrove, Eddie Jennings – though I suspect we probably know more about him than you do – Harry Cartwright and,' he swallowed, 'Juliette Darke.'

'OK, you've got a deal.' She read back the names to check. 'I've got someone I can put on to this – he's a bright kid doing work experience, and this'll keep him out of my hair for a bit.'

'Thanks. And look, Kay—' He paused.

'Yes?'

'This sounds melodramatic, but could you give him this number and have him get back to me with anything he finds, whenever he finds it? I feel as if somehow I'm being out-manoeuvred, and I'm afraid to speculate about what might happen next.'

'Sure. You don't want any more nice ladies getting hit over the head, do you?'

'No,' he agreed fervently, and thinking of Juliette he felt a cold shiver run down his spine.

Chapter Eighteen

———————————

Juliette Darke closed the door of her bedroom with a sigh. She sat down on the bed with its flounced white cover under the white muslin-draped canopy and looked about her with something approaching despair.

Well, it had to be better than being downstairs listening to Debbie, but how long could it be before she went completely stir-crazy?

Her bedroom looked almost exactly as it had done when she was a child. Her mother, at great expense, had imported the pretty pale grey French furniture, and with its blue-sprigged wallpaper and curtains and its powder-blue carpet it was a charming room – for a little girl.

As a teenager it had been embarrassing, when her friends' bedrooms were plastered with posters of pop idols and furnished with floor cushions and bunk beds. Yet, with her mother dead, it would have seemed somehow unfeeling and disrespectful to change it.

How sad, how foolish that had been, Juliette reflected now. She had only partial memories of her mother – pretty and gentle and a little colourless compared to Harry, who worked hard at being larger-than-life – but surely she wouldn't have wished to imprison her daughter in a monument to filial piety!

The trouble had been, she couldn't ask her. Death freezes relationships at the point of parting. There is only silence beyond the grave, and the questions remain forever unanswered.

Like the question about whether her mother had left her father for the terrible reason Betty and her cohorts were suggesting.

She couldn't ask Jay, either, about what lay behind that dreadful, macabre scenario he had devised – whether it was malicious invention, an interpretation of something he had seen and could have misinterpreted, or the simple terrible truth, suppressed until now for his own strange reasons.

Juliette sighed again. If he'd been alive, he'd probably have lied to her anyhow.

Restlessly she got up and began to pace to and fro. How many times was it now that she had gone over and over all this in her head?

For her own sanity, she mustn't stay in Burlow much longer. Plans would have to be made for Jay's funeral, too; she'd have to go back to London and learn to live with the ghosts there instead of the memories which haunted her here.

It couldn't be much before the middle of next week, though, and she had begun to feel that if she had to spend even the rest of the day between these four blue-sprigged walls she was going to start climbing them. She didn't plan, however, to repeat the disastrous experiment of going into Burlow, and if she took herself for a walk on the moors she'd find herself on the same mental merry-go-round as before. She'd considered phoning Abbie Bettison, but how could she avoid talking about the subject uppermost in everyone's minds?

Perhaps Debbie would lend her the car and she could drive to Sheffield – go to see a film or look at the shops. Anything, to give her something else to think about.

Juliette glanced at her watch. Twelve o'clock – an hour to put in before lunch. There were actually things she could do in preparation for a trawl for work on Monday, which would justify the excuse she had meanly used to escape poor Debbie.

There was a telephone in her bedroom. She took the jack from its point and connected up her lap-top, set it on her neat little desk, sat down, then logged on to her network.

The 'you've got mail' icon was flashing. Her heart missed

a beat and she pushed back her chair involuntarily.

Don't be a fool, she told herself savagely. It could be anyone – one of the very firms she had been planning to contact, even. It hadn't been there when she checked yesterday, and Jay was dead, remember? She clicked on the innocent, cheerful little picture of a tray piled high with letters.

There was only one item listed. It bore today's transmission date, and her eyes widened as she recognised Jay's e-mail address – *osiris.london,* it began, followed by the address of his server.

She began to shake. Who could be using Jay's terminal in this sadistic way? It took her two clumsy attempts to get the arrow to the right place to access the message.

'*I am One, who becomes Two, who becomes Four, who becomes Eight, and then I am One again.*'

The old Neters' incantation! Who *was* this?

'*From beyond the grave, my greetings! My grieving widow, are you suffering? Oh, I do trust so! It is right that you and Harry-the-bastard should suffer, for Anubis has weighed your hearts against the feather of truth, and found you wanting.*

'*You are none of you worthy. You judged me a failure as a man; I knew myself from the first as different, as greater. Yet you, Juliette, betrayed me not once but twice.*

'*Have the police fallen into the trap I laid with the suspiciously clean glass and bottle, and arrested Harry for my murder? Did you admire the finesse of my message to Bill, pointing the plods in the right direction?*

'*Then, what of the virtuous Abbie? Surely even she has found it hard to resist the seduction of the power I have put in her hands.*

'*And what have the pervert, the fraud, the sadist and the crook done to protect themselves?*

'*I shall know all these things now, being dead to the world. I am watching you, even as you read this, seeing into the innermost recesses of your mind as you would never let me do in life.*

'*From this you will understand that I, Osiris, died by my own hand. I shall return in power, as Osiris always does.*

'*I give you one third and final chance. Join me in death, and share my immortality; live, and though you know the truth no one will believe you. Dark suspicions will be your daily companions. How long can you bear that agony?*

'*Under the Curse of Anubis, a Neter to death and beyond.*'

It was unmistakably Jay's voice. The room seemed all at once to have become cold, as if something sly and evil had entered it, as if not even death had stilled that vengeful spirit. Perhaps she had been wrong, perhaps the grave was not silent. Everything began to swim before her eyes.

Instinctively she ducked her head to her knees, and felt the blood which had been drained by shock return to her brain. Cautiously she sat up again, colour coming back into her ashen cheeks and sanity returning with it. The room wasn't cold after all, and of course Jay didn't have supernatural powers; no one did. He was mad, quite mad, and he had been playing computer tricks. As his ultimate revenge, he was trying to psych her into killing herself too, and that was what the Egyptian Game CD had been about as well.

Suddenly, in reaction to her fright, she was very, very angry. She had had enough of Jay's power games. No proof, indeed! As if the e-mail itself – written before he killed himself and put out on a timed delay program, presumably – wasn't proof positive of how maliciously he had tried to frame Harry!

Gathering her scattered wits she grabbed the mouse and selected 'Save', but as she did so the screen went blank. Frantically she clicked back to the e-mail listing. It was gone, as if she had chosen 'Delete' instead of 'Save'.

Juliette thumped the desk and swore. More of Jay's sleight-of-hand: some sort of self-destruct program, leaving her without proof, just as he had said.

So Jay was still pulling the strings, still directing the Game. But if he had meant to reduce her to abject despair, he'd achieved the opposite. She had lived too long with the tyranny of the dead and all at once she was incandescent with rage and frustration.

Hardly knowing what she did, she climbed on the bed and tore down the incongruous muslin drapes. The bare canopy looked almost indecent in the fossilised perfection of the dainty room.

It gave Juliette enormous satisfaction to tear them into shreds. And she'd turn Debbie loose on the room; by the time it had frilly knicker blinds and cabbage rose wallpaper and white furniture with heavy gilt doorhandles, no vestige of ghostly good taste would remain.

She knew now for certain her father had no hand in Jay's death – and could that mean, none in Bonnie's either? She'd suspected Jay himself from the moment Ward told her the news.

What else had Jay planned, in his crazy final hours? She was no match for his agile mind and his technical expertise, but clearly he couldn't cause more trouble for Harry with the police, without incidentally exonerating him. Perhaps she should tell Harry what had happened – but wouldn't he erupt, do all the wrong things and make matters worse?

No, the person she needed to talk to was Sergeant Ward – Tom. He was in the enemy camp, of course – how strange it seemed to say that about the police! – but she trusted him, somehow.

After lunch she'd phone from her room, tell him they needn't go on looking for a killer, at least in Jay's case and very likely Bonnie's too. The nightmare she had been living in might be almost over.

It was only later she remembered the part about the pervert, the fraud, the sadist and the crook. And Abbie had been mentioned as well.

What was all *that* about?

'It's ever so good of you to look in, Kate.' Hearing Ms Cosgrove's voice, Doreen Archer, like some lurid orange rabbit, had popped out from the back room of the Three Tuns.

Kate, in neat pale grey drawstring trousers and a soft blue silk twin-set, smiled charmingly. 'It's always good to be back, Doreen.'

'*I'll* get Kate her gin and tonic, Jim,' Doreen said, deftly elbowing her husband aside.

Jim, allowing himself to be relegated, went back to his task of broaching a new keg. Doreen considered it beneath her to act as barmaid, except to offer a G&T on the house to their Liberal Democrat candidate, popularly considered a dead cert for the seat at the next election. It added tone to the place, to Doreen's way of thinking. She'd always wanted the pub to be a lot more toney than it was ever likely to be.

Ms Cosgrove – still to be just Kate to the gratified Doreen – always came in around twelve at weekends, when the locals began dropping in for a lunch-time drink.

'Hasn't forgotten us that knew her as a girl,' Doreen was forever pointing out. 'Could go to the Cavendish, couldn't she, but not her – still takes a proper interest in us all.'

Jim, less charitably, was inclined to think her proper interest was in their votes, and resented the free gins. She'd been weekending at the cottage for years before she showed up at the Three Tuns, just after she'd been selected for the seat. Funny, that.

Still, he was savvy enough to keep his opinion to himself. Doreen certainly wouldn't want to hear that he'd always thought there was something very calculating about Ms Cosgrove. He never felt comfortable calling her Kate.

When the phone rang, Jim looked up hopefully from his ticklish task under the bar towards his wife, but Doreen showed every sign of having developed selective deafness. Annie, meant to be setting tables, had edged over and was standing listening to the conversation, her mouth open.

He sighed, set down the plastic hose he'd been trying to connect, and went gloomily to take the call.

It was, as he had expected, one of Doreen's friends. At the other end Muriel Pook was in a state of such high excitement that she wouldn't even wait while he fetched his wife.

'I've other people to phone. Just tell her Abbie Bettison – Fenner as was – is at death's door in hospital, struck down in broad daylight in the Flitchford multi-storey! Now what do you think to that?'

Not even pausing for his reply, she went on, 'Tell Doreen I'll catch her later,' and rang off.

Feeling shaken, Jim put the phone down. It was unsettling,

that's what it was – not what you expected around here. Not at all.

He went slowly back into the bar. None of the women looked round; he cleared his throat.

'That was Muriel, Doreen.'

'Oh?' His wife, who would normally have treated such a call as top priority, waved it aside. 'Tell her I'll ring her back.'

'She just left a message. John Fenner's Abbie – she's been attacked in Flitchford – ever so poorly she is, in hospital.'

Annie gave a shriek of dismay, then burst into noisy tears. Doreen spun round and stared at him, slack-jawed. 'What?' she said stupidly.

'Oh no, how awful!' Kate's face was grave. 'That's terrible news! And she's got a young family too now, hasn't she? We were at school together, you know – I might phone her mother this afternoon and ask if there's anything I can do.'

Jim wasn't given to startling insights, but it came to him that this was why he didn't like her; she always had exactly the right response in every situation, and normal people didn't. Somehow that really put him off her, though after Annie had thrown an exaggerated fit of hysterics and wailed about there being a curse on Burlow, he did wonder if maybe he was being a bit harsh.

It took all Doreen's authority to quieten Annie and get her back to work, and by then people were drifting in. The story was circulating rapidly in Burlow, gathering details as it went, some presumably rather more accurate than others.

Ms Cosgrove stayed for about twenty minutes more; as he served drinks Jim saw her out of the corner of his eye moving round the groups, listening and talking soberly and shaking her head a lot. Perce Willis, who had arrived and taken up his usual perch in the corner, was recklessly ordering shorts in the expectation of another Press bonanza.

It was nearly two o'clock, however, before Eddie Jennings appeared. This was unusual; these days, with his wife gone with the kids back to her mother's, he'd been on the doormat with his tongue hanging out at opening time.

He looked as if he'd just got out of bed: unshaven and with

bloodshot eyes and a yellowish tinge to his complexion. As he eased himself on to a barstool, Jim stepped back involuntarily from the reek of stale alcohol on his breath.

It was the first duty of a landlord to be tactful, but Jim couldn't stop himself. 'Eddie, are you all right? You look terrible!'

Eddie gave him a darkling look, as if any other reaction would be too painful. He put down a five-pound note.

'Hair of the dog, that's what I need. And about three pints of water.'

Jim nodded, fetching the water first. 'Want an aspirin?' he asked sympathetically. 'And Scotch, is it?'

'Vodka. It's cleaner.' Eddie downed half a pint of water in one go, then set the pint mug down. 'And an aspirin wouldn't begin.'

'Bad as that?'

He grunted, holding out a hand that was shaking visibly. He looked at it, then at Jim. 'Got to stop this, don't I?'

'We-e-ell—'

He leaned closer across the counter, grabbing the other man's sleeve. 'Jim, as a mate, tell me something?'

He had lowered his voice; Jim braved his breath to lean forward and hear what he said. 'Sure, Eddie. What is it?'

'Do you reckon the dead come back?'

Taken aback, the landlord had no ready answer. Eddie muttered on, 'Really come back, I mean, like do things, like act on people?'

Jim cleared his throat. He was obviously in a bad way, was poor Eddie. 'No, can't say as I think they do. Course not. You know that, Eddie.'

The other's great shaggy head nodded slowly. 'That's what I reckon too. But there's sometimes it doesn't feel like that . . .' His voice tailed away.

'Maybe you should give the drink a rest,' Jim, ever a fool to himself, suggested. 'What about a nice tomato juice?'

'Vodka first.' Eddie was clear enough about that, at least. He took a cautious sip, shuddered, then lapsed into silence.

From the far end of the bar, Perce Willis, who had been an

interested spectator though out of earshot, chirruped, 'What about Abbie Bettison, then, Eddie?'

Eddie looked across at him with bleary loathing. 'What about her?'

'Not heard, then?'

'Look, Willis, do me a favour. I don't want to have to push your face in today, but I will if I have to.'

'Coshed in Flitchford, she was.' Undaunted, Perce paused to take an artistic sip of his fourth whisky. 'With a tyre lever, so they're saying. Funny that, isn't it? Makes you wonder who would have a tyre lever handy.'

The other man blinked at him, then shook his head as if to clear it, wincing at the pain. 'A tyre lever?'

'But you'd be at home with a hangover, wouldn't you?' Perce was enjoying himself.

'That true?' Eddie looked towards Jim for confirmation. 'Or is the stupid old git trying to wind me up? If he is—'

The landlord nodded. 'That's right, Eddie. Don't know if it's true, of course – you know what it's like around here – but that's what they're saying.'

He thought he would never forget the look of bleak despair on the other man's face.

Eddie hadn't even reached his house again when the police car drew up beside him. When they lifted him, he seemed almost apathetic. In reply to caution and charge, he said only, 'I never done it, but I'll get nailed any road.'

The arresting officers, to whom Eddie was no stranger, were unsympathetic, handcuffing him roughly and thrusting him into the police car with unnecessary force.

'Oops, did I bang your head?' asked one.

'Pity you couldn't have banged it with a tyre lever, sarge,' said the other. Eddie had to move his leg sharply to avoid having it slammed by the car door.

★

'A tyre lever?'

Over a mug of what passed for coffee in the police canteen, Tom Ward caught up with Alex Denholm, who had been checking out recent sales of tyre levers with suppliers, without any positive result.

'I hadn't heard that part,' Ward went on. 'Suggestive, wouldn't you say, when one of the people we've got our beady eye on runs a garage?'

Denholm gave him an old-fashioned look. '*Your* beady eye,' he pointed out. 'As far as everyone else is concerned it's a mugging—'

Hours spent grovelling on a concrete floor had not improved Ward's temper. 'And does no one see that it would save police time and public money, and just conceivably be a tad more productive, if we used our brains instead of our flat feet? Just what was achieved this morning by talking to dozens of people to establish that they didn't see anything? And this afternoon, I'm going to have to field calls from civic-minded members of the public who want someone to come and record the fact that they saw something totally irrelevant, or the ones who are several cards short of a full deck who want to confide either that they did it or it was Margaret Thatcher.'

'Or they noticed someone acting suspiciously, which might give us a lead,' Denholm said firmly. 'It's the normal method.'

'Oh yes,' Ward sneered, 'and wonderfully effective it is too. Have you looked at our clean-up rate lately? Says it all, I would say—'.

Denholm sighed. 'Tom, you're beginning to make a fool of yourself. You're running out of rope, you know that?'

Ward's face was mutinous. 'I'm only saying—'

The ringing of the mobile phone in his pocket interrupted him. His irritation spilling over, he snapped, 'Yes?'

He had no difficulty in recognising Juliette Darke's voice as she stammered, 'Oh – I'm sorry. Is this a bad time to call you? I'll ring back—'

'No, no,' he said hastily. 'Not at all. What can I do for you?'

'It's – it's a little complicated. Would there be any chance of meeting?'

'Yes, of course. Now, where? Do you have any suggestions?'

'Not here, and I haven't a car. Could you pick me up on the road out of Burlow, beyond our house? If you tell me when you're coming, I'll be there.'

Ward looked at his watch and made a rapid calculation. 'I could make it in about forty-five minutes, OK?'

Juliette sounded relieved. 'That's wonderful. I'll walk along the road until you come.'

Ward, switching off the phone, coloured under Denholm's questioning gaze.

'I thought you were to be here this afternoon, fielding calls.'

'Following up calls.' Ward was aware of sounding defensive. 'That was a call, and I'm going to follow it up.'

Denholm hesitated. 'That wasn't a call from a certain pretty suspect, by any chance, was it?'

'Oh, for God's sake—'

'Hear me out, Tom. You know I've never been an establishment man, leaping to the salute and washing Little's boots with my tongue if he stands still long enough, but there's a difference between being mildly insubordinate and asking to get yourself sacked. You know perfectly well it's crazy to get involved with her—'

'I'm not involved—'

Denholm went on as if he hadn't spoken, 'And it's affecting your judgement. I'm worried about you, because you're not even listening to what I'm saying. You're bright, Tom, but everyone else isn't a fool. I've been amused by you in the past, and I've been irritated, but this is the first time I've found myself trying to pick a quarrel, just to make you wake up to the risks you're taking. For some bizarre reason I care about what happens to you.'

Ward got up. 'I hear what you say. You're a good mate, Alex, and I'm not going to quarrel with you, whatever you say, and though you may find it hard to believe, I'm grateful. But I just can't stand by and watch the bleeding obvious being dangerously ignored any longer. And frankly, if they throw me out it won't break my heart. See you later.'

Ward was about half a mile past the Cartwright house, when he caught sight of Juliette walking up ahead. She glanced round as the couple of cars in front passed her, then as she saw him slowing down smiled and waved.

'I hadn't realised how much traffic there is now,' she said, climbing in. 'I had to take to the verge, and I was getting some funny looks too.'

'Where now?' he asked.

'It doesn't matter, as long as it's quiet.'

They were just coming to the signpost for the Long Moor. 'Up by the caves?' he suggested. 'If it wouldn't upset you.'

Juliette shrugged. 'No, that's fine.'

She clearly didn't want to tell him whatever it was piecemeal. He said, as they turned into the side road, 'That's a dreadful business about poor Abbie Bettison, isn't it?'

She hadn't heard. 'Abbie? What's happened?'

He told her; she listened intently, and when he glanced round he saw tears in her eyes.

'Oh poor, poor Abbie! And poor Sam, too – they're such a good pair. What a terrible thing to happen! Someone looking for money for drugs, do they think?'

'Not necessarily,' Ward said, and sensed her stiffen.

'You don't think – oh no, surely not!'

They had bumped up the walkers' path now. There were a couple of cars parked nearby, but no one to be seen.

'Let's go and sit on that boulder,' Ward suggested, pointing. She nodded, tight-lipped, and followed him.

Below them the slopes of the hills were patched with shadows of the passing clouds, and the indefinable scent of summer was in the air. The long straight stone walls dividing the fields looked like an oddly precise extension of the rocky outcrops marking out the less hospitable terrain above.

They sat down side by side. Ward said, 'Can we leave the

Abbie business for the moment? I haven't much time, and I take it there's something you want to talk about.'

'Of course.' With an obvious effort, she composed herself and began to explain about Jay's message. Then she took a piece of paper from her leather shoulder bag and held it out to him. She had beautiful hands, he noticed, and oval nails with deep moons at their base.

'I thought I should write it down while it was fresh in my mind,' she said, and he jerked himself back to considering the paper. 'That's not perfectly accurate, probably, but I don't think I've left out anything.'

He was puzzled by the opening; it was a well-known ancient text, she told him, Jay's invariable beginning to their meetings, just as 'A Neter to Death and Beyond' was their close. He read the record of posthumous persecution with revulsion and anger. Perhaps, as Dr Abbott had said, Jay had been unfortunate enough to have a mental condition, but it didn't excuse this. This was volitional, and he was a pernicious bastard.

'So you see,' Juliette said as he finished reading and looked up, 'it shows he was trying to frame Dad. And surely that suggests Jay was covering up for himself?'

She looked at him pleadingly.

'Hmmm. There's absolutely no trace of this message in your system?'

'No. It's obviously one of Jay's stunts – that was his job, making computers do things no one else had thought of. Maybe an expert might find some trace of the transmission—'

'But not of what it said?'

'I shouldn't think so.'

'So no proof.'

'But you believe me, don't you?' she cried.

'Yes, I do. But then, my colleagues would say I'm biased.' He smiled at her wryly, reluctant to say what he had to say next.

'And you see, in this –' he tapped the paper '– there is absolutely no hint that he killed Bonnie. He sounds to me, to tell you the truth, as if he's running through the list of suspects in his own mind – the pervert, the fraud, the sadist and the crook

– and giving Abbie some sort of hold over them.'

'So you think that Abbie's attacker—' Juliette had gone very pale.

'Let's put it this way – it wasn't Jay, was it?' He saw her wince, then added consolingly, 'Still, your father's in London so at least he's in the clear where this is concerned.'

She didn't say anything, and he looked at her sharply. 'Isn't he?'

She admitted reluctantly, 'He came home at half-past eleven.'

There was something else. He could feel it in his bones. 'There's something else you're not telling me,' he said.

She gasped. 'How do you know—' then stopped short.

He gripped her hand briefly. 'Juliette, if you ask me what I think, I don't think your father killed anyone. But if he did – *if* he did, you wouldn't shield him, would you?'

She hung her head. 'No,' she murmured.

'Then—'

'It's gossip, that's all, just gossip!' She was defiant now. 'Debbie's daily told her they're all saying my mother left my father because she knew what he had done to Bonnie. But how could they possibly know that?'

He was thinking. 'Surely your mother wouldn't go off leaving her daughter in the care of someone she knew to be a paedophile and a murderer?'

She winced at the word but seized the suggestion as if it had been a clear refutation.

'How stupid of me! Do you know, I never thought of that? Of course she wouldn't.'

'Perhaps your grandmother would know more about it. You could ask her – or better still, I could, officially—'

It was a step too far. She had withdrawn, shaking her head. 'I don't want to have Grandmère getting involved.'

'I promise I'd be tactful.'

'Tact is an entirely foreign concept to my grandmother. But she wouldn't speak to you, anyway. She hates the English.'

'I'd talk French.'

'No.' It was a flat refusal.

He was annoyed with himself. Inadvertently, he had reassured her of her father's innocence and she was undoubtedly shielding him now. From what, he wondered? Well, she certainly wasn't about to tell him.

He stood up. 'OK, don't worry about it. May I keep this?' He held up the transcript she had given him.

'Of course.' She was leading the way back to the car. The atmosphere was still awkward. As he turned the car he said, changing the subject and glancing towards the caves, 'I always thought it was incredibly brave of poor Bonnie to go by herself through the passages and across that huge cave with nothing but a pencil torch for light. I was spooked even with the best illumination the generators could produce.'

She looked at him blankly. 'Sorry? Oh, I see what you mean. No, she wouldn't have come from that end. There was a way in leading almost directly to the caves round Anubis's temple among some bushes there.' She gestured vaguely to the slope above them. 'It was our secret way in; a bush grew across it and you had to wriggle under to get in – I think it was Eddie who found it originally. For all I know it's blocked up now, but anyway when Bonnie was stalking us that's the way she would have come.'

He was intrigued. 'So you would all come in that way?'

'That's right. The moor road loops round below there, and when there was a Neters' meeting we'd ride up and hide our bikes in one of the thickets so that no one – well, mostly Bonnie, I suppose – would know we were there.'

'Did all of you come by bike?'

She considered. 'Most of us, I think, yes. Oh, not Kate – I don't think she had one. But everyone else.'

They were nearing the Cartwright's house. He pulled the car off the road into a convenient lane, and got out as she did.

'Just one final thing.' His trade mark.

Juliette pulled a face. 'The killer punch?' she said lightly.

'I hope not. It's just – I wondered if there was anything else you should tell me? I sort of had the impression last time that there was . . .'

Juliette looked at him with genuine puzzlement, then remembered. A tide of colour flooded her face. He waited, patiently.

'If – if there was something,' she said at last, 'something that didn't prove anything but might make matters worse if it was misinterpreted, would you have to deal with it officially?'

He knew he had to say yes. 'No,' he said.

Her smile was his reward. 'It was another of Jay's filthy little tricks. It wasn't a message on my lap-top – I told you the truth about that – but he had posted me a CD-Rom with a sort of crude scenario on it, like a preliminary sketch for one of his computer games, as another of his attempts to drive me to despair.

'It showed us in the cave and Dad following us and then coming back obviously having – well, assaulted Bonnie, and throwing down a rock.' She shuddered. 'It was horrible, so horrible! Jay was always brilliant at computer graphics, and he made it look as if that was what must have happened. It wasn't proof, but if you showed it to anyone . . .' Her voice tailed off.

'I take your point. It might be hard to prove that it was made up, not a description of something he'd seen.' He really ought to see it for himself sometime, of course, but he wasn't about to push his luck. For the moment it was enough that she had told him. 'Thank you for trusting me.'

'Thank you, too.' She smiled, an enchanting smile which lit up her whole face.

He looked down at her. 'Be very, very careful, won't you? Perhaps Abbie was just the victim of a casual mugger, but I don't think so.'

His hands went up, of their own accord, it seemed, to cup her face tenderly, and still smiling into his eyes, she didn't draw back. But as they stood there, in that moment out of time, Tom felt a sudden prickle of discomfort, as if they were being watched. He turned his head quickly, but apart from a couple of cars passing he could see no one.

Juliette looked at him, surprised, and he shrugged.

'I just thought I felt someone watching,' he said. 'Imagination, probably.'

She nodded, then gave him another of her glowing smiles before setting off along the road back to the house. He looked after her for a moment before getting back into the car.

Well, well, well – that was interesting, the driver of one of the passing cars thought. *Might even be useful, too – who knows?*

When Juliette got back into the house, the door to her father's study was standing open, and Harry and Debbie were in the hall engaged in some serious discussion. Harry was frowning and Debbie was fluttering at him nervously.

'If that's what Joe says, Harry, I'm sure he—' Then seeing Juliette she broke off and said with relief, 'Oh, here's Juliette. She'll know what you should do.'

'What about, Dad?' Juliette asked with a sinking heart.

Harry shifted uncomfortably. 'Well, Rickman says the Met are satisfied with my alibi for Tuesday night. That's the good news.'

'And the bad news?' she prompted.

'He says I should make a proper statement to the police about Bonnie. I'm not sure he's right.'

'*Bonnie?*' Her mission forgotten, Juliette stared at her father in horror.

Harry's scowl grew blacker. 'Don't look at me like that, girl! I'm not about to confess that I murdered her.'

'Harry, Harry! Juliette would *never* think that,' Debbie protested, and his daughter murmured, 'No, no, of course not,' a little self-consciously.

'The thing is,' Harry said reluctantly. 'I did give the wretched child a lift the day before she disappeared. Well, she was walking along the road there by herself – she'd some story about you kids running away from her – and I picked her up just like I would any other youngster. I took her home, and that was it, except that Bella wasn't exactly grateful.'

'But what was wrong with doing that?' His daughter was puzzled.

'Nothing, that's the point. But it didn't seem the smartest thing to mention to the police just now, with her mother accusing me of rape and murder – not that she actually started doing that till she went round the twist.

'To tell you the truth – well, I think she just had a grudge against me, and it all got confused. That's what Barry thinks.' He paused, then said, 'You might as well know – I'd taken her out a couple of times and she was fit to be tied when I dumped her for your mother, Juliette.'

The two women were as astonished by this admission as Rickman and Broughton had been earlier. 'You fancied *Mrs Bryant*?' Juliette asked in blank disbelief.

Harry went on the defensive. 'You only knew her after she'd let herself go. And you should have clocked the rest of the talent round here.'

'Harry! That's not nice,' Debbie scolded him.

Harry snorted. 'Anyway, that's beside the point. Do I tell the police, or not? Joe says I sounded evasive and it's better to give them the truth than having them sniff around thinking the worst.'

Juliette was firm. 'Dad, you're always better to level with the police – they'll probably find out anyway. Do what Joe says – tell them what you've told us. OK?'

He looked a little bemused by her decisiveness, as if he were seeing her for the first time as an adult – a competent, intelligent adult – instead of his little girl. 'Right, Juliette,' he said, almost humbly. 'Right. I'll do that.'

Then at last she was able to make her escape up to her bedroom. She had a lot to think about.

Chapter Nineteen

By half-past eight on Sunday morning, Tom Ward was at his desk in the CID room, moodily surveying the aftermath of yesterday's phonecalls.

He had blagged his way back in yesterday without questions being asked, and meekly taken a multitude of entirely pointless calls, creating a small mountain of notes which he would have to waste his time typing up so some other poor beggar could waste his time reading them.

By Saturday evening, there had been a pervading atmosphere of gloom; the latest hospital report suggested Abbie Bettison was deteriorating, and for all the interviews and legwork they hadn't a single solid lead.

Ward flicked through the pile distastefully. There was so much he could usefully be doing, if only he could get authorisation. He'd been going to try again to nobble Broughton, but the only time he'd seen him, he was with Little. He hadn't yet found the brass neck to go to the office and bend his ear – though it might come to that, if this dragged on much longer. Irritably he began typing up the first report.

It wasn't enough to occupy his mind. As eyes and hands worked mechanically, he found himself thinking once more about Juliette. Whatever Alex might say, he didn't question her innocence, and yesterday, as far as he was concerned, was still further proof.

It was awkward, though, that she wouldn't let him phone her

grandmother. What was she afraid of – that a spiteful mother-in-law might deliberately make things worse for Harry?

Not that he had to be bound by her wishes, of course. Juliette had told him where she lived, near Limoges somewhere. Ambys! The name popped into his head, and he stopped typing, staring straight ahead, eyes narrowed in concentration.

She'd mentioned her grandmother's name, too. What was it again? Grandmère – Grandmère something . . .

It wouldn't come. You could hardly phone directory enquiries and ask for Mme Something, Ambys. He went back to his task.

The next call he was typing up ran to two pages of notes. It had actually gone on longer than that, but he had realised that the caller was just going back and starting all over again. He had scrawled, amusingly as he had thought, '*Reprise*', and then doodled instead of taking down anything more. He couldn't remember why he'd thought it was so witty – brain damage due to terminal boredom, probably – but there certainly was some pretty fancy artwork.

Daubigny! Suddenly the name came to him. He'd thought of the artist when Juliette said it.

She might not want him to phone her grandmother, but if what she said knocked the rumour on the head Juliette would be pleased enough. And if it didn't – well, in that event what she felt couldn't be allowed to matter, could it?

The other detective on early shift had just gone out. Ward picked up the phone and dialled directory enquiries.

Elise Daubigny's voice when she answered the phone was brusque, as if a call was an unwarranted intrusion on her busy life. Ward announced himself in French, first and a little disingenuously as a friend of Juliette's; she sounded merely indifferent until he explained that he was also English, and a policeman.

'You are English?' There was disbelief in her tone. 'You have then, perhaps, a French mother?'

'No,' he explained patiently, 'only a love of the language and the country,' but it did nothing to placate her.

'Why would I want to speak to an Englishman?' Centuries

of French contempt were in her voice as she snarled '*Anglais*', and he was afraid she would slam the phone down. But then she hesitated, her voice sharpening with anxiety. 'Did you say – a policeman? Why should an English policeman want to speak to me? Oh, not Juliette—'

He was quick to reassure her. 'No, no, there's nothing wrong with Juliette. It's just a minor enquiry about her father, Harry Cartwright.'

'*Bah!*' She spat the French expletive down the phone. '*Mon beau-fils – l'assassin!*'

'My son-in-law, the murderer!' As she said it Ward felt his stomach lurch. He had not expected so direct an accusation. Poor Juliette! 'Murderer?' he echoed hollowly.

'Yes, murderer!' Her voice rang with passionate anger as she repeated the word. 'He killed my daughter, Marguérite.'

'But I thought—'

She cut across him. 'So are you all, all murderers! What did my parents do, living peacefully in Limoges, to have your wicked English bombs destroy their house, kill them? Leave me alone – I do not talk to murderers.'

It took him a moment to grasp what she was saying. 'Please don't cut me off, Madame – I'm trying to help Juliette. When you say that he killed your daughter—'

There was a silence, as if she were weighing up what he had said. Then she went on heavily, as if reluctantly forced to reopen painful, ancient wounds. 'She comes home sick, sick from a broken heart.'

'Why did she leave her husband and child?'

There was venom in her tone. 'She leaves him because there are other women. He does not understand her refinement, her delicacy. He is coarse, a brute! So when she becomes ill, she wants to die in the care of her mother, who goes on loving her, however foolish she may have been.'

He was sure she would hate to know that he had heard her stifled sob. 'And – Juliette?' he asked softly.

'She leaves Juliette with her father because she is a saint, an angel. They have told her that her time on earth is not long, and the little one is better with her father than watching her beloved mother die. But this too – this breaks her heart.'

'She must have been a very loving and unselfish mother.'

'Do I need an Englishman to tell me that?'

She had her protective armour well in place once more. Ward smiled. 'Of course not. Thank you, Madame, for your so great kindness in speaking to me. It's been very helpful.'

'I do not like to help the English.' Again there was the pause, then she said, as if compelled, very much against her will, to be fair, 'But you say you are Juliette's friend, and perhaps, since you speak good French, you are not so bad.'

'*Merci du compliment*,' he said, laughing, and rang off.

Had Juliette been used to hearing her father described as a murderer, and with recent events begun to wonder if it was for a more sinister reason than a mother's prejudice against the man who had made her daughter so unhappy? His impulse was to phone her immediately, but other officers had arrived now and were working at their desks. It would have to wait.

It was about half an hour later that his mobile phone rang. 'This is Jason Digby, *Midland Star*,' a young voice announced importantly.

Startled that a journalist should be calling on this number, Ward started to refer him to the press officer, but was interrupted impatiently.

'No, no. Miss Grattan told me to do some research for you.'

'Oh right, right! I'm sorry. Have you got something for me?'

'Might have. First of all I checked out Juliette Darke, but she seems clean. Do you want the gen? A levels—'

The boy was clearly determined to milk it for all it was worth. 'No, I only want to know about anything that doesn't seem to add up.'

'Right. That's what I was looking for. Then I did Eddie Jennings – well, he's got a criminal record, as you probably know – joyriding in 'eighty five, bound over in 'eighty six—'

He seemed to be planning to read out all of Eddie's previous, which could take some time. 'We know all about that. Anything else?'

'Not about him, no. But then I did come up with something interesting.'

Waiting for the drum-roll was he? 'Yes?' Ward prompted impatiently.

'Barry Bryant. I got his CV from our files at the time he was appointed headmaster, then ran a check. He claims to have a B.Ed. from the University of Taunton, but I've accessed their graduate rolls and he doesn't feature.'

Ward sat up straight. 'Doesn't he, indeed! That's interesting. That's very interesting. You've done a good job there, lad. And what about Cartwright and Cosgrove?'

'Give me a break! I've been up half the night at the computer just sorting out these three. Miss Grattan said to phone you at once if I struck pay-dirt.'

'Sure. You've done a great job. Keep digging.'

Ward switched off the phone and sank back down in his chair. Bryant! He'd been the logical choice all along, and if he had something like this to conceal—'

There was still a pile of irrelevant bumf on his desk, awaiting his attention. It was unappetising, to say the least, compared to the gourmet morsel of information he had just been offered. No contest, really.

He got up, picked up a sheet of notes at random and waved it at the officer working at the next desk.

'Something I ought to follow up,' he said.

The other man looked up indifferently from his machine and grunted.

Five minutes later, Tom Ward was once again on the road to Burlow.

'I wanted to give you this.'

Sam Bettison, unshaven, drawn, eyes red-rimmed from grief and dull from lack of sleep, held out a slim perspex box to Superintendent Broughton.

Broughton had come to the hospital for the latest report on Abbie Bettison's condition. She had held her own throughout the night, the sister told him as they stood together in the tense, hushed atmosphere of the Intensive Care unit. Through the glass walls of her cubicle they could see Abbie's still form, attached to wires and tubes leading to a series of monitors and drips.

Sam had been at his wife's bedside, holding her unresponsive hand; he looked up at their approach and recognising the policeman whom he had met yesterday he got up and came out.

Glancing at the box, Broughton could see the shiny silver of a CD-Rom.

'When I went home last night to fetch some things,' Sam explained, 'I found this in one of Abbie's drawers. You see, it's got this weird message written on it – I don't know what on earth it means. Abbie didn't say a word about it to me, and that's not like her. And we don't even have a computer. Maybe it hasn't anything to do with this, but I just thought—'

'Of course.' Broughton took it and glanced at the inscription. 'Odd, certainly. As you say, it may not be relevant – could be some silly advertising stunt, for instance – but it's the simplest thing in the world to take a look. I do promise you we're leaving no stone unturned to find whoever did this.' He looked sympathetically at the young man's ravaged face.

Tears stood in Sam's eyes. 'Thanks,' was all he said, and walking like an old man he went back to his wife's bedside, taking her hand again and bending over to talk earnestly to her, just as if she were listening.

Watching him, Sister sighed. 'Such a lovely family. It almost makes you believe there is a power of evil working in the world.'

'Will she make it?'

'Well, Superintendent, I'd put it this way – if you're a praying man don't wait till bedtime to start.'

'I've started already,' Broughton said, and left, putting the box safely into his pocket. There was a case conference he was scheduled to go to now, but after that he'd make time to get it checked out.

★

Barry Bryant appeared mildly surprised to see Tom Ward on his doorstep. He was casually dressed in tracksuit bottoms, trainers and a sweatshirt, and he was still looking strained, though less exhausted than he had been on Wednesday afternoon.

'Oh, sergeant,' he said. 'Good morning! Do you want to come in?'

Ward followed him into the dark front room where they had talked before. It was a mild enough day, but the sky was overcast and there was a lamp on beside the fireplace where the electric fire glowed. A Sunday newspaper lay on the floor, as if dropped there when the doorbell went, and a mug of coffee stood on a table by one of the chairs.

'Coffee for you?' Bryant offered, but Ward shook his head.

'I'll try not to take up too much of your Sunday morning. It's just that something rather curious has come up, and I thought you might be able to help me.'

'Curious?' Bryant's expression became guarded. 'What does that mean?'

'May I ask you what your qualifications are?'

'Well, yes, of course – but it's a matter of record with the education department. I have a Bachelor of Education degree from the University of Taunton.'

'Do you have documentary evidence of that?'

Bryant stared at him. 'Well, naturally! You don't imagine you can wander in off the streets and say you have a first from Oxford and be taken at your word, do you? Do you want to see the certificate?'

'If you wouldn't mind, sir.'

There was a stack of box-files at one end of the desk; Bryant went over and ran his fingers down the spines, squinting at the labels, and then pulled one out.

'It'll be somewhere in here,' he said, sitting down with it on his knee.

'I admire your efficiency.' Ward watched him riffle through the contents. 'I haven't the first idea where mine is.'

'I had to learn the hard way that I couldn't cope otherwise. Ah! Here it is!' He held up a sheet of thick creamy paper with a coloured crest at the top and passed it over to Ward.

He scrutinised it carefully, and it certainly looked authentic enough. It had the university's name below the crest and began, 'I hereby certify that BARRY BRYANT was admitted to the degree of BACHELOR of EDUCATION on 27 June 1991.' It was signed by the Academic Registrar and the Registrar's Clerk.

'Right,' Ward said. 'The only thing is, there isn't any record of this in the graduate rolls of the university.'

Bryant looked bemused. '*What?*' he said blankly.

'I've been checking out the backgrounds of all the Neters – just informally, you understand,' Ward felt obliged to explain. 'Your name doesn't appear anywhere.'

'But I don't get it—' Then he broke off. 'Oh God! Oh my God – how did you check? On the Net?'

Ward nodded.

'That sodding bastard!' Bryant leapt up and went over to his own PC. 'I want to see this for myself,' he fretted, waiting for his server to connect. When the search box appeared, he typed in 'University of Taunton'.

A minute later he was scanning the lists with feverish haste. Ward glanced over his shoulder, hoping that Kay's lad hadn't made a mistake, but no: there was no Barry Bryant in the B.Ed. lists for 1991.

When Bryant turned round from the keyboard he was shaking. 'You're not going to believe me, are you? No one's going to believe me. Jay Darke has simply wiped out my quali-fication to teach, and that's all I care about.'

He sank into his chair again, his head in his hands. 'He threat-ened me, you know. These last few days it's been like waiting for the other shoe to fall.' The words poured out. 'When we went to Grammar School, after Bonnie died and the Neters broke up, I wouldn't let him push me around any more. He persecuted me there – all sorts of petty nastinesses like spoiled work and lost books – but the staff were good and always made allowances. But he told me then he never forgave betrayal and one day I'd pay.

'Naturally enough I forgot all about it until I got this strange,

threatening e-mail saying that his vengeance was at hand. I'd no
idea what it would be – it's been dreadful.'

'You don't still have it, do you?' Ward interposed eagerly.

'No, I deleted it. By the time I'd accessed it fifteen times I
decided it was becoming a neurosis.'

'Right.' Ward got up, his mind racing. It all sounded
authentic Jay Darke, though of course they'd have to run further
checks later. 'Thanks for your help, sir.'

'But hang on – where does this leave me?'

'Presumably the university keeps printed records,' Ward
pointed out. 'You can contact the Registrar's office and get yourself reinstated.'

'Of course. Stupid of me.'

'Though I suppose they may be closed for the summer. Still,
it's unlikely that your employers will suddenly be inspired to
check out your qualifications in the middle of the school holidays.'

Bryant sighed. 'Unless he's e-mailed them as well,' he said
gloomily.

'Surely there's a limit even to Jay Darke's mischief-making?'

'Oh no, sergeant.' The man's expression was grim. 'Oh no.
That is where you are wrong. There is no limit to his evil, this
side of the grave – or beyond.'

Driving through Burlow, Ward noted with surprise that the
workshop doors at Eddie Jennings' garage were open, and on an
impulse he turned in and parked.

There was a car inside with its bonnet up, but there was no
sign of the man himself, or indeed of anyone else. Ward got out
of his car and peered into the workshop interior. The car that
was being worked on was at one side; at the other there was a
tyre repair section. He wandered over to look.

There were open boxes with tools casually stowed inside
along one wall, and in the box nearest to the stack of tyres he
could see at a cursory glance no fewer than three tyre levers.
He picked one up, hefted it thoughtfully in his hand and then
put it back.

He was on his way out again when he saw a youth in dirty overalls coming towards him from the office, a mug in one grimy hand, who glanced at Ward incuriously.

'Wanting something, then?' he said. 'Boss i'nt here today. T'i'nt rightly open, see – this 're a special rush job for a customer.'

'No, not really,' Ward said. 'Tell me, is it always this easy to walk into your workshop?'

The lad stared at him, then shrugged. 'You could say.'

'Isn't your boss worried about theft?'

'What're to take? 'Cept a car or a tyre maybe. And even her in there –' he jerked his head at the girl at the petrol till, 'might see that.' He went back to his task.

Ward got back into his car. Eddie Jennings wasn't the only person who could lay hands on a tyre lever, was he – indeed, you might be pardoned for thinking that the choice of a tyre lever might be precisely intended to divert suspicion his way.

DCI Brian Little came into the CID room, his face black with fury, and looked about.

'Where's Ward?' he snarled.

The officer who had been working at the next-door desk glanced up. 'He went out about a quarter of an hour ago, sir – checking up on something that came in yesterday, I think he said.'

DS Denholm was unfortunate enough to choose that moment to come in, and Little rounded on him.

'Denholm! Do you know where your sidekick Ward is?'

'No sir.'

'The Super wants him.' He paused, then prompted by a raging sense of injustice, went on, 'They've found a print on the tyre lever that matches Eddie Jennings', and they're bringing him in, but would the Super believe me when I pointed out that it's a natural criminal progression? Oh no! *He* has to take the notion that it's something to do with this Bonnie Bryant business that Ward's been giving himself airs about.'

Well, blow me, don't tell me the jammy devil's going to be proved right all along! Denholm thought, but said, 'I could try to contact him on his mobile, sir. I have the number.'

'Do that small thing, sergeant, and tell him to get himself back here PDQ. And he'd better have a solid reason for not being at his desk.'

'Oh, I'm sure he will, sir.' *When hasn't he?*

'You know something about it too, don't you? You'd better go up and explain to the Super. Keep him happy till your little chum gets here.'

Little went out, and Denholm dialled Ward's number. 'A word to the wise,' he began, and was relieved to be told Ward was already on his way back, though the traffic was slow as usual on a Sunday afternoon.

At the charge bar, Eddie Jennings agreed listlessly that he wanted to summon his solicitor, but refused the suggestion of the charge sergeant – a kindly man – that he should call his wife.

'Won't care, will she?' he said bitterly. 'She's at her mother's, and the old bitch always had it in for me.'

When his solicitor arrived, a man whose pleas in mitigation on Eddie's behalf were in the trade considered exemplars of that black art, he insisted that Sue be told.

'She's stuck by you all these years, Eddie,' he pointed out. 'She's a good wife, Sue, and believe me, you're going to need her. I'll phone her myself once I've finished up here.'

Sue, informed of her husband's arrest, was at first resigned and then, when she heard the charge, appalled.

'He couldn't of!' she protested, near to tears. 'Abbie's a lovely girl.'

'He swears he didn't, Sue. He's very down – says he had a hangover and was asleep till lunch time yesterday.'

'Well, that's no surprise. I went in, had to pick up clothes for me and the kids. And he were in his bed, snoring like a hog. Never so much as twitched.'

'What did you say? Sue, that's important. It was in the morning Abbie Bettison was attacked. What time did you go in?'

'After ten, or thereabouts. I were there for quite a bit, watering plants and such. Never think to notice they was shrivelling up, would he?'

'So you could tell the police that?'

There was no doubt she was relieved, but her tone was deliberately off-hand. 'Suppose so. Don't want the daft bugger locked up again, do I?'

The solicitor cleared his throat delicately. 'I'm not entirely sure it's as simple as that. The police have indicated there may be a number of other matters he could help them with.'

She sighed. 'Never should of married him, should I, just because I were up the spout. Jason would be just as well without a dad, for all he sees of him.'

When Tom Ward walked into the hall of the Flitchford headquarters, the desk sergeant called him over.

'The switchboard passed through a message. The caller said it was urgent.' He glanced down at a note lying on the desk and read out, '"Mrs Juliette Darke wanted you to know that she had sent you an e-mail."'

'That's the message?'

The sergeant nodded, 'Urgent, apparently.'

'That's odd. Thanks anyway.'

Ward headed for the CID room. There were files he needed for the Super, and he could collect Juliette's e-mail on the way. Strange that she should send an urgent e-mail instead of just phoning him.

Three other officers told him he was wanted by the Super and that Denholm was there already.

'Sure, sure,' he said, going to his desk. While he waited for access, he hastily shuffled together the notes he needed. At last Broughton seemed to have accepted the connection – better late than never.

'Come on, come on,' he muttered under his breath; at last the e-mail list appeared, with one entry which had Burlow something in the address. He clicked on it impatiently.

'*Tom,*' it read. '*The most wonderful thing! There's absolute proof my father's innocent, but I have to go to the caves immediately to be shown it. By tonight I'll have cleared his name. With love, Juliette.*'

His immediate reaction was a blind fury that she could possibly have been so naïve as to fall into such a blatant trap, then rage was swallowed up in a disabling terror he had never experienced before. In the vaults of those caves, in the darkness and the silence, what might happen to her, with no one to hear her cries? And afterwards – he thought of the gaping holes and pits where a body might lie undiscovered for ever, and realised what it meant to say your blood ran cold.

No wonder she hadn't phoned! She would know bloody well that he would forbid her to go, or anyway to go alone. At least she had had the sense to tell him where she was even if – he looked at the time record – it might be already too late. It was nearly three-quarters of an hour since she had sent this, and even on foot she'd have reached the caves by now, where a murderer would be lying in wait for her. Juliette's delicate features, transfigured by that glowing smile, came up before his eyes and it was all he could do not to groan aloud.

He had to go at once. There was at least a chance that he might reach her before – he shied away from the thought.

He'd been ordered upstairs, but if he had to explain, convince, it would take up time he dare not lose. In his panic fear for Juliette he could only think that he must get out of the place before anyone stopped him.

He wasn't fool enough, though, to think it would be smart to try to handle this unaided. Once he'd made his escape he'd want all the back-up they'd give him. Phone Alex once he was on the way – that was the answer.

Ward cleared his screen, grabbed the files and went out. He thrust them at the desk sergeant as he hurried through the hall.

'Could you see the Super gets these? I've been called to an emergency.'

He was out of the door before the sergeant could say, 'Fine.'

Chapter Twenty

Superintendent Broughton was getting impatient. 'Didn't you say Ward was on his way back here?' he demanded of DS Denholm, sitting nervously opposite.

'The traffic was heavy, apparently, but he should be here by now,' Denholm said, just as there was a knock on the door and a WPC came in with files which she laid on the desk.

'DS Ward asked that these should be brought up to you, sir.' She was turning to go when Broughton called her back.

'Constable! Are you telling me DS Ward is in the building?'

'No, sir. He went out about five minutes ago. He said you wanted the files.'

'I see. Thank you.'

Broughton turned to Denholm. It wasn't often he lost his temper, but when he did somewhere else was a good place to be. Denholm broke into a light sweat, transfixed by the gimlet eyes behind the spectacles.

'Perhaps you're in a position to suggest what the blazes your friend thinks he's playing at.'

Fighting the disloyal temptation to say, 'Friend – what friend?' Denholm was muttering, 'I'm afraid I've no idea—' when the mobile in his pocket bleeped. He hesitated, then at a brusque nod from Broughton took the call.

'Tom! Where on earth are you?' he exclaimed.

He listened, then forgetting his company, cried in dismay, 'For God's sake, Tom, don't be a bloody fool! Don't you see

– she could be laying a trap for you! Have you gone mad?'

Again he listened, then said, 'Well, it's not up to me, but I'll ask. But Tom, don't switch off—'

He found himself talking to a dead line and switched off himself, looking stunned.

'Well?' Broughton demanded.

'Well, sir,' Denholm swallowed 'I'm afraid he's not – well, he's kind of lost the plot where Mrs Darke is concerned. She's – she's a very attractive woman . . .'

'And?'

'And she's sent him an e-mail saying that some unnamed person's meeting her in the caves to show her some sort of proof that her father's innocent.'

'Sounds a pretty fishy story to me.'

'That's what I said, sir, but he's not rational about her. I'm just afraid he could be walking into some sort of ambush that the girl and her father have set up. He's on his way to the caves now – he's asking for back-up.'

Broughton sighed. 'Then I suppose we have to send a car, tempting though it is to let the arrogant young idiot— Come!'

The knock on the door heralded the arrival of a uniformed sergeant, looking shocked.

'Sorry to interrupt, sir, but I felt you should know about this without delay. We've been checking out the CD-Rom you gave us that was in Mrs Bettison's possession. The contents are very disturbing.'

Both men followed him back to the office where he had been working and gathered round the computer desk in the corner. There on the screen was Abbie's poisoned legacy from Jay Darke.

They read the allegation that Barry Bryant was a confidence trickster who had lied about having a degree. There was a list of dates and places of crimes committed in the locality, with names attached, to be found, according to this, in Eddie Jennings' computer. And there, most horribly of all, were copies of a series of polaroid pictures of maimed and executed animals. '*Kate keeps these in her computer so she can have a peek at them to cheer herself up when she feels down,*' the accompanying text read. '*She thought up the sacrifice idea and then she got hooked. Nice sort of hobby for an MP, don't you think?'*

The men stared at the screen in stunned silence. Looking at the photographs – rabbits, birds, a cat – Denholm felt sick.

'Get rid of it,' Broughton said testily, clearly feeling the same, and the screen went mercifully blank.

'Well,' he went on, taking a deep breath, 'where do we go from here? How much of this does Ward know, do you suppose? Give him a call, Alex—'

Denholm shook his head. 'No use. He was switching the mobile off.'

'Hmm.' Broughton's expression was darker than ever. 'As if things weren't difficult enough at the moment, without insubordinate officers making matters worse. He's gone too far this time, Alex.'

Denholm tried desperately to think of something he could say to excuse the inexcusable, but nothing came to mind.

'Yes, sir,' he said gloomily.

Broughton sighed. 'I suppose we'd better make a start by establishing whether anyone knows the woman's whereabouts.' He picked up the phone on his desk and a minute later was speaking to Debbie Cartwright.

'Juliette? She's upstairs in her room, I think. Do you want to speak to her?'

'If she's there.'

Broughton raised his brows, holding out the phone so that Denholm could hear Debbie call 'Juliette! Juliette!'

Then a second later, Juliette's voice. 'Hello?'

They were both taken aback that she was there. No, she told Broughton, she hadn't sent any e-mail to DS Ward. She hadn't spoken to him since yesterday. No, she had not told him she was going to the caves. Why ever should they think she had?

Broughton made some anodyne reply and put the phone down. 'You know what's happened, Alex? Someone knows Tom's involved with the girl, and they've used her as bait to get him rushing to the rescue. Who said there's no fool like a clever man? Well, he'll have to face the music later, if his suicide bid doesn't succeed. But for the moment—'

'There's a grid across the entrance,' Denholm recalled suddenly. 'You can't get in without a key. It's kept at the farmhouse there – maybe we could stop them giving it to him.'

It took some time to track down the number.

'Oh,' said the farmer's wife, 'I'm ever so sorry. Sergeant Ward collected the key a few minutes ago.'

'Are there any other keys, Mrs Hunter?' Broughton asked.

'Just the one hanging behind the door here.'

'Then I wonder – is your husband about? I'd be grateful if he could go out immediately and see no one follows DS Ward – lock the grid behind him, in fact. Thanks very much. We'll have someone there shortly.'

Broughton put the phone down. 'Well, at least we know the caves were locked until he got there, so with the grid locked again he'll be safe enough. And we can probably get a car there shortly to fetch him out and bring him back to explain himself.'

'Sir, may I go? I know the layout of the place.' Denholm was not altogether hopeful that he would get permission, but in his present state of anxiety he almost felt he'd do a Tom Ward and take matters into his own hands if he didn't.

Broughton considered. 'I'm inclined to say no – we've enough to do here without squandering more manpower. But I suppose it might save time in the long run. OK, Alex.'

Denholm departed like a dog released from its leash by its master.

Bewildered, Juliette put down the phone after her conversation with Superintendent Broughton, and sitting on her bed tried to make sense of the questions he had asked.

What on earth was all that about the caves, and why ever should they think she had sent Tom an e-mail?

E-mail! Suddenly the hairs rose on the back of her neck. It stank of Jay to her; what had he done now? Had he persuaded Tom to go to the caves, thinking she was there, in danger?

But how could he know about Tom Ward, and what could be the point of sending him to the caves? It was inexplicable – unless he truly possessed the supernatural powers he believed death would bestow on him.

Had he been watching her – was he watching her now, leaving her no privacy even in the recesses of her mind? And what depraved and evil creature was stalking the caves and passages dedicated with the unholy vows of children and the blood of innocent beasts to the carrion-eating jackal god?

In the grip of unreasoning terror she jumped to her feet and ran downstairs to borrow Debbie's car.

As Tom Ward opened the iron gate, the grating of the key in the lock and the clang of iron on stone as it swung back rang eerily down the passageway, the sound travelling as if rock spoke to rock. A breeze like a breath touched his face, bringing with it the miasma of stale, damp air. Ahead, the passage gaped like an open mouth, light penetrating only a short distance down the throat before being swallowed up in darkness.

He switched on his heavy-duty rubber torch, standard police issue, and stepped inside. God, it was dark! Around the brave beam of light, the blackness was dense as velvet. What sounds there were – the trickle of water, the noise of his own footfalls and his breathing – suggested pebbles dropping into an ocean of silence.

He had been walking as quickly as he safely could for about five minutes when from down the passage behind him suddenly came, echo-warped, the unmistakable sound of the entrance gate clanging shut. He stopped in his tracks, aghast, listening intently. Surely whoever had lured poor, trusting Juliette to the caves would be party to the secret of the Neters' entrance; was it possible, instead, that someone had been lurking outside, waiting for him?

Suppose Alex was right – suppose his fear for Juliette had completely distorted his judgement? Could someone have known he cared enough about Juliette to dash instantly, idiotically to her rescue? *Harry Cartwright*, he thought. *He could have known* . . .

If that was so, Juliette was presumably safe and danger lay behind and not ahead of him. But there was still the nagging doubt – how could he be sure? If he was wrong, if she was there, deep in the caves . . .

He simply could not risk turning back, and in any case, keeping out of trouble was smarter than confrontation. He pressed on until he reached the Cathedral cave and crossed it quickly, barely noticing its splendours. Only then did he pause to glance back over his shoulder and strain his ears, without success, for any telltale light or sound. Nothing.

He climbed quickly and neatly up the giant's staircase; once he was behind the calcite screen he knew he was out of sight of any pursuit. Now he must choose a suitable hiding-place from among the mouths of caves and passageways which yawned on either side. Tom flickered the torch across them.

He had come to the point where several passages met, a wide flat area just beside the crevice where they had found the Anubis figure, opposite the passage where animal bones had been found. The Neters' entrance must come in somewhere near here; he listened intently, but there was no sound other than the eternal murmuring and dripping of water. No cries for help, no demand for a heroic rescue . . .

So he had made a complete fool of himself, after all. He had scorned Alex's warnings, and he had walked into a trap which was so pathetic that he had been furious to think that Juliette should have fallen for it – yet another arrogant assumption. Now all he could do was keep himself out of trouble and wait for a patrol to come to rescue him, always supposing Alex had managed to galvanise them. Yes, it was humiliating; yes, it was probably the end of his police career, but right now he'd settle for that if it meant getting safely back up to daylight again.

His pursuer must be closing on him now. Hurriedly he flicked the torch about again –

The attack came from in front of him, to the right. Feeling the rush of air, he swung round, but taken at a disadvantage he was too late. A rock smashed onto his right wrist so that he dropped his torch, and a second later a violent push threw him off balance so that he staggered, caught his foot on a projection and fell hard against the side of the passage, hitting his head. The head-blow was painful though not disabling, but his right hand was useless and shafts of agony were shooting up his arm. The torch had gone out and darkness fell about him like a blanket thrown over his head. He struggled to his feet, but he was disorientated, with no idea of which way he was facing, nor had he any idea where his assailant was now.

Suddenly, shockingly in this silent place, laughter rang out, peal upon peal of high-pitched, theatrical laughter amplified by the space to a chorus of shrieking devils. Tom cringed back against the rock face under the sound.

At last it stopped and the echoes faded. Pain turned him almost sick, but he strained his ears. Was that someone else's breathing, or only the breath sobbing in his own throat?

He could give nothing away by speaking. 'Who's there?' he challenged, and the mimicking repetitions provided a defiant chorus.

It was a whisper which answered, a loud whisper, the sound blurred and amplified by more whispering echoes. 'I am Osiris, who have brought you here to the Kingdom of the Dead.'

Clinging desperately to reason, Tom told himself that it was not a dead man who spoke. It was someone who had come in by that other entrance, someone who had been waiting here at the dark heart of ancient evil. Which meant that—

'Juliette!' he yelled at the top of his voice, terror-stricken. 'Juliette!'

'Juliette-ette-ette Juliette-ette-ette-ette . . .'

The despairing cry faded at last, and then there was only silence and darkness and fear.

'I have taken it upon myself,' DCI Little grandly informed WPC Matthews as they drove to Burlow, 'to break the news to Ms Cosgrove. It's a kid-gloves job, you see. Needs a delicate touch.'

'Yes, sir,' Jenny Matthews agreed politely, keeping to herself the belief that if Kate Cosgrove wasn't likely to be their next MP and in addition a very attractive woman her lacerated feelings would have had to lump it.

'Not everyone would understand the shock,' he explained. 'For a lady like her to have a scumbag like Darke plant pictures like that on her, blackening her name— Well, it'll be a shock, I can tell you.'

'Yes, sir,' Jenny said again. She wasn't anything like as sure as he seemed to be that sadism would give Ms Cosgrove a fit of the vapours. Men always seemed to fall for her, but in Jenny's private opinion she was a hard-faced, toffee-nosed cow.

You couldn't fault her PR though, she thought ruefully, having managed to please no one in her own PR role over these past few days. There Cosgrove was, at every police charity do, seeing to it that she charmed everyone who mattered, even if she felt she could safely ignore a humble WPC as she jumped the queue in the Ladies'.

She certainly had Little eating out of her hand. He was rumbling on, 'Disgusting, I call it. Just as well the bastard's dead – suicide was too good for him.'

A niggling concern for justice prompted Jenny to say bravely, 'But it's funny, isn't it, what he said about Eddie Jennings? Sergeant Crozier said all the dates check out.'

Little turned his head to glare at her. 'Well, Jennings, of course. That's different.'

She wasn't that brave. She subsided.

Little went on with the attack. 'And what about all that rubbish about Barry Bryant? I was on the school board when he was appointed – do you think we just took his word? And are you really suggesting –' he was working himself up into a lather of indignation '– that *Kate Cosgrove* – a parliamentary candidate, mark you, as well as a partner in a distinguished firm of solicitors – would have anything to do with filth like that? I'm astonished at you, Matthews, I really am. Have you *seen* those pictures?'

Sinking further down in her seat, Jenny murmured that she had. She didn't want to think about them; she had a vivid imagination and was subject to nightmares.

She sat up again as they reached Burlow, checking the directions they'd been given for finding Cosgrove's cottage on the outskirts of the town.

'There it is,' Jenny said, spotting the long hedge they'd been told to look out for. Little swung the car in at the smartly painted white gate.

'Very nice,' he said approvingly as they drew up outside the pretty, extended cottage. There was a conservatory at one end, elegantly furnished with modern, pale wood chairs, low tables and a small jungle of expensive ferns.

'No car,' Jenny pointed out as they went to the door. 'And no garage.'

'Hmm.' Little scowled. He'd taken a risk, driving all this way; she hadn't been in when he phoned earlier, but he'd promised himself that he would be the one to receive her grateful thanks for his sympathetic and discreet handling of this distasteful affair. And Janine would be impressed – not to mention her sister Moira – when the invitations came to have drinks with an MP.

He rang the doorbell as if the force he put into it could somehow compel her presence.

There was no answer. He tried again, then in a sour mood returned to the car.

WPC Matthews followed him, sighing. It was a long way back to Flitchford.

'Where – is – she?' Tom Ward spoke the words into the anonymous dark, his teeth gritted against the pain as he cradled his useless hand.

'I saw you together. I knew you would be foolish as well as fond. But she's not here, not here.' The whisper sounded close at hand – or was that another trick of the acoustics? 'Just you, and Osiris, and hungry Anubis.'

Despite the dank cold, Tom felt sweat break out on his brow. The claustrophobic atmosphere, which he had barely noticed before in his fears for Juliette, was beginning to feel alarmingly oppressive. *Don't panic*, he told himself fiercely. *Panic, and you're finished. You have a brain – use it!*

But no amount of smart analysis could compensate for being disorientated, injured, without a light, without a weapon of any kind, and at the mercy of someone claiming to be a dead man. And conceit about his mental powers had got him into this mess in the first place. A judgement, or what?

Osiris. Jay Darke. But it wasn't Jay; Jay was dead. Even here, in the terrifying darkness, his mind was clear about that.

'Why are you calling yourself Osiris?' he said boldly. 'Osiris is dead.'

The sudden angry hiss of indrawn breath filled the air with the sound of a dozen snakes. 'This is Osiris's business, set to his account, not mine.'

He couldn't tell whether the hoarse whisper was male or female. 'What you do is set to your account, not anyone else's, when judgement comes,' he said, hoping to provoke a rebuttal. Engage them in conversation – that, they had been taught, was the proper procedure in a hostage situation. How richly ironic to find himself grasping desperately at procedure now, inspiration having failed!

There was no reply; he tried again. 'What are you going to do?'

Still no answer, only a stealthy movement, from his right, he thought. He braced himself against the wall, angled himself towards the sound.

'Are you going to – kill me?' There, he had said the words, but they sounded melodramatic, unreal.

Still silence, 'Let's talk about it,' Tom urged desperately. 'I don't know what all this is about – talk to me—'

'No use.'

Tom recognised finality in the breathy, passionless voice. So following procedure hadn't helped either – what was left?

'They know I'm here,' he gabbled frantically, the panic he had so far controlled starting to show in his voice. 'They're on their way here now, and it'll be a murder hunt – they'll never give up—'

'As well be hanged for a sheep as for a lamb.'

The homely phrase, in this macabre context, intensified his confusion. This couldn't be happening—

A powerful light was switched on, swivelling to shine directly into his eyes. He put up his good hand to shield them as it came closer.

Without warning, something was thrown over his head, something soft and smothering, and he was entangled in its folds. A blanket, a rug, perhaps; he fought it, but arms came round him from behind, pulling the material tight and sending dizzying pain through his injured arm. He mustn't vomit – he would choke—

A rope or something had been passed around the blanket now, trussing him below his bent arms. He lashed out with his feet but made no contact.

He had thought before, when he lost his torch, of the darkness coming down on him like a blanket, but he had been wrong. A blanket clung suffocatingly to your face, the wool damp with your breath. He had to struggle for air, struggle against the pain, struggle to hold on to the belief that somehow, having no further resources himself, rescue would come—

'Move!'

Tom found himself being propelled helplessly forwards. He tried to protest, but his voice was muffled by the folds of cloth. He tried to resist, stopping and digging his heels in, but he was unbalanced and afraid he would fall, to be as helpless as a beetle on its back.

He could breathe better with his head bent and see, looking down, his stumbling feet and the floor of the passageway in the jerky torchlight. The ground was sloping now rather more steeply, and the little shallow streams along the path seemed to be running more strongly.

Realisation came to him with a sick jolt to the pit of his stomach. He remembered the tape across the passageway beyond the temple cave; he recalled the SOCOs' inspector warning, 'It slopes into a shaft – we don't have the resources to get you out – not that you'd care, once you hit the bottom.'

They could be within feet of it now, and there was nothing Tom could do.

It wasn't far to the turning on to the single-track road which curved round the flank of the Long Moor, but the sun was shining now and its warmth had brought the tourists out, like maggots hatching.

Stuck behind a car which slowed erratically whenever its driver was struck by some fresh vista, Juliette had plenty of time to calm down and wonder whether she might not, after all, be on a fool's errand.

The police hadn't actually said that Tom was going to the caves, had they, and even if he did, he was a policeman, for heaven's sake, trained to look after himself. What on earth did she imagine she was going to be able to do?

Anyway, out here in the fresh air and sunshine, with the children in the car in front pulling grotesque faces at her in that very normal way, she didn't feel at all as she had felt within the four confining walls of her bedroom. Now, her fears of Jay's sinister omniscience seemed ridiculous superstition.

After all, she remembered suddenly, Tom had felt uncomfortable, as if someone had been spying on them as they stood together at the roadside yesterday. Anyone in a passing car could have seen them, guessed—

Guessed what? Embarrassed colour came into her cheeks, she certainly wasn't ready to think about that at the moment.

And then, too, supposing when she arrived, Tom *was* there, standing round chatting to colleagues, most likely. He'd be surprised to see her, unlikely to believe that she had been seized quite coincidentally with a desire to revisit old haunts. If he knew what the police had said to her, he might even guess at the quixotic impulse which had prompted her. She felt her cheeks grow even hotter at the thought.

Yet something was urging her on. She reached the turning and accelerated as the road ahead became clear.

What if all was quiet at the caves, as she half-believed it would be? What if there was no sign of Tom, or indication of any disturbance? What would she do then?

Juliette shrank from the thought of entering once more the caves she had not visited since that day of childhood horror so long ago. She could not be certain that there, in the dark nursery where they had all played with evil and learned cruelty, Jay's restless and power-hungry spirit would not still be in some sense alive, at least in her own unquiet mind.

She glanced for reassurance at the big halogen lamp lying on the passenger seat beside her which she had had the presence of mind to snatch up on her way out. Power-cuts were not unknown when winter storms lashed the Peaks, and Harry kept this to hand in the garage. It was very powerful; once she had crawled through the bushes into their secret entrance – if it wasn't completely overgrown by now – she need only go yards into the caves before with its intense beam she could see as far as the Temple of Anubis. Then she would know if anything – she corrected herself hastily, anyone – was there.

That was the turning for the bumpy track on to the moor now. She slowed down to turn in, then saw above her, up on the flank of the hill, a police car, and beyond it two other parked cars, one of which she recognised as Tom's. Two uniformed officers were getting out of the car; another man in plain clothes was coming over to greet them – was it the detective she had seen in London? – but of Tom there was no sign.

Juliette's heart skipped a beat. He should have been waiting for their arrival, surely, waiting until they could go in together. If he hadn't, it meant he had gone in already, most probably on his own.

Her fears came rushing back. Her instinct had been right after all. Somehow Tom had been lured into Jay's Kingdom of the Dead.

If she could reach the officers before they went in, she could take them there directly, to the passage opening just beyond the Temple of Anubis. But when she tried to speed up, the car bucked alarmingly on the rocky terrain, threatening to leave the track altogether, and with a steep drop on one side there was no alternative but to slow down. When she reached the parked cars, there was no sign of anyone.

She hesitated. Should she go after them, try to explain?

It would take too long, and the sense of urgency was growing. The old entrance was just above her now, and grabbing the lamp she launched herself up the hillside. It was more of a scramble than she had remembered, and the ground was muddy and treacherous, the grass slick with recent rain. Reaching for small outcrops and tufts of vegetation, she hauled herself up until she could grasp the stout branch of one of the bushes forming the little brake which had kept the secret of the Neters' access so effectively.

The bushes had grown; their branches were thicker and more resistant as she forced her way through, oblivious to the scratches on her face and hands. At last she reached the more open heart of the thicket, and looked to where the entrance should be.

There it still was. It was surprisingly clear – and now she looked, there were plants uprooted and dying round about. At the end opposite to the one she had come from, she could see a trail of broken twigs and branches like the one she had left herself.

Someone had come here before her, someone who knew the Neters' way in, someone who was no spirit, who presented a real, physical threat.

There was no doubt now what she must do. She bent to the low, narrow opening, so much smaller and narrower than she remembered, and crawled into the damp, earthy gloom.

After a couple of yards she was inside the caves. The earth under her feet gave way to rock, the roof arched and she could stand up cautiously, holding her breath.

That was a sound – a stone being kicked, perhaps? As she crept forward, the darkness seemed to come softly to meet her, gathering her into its embrace, and she shivered. She had to force herself to edge round the corner which would blot out the light and air from the upper world.

It all came flooding back to her; the smell, the clamminess, the hollow sounds of dripping water and soughing air. For a moment, she was Isis again, going below to reclaim the shadowy kingdom she shared with Osiris, ever-dying and ever-alive again when Isis came to restore him. She could almost hear the chants, see the distant lights of the bobbing torches—

She caught her breath in a sob of terror; shut her eyes to steady herself. When she opened them again, she realised that the bobbing torchlight had not been her imagination.

She was in the short passage just before the Temple of Anubis. In front of her, and to the right, there was a light and the sound of movement and ragged breathing.

Moving as soundlessly as she could, she edged out into the main passage. Ahead there was someone walking behind a torch with – something, a shape – in front.

With sudden decision she flicked the switch on her lamp, and the passage, with its occupants, sprang into harsh illumination.

Chapter Twenty-One

How far could it be to the gaping maw of the shaft? Tom had no means of knowing, but there could be at most only yards between him and certain death.

He had two alternatives. He could balk, fall down, scrabble and resist, or he could turn and hurl himself blindly backwards, hoping to make contact with his captor and achieve at least delay if nothing else.

He'd rather go down fighting than be rolled like a log to an ignominious end. And – was it his imagination? No, his bonds were starting to work their way down, loosening as he walked.

Tom slowed to a shuffle. 'Look, I don't understand.' He spoke as clearly as the muffling fabric would allow. 'You've got to explain – what's all this about? Where are you taking me?'

With his good hand, round at the front, he pushed at the rope. Yes, it was slipping . . .

'Move!' Again, there was no discussion, just the hoarse whisper and the hand in the small of his back propelling him on. He stumbled deliberately, swore.

'Come on,' he said roughly. 'Quit playing games. What's the idea?' Another second's stalling, and he'd be able to free himself, at least.

He had got his hand over the bonds now, they were slipping, slipping; he tensed himself—

Suddenly strong light flooded the ground under his feet. There was a gasp that was almost a groan from behind him, and throwing off the blanket Tom kicked his feet clear of the rope which had fallen about his ankles. He swung round, blinking in the brilliance of a huge lamp which was being shone on them from the mouth of one of the passages.

His attacker stood transfixed, as if the light beam were a lance which had pierced him through.

'Bryant!' Tom exclaimed, at the same moment as a voice which he recognised as Juliette's said from behind the beam, 'Oh God, Barry!'

Without conscious thought, Tom launched himself at the other man in a flying tackle. He brought him down, but he had forgotten his injury; searing pain told him that he had made it worse, and if Bryant chose to resist there was nothing he could do.

Barry lay, pinned by the policeman's sprawling weight to the floor of the cave, motionless, half-stunned. His eyes were closed. He could feel gravel against his face, and a sharp rock had gashed his cheek. Blood was trickling from it, warm and sticky. His thick fisherman's jersey was growing cold and sodden with water from the rivulets on the path.

He didn't want to move, or to open his eyes. He didn't want to see them seeing him: Barry, the good fellow. Barry the devoted son, Barry the admired headmaster. Barry the *murderer*.

There in the darkness he had been concealed, presenting himself as Osiris – justly, as he thought. After all, it wasn't Barry's fault; it was Osiris who had made all this happen so long ago by offering the poisoned gift – a present for the only woman Barry had ever been able to love – which had led him into temptation and thence to mortal sin.

Lead us not into temptation, he prayed daily with his pupils now, as he had prayed as a child then; how little protection it had been, against the ancient powers Jay Darke had invoked!

He had thought he had put that childhood behind him. He had stood tall, no longer the bad twin, the stupid twin, the *male* twin.

That wasn't Barry's fault either. That was Harry Cartwright's fault; his betrayal had made Bella sour and distrustful of men. It had warped her marriage, certainly, and even, Barry wanted to believe, her love for her son. It had pleased him to be able to foster her unbalanced suspicion of Harry's casual good deed to Bonnie, though heaven knew it was small enough revenge! Barry was conscious now that the weight on his back was shifting. The man was sitting up, and he heard an involuntary cry of pain. Poor interfering fool! Barry had wanted none of this – not the attack to silence Abbie, not this clumsy trap to stop the sergeant's mouth. It was Jay who had dictated these; Osiris at his old tricks, even from beyond the grave.

Bitterness rose in him like bile, the old, childish sense of injustice. It wasn't fair that Barry should have had to struggle and struggle to read and write like anyone else, or to seem stupid when he knew he was not, or to have his mother love Bonnie – ugly, sly, cruel Bonnie – and not him. Why should it be Barry now who—

Juliette's frightened voice broke into his thoughts. 'Tom! Are you – are you all right?' He heard the man's strained attempt at reassurance, and the murmur of their voices saying something he could not hear. Then Barry heard him say, more loudly, 'The rope – over there. Get it, can you?' and felt his arm being grasped. He made no resistance as first one then the other was lifted behind his back. Juliette's smaller hands grabbed at his, fastening the stiff, unwieldy rope round his wrists to secure them together.

The policeman's weight was removed, and Juliette's arm linked into his, trying to pull him to his feet. She wasn't strong enough. 'Get up, Barry,' she said, her voice high and nervous. 'Come on – get up and stand against the wall.'

He did as he was told. He had to open his eyes now.

He had always liked Juliette, and she had liked him. He felt shrivelled by her accusing gaze, by the dismayed contempt he read in her face.

He didn't like looking at the sergeant either, his face grey and glistening with the sweat of pain in the harsh light of the big lamp set on a rock shelf, a shard of bone poking out from his bloody and swollen wrist. Osiris was responsible for that too, just as much as if it were Jay himself who'd brought the rock smashing down. That wasn't the sort of thing Barry did.

They had moved nearer together, as if they were taking comfort from each other's closeness, his face mirroring her expression of horror and disgust. Barry bowed his head, groaning. It was all so unfair! He felt very sorry for himself.

How could he make them understand how it had happened – how he had known himself a teacher from the start, just as some know they are artists or musicians? Thoth the teacher, the god bringing learning to man – Jay had given him his Neters' identity as a cruel mockery, perhaps, but it had fitted his dreams. The Secondary Modern, he had convinced himself, would have been death to his hopes: better that greedy, spiteful Bonnie should die instead . . .

Juliette was talking to him now. He was having trouble focusing on what she said.

'Oh Barry, I can't believe it! Barry, how could it be you?'

'Not me,' he muttered. 'Osiris.'

But he could tell from the way they were looking at him that they didn't understand. It was getting darker, somehow, not outside, where the brightness of Juliette's lamp was almost painful to his eyes, but inside his head. It was as if a shadow were forming somewhere at the edge of his mind, the shadow of a jackal's head, perhaps. It might be easier not to fight it, just to let it in, sniffing, searching . . .

Leaning against the rock wall opposite, Tom Ward nursed his arm, fighting nausea and trying to blot out the pain. 'Stall,' he had muttered to Juliette, and she had been quick to understand.

'They're on their way,' she had murmured back, though he'd thought this was probably just to keep his spirits up. Then she had pulled Bryant to his feet.

He looked harmless enough, standing with his hands tied behind him and his head bowed, one cheek still bleeding from a triangular gash, his clothes wet and his face smeared with mud. His mild, pleasant face, though, was slack and strange.

'Barry, look at me,' Juliette was saying, her voice coaxing. 'I'll try to understand.'

Tom saw the man's eyes fill as if her kindness was unexpected and even painful. 'Bonnie would have told, Juliette – you know how she told tales! She found out about the cheating for the Grammar, and she was going to tell!

'Oh, it didn't matter for the rest of you. You, Jay, Kate – you'd have got there anyway, even if you'd had to sit another test. And for the others, it was a bit of a joke. But if my mother had found out—'

He paused, blinking away the tears which had gathered. 'You see, she was pleased,' he said simply. 'She was pleased with me, for the first time ever. Her dad was a teacher, and he was the only man she didn't hate. When I got in the Grammar, she was *pleased*.'

It was, Tom reflected with sudden compassion, a terrible insight into the effects of conditional love. He had heard how dutiful a son Barry still was to the mother who didn't even recognise him; was he, even now, desperately seeking the affection and approval that had been so cruelly denied him as a child?

And now, it all began to fall into place. Who would have found it easier than her brother to lure Bonnie to the caves by telling her where the Neters met? Had he even, perhaps, hoped for some accident amid the frenzy of heightened emotions their ceremony produced, so that he wouldn't have to take that ultimate step of hunting down and killing his twin?

And the bike, too, which had so strangely vanished from the caves to reappear at the Quarry Lake suggesting she had drowned, Bonnie's flashy silver birthday bike – it had been Barry's birthday too, and if he'd had one the same who would have noticed that he wasn't riding his own?

Juliette was valiantly keeping him talking, but the strain was obvious now. When she said, 'You didn't do very well at the Grammar School, though, did you, Barry?' there was an edge of hostility in her voice which he was quick to notice.

Bryant raised his voice, stirring the chorus of echoes. 'I was dyslexic!' he cried. 'Can you understand what that was like? Dyslexic, when no one understood, when you knew you were clever but everyone told you how thick you were?

'Do you think I've enjoyed having to deceive people – having to lie about retaking exams, and being at university when I was stacking the shelves in supermarkets? I did the work, though, and my certificates look good – don't they, Sergeant Ward? I'm good with computers. You have to be, if you're dyslexic.

'And once I got a job my references were brilliant, because I'm a brilliant teacher, just the way I knew I would be. I got back here, and there are dozens of Burlow children whose lives are better because of that – kids like me, only they've got a proper start. And my mother, if only she could know, would be proud – so proud! So that will weigh in the balance against the feather of truth Anubis uses to judge souls, won't it?'

His smile – the attractive, warm, generous smile Ward had remarked before – did not reach the cold, dead eyes. 'Anyway,' he added, almost conversationally, 'I hated Bonnie, didn't you? Didn't everyone?'

Tom felt Juliette flinch, and willed her not to show her revulsion at hearing Bonnie's epitaph, spoken thus casually, by her twin. He shifted uneasily himself; he wasn't comfortable about the change in Bryant's tone.

'I only did what Osiris wanted – what you wanted, what everyone wanted. I don't see why I should be the only one to pay.'

Tom tensed. Was that a threat? And, it suddenly occurred to him, had they managed to tie his wrists tightly enough, so that the stiff rope would not loosen as it had when Bryant had fastened it about Tom himself? The atmosphere was changing dangerously – where the hell was everybody?

Juliette had taken a step closer to him, and he could feel her nervous, uneven breathing. 'Keep talking,' he muttered, and obediently, after taking a steadying breath, she went on, 'But what about Abbie, Barry? What had she ever done to you?'

'Oh, poor, poor Abbie!' With another of the disconcerting,

unnatural changes of expression he looked concerned and sympathetic. 'That wasn't me, Juliette! That was Osiris pulling the strings, of course, wicked, all-powerful Osiris controlling us as he always did. Eddie, me, Kate, you, like enough—' 'Jay's dead. You know that.' Glancing down, Tom saw that Juliette's hands were clenched, as if she were digging her nails into her palms.

Bryant laughed, glancing round about him. As he moved, his shadow, grotesquely magnified by the light, crawled across the rock face behind. 'Is he? You can't see him, but isn't all this his doing – the pain, the suffering? Osiris? Are you there?'

He threw back his head and laughed again, shouting into the cacophony his laughter provoked, 'Your servants, Thoth and Isis!'

Juliette shrank back, and a small, frightened sound escaped her. Even Tom, with a prickling of the hairs at the base of his neck, could almost sense a presence in the darkness, an ancient malevolence slyly encroaching—

Then he realised that he had, indeed, heard something, a stealthy movement which had no supernatural cause.

The reverberating echoes were his allies now. To rouse them again, he demanded loudly, 'And what about me? What did I do, to make you decide I must die?'

'That was Osiris too!' Bryant raised his voice to be heard. 'You, and Abbie – he gave her the information and she told you how to destroy me—'

'But it wasn't Osiris.' Ward fixed Bryant's eyes with his own, hoping he would not turn his head to see the distant flicker of a light at the far end of the passage. 'I worked it out for myself. It was just plain, ordinary detective work. You were one of my chief suspects – I ran a straightforward background check—'

In the cold artificial light, Bryant's fair complexion was pale anyway; now it seemed, before Ward's eyes to take on a greyer hue, and his eyes go dark as if a shadow had swept across them. It seemed as if he had until this moment managed to believe himself blameless, the helpless agent of a greater power. 'Not – not Osiris?' he stammered. 'Not because of him?'

'No, because of you, Barry. *You* killed Bonnie, *you* tried to kill Abbie, *you* did your best to kill me. Stop trying to hide behind Jay Darke – he was an ordinary man like anyone else, and he's dead now, for God's sake! And even if he weren't, he couldn't make you do anything. No one *made* you kill. You had a choice, Barry, and *you chose evil!*'

He had spoken with vicious satisfaction, and as the words left his mouth Ward knew they were self-indulgent and wrong. He was badly shaken and in severe pain; he had been made to feel impotent and afraid, and he had lashed out from wounded pride with the express intention of making his tormentor suffer. It was unprofessional, in the most damning sense of that word.

Bryant, who had made no resistance from the moment Juliette's lamp had stripped away his anonymity, erupted into violent action. He wrestled his arms free of the inefficient bonds and jinked past Ward's clumsy, left-handed attempt to stop him, pushing him aside.

Juliette stepped bravely into his path. 'Barry, stop!' she cried, and he swivelled towards her.

'Let Anubis have his way! Come with me, Isis!' he shouted, and as Tom struggled to regain his balance he saw with horror Bryant grab Juliette and attempt to sweep her on along the path ahead of him.

Throwing her weight sideways and lashing out with arms and feet Juliette broke his hold on her and stumbled against the rock wall. He barely checked; running on down the sloping passage towards the shaft. Then Ward came after him, but he was a crucial few steps behind.

In less than twenty paces, Bryant was on the brink of the sheer drop. Ahead of him, a shower of small stones kicked by his flying feet, crashed and bounced down, down, down into the unplumbed depths below.

Ward flung himself into another desperate tackle. 'No, Tom, no!' Juliette screamed her terror, unleashing scream after echoed scream.

Alex Denholm, sprinting ahead of the other two officers, reached the scene as a shadowy figure toppled out of his sight and a woman threw herself across the legs of his spreadeagled colleague just in time to stop him being dragged to his death in the abyss below.

Late on Sunday afternoon, Juliette, pale but determinedly composed, was giving a full statement to DS Denholm and DC Gault in her father's sitting room. She had banished Harry, but couldn't stop Debbie popping in and out – presumably briefed to report what she heard – with offers of tea, coffee and, as it got later, 'something stronger' which the officers politely declined.

It took a long time, but at last she finished and DC Gault, a fresh-faced youth, set down his pen, flexing his cramped fingers. 'Thanks very much,' Denholm said. 'We'll get that typed up. Maybe you could drop into headquarters and read it through and sign it for us?'

'Of course.' Juliette was fidgeting with the lace on one of Debbie's hysterically frilly cushions. 'Sergeant, can you tell me – what will happen to Tom?'

Under her direct gaze, Denholm, about to make a soothing reply, changed his mind. 'There's no point in denying he's in a spot of bother. Defying orders, flouting every basic rule, then having a suspect commit suicide while he was technically in police care, even if he wasn't actually under arrest—'

'But he only went to the caves to save me!' Juliette cried. 'He explained what happened just before the ambulance came—'

Denholm pulled a face. 'Well, it may have been romantic,' he watched her blush with sardonic amusement, 'but it surely wasn't sensible. He endangered his own life and risked yours by going in unprepared and on his own.'

'By the time you got there,' she pointed out stubbornly, 'I could have been dead. If I'd been there, I mean.'

'If.' Denholm sighed. 'Tom's my good friend, but he's been a total idiot. There's going to have to be an inquiry and no one's going to be handing out medals for gallantry. Oh, except maybe to you for saving his life.'

Juliette was appalled. 'Oh, please don't say that! He'd be so humiliated!'

Both policemen laughed. 'Do him good,' Denholm said, with feeling. 'Now let me see – have we covered everything for the moment?'

He picked up the notes the constable had made and flicked through them. He paused, tapping one page.

'The CD-Rom and the e-mail your husband sent you – can we have a look at those?'

'The disk, yes,' Juliette said. 'I'll get it for you. But the e-mail disappeared when I tried to save it – another of Jay's little tricks.'

The young constable cleared his throat. 'Er – are you sure, miss? Sometimes things are still there somewhere, even though you think they've gone.'

Denholm winked at her. 'Fancies himself as a bit of a whizz with computers, does Andy here.'

Juliette smiled. 'Well, you're welcome to try if you like. I'll bring down my lap-top as well as the disk.'

When she came back in, Gault seized it eagerly, like a child being given a promised treat. She told him her password and a moment later her e-mail screen came up.

'There's one,' he said. '*osiris.london* – is that it?' He mispronounced the name, putting the stress on the first syllable. Even as Juliette exclaimed, 'Has it come back?' he clicked on it and the e-mail appeared.

'*I am One, who becomes Two, who becomes Four, who becomes Eight, and then I am One Again,*' it began, as the previous one had, but it went on differently.

'*Are you reading this, Juliette? Or have you come to join me as Isis in my eternal kingdom? Are there alien eyes reading this? I do not know the answer to that, though in time I believe I will.*

'*Now, when my earthly life is so nearly over, I wonder, could it all have been different – could we have loved and laughed and lived like ordinary mortals, we two?*

'*But no! I have known myself from the first a different breed – cleverer, more powerful, alien to this petty world. That knowledge gives me strength now to believe I have a different destiny.*

'*I have sown destruction, as gods among men ever do. I have punished with a god's vengeance. And you, Juliette – if you are reading this, as sadly I believe you are, for you never truly loved me – are lost to mortality. Farewell, for ever.*'

She had thought she hated Jay. She had certainly feared him. But now as she read his defiant, pathetic leave-taking she saw him in a different light, as a man handicapped by his nature, an outcast who had given himself up to this deadly fantasy of power beyond the grave to compensate for lack of human feeling. Tears began to stream down Juliette's face, and as she reached the end, she put her hands over her face and sobbed.

She did not see the text displaced by the black silhouette of the jackal god on a blood-red background, did not see that image begin to drip and melt all over the screen, or the young constable start frantically clicking at the mouse and pressing keys.

'It's a bloody virus!' he exclaimed, and when she looked up, he had gone pale with dismay. 'I'm really sorry, miss. I couldn't stop it. It's running right through your system – there won't be a thing left.'

'How very, very like Jay,' she said, and with the tears still wet on her cheeks she began to laugh. She couldn't stop until Denholm, apologetically, slapped her on the face.

DC Little set off promptly on Monday morning. He had an appointment with Kate Cosgrove at her office in Sheffield; she had been charmingly apologetic about being out when he called, but explained that she had been at the hospital visiting Abbie Bettison, whose condition, thankfully, was improving. She had been predictably shocked at what he had told her over the phone, and expressed herself delighted to see him 'to straighten things out', as she put it.

He had dispensed with WPC Matthews' company this time; with so much going on at HQ Matthews was needed there. It had been difficult enough to extricate himself.

When Kate Cosgrove came out of her office to greet him, she looked even more attractive than he had remembered her, and somehow younger. Her dark blonde hair was pinned on top of her head so that waving tendrils escaped to frame her face, and she was wearing a soft pink trouser suit.

'How kind of you to come all this way!' she said, taking his outstretched hand in both of hers. 'It's just so dreadful, isn't it? First poor Abbie, then the whole ghastly tragedy of Barry Bryant – such a charismatic headmaster! And then your own officer – how is he?'

'Hmmph.' She had led Little through into her office, drawing him down to sit beside her on the charcoal-grey sofa, and in such civilised surroundings bluntness seemed inappropriate. 'Oh, he'll mend,' he said at last, by way of compromise.

'I'm *so* glad.' The secretary had brought in a tray; Kate poured coffee from a tall white pot into a fine bone china cup and handed it to him.

'Now, inspector, I know we have to talk about these – these horrible pictures you told me about.'

She turned a troubled face to him, distress plain in her golden-brown eyes. He smiled at her reassuringly, grateful to have the difficult topic so straightforwardly introduced.

'Now, you mustn't upset yourself. We are fully aware that this constitutes an unsubstantiated allegation—'

Her soft pink lips trembled and she gave a great sigh. 'Oh, I can't tell you how relieved I am to hear you say that! I've gone over it and over it in my head, and I just couldn't see how I was to prove that this was just some horrible sick idea of Jay Darke's! Even if there was nothing in my computer, how could I prove it hadn't once been there?'

'I know, I know.' Little took a bite of the dainty macaroon biscuit which had come with his coffee. 'But of course, it works the other way, Ms Cosgrove—'

'Kate!' she corrected him, wagging a pink-tipped finger.

'– Kate,' he smirked. 'You see, your reputation is well known to us, and so is Darke's. It seems he may even have had a personality disorder which made him behave in a callous and inhuman manner. There's no way we could take his word against yours, in the absence of absolute proof.'

She rewarded him with a grateful smile. 'Well, as a lawyer of course I know you're innocent until proved guilty, but it's a relief to find the police so understanding.'

He smiled back, then with a waggish air said, 'But not so fast, young lady! I have to put one or two formal questions to you first, you know – just for the record.'

'Of course.' She composed her features into a mock-prim expression, sat up straight then folded her hands in her lap like a schoolgirl. 'Fire away.'

He had got out a notebook. 'You have been told of the existence of photographs of tortured animals, allegedly taken from your computer files. Did you have any such photographs?'

'No, absolutely not. It would be completely abhorrent to me.'

'Have you ever seen photographs of that description?'

'Never.'

'Would it have been possible for Jay Darke to have hacked into your computer?'

'Possible, I suppose.' She shrugged. 'Hackers seem able to get into anything they choose. I certainly wasn't aware of it, and of course he wouldn't have had to, would he, since the pictures weren't there.'

'Quite, quite.' Little scribbled that down too. There wasn't really much more to ask her, now he had recorded the formal denials, but he was still savouring his coffee. With a recollection of a half-heard discussion of e-mails the dead man had apparently sent, he asked, 'Have you had any recent communication with Darke?'

Her look was frank, her gaze limpid. 'Inspector, I hadn't so much as thought of Jay for years until your sergeant came asking questions last week. I haven't met him, spoken to him, or had contact with him since we were at school together.'

'No computer messages, for instance?'

'Not a single one. Cross my heart!' Smiling, she suited the action to the words.

Little beamed on her fatuously. 'You can't say fairer than that.' He had finished his coffee; somewhat reluctantly, he stood up to go.

Just as he did so there was a perfunctory knock at the door and a young man burst in, looking agitated. He seemed barely to notice Little's presence.

'Kate, it's a complete disaster. That virus that struck your computer this morning – it's going through the system like wildfire! The anti-virus software doesn't seem to recognise it – there's that dog-thing melting down every screen—'

She had jumped to her feet, speaking across him and drowning out his last words. 'That's awful, Simon. I'll be with you in a second, OK?'

The man, running a distracted hand through his hair, nodded and withdrew.

'So sorry, inspector.' Kate produced her most dazzling smile. 'I don't want to hurry you, but—'

'Of course, of course.' Little stuffed his notebook and pen into his pocket. 'Terrible things, these viruses. Not that I know much about computers – I have young men to know that sort of thing for me.'

On his way to the door he stopped suddenly, looking intently at the big semi-abstract painting on the wall. 'Now *that's* clever!' he exclaimed admiringly. 'I've only just got it, do you know that? It's a lioness all ready to attack, isn't it? My word, what an evil-looking beast!'

Kate turned to look at it, her golden-brown eyes suddenly cold.

'I'm thinking of selling it,' she said abruptly, ushering him out.

'My resignation, sir.'

Tom Ward's wrist was in plaster and his face was pale, with livid bruises on the right cheek and a long gash with stitches in it on the temple, but he was standing rigidly to attention as he handed the envelope to Superintendent Broughton.

Broughton leaned back in his chair, pushing up his spectacles to rub his weary eyes. He was looking very tired; the last few days, answering to the higher authorities and dealing with a rapacious media doggedly determined to get hold of the wrong end of any stick held out to them, had taken its toll.

He sighed. 'I can't try to dissuade you, Tom – always better to jump if there's a chance you will be pushed. But it's a pity, a great pity.'

'That's very kind. Thank you, sir. I also wish to make a formal apology, sir, for the trouble I've caused to the Force. I'll try to make it plain to the inquiry that the responsibility for Barry Bryant's death is entirely mine, sir, but—'

'You'll do no such thing!' Broughton rapped out. 'Oh, sit down, lad, for heaven's sake and stop striking poses and "sir"-ing me all over the place. You're not a policeman any more.'

'Breast-beating,' he said when Tom, somewhat reluctantly, had done as he was told, 'never helped anybody. Bryant, facing one charge of murder and two of attempted murder, opted to kill himself rather than stand trial. Despite a painful injury you gallantly attempted to stop him, risking your own life in the process, but sadly failed. You've read the press release.'

'But I shouldn't have been there, should I? And you see, it was something I said that made him do it, so—'

Broughton held up his hand. 'Hang on. No, you shouldn't have been there. You were disobeying a direct order, and if you hadn't resigned I'd be having to consider sacking you for gross insubordination.

'But where Bryant's concerned – well, let me put it this way. You can say anything you like to me, Tom – anything – and I promise I won't kill myself as a result. You can't, just by what you say, make someone kill themselves who wasn't minded to do it in the first place. Got that straight?'

Ward recalled saying something of the sort to Juliette – a long time ago, it seemed – and the ghost of a smile appeared round his mouth. 'Thank you, si— Well, thanks anyway. It's not that simple, is it, but I hear what you say. And I'll toe the line in public; I've caused enough trouble for you already.'

Broughton sighed again. 'You always were a bit of a maverick, Tom, but useful, useful. I've read your reports on the case, and they're first-class – meticulous, intelligent, quite exceptional.

You were well on your way to fingering Bryant before it all went pear-shaped.'

Ward actually smiled this time. 'To be absolutely honest, if Alex Denholm would have taken the bet, I'd have backed Cosgrove. She's a seriously unpleasant woman, even if she isn't a killer.'

'Hmm. DCI Little went to Sheffield to see her and has filed a report saying she doesn't know a thing about any sadistic pictures.'

'What?' Ward was amazed. 'But they were on the disk – Alex showed me—'

'That was just a nasty piece of character assassination by Darke, according to the lady. It would certainly be next to impossible to prove it wasn't. But I confess I'd like to see some healthy scepticism in the report. Little seemed perfectly happy to take her at her word.'

'Oh, she's good at innocent charm,' Ward said grimly. 'It'll stand her in good stead as a politician. Watch her go straight to the top.'

'That's a depressing thought! I shall miss your refreshingly cynical comments, you know. I really wish this didn't have to happen.'

'To tell you the truth, I'm not entirely sure how long I'd have stayed in any case.' Ward sighed. 'I find myself wondering, what did all that achieve? Burlow Primary's lost an excellent headmaster and Sam Bettison nearly lost his wife. I suppose Bonnie Bryant got what you might call justice – and from all I've heard about that very unpleasant child, she'd probably be pleased – but mightn't it have been better if they'd never found her bones at all? And if you think like that . . .' He shrugged.

'There wouldn't be a lot of point in being a policeman,' Broughton finished for him. 'I think I do still, against all the odds, believe in the importance of justice, but I take your point. So, Tom, what happens next? Had any thoughts yet?'

'I was thinking,' Ward said hesitantly, 'that perhaps I might take a course in teaching English as a foreign language and look for a job somewhere in France.'

'France?' Broughton's eyebrows rose, and then he smiled knowingly. 'Ah! I did hear she was half French, as well as being a charming young woman with a useful line in life-saving.'

Tom's face flamed. 'My plans have nothing to do with Mrs Darke,' he said stiffly, then, under the sceptical gaze of his former superior officer, gave a reluctant grin. 'Well – not yet, at any rate.'

They both got up, and Broughton held out his hand. 'You're a good man, Tom, and a loss to the Force. You've still got a lot to learn, but something tells me you may be a bit more receptive to learning it now. Good luck.'

Tom shook it awkwardly, left-handed, then went out and down the stairs. He had no wish to embark on an embarrassing round of leave-taking, and he crossed the reception area without even a glance towards the duty desk, and let himself out of the building. He'd arranged to meet Alex later in the pub.

But at the foot of the front steps, Tom Ward, DS no longer, stopped and turned to look at the police building which had been his world for so long. Inside, phones would be ringing and men and women – his former colleagues – would be carrying their daily burden of coping with whatever presented itself, whether a straying dog or disaster and sudden death.

He stood for a moment, then he shrugged, squared his shoulders and walked out into civilian life.